Praise for Linda Warren

"Linda Warren writes a story
overflowing with emotional twists and turns
that grabs the reader from the first page
and doesn't let go until the end."
—*Romance Junkies* on *Once A Cowboy*

"Linda Warren writes a novel not only
with romance but emotion. The emotions
run from joy to heartbreaking sadness,
from humor to horror and hits all the highs
and lows in between, making this one of the
best Harlequin romance novels written."
—*Love Romances* on *Adopted Son*

"Ms. Warren writes books that are gripping
and will put you through an emotional wringer—
in a good way."
—*The Best Reviews* on *Forgotten Son*

"Magnificent! Moving! Brilliant!"
—*CataRomance* on *The Christmas Cradle*

"Ms. Warren writes a wonderful romantic read and
her characters will burrow their way
into the hearts of readers."
—*RT Book Reviews* on *Son of Texas*

"Linda Warren writes about people discovering
their strengths and passions. Her gift with dialog
brings the characters to life and compels your
sympathy and caring."
—*Fresh Fiction Reviews* on *The Texan's Christmas*

LINDA WARREN

Two-time RITA® Award-nominated and award-winning author Linda Warren loves her job, writing happily-ever-after books for Harlequin. Drawing upon her years of growing up on a farm/ranch in Texas, she writes about sexy heroes, feisty heroines and broken families with an emotional punch, all set against the backdrop of Texas. Her favorite pastime is sitting on her patio with her husband watching the wildlife, especially the injured ones that are coming in pairs these days: two Canada geese with broken wings, two does with broken legs and a bobcat ready to pounce on anything tasty. Learn more about Linda and her books at her website, www.lindawarren.net, or on Facebook at www.facebook.com/authorlindawarren.

LINDA WARREN

Home on the Ranch: Texas

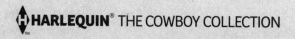

HARLEQUIN® THE COWBOY COLLECTION

Recycling programs
for this product may
not exist in your area.

ISBN-13: 978-0-373-60655-9

HOME ON THE RANCH: TEXAS

Copyright © 2014 by Harlequin Books S.A.

The publisher acknowledges the copyright holder
of the individual works as follows:

CAITLYN'S PRIZE
Copyright © 2009 by Linda Warren

MADISON'S CHILDREN
Copyright © 2009 by Linda Warren

This edition published by arrangement with Harlequin Books S.A.

For questions and comments about the quality of this book,
please contact us at CustomerService@Harlequin.com.

Printed in U.S.A.

CONTENTS

CAITLYN'S PRIZE

A special thanks to my editor, Kathleen Scheibling, and to Wanda Ottewell for making this series possible. Thanks to J.O., Bobby and Chris Siegert for refreshing my memory and answering my pesky questions about ranching, cattle, windmills, oil wells and the sand and gravel business. All errors are strictly mine.

DEDICATION

This past year has been especially difficult for me. I dedicate this book to my husband, Billy, my Sonny, who was always there to help me through it.

CHAPTER ONE

IT WAS RECKONING DAY.

Caitlyn Belle knew that with every beat of her racing heart.

She stopped at the entrance to the Southern Cross ranch and shoved the stick shift of her old Chevy truck into First. The gears protested with a grinding noise, which she ignored. Her brain cells could process only so much, and right now her full attention was on the ranch's owner, not a faulty transmission.

Once she crossed the cattle guard, there was a whole lot of reckoning waiting for her. Judd Calhoun, the man she'd jilted fourteen years ago, had requested a meeting with her. The question *why* kept jangling in her head like loose change.

Time to find out.

Reckoning or not.

She drove between the huge stone pillars that supported the decorative, arched wrought-iron sign that bore the name Southern Cross. White board fences flanked both sides of the graveled road, curling toward a massive ranch-style house with a red tile roof.

A circular drive with a magnificent horse-sculpture fountain made of limestone graced the front of the house. The place looked like something out of a magazine. The only things that signaled this was a working ranch were the corrals and barns in the distance and the white Brahman cattle that dotted the horizon.

High Five had once been like this, but not anymore. Cait felt a moment of sadness. She couldn't change the past. The future was her main concern.

The High Five, owned by the Belles, and the Southern Cross, owned by the Calhouns, were the two biggest ranches near High Cotton, Texas, a stop in the road of less than five hundred people. It had been both families' dream that someday the ranches would be one, joined by the marriage of Caitlyn, the oldest Belle daughter, and Judd, the only male Calhoun offspring.

But Caitlyn couldn't go through with it. No one understood her reasons, least of all her father, Dane Belle. He'd begged her to think about what she was doing and to reconsider. She couldn't. The rumor mill in High Cotton said she was spoiled, stubborn, but there had been a whole lot more to her decision than that.

The two families had been at odds ever since. The Calhouns prospered, while the Belles suffered financial losses one after another. Her father had passed away two months ago and High Five was barely holding on. The enormous debt Dane had incurred still angered Caitlyn. Without the royalties from the oil and gas leases, the ranch would fold. She was going to make sure that never happened.

She parked on the circular drive and took a moment to gather her wits. But her wits were scattered hither and yon, and might take more time to collect than she had. The fountain bubbled invitingly and memories knocked on the door of yesterday. She refused to open it.

Getting out, she hurried toward the huge walnut front doors and tapped the brass knocker before she lost her nerve. She studied the beautiful stained glass and saw her distorted reflection.

Maybe she should have worn makeup and a dress instead of her bare face, jeans and boots. The thought almost caused her to laugh hysterically. Judd Calhoun was not going to notice how she looked. This was business. It certainly wasn't personal. Personal feelings had taken a hike when she'd said, "I can't marry you."

Brenda Sue Beecham swung open the door. "Oh, Caitlyn, you're right on time."

Brenda Sue, a bleached blonde, had more curves than Harper's Road and was known for her friendly disposition. In high school she'd been called B.S. for obvious reasons. No one could B.S. like Brenda Sue. Her mouth was going at all times.

After a failed marriage, she was back home, living with her parents and working as a secretary in the Southern Cross office. There were very few jobs for women in High Cotton, and Cait could only imagine how Brenda Sue had gotten this one. But she shouldn't be catty. Brenda Sue's dad, Harvey, had worked on the Southern Cross for years before he retired because of a bad back. Cait felt sure he'd asked for Judd's help on her behalf.

"Come this way. Judd should be here any minute. You know how he loves his horses. Oh, what am I saying?" Brenda Sue gave a forced laugh. "You know everything about Judd. Sometimes I forget that, with you being such a stick-in-the-mud and all. Now, I don't mean that in an offensive way. You've just always been rather…you know…"

Caitlyn followed her into Judd's study, thinking that yellow hair would make a good dust mop. She pushed the thought aside. Brenda Sue and her endless digs and infinite "you know's" were the least of her worries.

"Judd will be right with you. I have to get back to the office. I help out in the house every now and then, you know. Gosh, it's good seeing you, Caitlyn." With that, Brenda Sue closed the door and disappeared.

Caitlyn hadn't said one word. She didn't need to. Brenda Sue was a one-woman show, no participation required. How did Judd put up with that airhead? But he was a man and probably enjoyed looking at her cleavage. Caitlyn didn't want to think about what else might be between them.

She took a seat in a burgundy leather wingback chair facing the enormous mahogany desk. Vibrant polished wood surrounded her. A man's room, she thought. There were no family photos, just framed pictures of prize Brahman bulls and thoroughbred horses, along with several bull and horse sculptures. A magnificent one sat on his desk, a smaller version of the one in the fountain. The stallion stood on his hind legs, his mane flowing in the wind as his front feet pawed the air.

If her nerves weren't hog-tied into knots, she'd take a closer look. Right now she had to focus on the next few minutes. She crossed her legs and tried to relax. It was only a meeting.

After fourteen years.

The knots grew tighter.

She touched her hair in a nervous gesture. After brushing it until her arms ached, she couldn't decide whether to wear it up or down. Judd had liked it loose and flowing, so she'd weaved it into a French braid, as usual. It hung down her back and conveniently kept her hair out of her face.

She recrossed her legs and stared in horror at the

horse crap on her boots. *Damn. Damn. Damn!* But
when you ran a working ranch it was hard not to step
in it every now and then.

Tissues in a brass holder on the desk caught her attention. Just what she needed. As she started to rise,
the door opened and Judd strolled in with Frank Gas-
ton, her father's attorney. Her butt hit the leather with
a swooshing sound, but Judd didn't seem to notice. He
didn't even look at her, though the lawyer nodded in
her direction.

Judd sank into his chair, placing a folder on the desk
in front of him. He was a big man with an even bigger
presence. His hair was dark brown, his eyes darker.
She'd once called them "midnight magic." Their color
rivaled the darkest night, and magic was what she'd felt
when he'd looked at her.

Oh, God! She'd been so naive.

The leather protested as she shifted uncomfortably.
Judd had changed very little over the years. He'd been
at her father's funeral, but had never gotten within
twenty feet of her. She'd seen him every now and then
when she was at the general store or the gas station in
High Cotton, but he'd always ignored her.

As he did now.

She'd never been this close before, though, breathing the same air, occupying the same space. There were
gray strands at his temples, but they only added to his
appeal. A white shirt stretched across his shoulders.
Had they always been that wide?

Reality check. Something serious was going on and
it required her undivided attention. What was Frank
doing here?

As she watched, Judd opened the folder and laid a
document on the desk in front of her.

"Two months before your father died, he sold me High Five's oil and gas royalties."

Everything in the room seemed to sway. Cait's fingers pressed into the leather and she felt its texture, its softness, its support, yet it felt unreal. The expression on Judd's face, though, was as real as it got.

Something was stuck in her throat. "Excuse me?" she managed to ask.

"Are you hard of hearing?" He looked at her then, his dark eyes nailing her like barbed wire to a post, hard, sure and without mercy.

"Of course not." She wouldn't let him get to her. She sprang to her feet, wanting answers. "I don't believe it. My father wouldn't do that to us."

"It's true, Caitlyn. I'm sorry," Frank said, a touch of sadness in his voice.

Judd poked the document with one finger. "Read it. The fifteenth will be your last check."

Grabbing the document, she sat down to see this debacle with her own eyes. She had to. Her knees were shaking. As she read, the shaking spread to her whole body. It was true. Her father's bold signature leaped out at her, sealing her fate and the fate of High Five.

How could he?

Judd Calhoun had found his revenge.

She was lost somewhere between feeling like a nineteen-year-old girl with her head in the clouds and a woman of thirty-three with her feet planted firmly on the ground. Shaky ground. What happened next? The adult Caitlyn should know, but she didn't.

Judd did, and she was very aware of that as she heard his strong, confident voice. "Dane worried about the welfare of his daughters and his mother."

"So he sold everything that was keeping us solvent.

Why?" She fired the question at him with all the anger she was feeling.

"Gambling debts. He didn't want those people coming after you or your grandmother."

"So he leaves us with nothing?"

"You have the ranch."

She stood on her less-than-stable legs, but she would not show one sign of weakness to this man. He had somehow finagled her father into doing this. That was the only explanation.

Judd pulled another paper from the folder. "There was nothing he could do about the gambling debts but pay them. He felt, though, that he should made arrangements for you, your sisters and your grandmother. I agreed to honor them as best as I could."

That was her father. He was of the older generation and believed a woman had to be taken care of. That her place was in the home, kitchen or bed. Daughters were pampered and spoiled and did what they were told, like marrying a man of their father's choosing.

Caitlyn had lived with that mindset all her life. She had defied it once, to her regret.

Pushing those thoughts away, she concentrated on what Judd had said. *Agreed to what?*

"What are you talking about?"

"With his enormous debt, Dane had very few options, and he asked for my help." The rancher paused and picked up a gold pen, twirling it between his fingers. "Dane was also very aware of your stubborn, independent streak."

She stiffened. "So?" As if she wasn't reminded of it every freakin' day of her life.

"Here's Dane's deal…." His dark eyes swept over her. "If the ranch is not making a profit within six months, you will sell High Five to me at a fair market price."

"What!" His words hit her in the chest like a shot of her dad's Tennessee whiskey.

"Still have that hearing problem?"

She ignored the sarcastic remark. "You can't be serious."

"It's true," the lawyer interjected.

"Shut up, Frank." She pointed a finger at him. "What are you doing here? You're the Belles' attorney. Shouldn't you be on my side?"

"Caitlyn…"

Ignoring her outburst, Judd read from the paper in front of him. "'I'm giving Caitlyn the option to operate High Five or sell. This decision is hers, not Madison's nor Skylar's. It is my wish, though, that she consult with her sisters. To die with a clear conscience, I have to give Caitlyn a chance. But if the ranch continues to decline six months after my death, then High Five ranch and all its entities will be sold to Judd Calhoun. Dorothea Belle will continue to live on the property as long as she lives.'"

Caitlyn was speechless, completely speechless. Her father, in his antiquated thinking, had given Judd a golden opportunity to exact his revenge. But she would not give in so easily. She would not fail.

"I…I think I'll go and let you two sort this out." The attorney glanced at her. "If you need anything, Caitlyn, just call."

"Yeah, right."

Frank shrugged and walked out.

She looked straight at Judd, her eyes unwavering. "You think you've won, don't you?"

He leaned back in his chair, the cotton fabric of his

shirt stretching taut across his chest. "Yes, I've won. But knowing you, I'm sure you'll flounder along for six months. In the end I will take everything you love."

Her heart fell to her boots and her words tangled in the remnants of her shattered pride.

"Nothing to say?" he mocked.

"I think you've said it all, Judd. If you're waiting for me to beg, I'd advise you to take a breath, because it's going to be a long wait."

He lifted an eyebrow. "Beg, Caitlyn? For what?"

"Go to hell."

He shrugged. "Thanks to you, I've been there, and I'm not planning a return trip."

"What do you want from me?"

"Nothing. Absolutely nothing."

She swallowed. "Then this meeting is over."

"Not quite. I take it you are planning to operate High Five."

"You got it."

"Your sisters have to be informed of this development. Do you want to do the honors or should I?"

"I will speak to my sisters. We do not need your interference."

"Fine." He rested a forearm on the desk, his eyes holding hers. "Give it up, Caitlyn. You can't win this. Even Dane knew that. Sell now and save yourself the aggravation."

"You are not God, Judd, and you can't control people's lives."

"Control?" His laugh bruised her senses. "I never said anything about control. I'm helping a friend. Out of respect for your father, I've agreed to this arrangement and I will not go back on my word."

Respect? He didn't know the meaning of the word.

"You're a conniving bastard, Judd. I don't know how you got my father to agree to this."

"Dane came looking for me, not the other way around." He spoke calmly, but she couldn't help but note the curl in his lip.

"And you were there, eager to oblige."

He suddenly stood, and instinctively, she took a step backward. "I will own High Five and I will take great pleasure in taking it from you."

She held her head high. "I've often thought you were heartless, sort of like the Tin Man from *The Wizard of Oz,* except he *wanted* a heart. You, Judd, are lost forever. May God have mercy on your conniving soul."

"I had a heart but you ripped it out by the roots." The glimmer in his eyes was the only sign his emotions were involved. "This is reckoning day. I'm taking it all. It's just a matter of time. I see it as sweet justice."

She walked out of the room with only her dignity, which didn't feel like much. Stoically, she marched to the front door. On the silk Persian rug, she paused and wiped the crap from her boots.

Now that was sweet justice.

CHAPTER TWO

"You can't stop watching her, can you?"

Judd tensed, but his eyes never left Caitlyn as she jumped into her truck and raced down the driveway, tires squealing. Fourteen years and she was still the same—breathtakingly beautiful with Hollywood curves, glossy black hair and a smooth olive complexion.

But it was her forget-me-not-blue eyes that always got him. They reminded him of crystal marbles his grandfather had once given him: bright, shiny and irresistible. He still owned them, tucked away in a box somewhere, but he'd long ago found that Caitlyn wasn't a thing to be possessed.

He turned from the window to face his mother. "Did you need something?"

Renee motioned over her shoulder. "I just saw Caitlyn leave."

"Yes."

"Then you told her?"

"Yes."

"Why aren't you smiling? Why aren't you happy?"

He blew out a breath. "I don't really want to get into this."

"Well, sorry. I do." His mother walked farther into the room, flaunting her usual you'd-better-listen stance.

As a kid, he'd hated that tone in her voice. He wasn't crazy about it now.

"I'm not in the mood."

Renee placed her hands on her hips. In her late sixties, she was an active woman. After Judd's dad's death, shopping had become her favorite exercise and pastime. She never interfered in Judd's life and he liked it that way.

Of course, she'd never been a big part of his life. Judd had been five when she'd left Jack Calhoun and him. Judd then had the stepmother from hell.

After that marriage fell apart, his parents had miraculously reconnected, remarrying when Judd was twelve. By then there was a gulf between him and his mother that couldn't be bridged.

"From the tires squealing on our driveway, I assume she didn't receive the news well. But what woman would? You take her livelihood away from her and—"

"I did not take it." He tried to control his voice, but the words came out too loud. "Her father sold it."

"Why couldn't you have worked out a loan so payments could have been made? That way Caitlyn would have had a fighting chance."

"Why should I care about giving that woman a fighting chance?"

"Because—" his mother lifted an eyebrow that said she knew him better than he thought "—in fourteen years I've lost track of the number of women you've gone through to forget Caitlyn. I thought Deanna was the one, but the next thing I knew you weren't seeing her anymore." Renee took a step closer. "You haven't forgotten Caitlyn, so why not admit it and try to make this work?"

"Mom, you know nothing about this. You have no idea how much money Dane owed."

"It couldn't have been that much."

"Try six hundred fifty-two thousand dollars."

"Oh, my God!" Renee clutched her chest. "How could he gamble away that much money?"

"It's easy when you're losing."

The lines on his mom's forehead deepened. "Are the oil and gas royalties worth that much?"

"Yes. In a few years I'll recoup my investment. That is, if oil and gas prices don't drop. It's a gamble."

"So in a way you're doing a nice thing?"

He hooked his thumbs into his jeans pockets. "What?"

"If you hadn't paid off Dane's gambling debts, those people would have come looking for Caitlyn, her sisters and Dorie."

He rocked back on his heels. "Yep."

"So you did a good thing?"

"Ah, Mom. You have to see some good in me, don't you?"

"As a mother, I know there's good in you."

"Not this time." He walked to his desk with sure steps. "I was glad Dane asked for my help. As a neighbor, I would never have said no. As the man his daughter jilted, I was more than eager to oblige. I'm going to take Caitlyn down hard. She will beg me for mercy before this is over."

"Son, son." Renee clicked her tongue. "It's been fourteen years. Just let it go."

"I can't." He raked his fingers through his hair. "She destroyed everything I believed about relationships and trust. I'm thirty-six years old and should have a family. Caitlyn Belle will pay for what she did to me. And it's only just starting."

"Why, son? Why do you need this revenge?"

"I don't have to justify my actions."

"You can't even see the forest for the trees."

He frowned. "What does that mean?"

"It means Caitlyn loved you, but you pushed too hard and so did Dane. She was nineteen years old and all she wanted was to finish college, to be young and have fun. But neither you nor Dane would listen to her wishes. Y'all had to control her every move, and look what happened. If you had given her the time she'd wanted, you'd be married today."

"Loved me?" His jaw clenched. "Why do women have to always drag out the *L* word? It was a business arrangement solely."

"A pity no one mentioned that to Caitlyn."

"She couldn't handle it. She was weak."

Renee gave a laugh that grated on his nerves. "Weak? Caitlyn Belle? Oh, son, you're in for a rude awakening."

"Mom, just drop it."

But his mother never listened to him. "You can't see Caitlyn as a person. All you see is a woman who has to be controlled. You get that from Jack. But Caitlyn proved she can't be controlled, not by you and not by her father."

His eyes narrowed. "This doesn't concern you."

Renee waved a hand. "You sound just like your dad. He thought I needed to be told what to do. And I was to overlook his little infidelities. I couldn't, so I walked away and lost my son."

"I don't want to go over this again." Judd had heard

the story so many times it was burned like a brand into his brain.

"He said he wasn't cheating on me with that bitch, Blanche, but he was lying. As soon as the divorce was final, he married her."

"You left a five-year-old kid behind." Judd couldn't keep the accusation out of his voice.

She brushed back her blond hair, pain evident in her green eyes, pain he didn't want to see. But it was hard to ignore. "I had no choice. I couldn't continue to take that type of humiliation, but I never planned to lose my son. Jack had the money to make sure I stayed away from you."

"Mom, it's over, and you and Dad had twenty years together before his death."

"Yes, and we learned from our mistakes. Jack didn't cheat again. At least, not to my knowledge." She gazed at Judd. "You were the casualty of our mistakes. Do you remember what you did when your father brought me back here?"

He stared at the horse sculpture on his desk, not willing to speak.

"You walked out of the room and wouldn't say a word to me. That hurt. I cried and cried. Your father said you'd come around. It took a solid year before you accepted me back into your life."

Back then he couldn't understand how a mother could leave her only child. He still didn't, but she was his mom....

"Sometimes I don't think you've ever forgiven me, or that you can forgive anyone. That's my fault and—"

"This trip down memory lane is over. I'm going to check on the cowboys."

"Dear son, listen to me. I was weak, but Caitlyn

Belle is not. She will come back fighting. I've known her all her life and she will not bow easily. Be careful you're not the one who ends up begging."

"Mom…"

"I've said enough." She raised a hand. "I'm not arguing with you. I came to tell you that if you don't get rid of Brenda Sue, I'm going to strangle her."

"Just don't listen to her."

"Not listen to her? I'd have to be stone deaf not to. Her voice rivals nails on a chalkboard. The woman never shuts up."

"I'll handle it."

"If you don't, I'm buying a gun."

"Okay, okay." He strolled from the room, headed for the back door and freedom from his mother's words.

And freedom from the shattered look in Caitlyn's blue forget-me-not eyes.

CAITLYN SLAMMED ON HER brakes at the barn, causing dust to blanket the truck. Unheeding, she jumped out and ran for the corral, whistling sharply.

Whiskey Red, a prize thoroughbred, her father's last gift to her, trotted into the open corral. Cait hurried into the barn and Red followed. Within minutes, she had her saddled.

Cooper Yates and Rufus Johns, her only cowhands, came out of the tack room. "Hey, Cait, what are you doing?" Coop asked. "We just checked the herd."

She swung into the saddle. "I'll catch you later." Kneeing Red, she bolted for fresh air.

"Hey, what's wrong?" Coop shouted after her.

She didn't pause. Red's hooves kicked up dirt as they picked up speed, moving faster and faster. If she was lucky, maybe she could outrun the pain in her chest.

Thirty minutes later, she lay in the green grass along Crooked Creek, her body soaked with sweat, her heart bounding off the walls of her lungs.

She sucked in a much needed breath and stared up at the bright May sky. The temperature was in the upper eighties, a perfect day.

A squeak of a laugh left her throat. Perfect? Far from it.

Your father sold me your oil and gas royalties.

Now what should she do?

I'm taking it all. It's just a matter of time.

Not as long as she had breath in her body.

She sat up and stared at the plum trees growing close to the creek, dried dewberry vines nestled beneath them. She and her sisters often got sick from eating too many sweet plums in the summer, and they'd gotten drunk a time or two sneaking Etta's dewberry wine.

Memories. High Five. A piece of her childhood. Her life.

It seemed as if her father had reached out from the grave to try and still control her. He'd never understood her need to be a person in her own right and not a trophy on some man's arm.

The fight for independence probably began when she was small. Her great-grandfather, Elias Cotton, had had three daughters, and it was a woeful happenstance that God had given him daughters instead of sons to carry on the tradition of High Five.

Dorothea, Caitlyn's grandmother, had married Bartholomew Belle. Bart eventually bought out the sisters, and he and Dorie had run the ranch. After several miscarriages, they were blessed with a boy, Dane. All was aligned in the heavens. At last there was a son.

But once again fate struck. Dane had the misfortune to produce daughters. It wasn't for lack of trying. Dane and Meredith, Caitlyn's mother, had been high school sweethearts. They broke up when Dane went off to college. Years later they met again and married, but it wasn't meant to be. Meredith died giving birth to Caitlyn.

He didn't grieve for long. Six months later he'd married Audrey, but again the marriage didn't last. Audrey was very religious and didn't take to Dane's gambling trips to Vegas and Atlantic City, or to his weekly poker games with his buddies. A year later she moved out with her newborn daughter, Madison.

Dane met Julia, Skylar's mother, in Vegas, and felt he'd finally met the woman for him. Julia was from a Kentucky horse family, so it had to be a match made in heaven. It wasn't. Although Julia knew Dane's bad habits, she didn't enjoy living with them on a daily basis. After two years, she'd packed her things, including her baby daughter, and left.

Three wives. Two divorces. And three daughters, all with different mothers. After the third wife, Dane gave up and accepted his fate. Without sons, High Five was doomed.

Cait had heard that all her life and didn't understand it. She'd told her father many times that she could run High Five as well as any man. That always brought on a sermon about how a woman's place was in the home, producing heirs.

That stung like a rope burn. But nothing had ever changed her father's thinking.

Then she'd fallen hard for Judd, to the point that all she could see was his dark eyes, all she could feel was excitement when he looked at her. He was three years older, more experienced and more man than she'd ever met before.

Judd was popular in school, but he never glanced her way. Then one summer Renee threw a party and the Belle daughters were invited. Judd asked her to dance and Caitlyn thought she was in heaven.

After that, they met often, and before long heated kisses were taking her places she'd never been before. She was so in love that she never questioned Judd's love or his attention.

He had a power about him that frightened and attracted her at the same time. When she was around him she couldn't think. All she could do was feel.

And that caused her to fall right into her father's plan. Marrying Judd would unite two powerful ranching families, and High Five would continue to prosper.

Cait was prepared to fulfill her duty. She loved Judd and wanted to spend her life with him. Her first year in college was fun, but nothing was more exciting than rushing home to spend a weekend in his arms. It was bliss. It was perfect.

Then Dane had said there was no need for her to return to school in the fall, that doing so would be a waste of money. She needed to focus on Judd, a home and babies. They'd had words, and she'd run to Judd, wanting him to take her side.

But he hadn't. He didn't understand her viewpoint. Why *wouldn't* she want to think about a home for them and babies? he'd practically shouted. That's what a married woman should want.

In that instant Cait saw her future. She would be like his mother, Renee, ruled by her domineering husband. She would decorate his home, serve his dinner guests, warm his bed and produce children. As Judd's trophy wife, she would want for nothing. Except being treated as an equal.

Caitlyn made the toughest decision of her life in a heartbeat. Taking off her engagement ring, she'd said, "I can't marry you. I can't marry a man who doesn't respect me as a woman."

She waited for the magic words, his profession of love and respect, but they never came. He slipped her beautiful ring into his jeans pocket and walked out of the room. Her heart broke, but she held it all inside.

Her father wouldn't speak to her for six months. Judd spoke to her for the first time today. But she'd gotten that education and she'd traveled. In the end, it brought her home to High Five.

Her grandfather had passed on and Gran had grown older. Cait was needed at home. Her father was gambling heavily and the ranch was neglected and in disrepair.

Cait had a degree in agriculture management and worked her butt off to keep High Five afloat, but her father's debts were slowly taking them under.

Then they got the news: Dane had lung cancer and was given mere weeks to live. Cait was blindsided by grief, love and anger. Through it all she was determined to prove to him she could be the son he'd always wanted.

Sadly, he never saw her as a competent woman and rancher—only a beautiful daughter who needed a husband.

Lying in the grass, remembering, Caitlyn glanced toward the sky. "You never gave me a chance. And now…"

Tears stung the back of her eyes, but she refused to

shed a single one. No one was taking High Five, especially not Judd.

Reaching for Red's reins, she stood. In a flash, she was headed back to the ranch. She had to call her sisters. Maybe together they could save their home.

But the ranch wasn't Madison's or Skylar's home. They'd been raised by their mothers, and spent only summers and a week at Christmas here. Cait had always looked forward to those times. Back then money hadn't been a problem and their father had spoiled them terribly, giving them anything they'd wanted. But their best times had been just being together as sisters, racing their horses and exploring all the special places on the High Five ranch. It was always sad when the others left to return home for school in the fall.

For Caitlyn, the ranch had always been her home.

And always would be.

She glanced east to the Southern Cross.

Cait knew she had a fight on her hands, the biggest one of her life. There was no room for error, no room for losing.

And no room for feminine emotion.

CHAPTER THREE

CAITLYN RODE INTO the barn, feeling more determined than ever. Judd Calhoun would not take everything she loved.

As she unsaddled Red, it crossed her mind that she had once loved Judd. And if a psychologist chiseled through the stubborn layers of pride encased around her heart, a flicker of love might still be there. But Judd had just killed whatever remaining emotion she had ever felt for him. Guilt, her constant companion for years, had just vanished.

Now she was fighting mad.

"Hey, where did you take off to?" Cooper asked, walking into the barn, with Rufus a step behind him.

Her cowhands were outcasts, both of them ex-cons who worked cheap. She trusted them with her life.

Cooper Yates was bad to the bone—that's what people in High Cotton said about him. He'd had a nightmarish childhood, with a father who beat him regularly. In his teens he'd been in and out of juvenile hall.

Coop had been a year ahead of her in school and she'd always liked him. They were friends, sharing a love of horses.

After high school, Coop worked on several horse farms, determined to stay out of trouble. But trouble always seemed to follow him. When he'd hired on at an operation in Weatherford, Texas, several thoroughbred horses died unexpectedly. An investigation determined that the pesticide mixed with the feed to kill weevils had been incorrectly applied.

The owner pointed the finger at Coop. They'd gotten into a fight and the owner had filed charges. Cooper was arrested, tried and convicted. He'd spent six months in a Huntsville prison.

When Caitlyn heard the news, she was convinced Coop was innocent. There was nothing he didn't know about horses or their feed. She'd been proved right. The cover-up soon unraveled. The owner had mixed the feed and had used Coop as a scapegoat. Her friend was released, but the damage had been done. No one would hire him.

Caitlyn had urged her father to take a chance on Coop. He'd been working on High Five for three years now.

Rufus, the husband of Etta, their housekeeper, was now in his seventies. Years ago he'd been in a bar with friends when he saw a guy slap his girlfriend and slam her against the wall. Rufus pulled him off her and the man took a swing at him. Rufus ducked and managed to swing back, hard. The man went down and out—for good. His head hit a table and that was it.

Rufus had been tried and convicted. He'd spent three years in a Huntsville prison for involuntary manslaughter. When he was released, he came home to Etta and High Five. They were a part of the Belle extended family.

Cait threw Red's saddle over a sawhorse, then pushed back her hat. "I have a heap of problems, guys."

"What happened?" Coop asked. He was always the protective one.

She figured honesty was the best policy, so she told them the news.

"Shit," Rufus said, and quickly caught himself. "Sorry, Miss Caitlyn. Didn't mean to curse. It just slipped out."

"Don't worry, Ru. I'll be doing a lot of that in the days to come." She took a breath. "I don't know how much I'll be able to pay you, so it's up to you whether you go or stay."

"I'm staying," Coop replied without hesitation. "I'm here until Judd forces us out."

Rufus rubbed his face in thought. "I go where my Etta goes, and she ain't leaving High Five or Miss Dorie. I'm staying, too."

"Thanks, guys. Now I have to go tell Gran." Cait had had no doubt about the men staying. They were close. They were family.

"We're going to fix that fence in the northeast pasture," Coop said. "I guess we now have to play nice with the lofty Calhouns."

A smile touched her lips for the first time all day. "We're going to play, but I'm not thinking nice."

Coop grinned and it softened the harshness she often saw on his face.

She waved toward her horse. "Would you please rub down Red and feed her? I have to see Gran."

"You're gonna let me take care of Red?" One of Coop's eyebrows shot to the brim of his worn Stetson. "Did you hear that, Ru?"

"Yes, siree, I did."

She placed her hands on her hips. "Okay, I don't like other people taking care of my horse, so what?"

Cooper bowed from the waist. "I'll treat her with the utmost care, ma'am."

She shook her head and walked toward the house. The two-story wood-frame dwelling wasn't as fancy as the Calhoun spread. John Cotton, her great-great-grandfather, who'd settled High Cotton with Will Calhoun in the late 1800s, had had simpler taste.

The exterior was weatherboard siding that desperately needed a coat of paint. The hip roof sported four chimneys, but since Grandfather Bart had installed central air and heat, they were rarely used.

Brick piers supported Doric half columns along three sides of the wraparound porch. A slat-wood balustrade enclosed the porch with a decorative touch. Black plantation shutters added another touch, as did the beveled glass door that had been there since the house was built.

In the summers Cait and her sisters used to sleep out on the porch in sleeping bags, laughing and sharing secrets. What she had to share now wasn't going to be easy.

She picked up her stride and breezed through the back veranda into the kitchen. Etta was at the stove, stirring something in a pot.

"Where's Gran?"

"In her room." Etta always seemed to have a spoon in her hand, and she waved it now. "I'm almost afraid to go up there." The housekeeper was tiny and spry, with short gray hair, a loyal and honest woman with a heart of gold. Cait had never met a better person.

Etta was fiercely loyal to Dorie, and worried about her. Since her son's death, Dorie tended to live in a world removed from reality. As kids, playing make-believe with Gran had been a favorite pastime for Caitlyn and her sisters. But lately it had gotten out of hand.

"What is she doing?" Cait asked.

"She had me help her get that old trunk out of the attic. She was pulling clothes out of it when I came down to start supper. We're having stew and cornbread."

"Etta…" Cait sighed. "Neither you nor Gran are to pull trunks out of the attic. I'll do it or Coop will."

"She was in a hurry, and you know how Miss Dorie is."

"Yes." Cait turned toward the stairs in the big kitchen. "I'll go talk to her."

Cait knocked on her grandmother's door, stepping into the room when she heard her call, "Come in." Then she stopped and stared.

Gran stood in front of a full-length mirror, in a dress from the 1930s. It fit her slim figure perfectly. She wore heels and a jaunty hat that were also of that era.

"Gran, what are you doing?"

"'I've been betrayed so often by tomorrows, I don't dare promise them.'"

Cait blinked. That made no sense. Though it kinda, sorta exemplified their situation, she thought.

"Remember that line, baby?" Gran primped in front of the mirror, turning this way and that way.

"No, I don't." Cait was thirty-three and her grandmother still called her "baby." She wondered if Gran would ever see her as an adult.

"Bette Davis." Dorie whirled to face her. "As Joyce Heath in *Dangerous*. Let's play movies of the thirties."

"I really need to talk to you."

"Oh, posh." Gran knelt at the trunk, pulling out more clothes. She held up a white blouse with a big bow. "I know you remember this line. 'Fasten your seat belts. It's going to be a bumpy night.'"

Cait could say that was apt, but decided to leave her grandmother with her playful memories for the moment. Cait was worried whether Gran was ever going to be able to cope with her son's death. Soon, though, she was going to have to face facts. Cait hoped to make it as easy as possible.

She hurried down the wooden staircase and across the wide plank floors to her study. She had to call her sisters. Since Cait was in charge of their inheritance, they depended on her to make decisions that would benefit them. How did she tell them they wouldn't be receiving any more checks? *By being honest.*

She called Madison first. Their middle sister was easy—that's what she and Skylar often said. Not easy in the sexual sense, but with her emotions. Madison was easygoing, loving, compassionate, and felt other people's pain. Cait and Sky often played on Maddie's sensitive nature because they knew she would never do anything to hurt or disappoint them. Cait was counting on her understanding today.

Madison answered on the second ring.

"Maddie, it's Cait."

"Hi, big sister. What's going on? Is there a ranch crisis?"

It was the opening Caitlyn needed. "Yes." She told her about her meeting with Judd.

There was a long pause on the other end. "Cait, I need that money. I depend on it."

Cait was taken aback. This didn't sound like her easy, understanding sister.

"I'm sorry, but it's gone."

"Can't you do something?"

Cait heard the desperation in her voice. "You need to come home so we can discuss this."

"I… I can't."

"Why not?"

"I just can't, okay?"

"Maddie, we need to discuss our options face-to-face. That's all I know to do."

There was another long pause.

"I'll try to get the next flight out of Philadelphia. I'll let you know."

"Good. I can't wait to see you."

"Cait…"

"What?"

"Nothing. We'll talk when I get there."

Cait hung up, knowing something was going on with Maddie. But what? She'd find out soon enough.

Sadly, as they grew older, the sisters spent less and less time together. Maddie had come home when their father became ill, and had stayed until he died. Before that Cait hadn't seen her in three years.

Maybe they could reconnect and become family again. There was that hope, but she knew her sisters would pressure her to sell. She closed her eyes briefly, realizing she was facing the biggest fight of her life. And not only with Judd.

Calling Skylar was more difficult. She was the wild, defiant one, and was not going to take this news well. When Sky came to visit their father in his last days, it had been four years since Cait had seen her. Skylar had her own life, living in Lexington, Kentucky, with her mother, but had a stake here, too.

Without another thought, Cait made the call. Usually she had to leave a message on voice mail, but today her sister answered.

"Hi, Sky. It's Caitlyn."

"What's wrong? You only phone when something's wrong."

As with Maddie, she told her the truth, not sugar-coating any of it.

"You're kidding me."

"No. The cash flow has stopped and the ranch is in dire straits."

"Why, Caitlyn? Why isn't High Five making a profit? It's a big ranch with a lot of cattle, and it's always been profitable. What's the problem?"

Skylar was pointing the finger straight at her. How dare she! "Maybe if you came home more often, you'd know."

"Maybe if you were a better manager we wouldn't be in this fix."

"If you think you can do a better job, then get your ass here and try."

"Don't get huffy with me. If you'd just married the damn man, we wouldn't be in this mess."

"Excuse me?" Both of their tempers had flown the coop, so to speak, and Caitlyn wasn't backing down or admitting fault. This was typical of their relationship, with the two of them always at loggerheads.

"You know what I mean."

"My relationship with Judd or lack thereof has nothing to do with this. Dad sold our oil and gas royalties and now we have to decide what we're going to do. You need to come home."

"There is no way I can just drop everything and leave at a moment's notice."

"That's up to you. Maddie and I will make decisions without you."

"Like hell." There was a momentary pause. "Listen, Cait. I need that money."

"I heard the same thing from Maddie. And I might remind you that I put my money back into High Five. You two have been living free and easy. That's going to stop. I'm sorry, but it is. If you want to change things, then come home. That's my last word."

"Cait—"

"No, Sky. I'm not listening to any more of your mouth. If you think you can run this ranch better, you're welcome to try. *Just get here!*" She shouted the last words into the receiver and slammed it down.

Caitlyn stood and paced, trying to release her pent-up emotions. Sky didn't know how bad their father's drinking and gambling habits had been, nor did she know about Gran's fragile state of mind. Neither did Maddie.

Cait had shouldered the burden, while her sisters had lived a life of luxury. She ran her hands over her face with a deep, torturous sigh. She should have told them. Was this her fault?

Dropping her hands, she glanced out the window toward the Southern Cross. *I'll take everything you love.* Judd's words took root in her thoughts, her emotions. Yes, it was her fault. All because she wouldn't marry a man who didn't love her.

At nineteen, she'd believed in love and happily ever after. She'd thought she'd hit the jackpot, only to discover that the marriage had been arranged between Jack Calhoun and her father. That's why Judd had shown an interest in her, after ignoring her for years.

It was all planned. Caitlyn was to do as she was told. But her father didn't count on her stubborn streak.

She'd wanted to marry for love, and wouldn't settle for less.

Now, years later, she had to wonder if love was real

or just a fantasy that lived inside foolish women's hearts and minds.

For her, it was something she'd never experience again.

Love had died.

Only revenge remained.

CHAPTER FOUR

"CAITLYN, WHERE ARE YOU? I can't traipse all over the house looking for you. I'm too old for this. You have a visitor, so get your butt out here."

Etta's annoyed voice snapped Caitlyn out of her malaise. She hurried to the door and yanked it open, finding the housekeeper there with a wooden spoon in her hand.

As a kid, Cait had often felt the sting of that spoon on her legs, mostly for doing something she'd been told not to. She had a feeling Etta wanted to swat her with it now.

"What is it?"

"You have a visitor. He's in the parlor."

"He, who?"

"Mr. Calhoun."

Oh great, just what she needed. Two encounters with the man in one day. What did he want now? Her blood?

Etta leaned in and whispered, "What's he doing here?" Those faded brown eyes demanded an answer. Gran's faculties might be faulty, but Etta's were not. Cait knew she couldn't slip anything past her.

"I'm not sure. I'll go see."

Etta's bony fingers wrapped around her forearm, stopping her. "Don't lie to me, girl."

"High Five's in trouble. I'll explain later."

"Fine." She released her hold. "Did you check on Miss Dorie?"

"Yes. She's digging clothes out of the trunk and re-living happier times."

"Lordy, Lordy, is she ever gonna snap out of it?"

"We just have to be patient and gentle with her."

"Yeah." Etta glanced toward the parlor. "What are you waiting for?"

Cait smiled briefly. "Maybe a shot of courage."

Etta held up the spoon. "Will this help?"

"You bet."

Moments later, Caitlyn walked into the room, her boots dragging on the hardwood floor. The parlor looked the same as it had in the seventies, with velvet drapes and heavy antique furniture. Judd stood in the middle of the room on an Oriental rug that had seen better days. He held his hat in his hand, along with more blasted papers.

Oh, yes, a gentleman always removed his hat in the company of a lady. Judd had always had impeccable manners. Too bad they didn't come with real emotion, real feelings.

"What is it, Judd?" She stood a good twelve feet away, but still felt the power of his presence. Her lungs squeezed tight and a feeling from her past surfaced. She was nineteen, young and in—oops... The four-letter word wasn't in her vocabulary anymore. She'd replaced it with one that would scorch his ears.

"You left in such a hurry you forgot your copy of the sale of the royalties and your father's codicil to his will. You might need them to show your sisters." Judd held the papers toward her.

She crossed her arms and made no move to take them. "You could have sent someone with them. Brenda

Sue goes right by here on her way home. Why are *you* here?"

Her direct question didn't faze him. He laid the papers on an end table by the settee. Cait noticed the film of dust there. Damn! Etta's eyes weren't the best anymore and Cait didn't have time for housework. She had a ranch to run. And what did she care if Judd saw their home wasn't immaculate.

"I had a reason for coming," he said, jolting her out of her thoughts.

"What would that be?"

His eyes caught and held hers. She wanted to look away but couldn't. "I wanted to urge you once again to sell now and get it over with."

She cocked an eyebrow. "You don't think I can run this ranch successfully without the royalties?"

"You haven't so far."

"I—"

He held up a hand. "Don't make this about you and me. Do what's right for your family."

"*You* made this about you and me." Her voice rose with anger. "You want me to pay for daring to walk away from Judd Calhoun. Maybe even beg. It ain't happening, mister."

His lips formed a thin line. "I was harsh this afternoon. A lot of that old resentment came back. Bottom line, Caitlyn, you lived away from here a lot of years. It shouldn't be a problem to do that again."

"I lived away because my father didn't want me here. It wasn't voluntary." Despite every effort, she couldn't keep the hurt out of her voice.

"You made that decision. No one else."

She stepped closer to him, his woodsy masculine scent doing a number on her senses. "Yes, I did. At the time, you didn't even care enough to ask why I made that decision."

He gripped his Stetson so tight he bent the rim. "You wanted me to beg you to stay?"

"No. I wanted to talk. I wanted to have a say in our wedding, our marriage, our life."

He drew back. "I don't know what the hell you're talking about. You planned the wedding."

"Oh, please." She rolled her eyes. "I was to wear your mother's wedding dress and the wedding would be at Southern Cross. Soon after, I was to produce babies and heirs, preferably all male."

He frowned deeply. "My father requested that you wear my mother's dress and—"

"No. He demanded, and you backed him up." She cut him off faster than a road hog on the freeway. "I was never asked. Every freaking woman on the planet dreams of picking out her own damn wedding dress."

"It's a little late to be discussing this now."

"You got it, so take your offer of a sale and stuff it. I have six months and I'm taking every second of that time."

"Your sisters might have something to say about that."

"I can handle my sisters."

He stared at her and she resisted the urge to move away. He was too close, too powerful. But she stood her ground, despite shaky knees and an even shakier disposition.

"You've gotten hard, Caitlyn," he remarked, his eyes roaming over her face. Heat rose in her abdomen and traveled up to bathe her cheeks.

"Really? Your own edges are so hard they'd cut glass," she retorted.

His eyes met hers then. "That's what you did to us." Saying that, he walked out.

She sucked in a breath and an errant tear slipped from her eye. He had to have the last word, and it was effective, engaging all her feminine emotions. Guilt invaded her conscience and that made her mad.

Judd Calhoun would not get to her.

AFTER SUPPER, they sat at the kitchen table and talked about the future. Etta, Rufus and Cooper were all the help Caitlyn had, and they always ate together. Cooper lived in the bunkhouse, and Etta and Rufus's home was the first log cabin that Caitlyn's forefathers had built on the property.

Etta took a seat after checking on Gran. Cait had decided not to tell her grandmother until she felt Gran was ready to hear the news.

"How is she?" Cait asked.

"Still playing with those old clothes. Miss Dorie needs to get a grip on reality, but I don't know how she's going to handle what's happening now. Lordy, Lordy." Etta shook her head. "But I know one thing. I'm not playing Prissy from *Gone with the Wind* again. Enough is enough."

"Now you'd make a good Prissy," Ru said, chewing on a toothpick. "A mite too skinny, though."

"Now you listen here—"

Caitlyn made a time-out sign. "Take a breather. We have bigger problems than Gran's make-believe. I'm open for suggestions."

Coop rested his forearms on the old oak table. "June is a couple of days away and we'll have plenty of hay to bale. We can keep what we need and sell the rest. And, of course, sell some of the stock."

Cait took a sip of her tea. "I only want to do that as a last resort. Without cattle we can't operate this ranch."

"Don't worry about my wages, Cait," Coop said. "I have a place to live, and food. All I need are a few bucks for beer, and gas for my truck."

"Same goes for Etta and me," Rufus added.

"I appreciate everyone's help. My sisters will be here in a few days and we'll decide what to do."

"No offense—" Coop swiped a hand through his sandy-blond hair "—but they're city girls. They don't know much about ranching."

"They're owners of High Five, though, same as me."

"Yep." Ru reached for his worn hat. "Things are getting rough around here. I think I'll mosey over to our place and stretch out for a while."

"Just wipe your feet before you go in," Etta told him.

"Woman, don't be a pain in my ass."

Cait was in the process of interrupting when there was a loud knock on the back door.

Chance Hardin, Etta and Rufus's nephew, poked his head in. "Hey, I wondered where everyone was."

When Etta's brother and sister-in-law were killed in a car accident, Etta and Rufus had taken in their three boys. Chance was the only one still around High Cotton, and he checked on his aunt and uncle often.

"Chance." Etta threw herself at him and hugged him tightly.

"Let him go, for heaven sakes," Ru said. "You're gonna choke him to death."

Cait noticed Ru squeezing Chance's shoulder, too. They were both glad to see him.

Etta drew back, her bony fingers smoothing her nephew's chambray shirt. "Why didn't you call and let us know you were coming? We'd have waited supper. Are you hungry? We have plenty."

"No. I've already eaten. I was just passing by and wanted to say hi."

"Hi, Chance," Caitlyn said.

"Ah, Cait, the most beautiful woman in High Cotton."

She grinned. "Yeah. Me and every woman you meet."

He met her grin with a stellar one of his own. "Damn. Beautiful and smart. Can't beat that with a sledgehammer." He turned to Cooper. "Hey, Coop."

"Chance." The cowboy shook his hand. "What are you doing these days?"

"Working my butt off for the big oil companies."

"You still out on the rigs?"

"You bet. Pays good money. We're drilling over at the McGruder place, about thirty miles from here."

"I know. I've been by the place a few times and saw a lot dump trucks going in and out of there."

"Yeah. Old man McGruder is smart as a whip. This is the second well we've drilled on his property, and he probably has money coming out the wazoo. But now he's selling sand and gravel off his land."

"Who buys it, and for what?" Cait asked curiously.

"He sold a lot of sand and gravel to the oil company. They have to have it to build roads to the oil pads, so the big rig and trucks can go in and out without getting stuck. Of course, we had to have water for drilling, so Mr. McGruder got a new water well. They use the pea gravel for drilling, too. He's also selling sand to a home builder who uses it for the foundation of new houses."

"Bart did that back in the eighties when things got a little tight," Rufus said.

"Where?" Cait asked, not remembering that.

"The southwest pasture. We don't run cattle there."

"How about some pie?" Etta interrupted.

Caitlyn picked up the leftover chocolate pie from the table and handed it to her. "Go spend some time with Chance. I'll clean the kitchen."

"No, I—"

Cait gently nudged them out the door, knowing they wanted to visit.

"I'll help," Coop offered.

Within minutes they had the kitchen clean. Cait laid the dish towel over the edge of the sink.

"Are you okay?" the cowboy asked.

She wiped her hands down her faded jeans. "Not really. I don't know how I'm going to save this ranch. With the oil and gas royalties, I was able to rebuild the herd Dad had sold. We were just getting to a point were we might show a profit. But if we have to sell off cows that won't happen."

"A calf crop will be ready to market in June. That will help."

"Yeah, but it won't be enough to see us through a dry summer." She massaged her temples. "It's a bitch when the past comes back and bites you in the butt."

Coop leaned against the cabinet. "How much gambling money did your dad owe?"

Cait dropped her hands. "I didn't ask." And she should have. Where was her brain? Going down guilt avenue at full throttle. Damn it. That should have been her first question. But her senses were too busy remembering what it was like to be in love with Judd.

"Those people are not pleasant when they don't get their money."

"Judd mentioned that."

"Maybe Judd was the only solution for Dane, for High Five."

She pointed a finger at Cooper. "Oh, please. Don't you dare go over to his side."

"I'm not, but you know how your father was. He never had a spending limit."

"I know." She stretched her shoulders, wishing she could close her eyes and the nightmare would go away.

"I saw Judd's truck here this afternoon."

"Yeah. He was doing what he does best, pressuring me to sell."

There was silence for a moment.

"I wasn't here all those years ago when you broke the engagement, but I assume you had a good reason."

Cait thought about that. Would a man understand? Cooper was her best friend. She told him a lot of things, but sharing her feelings about Judd wasn't on the table.

"Okay, that's a little personal, and I don't do personal," Coop said quickly. "Think I'll head to the bunkhouse and nurse a beer."

"Think I'll head to the study and nurse a gigantic headache named Judd Calhoun."

Coop smiled. "See you in the morning."

Caitlyn walked upstairs to check on Gran. She was curled up on a chaise longue, asleep in a dress from the forties, with her long white hair cascading over her shoulder.

Kissing her wrinkled cheek, Cait whispered, "Dream on, Gran." With a sigh, she sank down to the floor beside her. Resting her head on her grandmother's hand, she picked up a high-necked dress from the thirties.

So many people depended on her: Gran, her sisters, Etta, Rufus and Cooper. What would they do if High Five was sold?

Judd had her by... What was it that guys said? By the short hairs? All she knew was that Judd had her where it hurt. Bad.

She fingered the dress, which smelled of mothballs, willing herself to come up with a way to get the money she needed to save her home.

Wait a minute. She sat up straight and threw the dress into the trunk. Why hadn't she thought of it before?

CHAPTER FIVE

EARLY THE NEXT MORNING Caitlyn was on the way to Mr. McGruder's. She wanted information about selling sand and gravel. She could have called, but Mr. McGruder was the kind of man who responded better when talking face-to-face. Being of the older generation, he didn't care for phones all that much. He liked the personal touch.

It didn't take her long to get the buyer's name and number. She didn't ask about price because she knew McGruder wouldn't divulge it.

Back in her office, she called only to learn the man had all the suppliers he needed. Damn! She told him to keep her in mind if he ever needed another one, and gave him her name and phone number.

By the time she hung up, all the excitement had oozed out of her and she felt stupid. Their financial situation wasn't going to be that easy to fix. There must be a black cloud over her head or something, but she didn't have time to wallow in misery. There was work to be done.

She saddled Jazzy, her brown quarter horse, and set out to join Coop and Rufus. Red neighed from across the fence. The mare didn't like it when Cait rode another horse, but Jaz was for work. Red she rode for pleasure.

The day was already getting hot. Cait pulled her

straw hat lower to shade her face. Her arms were protected from the sun by a long-sleeved, pearl-snap shirt. The sun was hell on a woman's skin.

Coop came to meet her riding a bay gelding. "We have a good count of calves in this pasture to go in June, and we have a lot more on the ground, maybe a September sale."

They ran a mixed-breed cow-and-calf operation now. Cait's father had sold the registered stock years ago. In High Five's heyday her great-grandfather would have nothing but purebreds on his property. But it took time and money to keep records of an animal's ancestry, so that wasn't an option for the ranch anymore.

"We can make this work." Coop glanced around at the knee-deep coastal the cows and calves were standing in. "They have plenty to eat and all we have to do is supply water, salt and minerals."

Cait moved restlessly in the saddle. "It's the summer I'm worried about. When the coastal has been eaten and we have barren dry ground."

"We'll rotate the pastures like always."

Cait's gaze swept over the grazing cattle. "Where's Ru?"

"Checking the windmill."

"Good. We have to make sure they have water at all times."

"I'm heading for the northeast pasture. Catch you later." Coop kneed his horse and then pulled up again. "Whoa, we got company."

Cait noticed the riders, too—Albert Harland, the Southern Cross foreman, and two cowboys. Harland was mean as a rattlesnake, sneaky as a ferret, and resembled the latter. His number one goal was to make life as miserable as possible for Caitlyn. He thought she was uppity and didn't know her place.

He stopped just short of galloping into her. If he thought she was going to show fear, then the man didn't have a brain cell that was actively working.

"Mornin', Miss Belle." He tipped his hat and grinned like a possum eating persimmons.

"Harland." She folded her hands over the saddle horn. "Is there a problem?"

"Yep." The saddle protested from his weight. "The fence is down again on this pasture. One of your bulls, the big black one, keeps getting into our registered cows, and Mr. Calhoun would appreciate it if you'd take care of your fences and keep your mangy bull away. It costs us money every time he breeds a cow. You got it?"

Anger shot through her veins like a rocket. "I got it."

"And if I catch that bull on the Southern Cross again, I'll shoot him. Do I make myself clear?"

"You bag of—"

Harland broke into Coop's effusive tirade. "Yates, if I catch you on the Southern Cross, I'll shoot first and ask questions later. Ex-cons aren't welcome there." He jerked his reins to turn his horse, but Caitlyn reached out and grabbed them, effectively stopping the horse. And rider.

"What the hell?" the foreman spluttered.

"Let's get one thing straight, Harland. That gun business works both ways. If Judd Calhoun doesn't want to see a lot of dead registered cows sprawled on his property, then I suggest you think twice before shooting my bull."

"Why, you—"

"And if you even look crossways at Cooper, you're

gonna have a whole lot of mad woman coming your way. Got it?"

"Bitch," Harland muttered, and jerked his horse away.

"Give your boss the message," she shouted as they rode off her land.

"Damn, Cait." Coop stared at her with a startled expression. "You can bullshit better than anyone I know." His eyes narrowed. "Or did you mean that?"

She shifted uncomfortably in the saddle. "Actually, if I had to shoot any living thing, I'd probably throw up." She lifted an eyebrow. "But I can talk a good game. I did mean what I said about you, though." She turned her horse. "Now let's go get ol' Boss before he gets us into any more trouble."

They'd named the bull Boss because he fought every bull that came within his chosen territory. He liked having the cream of the crop, and usually that included their neighbor's cows.

Caitlyn and Cooper crossed onto Judd's ranch through the broken barbed wire, and found the bull easily, smack-dab in the middle of a herd of high-class registered cows. He was busy sniffing every animal in sight.

"This could prove to be a little difficult," Coop said, pulling up alongside Cait. The two of them watched the two-thousand-pound bull chasing cows. "He's not going to like having his fun interrupted."

"Any ideas?" she asked as she caught sight of Harland and his cowboys on the horizon. They were watching, waiting for her to make a fool of herself.

"The old-fashioned way?" Coop suggested.

"Okay." She knew cattle and she knew horses, and both were unpredictable. Cait wasn't counting on Boss being docile and following her to High Five. He was in the midst of sealing a thirty-second love affair with a high-priced cow, and he wasn't going to take their intrusion kindly. "Let's give our quarter horses a workout. Ready?"

"Yep. Watch those sawed-off horns."

"I'll take the left," Cait said as she meandered into the herd. Coop moved to the right of the bull.

The cows scattered, and as soon as Boss spotted the riders, he swung his head in an agitated manner and pawed at the ground with a you'll-never-take-me stance. Cait patted Jaz's neck. "Okay, let's show him who's the boss."

They effectively cut him away from the herd, and Boss wasn't happy. He charged, but Jaz did her magic, swinging back and forth, not letting him get by. The bull charged the other way, but Coop was there, blocking his path. Boss swung toward Cait again and she let Jaz work the way she'd been trained. The quick moves had Cait on full alert. She had to stay focused and not lose her balance.

As the bull switched gears and charged toward Coop yet again, Caitlyn pulled the Hot-Shot cattle prod from her saddle and rode in and zapped the animal from the rear.

Not liking the sting, Boss spun round and round, snot flying from his nose, and then made a dead run for High Five.

"Hot damn," Coop shouted. He rode right on the bull's tail, whooping and hollering.

Jaz was ready to run, too, and Cait had a hard time controlling her. As Jaz pranced around, Cait saw that Judd had joined Harland and the boys. There was no mistaking him. She backed up Jaz with a quick step, thumbed her nose at the watching crowd, then high-tailed it for High Five. She didn't even mind eating Coop's and Boss's dust.

"Yee haw," she cried, just for the hell of it, immensely grateful she hadn't made a fool of herself. Or maybe that was a matter of opinion.

When she caught up with Coop, he was watching Boss refamiliarize himself with the High Five herd, sniffing each cow to make sure he hadn't missed one while he was rambling.

"That bull has one insatiable appetite."

"It keeps calves on the ground," Cait said, trying not to smile. "Now let's fix that fence." She turned Jaz and saw the rider coming their way. "Now what?"

Judd, tall and impressive in the saddle, was headed toward her. He rode a magnificent black stallion, as magnificent as the man himself. Both exuded strength, power and a touch of splendor. And she could be suffering from too much sun, because Judd had more of a touch of the devil than of splendor.

"I'm going to get Rufus," Coop said. "You're on your own."

"Gee, thanks." She nudged her horse forward to meet her neighbor, wiping dust from her mouth with the back of her hand. At that moment she realized what a sight she must look, with dust from her hat to her boots and sweat staining her blouse. She smelled as foul as her horse, and the fact rubbed like a cocklebur against the feminine side of her nature.

"Why are you playing rodeo in my herd?"

"I was told to get my bull out, and that's what I did." She kept her voice neutral and didn't react to his angry tone.

"My boys could have cut him out much easier." His tone didn't change.

She rose a bit in the saddle and the leather creaked. "I thought I did a damn good job myself, considering time was of the essence."

He squinted against the noonday sun. "What do you mean?"

"Harland said he was going to shoot him if I didn't get him out in a nanosecond. Something about 'registered cows' and 'Judd Calhoun wasn't pleased.'"

His face tightened into those taut lines she knew so well. "I never said anything about shooting the bull. You have my word he won't be shot. Just keep the damn animal on your property."

A quick thank-you rose in her throat, but his last sentence killed the idea like a blast from a shotgun, successfully scattering it to the saner regions of her mind.

"That's what I'm doing," she said through clenched teeth.

He motioned over his shoulder. "I'll have the fence repaired."

"I can fix the fence."

"I want it done right and not half-ass."

Any other time she would have spat holy hell at his high-handedness. But it would take money to repair the fence properly, money she didn't have. For the sake of High Five she pushed her pride aside. And the weight was heavy. It took her a full minute to nod her head.

He stood in the stirrups and picked up his reins. Suddenly he eased his butt back against the leather, his black eyes holding hers with a gleam she remembered from her younger days—a gleam of playful teasing. Talk about a blast from the past. It was so unexpected it almost knocked her out of the saddle.

"Your blouse is open."

She glanced down and saw that two snaps were un-done, revealing the white lace of her bra. They must have come open when she was bulldogging Boss. *Oh, sh…*

Raising her eyes to his, she replied, "I know. I like it that way. It's cooler."

"It might give Yates the wrong idea."

"Maybe. But that's none of your business."

He inclined his head, and she wondered if he re-membered all the times he had undone her blouse, and what had followed afterward. With all the women who'd followed her in his life, she doubted it. But she remembered the tantalizing brush of his fingers and the excitement that had leaped through her—much as it was doing now. Some memories were gold plated and stored in secret places. Why she'd chosen this moment to review them was unclear.

"Enjoy the fresh air." He kneed the stallion, and the horse responded beautifully, turning on a dime and kicking up dirt. She watched rider and horse until they disappeared into the distance.

Then she slowly snapped her shirt closed.

JUDD GAVE BARON HIS HEAD and they flew through fields of coastal and herds of cattle. They sliced through the wind effortlessly, but no matter how fast the stallion ran, Judd couldn't outrun the fire in his gut from when he'd looked at Caitlyn.

He shouldn't feel this way after all these years. How could he hate her and react like this? All he could think about was reaching out and undoing the rest of those snaps, lifting her from the saddle and then slid-ing with her to the grass. Nothing existed but the two of them, and together they rode to places only lovers knew about....

His hat flew off and he slowed. He turned Baron and headed back for it. Reaching down, he swiped it from the ground. After dusting it off, he galloped toward home. And put every memory of Caitlyn out of his mind. That came easy. He'd been doing it for years.

Over the ridge, Harland and the cowboys were waiting. Judd stopped.

"Get supplies and fix that fence today," he said to the foreman. "I don't want that bull back in my herd."

"You want us to fix the fence?" Harland asked, a touch of sarcasm in his voice.

Being second-guessed rubbed Judd the wrong way. Harland questioned too many of his orders, and he wanted it stopped.

"Do you have a problem with that?" he asked, his eyes locking with the other man's.

"No, sir, but—"

"On the Southern Cross, I'm the boss and what I say goes. If that doesn't suit you, you're welcome to leave. Now."

"C'mon, Judd, I've worked here a long time. I just thought Miss Belle should be the one to fix the fence. Her bull broke it."

"Miss Belle would only patch it. I want it fixed right. In a few months her place will become a part of Southern Cross and I don't want to have to redo it."

Harland grinned. "I knew you had a damn good reason. I'll get the boys right on it."

"Another thing, and I hope I'm clear about this— do not shoot that bull or any neighbor's animal that strays onto our property. I don't do business that way. Am I clear?"

"Yes, sir. I was only trying to scare her."

"Miss Belle doesn't scare that easily."

Judd kneed Baron and rode on toward the barn. Nothing scared Caitlyn, except losing High Five. That was her deepest fear and he knew it. Knowing your enemy's weakness was half the battle. Victory was just a matter of time.

It was his goal, what he'd dreamed about for fourteen years. But as he dismounted, all he could see and think about was her open blouse and the curve of her breast.

CHAPTER SIX

CAITLYN RODE BACK TO THE house about two to check on Gran. She hadn't been up when Cait had left that morning.

Chance's truck was parked outside, and when she went in, Gran, Etta and he were at the table, just finishing lunch. Gran was dressed in her normal slacks and blouse, and her hair was pinned at her nape. She looked like she used to, and Cait prayed her grandmother was back to her old self.

"Caitlyn, baby, we have a visitor," Gran said. "Chance is having lunch with us."

He winked. "Etta wouldn't let me leave without eating one of her home-cooked meals."

"We see you so little." Etta carried dishes to the sink.

Caitlyn placed her hat on the rack. "Leaving so soon?"

"Yep." Chance stood. "We're through at the Mc-Gruders and we're packing up and heading for east Texas." He kissed his aunt's cheek. "I'll call. Thanks for the lunch, Miss Dorie."

Caitlyn followed him outside. "Would you do me a favor, please?"

Chance settled his hat on his head. "Anything, beautiful lady."

"If you hear of anyone needing sand or gravel, would you send them my way?"

"Sure. Etta told me about High Five's problem. I'm sorry, Cait."

"Thank you. Find me a buyer and I'll love you forever."

"Yeah." He smiled broadly. "They all say that."

She waved as he drove away, and then she went back inside.

Gran was on the phone. Replacing the receiver, she smiled at Caitlyn. "That was Madison. She's coming for a visit." Dorie looked past Cait. "Is your father with you? He's going to be so excited."

Cait felt as if someone had just lassoed her around the neck and yanked the rope tight. She struggled to breathe. Gran was not back to normal. The doctors had said to tell her the truth, so that's what Cait did, even though it made her throat feel rusty and dry.

"Gran, Dad is dead."

"Yes." A look of sadness clouded her brown eyes. "I forget sometimes."

Caitlyn hugged her. "It's okay to forget—sometimes."

But Cait never forgot, not for a second. Her father's death filled her every waking moment and all the dreams that tortured her nights. She wasn't the son he'd wanted. At her age she should be beyond that childhood feeling of inadequacy. Why wasn't she?

Gran drew back, her eyes bright with unshed tears. "But it's exciting that Maddie's coming home, isn't it?"

"Yes, it is. When is she arriving?"

Gran frowned. "I forget."

"Don't worry about it," Cait reassured her. She would call Maddie back.

"Okay. I'm going upstairs, to pull out all the dresses that will look great on Madison. With her blond hair and blue eyes, she'd make a great Ingrid Bergman. *Casablanca.* Oh, yes, we're going to have so much fun."

Cait sighed and scrubbed her face with her hands. She wanted her grandmother back—the one who didn't live in a make-believe world.

Etta patted her shoulder. "Dorie will be fine. She's just grieving."

"I don't know. It's been over two months now."

"Stop worrying. You have to get a move on. Maddie's plane lands in Austin at four."

Cait whirled around. "What?"

"I answered the phone and that's what she said."

"Good grief, I could use a little notice. It's not like I'm sitting here cleaning the dirt from under my nails."

"Well, I'm sure they could use it." Etta reached for the plate of leftover fried chicken.

Caitlyn looked at her nails. Holy moly. They were broken off short and caked with dirt. How unattractive was that? They were a worker's hands. She'd almost forgotten how to feel feminine.

She touched the collar of her shirt. No, she hadn't forgotten. She'd felt it today when Judd had stared at her breasts.

She threw that emotion into the trash bin of her thoughts. That's where it needed to stay. And that's where Judd Calhoun would stay, too.

A few minutes later, Caitlyn was driving Gran's old Lincoln, munching on a chicken leg and heading for Austin, almost two hours away. She'd taken the sedan because she was afraid her truck wouldn't make it. Turning up the radio, she leaned back and enjoyed the ride.

The traffic wasn't bad on U.S. 290 or Texas 21. As she neared Bastrop Highway it became a little congested, as it was on Presidential Boulevard in Austin, leading to the terminal.

Glancing at her watch, she saw it was already after four. By the time she reached the baggage and pickup area she was definitely late.

With her blond hair, her sister was easy to spot. Maddie placed her case on the backseat and slipped into the passenger side. She wore gray slacks and a powder-blue top, with her hair in a neat bob around her face.

"Hey, big sis." Madison hugged and kissed her, then wrinkled her nose. "Whatever perfume you're using, it's not working."

"Very funny. I was on the range and didn't get your message until almost two. I didn't have time to change, so don't give me any lip."

A car honked behind them.

"Keep your britches on," Cait said into her rearview mirror, and drove off.

"We can't go far," Maddie told her.

"Why not?"

"I got a call from Sky, and her plane is coming in at five."

"It would be nice if the two of you would call me and let me know these things."

"I tried three times this morning and no one answered, so don't give *me* any lip." Maddie held up a hand for a high five, something they'd done since they were kids.

They slapped hands. "I was out early, Gran was asleep and Chance was at Etta's, so I guess she was late."

"Sky tried, too, and couldn't get anyone. That's why she called me."

Cait maneuvered through the traffic. "I'll have to go out and circle back."

"Sky should be there by then."

Cait's full attention was on the traffic zooming by the old Lincoln, and nothing else was said.

"How's Gran?" Maddie finally asked, keeping an eye on the traffic, too.

"Not good. She hasn't adjusted to Dad's death. She even forgets he is dead. Most of the time she plays make-believe with those old clothes she's saved from her Broadway days."

"I love playing make-believe with Gran. It's a special memory of my childhood."

"Mine, too, but it's different now." Cait made the turn onto Presidential Boulevard. "You'll see when you get home."

"It won't be the same without Dad there," Maddie said, her voice laced with sadness.

"I know. I—"

"There's Skylar." Maddie pointed to the striking redhead with the impatient expression, standing at the curb.

Cait knew it was Sky, but it didn't look like her flashy sister. Her hair was clipped back and she wore black slacks, a white blouse and no-nonsense shoes. No jewelry. Very little makeup. She could pass for a nun. This couldn't be her sister—the one whose best friend was a mirror.

Cait pulled up and Skylar slid into the backseat. "Where in the hell have you been? I've been standing out here for ten minutes."

Oh, yeah. Now *this* was her sister.

"I'm sorry, your highness. I'm a little late with my pick-up schedule."

"Shut up, Cait."

"*You* shut up," she retorted.

Suddenly all three burst out laughing. Sky leaned over the seat and patted Cait's and Maddie's shoulders. "It's so good to see both of you. Sorry I'm so bitchy. I think I have permanent PMS."

"You've been that way since you were about five, so I don't think you can blame it on that." Cait snickered.

"Don't start with me!" Skylar warned. Without a pause, she added, "How's Gran?"

Cait told her what she'd told Maddie.

"Gran has always loved to play make-believe. That's nothing new." Sky looked behind them. "I think you just ran a red light."

"I did not. It was yellow."

"And you're always right."

Cait glanced at her in the rearview mirror. "Remember that when we discuss the ranch, which we'll do at home and not in the car."

"You're bossy, but you've always been that way."

"We have bitchy and bossy, so what am I?" Maddie asked.

"Hmm." Cait thought about it. "How about Betty Crocker sweet?"

"Oh, please." Maddie sighed. "I can be bitchy and bossy."

Both her sisters guffawed at that and then Sky leaned over the seat. "I don't think the ranch is in as bad a shape as you say, and I think Gran is fine, too. You're exaggerating."

Cait gritted her teeth and changed the subject. The rest of the way home they talked about their childhood. Maddie and Sky would have to see the ranch for themselves. It wasn't the showplace it once was. Sky had only stayed for a little while when their father had passed. Maddie knew more of the situation, but didn't offer any comments.

They reached Giddings and turned onto a county road that led to High Cotton. The place was barely a stop in the road—a convenience store–gas station combo; a general store that sold feed and hardware; a post office, community center, water and utilities building; two beer joints, one on each side of the road.

Caitlyn pulled into the gas station. "I better fill up before we go home. Gran gets really mad if the tank is empty."

They all climbed out. Cait undid the gas cap and inserted the nozzle just as Brenda Sue drove up in her Corolla.

"Hi, there, Caitlyn," the blonde gushed as she got out. "I have to get my kids snacks. You know how kids are—always wanting something." Her gaze swung to her passengers. "You don't have to tell me. I know these are your sisters. I met y'all years ago at a Fourth of July barbecue on High Five. Your dad sure knew how to throw a party, and he was showing off his girls. You probably don't remember me because I didn't stay around long. I had a big crush on Chance Hardin and I was more interested in seeing him. You know how that is. I'll catch y'all later."

Sky and Maddie stared after her. "What the hell was that?" Sky asked. "My head is buzzing."

"A girl I went to school with. She has a hard time taking a breath." Cait grinned.

"Talk about a run-on sentence," Maddie declared.

Sky looked around. "How do you live in this hick place?"

"It's home. It's all I know and it's everything I love."

Sky and Maddie exchanged glances.

"I'll pay for the gas and we'll be on our way to see Gran." Walking away, she felt the dent in her heart and in her pride. Her sisters had never viewed High Five the way she had, and she knew she had a big fight coming.

CAIT DROVE DOWN the dirt road to High Five, dust billowing behind them. The garages Grandpa Bart had built were in back. A covered walkway connected them to the house. He'd put in the garage for his beloved Dorie, so she could have easy access in inclement weather.

Pulling into Gran's spot, Cait slid the gearshift into Park and got out. Madison and Skylar followed.

Sky looked toward the barn. "When I was here for Dad's funeral, I did notice things were in disrepair. Maybe you didn't exaggerate that part."

"I haven't exaggerated anything."

At that moment, Coop and Rufus rode in from a day's work on the range.

Sky watched Cooper closely. "Why you hired an ex-con is beyond me. Have you thought he might be stealing from you? Maybe that's the reason we're in such a mess."

"Cooper is a fine, honest, hardworking man, and I trust him. If you want to keep all that red hair on your head, then I suggest you button your bitchy mouth."

"And I suggest—"

"Stop it." Madison stomped her foot. "I'm not spending this visit refereeing you two. Grow up, for heaven sakes."

Caitlyn shrugged. "Betty Crocker has spoken."

They laughed, linked arms and made their way into the house. They'd always been like that—fighting like hellcats and in the next instant smiling and hugging. They were sisters and could make each other madder than anyone. And they loved one another just as fiercely. Cait hoped they could remember that in the days ahead.

CHAPTER SEVEN

A STOMACH-RUMBLING AROMA greeted them. Clearly, Etta had been preparing a special meal.

Madison hugged the older woman. "I could gain five pounds just by the smell in your kitchen."

"Lordy, Lordy." Etta smiled at them. "You girls are a sight for these sore old eyes. I made chicken and dressing with all the trimmings and I don't want to hear one word about any diets. Tonight we're celebrating."

"You won't get any complaints from me." Sky embraced Etta. "I love your cooking."

"Where's Gran?" Maddie asked.

"Upstairs trying on dresses, and I'm not running up those stairs one more time to see how a gown looks on her. My patience and bony legs only go so far."

"I'll check on her." Cait hurried through the dining room, then stopped so suddenly that Maddie and Sky bumped into her.

"Good heavens, Cait, you could at least…" Sky's voice trailed off as they stared up at their grandmother on the staircase.

She wore a white muslin slip that had to be at least fifty years old. Her long white hair tumbled down her back and across her shoulders was draped… No, it couldn't be. But Cait glanced toward the parlor and saw that it most definitely *was*—the old hunter-green velvet curtain.

"'War, war, war.'" Gran placed the back of her hand against her forehead. "'I get so bored I could scream.'"

Oh, my God! Cait darted up the stairs. "Gran," she said softly.

The elderly woman looked at her, her eyes a little dazed. "Hi, baby. Scarlett O'Hara from *Gone with the Wind,* remember?"

Cait swallowed. "Yes, Gran. Let me take this." She removed the heavy drape. "Look who's here." Maddie and Sky came up the stairs.

Gran held out her arms. "Oh, my babies are home." Maddie and Sky hugged their grandmother, then Gran brushed away a tear. "Caitlyn, go get your father. He's going to be so happy."

The three sisters stood transfixed, almost paralyzed. Cait's throat felt raw and she didn't know if she could say those words again today. They hurt too much.

Maddie came to the rescue, sliding her arm around Gran's waist. "Let's go upstairs so you can lie down."

"Okay."

Cait took Gran's free arm and they all walked her to her room. Sky threw back the comforter on the four-poster bed and Gran crawled in. Cait arranged the big pillows under her head the way she liked.

"Comfy?" she asked.

"Oh, yes. My girls are home." Gran closed her eyes, holding on to Maddie's and Sky's hands.

Cait left the room. She had to or she was going to burst into tears. It broke her heart to see their grandmother like this.

On the stairs, she picked up the drape where she'd left it, and carried it to the parlor. It smelled of dust and age.

The stool Gran had used to take down the curtain

stood by the windows. She could have fallen, broken something. Suddenly everything was too much, and Cait sank to the floor, the velvet drape settling in a heap around her. She drew her knees up and rested her forehead on them. Tears she couldn't stop spilled from her eyes. She couldn't be this weak! But Gran was her soft spot, her Achilles' heel.

"Cait." Sky sat beside her. "You weren't exaggerating. I can't stand to see Gran like that."

She raised her head. "I can't either, and I don't know how to help her."

"Me neither, but I'll be here for a few days, so I can at least help out."

"That would be nice."

Maddie came into the room. "Gran's asleep. She's exhausted from trying on clothes." She picked up the velvet fabric. "Let's hang this."

Together they put the drape back in place. Maddie wiggled her nose. "It's very dusty."

"I don't have time for housework. That can be your job while you're here."

"Gee, thanks."

"Supper's ready," Etta called.

The sisters made their way into the kitchen, to find Rufus sitting at the table.

"Where's Cooper?" Cait asked.

The old cowboy shifted nervously in his chair. "He's at the bunkhouse. I'll take him a plate."

"Nonsense…"

"I'm glad he respects our privacy," Sky said. "I feel more comfortable that way."

Cait placed her hands on her hips. "I hope you never have to eat those words."

"Now, listen—"

"Sit down and stop this bickering," Etta added, and the two of them complied.

Supper was a subdued affair. They were thinking about Gran.

IN THE MORNING, Cait awoke early and went down to make coffee. She carried Gran a cup.

"Mornin', baby." Gran scooted up in bed. "It's always refreshing to see my sweet baby's face first thing in the day."

Cait handed her the coffee. "Gran, I'm hardly a baby."

"I know. You should be married." Her grandmother took a sip. "Have you seen Judd lately?"

The change of subject took her by surprise. She wanted Gran back to normal, but not where she could gauge her emotions and read her mind. Caitlyn fidgeted as she felt the old woman's eyes filleting her like a crappie, getting to the tasty part.

She gave her best I-couldn't-care-less impression. "In a town as small as High Cotton, it's hard to miss Judd Calhoun."

"Because he stands a head taller than the rest, and your heart goes pitter-patter every time you see him."

Cait kissed Gran's forehead, wanting to tell her what a snake in the grass Judd really was. But she could never hurt her. "Not exactly." It felt more like she'd been hit in the chest with a rock from a slingshot, and her heart reacted in spasms of pain and regret. "I have to go to work, and you have company."

Dorie's face scrunched into a frown—like the one she'd told Cait, as a child, never to make in case it caused wrinkles. That must be true, because Gran had very few wrinkles. On the other hand, Caitlyn could feel hers deepening daily.

"Company?" Gran sat up straight. "Oh, my, Madison and Skylar are here, aren't they? I remember now."

"Yes." Cait clenched her jaw and waited. *Please, please, don't ask me to go get my father.*

Gran handed Cait her cup and swung her feet over the side of the bed. "I have to see them."

The door swung open just then and Maddie and Sky rushed in, dressed in their sleeping attire, shorts and tanks tops. Not for the first time, Cait realized Maddie was way too thin.

Amid hugs, kisses and laughter, Caitlyn said, "I have to get Cooper and Rufus started for the day. I'll be back later."

"Cait?" Sky called.

She glanced back.

"We need to talk."

She nodded shortly, resenting that her sister felt she needed to remind her.

An hour later, Cait joined Skylar and Madison in the study. Her sisters sat across the desk, where she laid out the document their father had signed, selling High Five's oil and gas royalties. Sky whipped it up, quickly read through it and then shoved it at Maddie.

"It says you get to make the decision whether to sell or not. So what the hell are we doing here?" Anger laced Sky's accusing words.

"You're both part owners of High Five."

"But you can keep us in limbo for six months?"

"Yes. And I just might make a success of this ranch."

Sky laughed, a sound that ricocheted off Cait's nerve endings. "Keep dreaming and we're going to wind up with nothing. I can't believe Dad would do this to us."

Maddie placed the document on the desk. "I know how you feel about High Five, Cait, but…but I depend on my share of the money."

"I do, too," Sky added. "I'm barely getting by the way things are now. I'm sorry, but we need to sell."

Cait swallowed the retort that leaped to her throat. "What about Gran?"

Skylar crossed her legs and stared at a speck on her jeans. Maddie kept her eyes downward. Cait knew this wasn't easy for them. It wasn't easy for her, either.

She leaned forward, trying to make her point. "Every dime I've gotten from royalties has gone back into High Five. Dad pretty much left us penniless. Regardless, every month I mail you a check, and you're able to live a life of luxury. Not once have I asked for you to give any of it back. Now I'm asking for your understanding, for Gran and for me. High Five is her home, and I will fight tooth and nail to keep her here."

Sky looked straight at her. "We're not heartless. You're just fighting a losing battle. You're fighting Judd Calhoun."

"I'm aware of that."

"He's powerful and he'll squash you like a pesky roach. Heaven forbid that you would apologize and put an end to all this."

"What?" Cait went on red alert, a state she and Maddie had been familiar with when they were teenagers and Sky got in their faces. It was usually an all-out war when the stubborn, strong Belle sisters butted heads, as they were now.

"Tell Judd you're sorry, that you'll sleep with him, have his children, marry him and otherwise grovel at his feet every chance you get. You love High Five. That's what you have to do to make this problem go away. I know it. Maddie knows it. The whole damn world knows it. Why in the hell don't you?"

Cait leaped to her feet. "Shut up, Sky."

The redhead lifted an eyebrow. "You can't deny the truth. Judd's been waiting years for this opportunity, and Dad just handed it to him like a blank check. Could that be because Dad was still pissed at you for walking away from the best thing that could have happened to you? The best thing that could have happened to High Five? Now we're all paying for your mistakes. Your choices."

Cait wanted to jump across the desk and yank every red hair from Sky's head. But truth kept her rooted to the spot. Sometimes the evil monster was a hard foe to beat, and her sister wielded it better than anyone.

A whimpered, tortured sound left their other sister's throat. Cait was instantly at her side. "Maddie, what is it?"

She wiped away a tear. "I hate all this bickering. We can't go back and change the past. We have to deal with the now, the future."

Caitlyn knelt and leaned back on her heels. "There's something else, isn't there?" She knew that by Maddie's pale complexion and her trembling hands.

"I'm very emotional these days."

"Tell us why."

Madison wiped away another tear. "You remember about three years ago, when I got a job at a hospital as a counselor?"

"Yes." Cait caught Maddie's hands.

"Well, I had to have a physical. At the time I was having a lot of cramping and excessive bleeding, so I had a complete checkup. Routine stuff, but…but the tumors on my ovaries weren't."

Cait's throat worked but no sound came out. Sky was also speechless.

"I had to have them removed, and then radiation and chemo. They said that, to save my life, I didn't have any options. Funny how they saved my life and took it away at the same time." She hiccupped. "I'll never be able to have a child."

"Oh, Maddie!" Cait hugged her, and Sky joined in. "I'm so sorry." She drew back. "That's why you're so thin and your hair is short."

"Yeah." Self-consciously, she lifted her hand to her head. "I'm growing a new batch."

"Why did you never tell us?" Cait asked.

"I just couldn't talk to anyone."

"Did Dad know?"

"I was getting chemo one day when he came for a visit, and my mom told him. I asked him not to tell anyone. I didn't want Gran or you all to worry."

"Are you okay now?"

Maddie shrugged. "As good as I'm going to get. I've been cancer free for two years, but I have enormous medical bills. That's why I need the money."

"Oh, Maddie. I'm sorry I was such a bitch." Cait hugged her again.

"I love High Five, but I have all these debts...."

Cait squeezed her hands. "Don't worry. We'll figure out something."

"I have a reason for needing the money, too," Sky said in a low voice.

"What reason?" Cait braced herself.

Sky got into a comfortable position, sitting cross-legged. "I need the money because I have...well, a child."

"Excuse me?"

"I have a child and…"

"You kept a child from us, your sisters and your grandmother?" Cait rose to her feet, feeling ticked off, really angry. "How could you do that?"

"It wasn't intentional. I was embarrassed, ashamed that I was so stupid. Todd told me repeatedly that he didn't want children. When he found out about the baby, he ended our affair and left. But his parents, who are wealthy, started calling and asking questions. I heard through a friend that they know about Kira and intend to gain custody. I can't let that happen, so I have to keep her hidden and a secret."

"Her name is Kira?" Maddie asked wistfully.

"Yes. She's three years old now, but from birth she cried all the time, and I had her in and out of the doctor's office for high fevers. I knew something was wrong, but the doc could never figure out what until her knee turned red and swollen. She has juvenile rheumatoid arthritis."

"Oh, no! I'm so sorry!" Cait's anger turned to sadness. "Did Dad know?"

Sky nodded. "Like with Maddie, he showed up one day unexpectedly, but he understood my reasons for secrecy. He wanted me to keep my child."

"Where is she now?" Maddie asked quietly.

"She's with my mother, which is why I can only stay a few days. I hope we'll be able to resolve this situation quickly. And for the record, I'm not enjoying a life of luxury. I live in a small apartment, and every dime goes toward my daughter's well-being."

Two pairs of eyes turned to Caitlyn. "Well, I think I have mud and egg on my face," she stated. "Anyone care to smack me?"

"Don't tempt me," Sky said with a grin, and then

added, "Sometimes you're obsessed with High Five. Please look at this realistically, for all of us."

Cait sank to the floor again, unsure how to explain how she felt to her sisters.

When she remained silent, Maddie spoke up. "All those years ago, I know you loved Judd. I'd never seen you so happy. Gran and Renee were knee-deep in wedding plans, and Sky and I had been fitted for our dresses. Dad had five hundred people on the wedding list. It was going to be the biggest affair this small town had ever seen. What happened, Cait? You never told us what made you walk away."

She played with the French braid hanging over her shoulder, and suddenly the words came pouring out. "I was floating on a cloud back then. The most eligible, most handsome bachelor in the county had asked me to marry him. Suddenly I was the center of his world."

"That was good, right?" Sky asked.

Cait twisted the braid. "It would have been wonderful, except I heard Jack Calhoun and Dad talking. They had arranged the marriage, and Judd went along with it. It would be beneficial to both families."

Sky's mouth formed a big *O*.

"I could have lived with that, and all the plans being made without my input, even wearing Judd's mother's wedding dress. But there was one thing I couldn't live without."

"What?" Maddie voice was breathless.

"Judd's love."

"But he loved you," Sky pointed out. "He couldn't take his eyes off you."

"I thought so, too." Cait pulled the braid until her head hurt. "So I *asked* him if he loved me. Do you know what he said?"

"What? What?" Sky sounded like an excited child.

"He said we'd have a strong marriage and we'd be happy." The words still stung like a bull nettle. "In that instant I knew I'd be a yes-wife like Renee, always bowing to my husband's wishes. I wanted more. I wanted a man who would love me above everything, even his family. I took off the ring and gave it back, saying I couldn't marry him. I waited and waited for Judd to come and confess his undying love. I'm still waiting." She laughed, a pitiful sound that revealed how weak she felt.

"Oh, Cait. I didn't know." Maddie slipped from the chair and held her tightly.

"Me, neither." Sky hugged her in turn, then leaned away with a mischievous glint in her eyes. "You know, Cait, a woman has ways to bring a man to his knees."

"I think I missed that course in college."

"Oh, please." Sky undid a couple of snaps on Cait's shirt. "Get my drift?"

Caitlyn remembered yesterday, and how Judd had looked at her breasts. Oh, yeah, she got it. "So you don't want me to apologize?"

"Not on your life." Skylar laughed and held up her hand for a high five.

"I just need some time," Cait said. "Two weeks tops to find a solution."

"Okay," her sisters said in unison.

Cait prayed that somehow she could work out a plan to help them all.

CHAPTER EIGHT

"YOU'LL NEVER GUESS who I saw yesterday. The Belle sisters, all three of them. You know the other two are kind of like Caitlyn, uppity but with a northern flair. They never said a word to me. How rude is that? Believe me, Southerners have much better manners. But you know, if I had looks like that I wouldn't have to worry for the rest of my life. I'd be on easy street, with a rich hunk of my choosing. All I'd have to do is spend his money and look oh, so pretty. Now that I—"

"Brenda Sue!"

She jumped at the sound of his voice.

"Is there a reason you're in my study?" Judd asked, his tone peppered with impatience.

"Oh, you don't have to shout."

"And you need to take a breath."

"What?"

The woman looked genuinely puzzled. Did she not have a clue? Damn it! "What are you doing in my study? This isn't the office."

"Sometimes, Judd, you can be rude," she replied in a haughty tone.

He leaned back, her voice wearing holes in whatever patience he had left. "You have five seconds to tell me in one sentence what you're doing in here or you're fired. Is that rude enough for you?"

She flipped back her yellowish-blond hair. "Harland finished repairing the fence between the ranch and High Five, and wanted you to know. He double wired it or something, so the Belles' bull can't get onto Southern Cross. Why couldn't Caitlyn fix it? It seemed—"

Judd pointed to the door. "Go, as fast as you can."

She fled.

His mother walked through the open door, glancing at Brenda Sue's retreating figure. "Dare I ask if you made her mad enough to quit?"

"She has two kids. She needs a job."

"Mmm. What's wrong with this picture?"

"What do you mean?" He kept signing checks for bills. He usually did that in the office, but there was just so much of Brenda Sue he could tolerate on any given day.

"You keep her on and put up with her endless marathon of drivel because she needs a job. You better be careful or people might start calling you a nice guy."

He signed another check. "I did it as a favor to Harvey. Is there something you need?"

"Yes." His mother clasped her hands together. "As I'm sure Brenda Sue has relayed to you, the Belle sisters are here, and I want to throw a party. A ball, actually, with formal attire."

He glanced up. "Have you lost your mind?"

"No. My faculties are all intact, thank you. It'll be like the old days, when we had such wonderful parties at Southern Cross."

"No," he said, and went back to signing checks.

Renee yanked the pen from his hand. His brows knotted so tightly he could feel them almost meeting.

"We're having a party. Get used to the idea. And you're wearing your tuxedo. The first dance is with me. After that you can have your choice of all the nice young ladies who will be here. Think marriage. Think babies. Think of making your mama happy. Other than that, I don't want to hear a word out of you. Oh, and of course, write me a very big check. The ball will take place Saturday night, so I have to get moving."

He grabbed his pen from her hand. "You've been around Brenda Sue too long. You need to breathe when you're issuing orders and otherwise annoying the living hell out of me."

"We're having a party, Judd."

"Don't count on me being there." He signed yet another check with a flourish.

"Well, I suppose you don't have to attend. I'll invite sons of your father's friends who would love to dance with the Belle sisters."

"Whatever."

"Mmm. You and Caitlyn couldn't make it work. Have you thought of Madison or Skylar? Very striking women."

"I'm not in the market for a wife." He kept signing.

"I want grandbabies."

"Rent one."

"Write me a very fat check, then. Babies on the black market cost a fortune."

He turned the page in the checkbook. "Go away, Mom. This is getting tiring."

"There will be other women here besides the Belles. This is your night to choose, so you'd better make good use of it. I'll even buy a gown for Brenda Sue and trot her out."

He couldn't hide a grin. "You must be getting desperate."

"I am, and you already have one desperate woman on your tail. You certainly don't want another, especially when she's your mother."

"Okay. Okay." He threw the pen down. "Have the damn party."

His mom flew around the desk and hugged him. "You really are a sweetie."

He let that pass. "Nothing excessive."

"There's no fun in that. I'll just surprise you." She hurried to the door, and he wondered if she'd heard anything he said. "I'll take your tux to the cleaners, so don't worry about that."

"That's a load off my mind."

"Don't be sarcastic."

"Don't bother me, then," Judd muttered. But the doorway was empty.

He glanced down at the checks. Damn it! The last two he'd signed as "Caitlyn Belle." Ripping them out, he tore the checks into tiny pieces and swore a few more cuss words.

Judd stood and walked to the window, flexing his shoulders to relieve the tension. Ever since he'd seen Caitlyn yesterday, he hadn't been able to get her out of his mind. He wasn't a sentimental person; his father had made sure of that. Men didn't cry or show their emotions. It made them weak. And Jack Calhoun had wanted Judd to be strong. Strong enough to rule Southern Cross. Strong enough to marry the right woman to ensure the lineage of the Calhoun name.

You'll marry Caitlyn Belle. She's a fine woman and will produce strong sons. She's young and stubborn, but Dane will keep her in line. The union will make both families stronger.

At the time, Judd hadn't balked at the idea. He didn't believe in falling in love or living happily ever after. His mother had pretty much killed all those feelings when she'd left him alone, to be raised by a domineering father.

And Judd had been watching Caitlyn Belle for a long time. He'd thought she was too young for him, though; he liked his women more experienced. That didn't keep him from admiring her beauty when he saw her riding, her black hair flying in the wind. In tight jeans and an even tighter blouse, she sat a saddle better than any woman he'd ever seen.

She rode into his dreams many nights, beguiling, tempting him with her blue forget-me-not eyes, full lips and a body that was made for a man's enjoyment. Caitlyn could arouse him more in his thoughts than other women could in the flesh.

Marrying her wasn't a problem. It would be a pleasure. But she wanted something he wasn't willing to give her—couldn't give her. She wanted his love.

How could he tell her he didn't know anything about the fickle emotion? Nor did he want to learn. It only brought pain. To his shock, she'd walked away. He knew she'd come back, though. Dane would make her. And women did what men told them. His father had drilled that concept into him all his life.

But Caitlyn wasn't like a willow that bent easily. She was more like a mighty oak, and stood strong in her convictions. Ultimately, neither Dane nor his father could change her mind.

She either wanted to marry him or she didn't. That was Judd's bottom line.

He quirked his lips. Man, they had sexual chemistry, though. It was obvious every time he was around her. Kissing her, having sex with her could generate enough electricity to light up the Astrodome.

His gut tightened and he cursed again. Thoughts of her made him need a cold shower in the middle of the day.

He turned his attention to the sisters. Since Madison and Skylar didn't live here, he was almost positive they'd apply pressure to sell. How would Caitlyn handle that?

He'd used bravado when he'd talked about buying the royalties from Dane, claiming he would take everything she loved. Judd didn't quite understand why he felt he had to do that. Maybe because she actually *could* love, and he couldn't.

What was his success going to prove when it was all over? He would have money and power, but he wouldn't have her.

CAIT STARED AT RED as the horse threw up her head and neighed, clearly wanting to be ridden.

"She's a beautiful animal," Cooper said, leaning on the fence beside her.

"Yep. My dad knew horseflesh. She's all rippling muscle, and she rides faster and smoother than a brand-new Cadillac."

"Since you won't allow anyone else to ride her, I wouldn't know."

Cait yanked Coop's hat lower. "Don't give me that woebegone puppy-dog look. She's my horse and…"

He straightened his hat. "And what?"

"I have to sell her." The words went down like a jalapeño pepper, burning all the way.

"Whoa." Coop removed his hat and scratched his head. "Didn't see that one coming. You love that horse."

"I love Gran and High Five more."

Somewhere through her chaotic and tangled thoughts, she knew what she had to do. Besides High Five, Whiskey Red was the only thing of value she owned.

Coop settled his hat on his head with a wry expression. "Your sisters have something to do with that decision?"

"I'm asking them to make sacrifices, so I have to be willing to do the same."

"Mmm."

All her life she had thought her sisters were living a fairy tale, with luxury at their fingertips. The truth was so different than what she'd imagined. They had heartaches and problems, too.

As much as she hated to let Red go, she knew it was the only way to help Maddie and Sky. The sale would give them money to live on, and Cait time to form a plan to save the ranch. It would solve their problems for now.

"I'm setting the sale for Friday at ten. Tell Rufus to get the word out to all the horse people who might be interested. I'll make a few calls, too."

"That's mighty quick."

"Yeah." Her gaze swung to Red again. *Sorry, girl.* "I better make those calls." She hurried toward the house.

"Cait?"

She turned, shading her eyes against the glare of the sun.

"I'm sorry."

She nodded and continued on her way. Tears stung the back of her eyes and she knew this was the start of Judd taking everything she loved. He wasn't taking Red; Cait was selling her.

But somehow it felt the same.

PHOTO ALBUMS AND PICTURES were strewn all over the parlor. Whenever her sisters came home, Gran's favorite thing was to reminisce about their childhood and happier times.

"Caitlyn, come look," her grandmother said. "We're having so much fun."

She sat on the sofa. Maddie and Sky were at her feet, albums in their laps. Cait plopped down to join them. She'd worry later.

They were giggling over the frizzy red hair Sky had had as a child when there was a knock at the door. Cait pushed herself to her feet. "I'll get it."

She swung open the door and shock ran through her. Renee Calhoun stood there, dressed to the nines in a pale pink linen pantsuit and heels. Her blond hair hung in a pageboy around her face. Judd looked nothing like his beautiful mother. He favored his father, with chiseled features and a dark, brooding personality.

"Caitlyn, dear, it's so good to see you."

Cait inclined her head, feeling a knot the size of a baseball forming in her stomach. "What can I do for you, Mrs. Calhoun?"

"Oh, please. You used to call me Renee."

"That was a long time ago." She kept her voice neutral, wondering what the woman wanted.

Renee touched her arm. "Too long, my dear." She looked past Cait. "Is your grandmother home?"

The knot expanded. "Yes, but—"

"Relax, Caitlyn. This will only take a minute and it'll be painless." Before Cait could stop her, Renee marched into the parlor.

Damn woman. What did she want?

Cait hurried after her. Maddie and Sky got to their feet. Gran stared at Renee with a startled expression.

"Dorie, I'm sorry for intruding."

"Oh, Renee." Gran shook her head as if to clear it, then patted the cushion. "Sit down, please. You've met my granddaughters."

"Oh, yes. Many times." She settled on the sofa and placed her bag beside her. "Very beautiful young women."

Maddie eased down on the other side of Gran, who reached for her hand. "I've been very blessed," the elderly woman said. "My granddaughters are a special gift from my son."

A look of discomfort crossed Renee's face. "I am so sorry about Dane."

"Thank you." Gran nodded and dropped her gaze.

Cait wanted to rush in and stop whatever was about to happen. Anything to protect Gran. But she didn't believe, not for one minute, that Renee would intentionally hurt her grandmother.

Their visitor pulled an ivory linen envelope from her purse. "I have some exciting news. I'm throwing a big party—a ball with formal attire—and I would love for you and your lovely granddaughters to attend."

A ball! Was the woman out of her mind?

Gran raised one hand to her breasts. "A party? Oh, my, we haven't had a party in ages."

Not since Caitlyn and Judd's engagement party. Everyone was thinking it, but no one said the words out loud. If they did, Cait was going to hurt them.

"It sounds like a very nice party." Sky picked up an album and laid it on a table. "But I'm leaving early Sunday morning."

"The party is Saturday evening, so you have plenty of time. It will be fun—something we all need."

"Thank you for the invitation, but I didn't bring any clothes to wear to a fancy ball." Maddie smiled politely.

Cait thought it was time to step in. "I'm sorry, Renee, but neither my sisters nor I will be attending any party at Southern Cross. I'm sure you understand." She headed for the kitchen to ease the knot in her stomach.

"Caitlyn Dane Belle!"

Gran's voice stopped her as effectively as a bullet. Her tone had the power to squeeze the stubbornness right out of her.

"We do not treat guests in our home that way."

Like a dutiful granddaughter, Cait turned and faced the woman who meant more to her than life itself.

"Yes, ma'am."

Sometimes Gran's Southern manners grated on her nerves like a squeaky screen door. But Cait would never show her any disrespect.

Gran rose to her full height, which was barely five feet three inches. "Our neighbor has invited us to a fancy party and, as good neighbors, we will accept."

Like hell. Cait stopped the words just in time. Gran didn't know about the latest incident with the Calhouns, and Cait couldn't tell her. She caught the glint in Renee's eyes. Oh, Judd's mother was counting on that. Conniving witch.

Gran walked to Caitlyn and linked her arm through hers. "You work too hard. You need some fun." She patted her hand. "This is what you need, my baby. We'll get all dressed up and have the time of our lives."

"Gran…" She wanted to shout that the party wasn't about dressing up or Southern manners. It was about a black-hearted devil trying to steal High Five.

As if she understood Cait's hesitation, Dorie said, "I know Judd will be there, but it's been a long time. We're neighbors, so we have to be civil."

"Oh, this is wonderful." Renee rose to her feet. "I look forward to seeing you all. Ta-ta."

Caitlyn beat her to the door. "What are you trying to pull? We are not attending any stupid ball."

Renee tapped a French manicured nail against her lips. "Judd said the same thing."

"Then why are you doing this?"

"For fun."

"For fun?" She arched an eyebrow. "How about spite?"

"Now, Caitlyn…"

"Haven't you Calhouns hurt us enough? What else can you take from me?"

Renee slipped her bag over her shoulder. "Maybe I'm trying to give you something back." After delivering that ridiculous message, she sashayed out to her car.

Cait slammed the door so hard her ancestors could hear the echo.

CHAPTER NINE

THE NEXT TWO DAYS were hectic as Caitlyn ran the ranch and tried to get ready for Friday's sale. It helped that Maddie and Sky were home. She didn't have to run back to the house to check on Gran. Her sisters took very good care of her, and Dorie was happy.

They'd decided not to mention the ball again in hopes she would forget about it. Attending wasn't in their plans.

The day was hot and Cait felt sweat trickling down her back and staining her clothes. She smelled as fresh as cow manure.

Coop and Rufus had cut the hay three days ago. It was now cured, so they were racking it into windrows to bale. There were three one-hundred-acre tracts of coastal, and it would take them at least the month of June, if not more, to get all the hay off the ground.

But they'd have enough to see them through a dry summer and a bad winter. She planned to sell what she didn't need. That would help with expenses.

While Coop and Rufus worked with the hay, she took care of the cattle. Since it was already getting dry, she had to keep a close watch on the stock tanks, wells and windmills. It was crucial that the herds had water, especially in this heat.

It was getting late and Cait had one more windmill

to check. She was so ready to head back to the air-conditioned ranch house and a bath.

But something was wrong. She knew that the moment she saw the cows huddled around the trough, bellowing. She rode in quickly, the dogs trotting behind her, and the animals scattered. Dismounting, she saw the trough was empty. That meant the storage tank was empty, too. Damn!

Glancing up, she watched the windmill's blades spinning in the breeze. But water wasn't pouring out of the pipe from the storage tank, as per normal.

It was a long way up the tower. Cait felt dizzy just looking upward. This had happened about three weeks ago, when the clevis and cotter pins had been broken. Could it be the same problem? She didn't understand how they could break again so soon. She had no recourse but to climb the tower to find out why the sucker rod wasn't pumping water into the trough.

Either that or the leathers needed changing. She'd have to call someone to repair that. If the gears or the pump were broken, fixing them would be a big expense.

A cow butted her, sending Cait staggering. "Be patient, old gal. I'll see what I can do, and stop pushing me around. I'm your only salvation." She whistled for the dogs and they responded, yapping and nipping at the cows until they shuffled away from the trough.

Cait searched her saddlebags for cotter and clevis pins. She'd bought some when the device had broken last time. If that was the problem, she could easily fix it.

On the horizon, beyond the High Five fence line, she glimpsed Southern Cross cowboys. Had they sabotaged the windmill? She wouldn't put it past them. And she wouldn't put it past Judd.

She found the pins and stuffed them into her jeans

pocket. Glancing up, she trembled. She wasn't afraid of heights. Normal heights, that is. But the tower had to be at least forty feet high, and was old and shaky. She always felt a little jittery when she had to climb it.

The cattle needed water, however, so she tucked away her fears and marched to the tower.

Reaching it, she yanked off her shirt. She would need her arms free and unrestricted. Luckily, she had a white cotton tank top on underneath.

The dogs dutifully worked the cattle, keeping them away as Cait placed a booted foot on the first steel rung of the ladder and started up. The sun torched her skin, but she kept climbing, staying focused and not looking down. She felt as if she were climbing into a hot tunnel of hell.

Reaching the hub, she took care not to get her head or anything else she might need chopped off. Quickly, Cait pulled the brake to stop the blades. The swooshing sound died away.

Don't look down.

Her breathing was labored, but that was normal under the circumstances. She concentrated on the C-shaped shackle that worked the sucker rod. It was missing both pins. Damn! She'd found the problem. Now to fix it.

Holding on with one hand, she slipped the other in her pocket for the pins. The clevis consisted of a head, shank and hole. The cotter pin went through the hole to hold it in place. She placed the cotter pin between her teeth.

Stretching out her arm, she grabbed the shackle and inserted the clevis, or at least tried. It was stubborn and didn't budge. Cait shoved with all her might, trying to position it back in place so she could insert the cotter pin.

The wind blew off her hat and fear tightened her throat, but she didn't lose her concentration. Nor did she look down.

"Come on, you stupid pin. Move." With all her strength she pushed until it slid into place, all the while trying to keep her balance. It took every muscle she had to hold it there as she slipped the cotter pin through the hole. Then and only then did she take a breath, scraping precious air from the bottom of her lungs.

The wind tugged and she quickly released the brake, waiting as the blades revved up again. Slowly the sucker rod began to move up and down, hopefully pumping water from beneath the ground into the storage tank, and then into the trough. Cait didn't see if it was happening, because she refused to look down. She'd find out soon enough....

Now she had to climb down. But first she had to loosen her grip and move her feet. One, two, three... She lowered one foot and then the other. All the way to the precious earth, which she wanted to kiss the moment her boots touched it.

But she had other problems. The water was not going into the trough. The cows must have dislocated a pipe, and water was spurting everywhere.

Damn! Damn! Damn!

JUDD WATCHED HER from a hill and had no intention of helping or interfering. But he could see water puddling on the ground, the sun glistening off its surface. The cows bellowed, shifting restlessly, and though the dogs worked to keep them at bay, the big animals smelled water. The dogs would not hold them long.

Without a second thought, Judd jumped Baron over the fence onto the High Five ranch. He gave the horse his lead and they flew over the dried grass. As he neared the windmill, cattle broke free, running and bellowing for the water.

Caitlyn glanced at the stampeding cows and made a dash for her horse, just as Judd swept in, grabbed her around the waist and rode to safety.

"Let me go," she screeched, her heart pounding against his hand. His fingers touched the underside of her breast, and even riding full tilt, he felt a powerful response.

"Let me go!" She flailed her arms, and he pulled up and released her. Cait fell to the ground on her butt, her eyes firing blue flames at him. "You bastard."

He sat back in the saddle, staring down at her. "Is that any way to talk to a man who just saved your life?"

She stood and dusted off the back of her jeans. "You're trespassing, Judd. Get off my property." She swung her cute butt around and headed back to the cattle jostling around the trough, fighting to get a drink of water.

Placing two fingers in her mouth, she whistled. The dogs trotted over, looking eagerly up at her. "Go. Go. Go." She clapped her hands. "Get 'em."

In a frenzy, the dogs went after the cows, herding them away from the trough once more. Caitlyn stepped into the mud without hesitation and bent to a pipe that was gushing water.

Judd slid from the saddle and went to help her. His head told him to ride away; this woman had hurt him more than anyone in his life. But his heart was a traitor, urging him forward.

The pipe ran along the ground and up into the

trough. The top part had come undone. Caitlyn grabbed the pipe to force it back in place, but the water pressure made that difficult. Judd placed his hands over hers and pushed.

She stilled for a moment and he expected more fireworks, but her fingers tightened under his and the two of them pushed together. Water squirted him in the face and chest, as it did her, but they focused on their goal. Neither spoke. The stubborn pipe finally moved into the trough and water spilled into its depth.

Caitlyn let out a sigh and wiped water from her cheeks. Her eyes pinned him like a target to a wall. "I didn't ask for your help, so please leave. You're not welcome here." Her words were like darts. If he was a soft man, they might hurt, but they didn't. They only irritated him.

"I thought your grandmother had at least taught you some manners. And she should have told you not to climb a windmill out here when no one is around."

"Evidently someone was, and I'm wondering why all of a sudden you're on High Five. And your cowboys. I saw them a little while ago. I'm beginning to think maybe the cotter pin was taken out."

He straightened. "Are you accusing me of deliberately breaking the windmill?"

Her eyes zoomed to his. "Maybe."

"Caitlyn, I don't have to sabotage you. You'll fail all on your own. Even Dane knew that."

"Don't say one word about my father." Her chest swelled with anger and her breasts pressed against the tank top. Since it was wet, he saw just about everything, and felt that familiar kick in his groin. That irritated him more.

The cows began to outmaneuver the dogs again,

hurrying to the water. One rushed in and bumped Caitlyn, and she landed on her back in the mud, arms and legs flying.

Once Judd saw that she was okay, he wanted to laugh, which he did. Not much, just a chuckle he couldn't suppress. Mud caked her body, her skin.

Her face froze into a mask of disbelief.

More cows made their way to the trough. He'd help her, but he knew she didn't want his assistance. "Get up or you're going to get trampled."

She rose to her hands and knees, and flipped and flopped like a beetle on its back. Unable to stand the sight a moment longer, he stretched out his hand. She didn't take it.

"Don't be a stubborn fool."

She latched on to it then and yanked. He went flying into the muck beside her. That, he didn't find funny. Mud soaked his clothes. His boots! He groaned. His favorite boots were ruined.

"Why aren't you laughing?" she asked, leaning back in the mud as if it were whipped cream. And she was the cat who had just had her fill.

He slipped and slid, but managed to get to his feet and to solid ground. Using the trough for leverage, she pulled herself up and waded out as well.

"You need a damn good spanking." The words were out before he could corral them.

She cocked her head, water dripping from her braid and other parts of her body. "A little mud make you cranky?" Her eyes slid down his body to his crotch. "Or horny?"

Before he knew what he was doing, he'd jerked her into his arms. Their mud-coated bodies welded together, every soft curve of hers pressed into his hardness, and he wanted her more than he ever had.

Her open mouth was a breath away. Her tongue touched her upper lip, and he realized she was the one in control, taking him places he'd sworn he'd never go again.

With more restraint than he knew he had, he pushed her away and strolled to his horse.

"Stay off my property, Judd Calhoun," she shouted after him.

He swung into the saddle, cursing. Baron pranced around and Judd rode to within a few feet of her.

"It won't be yours long, Caitlyn. Not for long."

"Go to hell!" Her words carried on the wind as he galloped away.

AIR GUSHED INTO Cait's lungs, hot and furious, just the way Judd made her feel. How dare he! As the anger oozed out of her, her heart rate returned to normal. Or as close as it was going to get today.

She glanced down at her mud-covered body and felt Judd's male imprint there. Her nipples hardened and her lower abdomen ached. Oh, she was so easy. All he had to do was kiss her… But he hadn't. Her mouth watered for what she'd been deprived of. It felt good, though, to know she had some power over him. Still.

Maybe Sky was right.

Could Cait work this to her advantage? It would be like sleeping with the enemy, and that had to be bad. Though her body was telling her something else…

Mooing cows brought her out of her insanity. They were fighting to get to the trough, butting heads. She clapped her hands again. "Go, go, boys."

The dogs went back into action, keeping the cattle busy and frustrated while the trough filled up. Finally satisfied they had enough water, she plucked her shirt and hat from the mud. They were ruined, but she couldn't leave them out here. The cows, being very curious, would try to make a snack out of the items.

With her shirt and hat rolled into a ball, she climbed into the saddle and headed for home.

THE SALE WAS Friday morning and Cait put the encounter with Judd out of her mind. Or at least she tried.

Coop wanted to stay and help, but she needed him in the hay field. Soon trucks pulling trailers nosed up to the fence at the corral. Her father's poker buddies hadn't let her down; they were here in full force. Red would bring a good price. But her heart was breaking. That, she wouldn't let anyone see.

Maddie hugged her. "I'm sorry you have to sell Red."

"It's to help us all." The three sisters stood in the barn and Cait rubbed Red down for the last time. The thoroughbred's muscles rippled and her coat was shiny. Someone would get a very good horse.

Sky stroked Red's long neck. "I wish there was another way."

"There isn't, so let's be big girls and pull up our panties and get this done."

They laughed at one of Gran's sayings from their childhood. That Cait could join in was a good sign. She'd survive this.

She held Whiskey Red's face and kissed her nose. "Goodbye, girl." Swallowing her emotions, she took the bridle and led her into the corral.

Six buyers walked around Red, running their hands along her back, her butt, her neck, her legs.

Red threw up her head and neighed, clearly not liking this inspection. "Easy, girl," Cait soothed.

"She's a fine looking animal," Dale Eddy said, chewing on a cigar.

"Yes, she is," Cait replied. "Let's get the bidding started."

"Twenty thousand." Dale made the first offer.

Bill Lightfoot eyed the column of Red's strong neck. "Twenty-five."

"Thirty." Dale upped his bid.

"Thirty-five," Charley Bowers said.

Frank Upton shook his head. "Too rich for my blood."

"Forty." Dale bid again, the cigar working overtime. Caitlyn knew he really wanted Red, and the horse would have a good home at Dale's ranch.

Bob O'Neal had walked around Red several times, but hadn't yet bid. "Forty-five," he said suddenly.

This was going better than Cait had expected. She'd been hoping for forty. More would make life a lot easier.

"Seventy-five thousand dollars."

Cait swung her head in the direction of the voice. No! He couldn't take Red. Not Judd. She wouldn't allow it.

"She's not for sale to you."

Judd walked farther into the corral. "So you posted the sale in bad faith?"

Maddie and Sky came to stand beside her. Cait thought of Kira, of Maddie's medical bills and her own pride. She had no choice. A buyer was a buyer. Even if he was the devil.

"You don't have to do this," Sky said in a whisper.

But Cait did. She couldn't renege on a sale, and they needed the money, even if it came from Judd Calhoun.

"No." Pride went down hard and bitter. "Red is for sale."

Judd looked at the other men. "Anyone want to top my bid?"

Dale patted Red's rump. "I was there the day Dane bought this horse. She has great bloodlines and she's worth every penny."

"That's not a bid, Dale," Judd told him.

The man shook his head. "That's out of my price range."

The others walked off and Caitlyn faced Judd. Maddie and Sky stood behind her like her wingmen.

"Why are you doing this?" she asked as calmly as she could.

"I can never pass up good horseflesh."

"Or sticking it to me."

He nodded. "That's always a plus."

Sky stepped forward. "You've gotten hard, Judd."

"Hello, Sky, Maddie." He tipped his hat. "I had a very good teacher."

"Oh, please, no one had to teach you a thing."

Cait placed a hand on Sky's arm before her sister went on full alert. "He's paying a lot of money for Red. Money we need." Her eyes probed the dark depths of his. "I find that a little strange. You're giving me money to succeed."

"But I'm taking something you love." His gaze never wavered as he delivered a blow that left her speechless. She found there was no response, other than to burst into tears. And she would never do that.

"I'd like a cashier's check by the end of the day."

He seemed taken aback. "Don't you trust me?"

When she didn't respond, he shrugged. "I'll have a check and a trailer here later."

"If you don't, the sale is off."

She watched as he walked out of the corral. He went to the end of the barn, where his horse was tethered. No wonder she hadn't heard him arrive. Sneaky devil!

But his scheme had started.

Would he completely destroy her?

CHAPTER TEN

JUDD WALKED IN the back door and stopped short. People were everywhere. People he didn't know. Damn party! He made his way down the hall toward his study, side-stepping tables, chairs and startled maids.

His mother hurried from the dining room. "Oh, Judd…"

"Do you really need all this help to get ready for a party?"

Renee glanced at the women arranging flowers in the entry. "Why, of course. We need decorators, caterers, maids and servers. Several guests will be spending the night."

He shook his head and went into his study. "Keep everyone, and I mean everyone, out of my space."

As always, his mother paid him no attention and followed him.

"Everyone meant you, too, Mom." He sank into his leather chair.

"Did I see Harland unloading that beautiful red horse of Caitlyn's?"

"Yes." Judd picked up his mail.

"Why is it here?"

"I bought her."

"What?"

He laid down his mail. "Don't you have a party to plan?"

Renee closed the door and walked to his desk. "Now, let me get this straight. Caitlyn put her horse up for sale and you bought it. I'm guessing at a very high price."

"You got it."

"Why, son? Why would you do that? It doesn't make any sense."

"It doesn't have to."

"This woman you want to bring down. This woman who hurt you. You're now giving her money."

"I bought a good horse. That's it. I'm getting tired of this interrogation." He rose to his feet and shoved his hands into his pockets.

"Son…"

"It wasn't about the money, okay? I took something she loved."

"Oh, well, that's just dandy," Renee said, narrowing her green eyes on his face. He hated when she did that. He didn't want her to see too much. "You're not this hard."

He moved toward the window. "You don't really know me."

"It all comes back to the bad mother, doesn't it?"

"Leave it alone, Mom."

"I can't when it's destroying your whole life."

"Mom…"

"I've told you a million times, I had to go in order to survive. I never planned to leave you here. I had you in my arms, but Jack ripped you away. When I tried to stay then, he forced me out. I had no choice. I left, but I fully intended to get custody. I never counted on your father's vindictiveness."

Judd clenched his jaw. "I've heard this story before."

"I tried twice to kidnap you. I even made it to the upstairs landing the second time before I was caught."

"What?" He swung around. "I never knew that. Dad said you never came back."

"Your father was very good at turning every situation to his advantage."

Judd removed his hat and placed it carefully on his desk. "I'll never understand why you married him again."

"Yes, you do. I've told you many times. When your father came into that diner where I was working, I was a bit nervous. But the moment he showed he was still interested, I worked it to my advantage. I learned from him. I'd have done anything to be back with my son. And I did."

Judd raked his fingers through his hair. He didn't want to hear this story, and didn't understand why he was still listening.

"The marriage worked out well, though. Jack had mellowed and we formed a stronger relationship. That's the funny thing about love. Once it's given it's almost impossible to destroy."

Judd didn't have anything to say, and a response didn't seem to be required.

"You're the casualty of our dysfunctional lives. Jack filled your head with his misguided, outdated views of women, and sadly, nothing I said or tried to do changed your thinking. But deep down I know you're a caring, compassionate man who can love deeply."

He had his doubts about that. He flung a hand toward the door. "Go plan your party, and stop spending so damn much money."

His mother lifted her chin. "I'll spend however much I please. Since you've irritated Caitlyn, the Belles probably won't come. It's not going to be much of a party without them."

"Good. Then we can forget this whole crazy idea."

"Not on your life. I bought this beautiful gold gown and I'm wearing it." She cocked her head. "I see myself as a fairy godmother."

"I see you as insane."

"Tut-tut." She shook a finger at him. "Don't talk like that to your mother."

He sighed. "You try my patience, you know that?"

"Yes, my dear son." She turned toward the door, then swung back. "I do love you, Judd, and Caitlyn did, too. One day you're going to realize that, and I hope it's not too late."

He plopped back into his chair as her words hit him right between the eyes. *Love?* Why did women brandish that word like a weapon? They wanted everything wrapped in a neat package with *married* and *happily ever after* written on it. But it never turned out that way. There always seemed to be more pain than happiness. A cynical outlook, perhaps, but he was a cynical, unfeeling man. That's the way Caitlyn thought of him.

Time and again he'd proved he could feel deeply— sexually. But she wanted the package with the vows of undying love.

He shifted restlessly. Their encounter at the windmill epitomized their relationship. They both felt a powerful attraction. Why wasn't that enough for her? It was for him.

Damn. He flexed his shoulders. He was so tired of thinking of her. When he'd heard of the sale, he'd had no intention of buying her horse. He had all the horses he needed, but against every sane thought in his head, he'd found his way there.

Another way to stick it to me.

Maybe. He wasn't quite sure why he'd done it. All

he knew was that he could and he had. Maybe it was a way to regain some of the ground she'd stolen at the windmill. Even he had to admit that little by little she was making inroads into his control. Into his resolve.

She made him weak when he wanted to be strong. She made him caring when he wanted to be tough. She made him feel pain when he wanted to be oblivious.

But he was never oblivious to her.

He could still see the hurt in her eyes when he'd bought Whiskey Red. That's what he wanted, wasn't it? Where was his feeling of victory?

"Judd."

He turned around and tried not to groan at Brenda Sue's interruption.

"My goodness, it's hard not to trip over maids, florists and whoever these people are. Your mother didn't ask for my opinion. She can be rather snotty sometimes. I don't think she likes me, but gosh, she knows how to throw a party. Crystal, flowers and a band—the whole nine yards. No plastic at this shindig. Everything is oh, so nice, and you should see the flower arrangement in the foyer. I could live a week on what that cost. But I've never—"

"Brenda Sue." Judd had to shout to get her attention. "Is there a reason you're in my study—again?"

She blinked like a raccoon with a light shining in its face. "Oh—oh, yes. Harland sent me to tell you that the new horse…" She wrinkled her nose. "Isn't that Caitlyn's horse? Sure looks like it. Anyway, Harland said the horse is not settling down, and he wants to know if you want him to give her something to calm her. Like, wow, I didn't even know you could do that. How…"

Judd grabbed his hat and hit the door, leaving

Brenda Sue in midsentence. It would probably be five minutes before she realized he wasn't there.

He ran out the back and headed for the stables. No one was touching that horse. No one was touching Whiskey Red but him.

CAITLYN COULDN'T SLEEP. She kept wondering how Red was adjusting to the stables at Southern Cross. She was a thoroughbred and temperamental, but Cait was sure Judd had professional people to deal with her. That didn't make her feel better, though.

She'd received the payment early enough to go into Giddings and deposit the money. When Maddie and Sky left on Sunday, she'd write them each a check for their part. Her share would go back into the ranch.

It was a solution for now.

She was up the next morning before everyone. She grabbed some cereal bars and bottled water and headed for the bunkhouse. Today would be a full day of baling hay.

Rufus ran the tractor with the baler. It would break every now and then, but she knew the two ranch hands could fix it. Cooper worked the hay carrier that loaded each bale and carted it to a fence line, where it would be stacked until it was sold or fed to the cattle.

Cooper and Rufus had a system, so Caitlyn soon left to check the herds.

The windmill was working fine, the trough full of water. She stared at the mud puddle and briefly thought of yesterday.

And Judd.

He'd seemed to want to help, but then he… She shut out the memory and went on to the next pasture.

This one had a stock tank and it was already getting

low. A good rain would help tremendously. The summers were always hell. But then the winters weren't a picnic, either.

Ranching was tough on a good day, and she wondered why she was killing herself to preserve something no one cared about but her. She knew, though. *For Gran. For her heritage.* Gran was the only mother Cait had ever known, and she would do everything to keep her on High Five.

The royalty sale ensured that Dorie could stay at the ranch until her death. But what would that be like for her? Dorie's childhood home would no longer be High Five, but part of the Southern Cross. Once Gran knew that, she wouldn't stay in the house. Cait knew her grandmother's pride wouldn't let her.

Somehow Caitlyn had to make the ranch work.

By the time Cait reached home that evening, she was exhausted. She wanted a bath, some food and…

She paused in the kitchen doorway. Etta, Maddie and Sky stood there, looking anxious.

Cait whipped off her hat. "What's wrong? Is it Gran?"

"Where have you been? It's six o'clock." Sky didn't bother to hide her temper.

"Where do you think I've been? I'm working this ranch."

"Calm down." Maddie was quick to intervene.

"You girls better get a move on," Etta said. "Miss Dorie doesn't like to be late."

"Late? For what?"

"Have you forgotten what today is?" Sky asked, rather tartly. At Cait's blank look, she added, "The ball."

Caitlyn frowned. "I'm not going to that. I refuse to. No way in hell can anyone make me."

"Go upstairs and tell your grandmother." Etta removed her apron. "I'm heading home. Food's in the refrigerator."

As the housekeeper went out the screen door, Maddie and Sky grabbed Cait by her arms and pulled her toward the staircase.

"What are you doing?"

"I'm going to make this short and sweet," Sky said as they climbed the stairs. "Renee called this morning to make sure we were coming, and Gran's been in a tizzy all day getting ready."

"What?"

"Oh, yeah." Maddie opened the door. "Wait till you see."

Cait stood aghast at the chaos in Gran's room. Gowns were everywhere, strewn over chairs, the lounger and the bed. The same with shoes.

The elderly woman came from the bathroom in a long slip, patting her hair, which was in an elegant knot at her nape. "Oh, Caitlyn, baby," she said when she saw her. "Go take a bath. We don't have much time. Your dress is all ready."

"Welcome to bizarro world," Sky whispered.

"Wait till you see the dress." Maddie nudged her.

"I can't believe you couldn't dissuade her from this," Cait muttered with a touch of anger. "We're not going."

Sky lifted an eyebrow. "Tell Gran that, Miss Can-Do-Everything."

Cait shot her a thousand-watt glare and walked to Dorie, who was inspecting a silver, satiny creation.

"Gran." She spoke softly.

Her grandmother blinked at her. "Caitlyn, go take a bath. How many times do I have to tell you?"

She caught her hands. "Gran, listen to me. We're not going to any party at the Southern Cross."

"Oh, my baby." Gran cupped Cait's face in frail fingers, but Cait only felt their power. "I know you don't want to see Judd, but my precious, you made the choice long ago. And I know my baby has the strength to hold her head up and be a lady. To be a Belle. With Southern manners."

All her *no*s deflated into a big *oh*. She could hold her head up and face anybody, but she didn't want to go to the Calhouns' ranch. How could she get through to Gran?

"Gran, I'm tired. I've been working all day and I don't have a thing to wear."

Behind her, Sky snickered. That was not the right thing to say in a room full of gowns.

"I don't know why you fool around on the ranch. Your father encouraged that and I never liked it. Leave the ranch to Dane. He runs it effortlessly."

Oh, God. Not today. Cait didn't want to say those words today.

Maddie put an arm around their grandmother's shoulders. "Gran, Dad is dead. He can't run the ranch."

"I know that." Dorie turned and picked up a gown from the bed. "Here's your dress, Caitlyn. I've already chosen it for you."

Cait stared at the garment. Staring was all she could do. It was red, strapless and tight fitting, with a slit up one leg.

"Daring little number, isn't it?" Sky said, tongue in cheek.

"Now, my babies, I'm going to finish my makeup, and you get dressed. Hurry."

The three of them stared at her as she closed the bathroom door.

"You handled that very well," Sky said, holding up the red dress with a lifted brow.

"I'm not going and I'm not wearing that. I'll look like a hooker."

Maddie reached for a white gown trimmed in pink, with capped sleeves and a full skirt. "Does this say Barbie? Virginal?"

Cait choked back a laugh even though there was nothing funny about this situation.

"Wait for this." Sky leaned over and plucked a black gown from the mix on the bed. "Does this say matronly?" It was a very simple sleeveless, long black dress with a V neckline. "Gran says I can wear a strand of her pearls. Oh, yeah, I'm going to party hearty."

Cait sank onto the bed, not caring about the gowns. "I don't know what to do."

Sky sat beside her, frowning at the black number. "We can just refuse to go. We're grown women and Gran can't force us."

"Yeah." Cait looked into Sky's eyes. "But are you willing to hurt her like that?"

"I'm not," Maddie said, plopping down beside them. "I'll wear this nightmare and smile, as long as it makes her happy."

"I think that's our bottom line," Cait murmured.

She hadn't thought about the ball all day, never had any intention of stepping foot onto Southern Cross property. But she had to give Renee credit. The conniving witch had found a way to get the Belles to the ball.

CHAPTER ELEVEN

CAIT WANTED TO LINGER in the bath, but she didn't have time. Damn party! Whoever heard of having a ball in Texas? She griped to herself the whole time she was dressing.

She lathered herself in scented lotion called *Moonlight Madness*. She was feeling a little mad tonight. The red dress lay on the bed. Strapless. It had been ages since she'd worn anything like that. Probably since college.

She dug in her dresser drawers until she found what she wanted—a strapless, push-up bra. A little old, but it still worked. She shimmied into it just as Maddie and Sky walked in dressed in their gowns, their faces somber.

"Hey, you don't look all that bad," she said. "Actually, you look damn good." She cast a not-so-nice glance at the red number. "I don't know how I'm going to hold up my dress."

"By those babes poking out of your chest there," Sky told her.

"Very funny." She grabbed the dress. "It's too revealing. It's not me."

"And you think this black nightmare is me?"

Cait looked her up and down. "Yeah. It's sassy and tempting, just revealing enough."

"Compliments won't work." Sky shoved the red dress into her hands. "Put it on."

Cait made a face and stared at the crimson fabric before wiggling into it. She held her breath and Maddie zipped her up. After shifting her breasts into the right position, she glanced in the mirror.

OhmyGod!

"Wow," Maddie said. "You look…"

"Like a hooker."

"No, sexy and wild, with your black hair hanging down your back like that."

"We need to do something with your mop." Sky grabbed a brush and wielded it through her locks.

"Ouch," she cried, and yanked the brush away. "I can fix my own damn hairdo, thank you." Then she smiled. "Remember all the times we did each other's hair?"

"Yeah," Maddie replied wistfully.

"Come on, you two," Sky urged. "We don't have time to go down memory lane. We're running late."

"Put your hair up," Maddie suggested. "It will look better that way."

Since Cait wore it in a braid most of the time, it was wavy and easy to loop into a knot of curls on top of her head. Several strands hung loose around her face. Good enough.

She put diamond studs, a gift from her father, into her ears and stood. The dress covered her feet. "Oh, crap. This skirt is too long."

"No problem." Maddie handed her four-inch-high red heels.

Slipping them on, Cait asked, "Where does Gran get all this stuff?"

"From the trunks in the attic." Maddie held up her

skirt to glance at her own shoes. "Mine are outdated, and so are yours, but who's going to notice?"

Thirty minutes later, they drove the Lincoln up the driveway at Southern Cross, Caitlyn at the wheel. The place was ablaze like Christmas at Graceland. Decorative lights lined the front of the house, but Cait didn't feel festive. She was more in the mood for a funeral.

A young man in black slacks and a white shirt came to her door with a big grin. Good grief, Renee had guys parking cars, probably in a cow pasture. Oh, yeah, this was Texas.

"Help Maddie with Gran," Cait said to Sky. "I'll have my hands full holding up this dress."

"Will you give it a rest?" Sky slipped a small beaded bag over her wrist. "You have plenty to hold it up. It's not like the summer we stuffed you with tissue."

Cait smiled as she slid out of the car, remembering her sixteenth birthday party. Breastwise, she'd grown since then, but at times she still felt like that young girl trying to prove she was a woman. To herself. Her father. Everyone.

She caught the boy staring at her skirt. The slit was cut up to way-past-decent and showed a lot of leg. Caitlyn handed him the keys. He kept staring. She wiggled them in front of his face. With a bashful grin, he grabbed them.

The little encounter gave her a burst of confidence. She could do this. If Judd could stick it to her, then she could stick it to him, even if she looked like something out of a 1950s movie. A sexy 1950s movie—with a streetwalker as a heroine.

They made their way up the walk, Maddie and Sky flanking Gran. Cait trailed behind with a sense of trepidation and excitement.

Renee was at the door, greeting guests, as they arrived. She looked years younger in a gold gossamer
creation with a boat neck and sheer sleeves. The diamond pendant sparkling around her neck could support a family for a year.

The foyer showcased a huge flower arrangement,
the fragrance of which wafted around them. For some
reason it made Cait think of a night in the Garden of
Eden. She knew the serpent was not far away.

But Judd was not standing with his mother.

"Oh, Dorie." Renee gave her grandmother an air
hug. "I'm so glad you're here." Her gaze swung to the
sisters. "And your granddaughters are lovely."

"Thank you. I'm very proud of them."

Renee's eyes settled on Caitlyn. "Oh, my dear. I wish
I was young enough to wear red."

Did that require a response? Cait didn't think so.

"There's plenty of food and drink. Enjoy your-
selves."

They trailed into the party room, speaking to neighbors as they went. A band played softly in the background. A buffet was set up at one end of the room, and
guests milled around it. Tables bedecked with white
linens and centerpieces of azalea sprigs and tea-light
candles floating in crystal bowls were placed around
the room. The double French doors were flung open,
with more tables outside.

A déjà vu feeling came over Caitlyn. This was almost identical to their engagement party fourteen
years ago. She'd been young and so much in love.
She'd thought she'd found her prince. She'd thought
he loved her.

But he'd only desired her.

Just as she was sinking into despair, Sky grabbed

her arm. "We found a table. Let's get some food. Remember at your engagement party they had all those delicious appetizers? I hope they have some tonight."

"Could we not talk about my engagement party, please?"

"Touchy subject, huh?" Sky looked around. "I wonder where Judd is?"

"Maybe he has enough sense to stay away."

"Caitlyn."

"Oh, hi, Mr. and Mrs. Wakefield." She shook hands with a neighbor and his wife.

"You remember Sherry, our daughter?"

"Yes, of course." She smiled at the tall blonde, but the smile was not returned. "And I'm sure you remember my sister Skylar."

"Oh, yes," Mr. Wakefield replied. "I'm always struck at how different Dane's daughters look."

"Yes." Caitlyn's heart squeezed. "Dad said he marked us with his blue eyes so that he'd know we were his."

Mrs. Wakefield glanced toward her grandmother. "How is Dorie?"

"She's coping." Cait didn't want to discuss Gran in a room full of people. "If you'll excuse us, we were going to the buffet table."

"Oh, yes, yes." Mr. Wakefield waved them away.

"That blonde was glaring at you," Sky whispered.

"Yeah. She thought Judd should have proposed to her instead of me."

"Well, the nerve."

They reached the buffet. There was prime rib, shrimp on ice and everything in between. Cait reached for two plates, one for Gran and one for her.

Sky filled Maddie's and her own.

"Maddie trusts you to choose for her?"

"She eats like a bird and I'm stuffing everything imaginable on here."

Plates full, the sisters headed to their table.

"Why haven't Judd and the blonde hooked up since then?" Sky asked.

"I don't know and I don't care."

"Caitlyn?"

She turned to Joe Bob Shoemaker, a rancher who bought hay from her.

"Is that you?" He eyed her up and down, clutching a drink in his hand. "Hot damn, I didn't know you had some of those things." He gestured with his glass at her breasts.

She sighed. "Yeah, every woman comes equipped with boobs. It's pretty much standard."

"And, damn, you got legs, too. Never see 'em in those jeans and boots you wear."

"Is there a problem?" Walker, the constable and only law in High Cotton, strolled over. An ex-marine, he was big and impressive. Everyone called him Walker. Most people didn't know his first name, and those who did never used it.

"Just Joe Bob being an ass," Cait replied.

"Ooh, I'm wounded." Joe Bob clutched his chest.

"Excuse my husband." Charlene, his wife, came up behind him. "Go get some food or I'm leaving."

Joe Bob saluted with the glass.

Charlene yanked it out of his hand and pointed to the buffet. "Food."

The rancher stomped off, muttering, "Damn wife. Free booze and she won't let me drink."

"I'm sorry, Cait," Charlene exclaimed. "Liquor short-circuits his manners."

"Don't worry about it."

"You look gorgeous in that dress."

"Thank you. Nice seeing you, Charlene." Cait held up the plates. "We better go. Our food is getting cold."

"See you later."

Maddie rushed forward to help with the plates, and since Walker still stood there, Cait felt she should introduce them.

"This is Walker, our constable, and Walker, these are my sisters, Madison and Skylar."

"Nice to finally meet y'all. I do remember seeing y'all at the funeral, but I was on duty and didn't get a chance to visit." As they shook hands, he said to Maddie, "Ma'am, I must say you look as young as my daughter."

"How old is she?" Maddie asked in her polite manner.

"Ten."

"Ten!"

Unflappable, understanding Maddie glared at him, and Cait knew her sister was about to lose her cool. "Bye, Walker." She shuffled Maddie toward their table.

"He said I looked like a ten-year-old. The nerve of him!"

"He was just being nice." Cait brushed it off.

"Yeah, and he's not bad looking," Sky quipped.

They shared a chuckle as they joined their grandmother.

"Here you go, Gran." Cait placed her plate in front of her. "Prime rib, shrimp, roasted potatoes with parsley and grilled asparagus."

"Thank you, baby."

Maddie looked aghast at her plate. "Sky, I can't eat all this."

"Just try."

The party wore on and Cait found she kept watching the door. Where was Judd? Was he not coming?

What did she care?

Once Gran grew tired, they were leaving. It couldn't be soon enough for her.

JUDD SAT AT HIS DESK in his bedroom, going over the feed ledger and inputting information into his laptop. He heard faint noises from downstairs, but ignored them.

He wasn't planning on making an appearance.

His door swung open and his mother stood there. My God, she did look like a fairy godmother in that cloud of gold. She glanced at his tux, still in the plastic from the cleaners, on his bed.

"Not coming to the party?"

"Nope."

She walked in, her long skirt rustling like feathers against tinfoil.

"Everyone in High Cotton is here, and some of our friends from Austin. Janna Durham came especially to see you."

"I didn't invite her." He turned back to his laptop. Janna was one of those women who tried her best to get him to the altar. She never understood that he wasn't interested in marriage. He didn't relish another foray into that minefield. Caitlyn had broken him of the marriage bug. He'd rather stay single.

"And the Belles made it."

He didn't respond.

"Madison and Skylar are lovely, but Caitlyn is causing quite a stir in a red strapless dress. Every man in the room finds he can't take his eyes off her. The band is fixing to start playing, and she'll be dancing the rest of the night. Enjoy your solitude."

"If that's your subtle way of getting me downstairs, you're out of luck. I don't care what Caitlyn's wearing or not wearing."

In his mind's eye he saw her at the windmill with sweat and mud trickling down her cleavage. It irritated him that he remembered that so vividly.

"My dear son, I would never pressure you to do anything. I'm not your father."

He turned to frown at her. "What are you talking about?"

"Jack pressured you to marry Caitlyn."

He slammed the laptop shut and stood. "Dad didn't force me to do anything I didn't want to."

"Does Caitlyn know that?"

"It doesn't matter." His voice rose as he talked. "It happened fourteen years ago and it's over. Done. Kaput. Do you understand?"

"Good." She walked to him and slipped her arm through his. He stiffened; he couldn't help it. His re-action was a reflex from years of pretending she didn't exist. Much the same feeling he had for Caitlyn. "There are so many beautiful young women downstairs just waiting for you to make their night. I'd hate to think that Caitlyn has you hiding up here in your room."

"Caitlyn has no control over me, and I told you from the start I wasn't taking part in this fiasco."

"Tut-tut." Renee tapped his nose with an artificial, manicured nail. "You seem rather defensive."

"Go to your party," he said through clenched teeth, "and leave me the hell alone."

"Whatever you say, dear son." She swished out the door in a cloud of gold.

He sat on his bed and the party noise vibrated around him. Something his mother had said stuck with him. Did people think he was hiding? And when had he ever cared what people thought?

But it still stung.

He jumped up. He was getting out of the house and away from the party. At the door, he stared back at the tux on his bed.

Was he running?

THE BALL WAS in full swing and the band was revving up to something lively. Some of the tables had been removed to make room for people to dance.

Caitlyn thought this would be a good time to leave. She leaned over and whispered to her grandmother. "Gran, are you ready to go home?"

"Where are your manners? We can't leave in the middle of a party. It's just not done."

Yes, heaven forbid.

"Here comes a waiter," Sky said. "Let's have some champagne."

"And lots of it." Cait reached for a glass.

Renee appeared in the doorway and a hush fell over the crowd. "I would like to thank everyone for coming tonight and—"

"My mother and I would like to thank you." Suddenly Judd was there, and contrary to every sane thought in her head, Cait couldn't look away. Not from his handsome face. And not from the years that stretched behind her like a path covered with thorns. Painful. And littered with what-could-have-beens.

His tux fit like a movie star's across broad shoulders and that long, muscled body. Expensive cowboy boots covered his feet—only in Texas could you wear boots with a tuxedo, but it suited the man as he gave a perfunctory smile to his guests.

He was a rancher with money and power, and it showed in every chiseled Clint Eastwood-like feature on his face. It showed in the way he moved and in the way he spoke. He was a man to be reckoned with. A man only a fool would cross.

Cait moved uneasily and realized she was spilling champagne into her cleavage. Good grief. She grabbed a napkin and dabbed, under several men's watchful eyes.

Old fools!

A Texas waltz played, and Renee and Judd took to the floor, dancing round and round. And the night dragged on. Judd danced with every woman in the room, including Gran, Maddie and Sky. Not once did he look in Cait's direction. Not once did he ask her to dance.

That was fine with her. She had plenty of partners. And she didn't *want* to dance with him. It was better if he didn't touch her. Southern manners only went so far.

She escaped to the powder room and turned on the gold faucets. Patting her face with a tissue, she soaked up the coolness and stared at the ornate wood trim, the crimson and soft pink walls. A fresh bouquet of pink irises graced the vanity, as did monogrammed towels and soaps. Everything was elegant. Everything was Renee.

Cait yanked opened the door and ran into Brenda Sue. Someone up there was testing her patience.

"Wow, Caitlyn, where did you get that dress? I want one just like it. I never knew you had it in you to wear something like that. You know, you never did in high school. But tonight you're showing actual cleavage. I'm surprised your grandmother allowed it. She's like, you know, rather high on morals and manners and things I've never heard about. Is anyone in the bathroom? I really have to pee. But I don't want to miss any of the action." She knocked on the door without taking a breath. "I'll just use one of the other bathrooms. You know I have the run of the place and…"

Caitlyn walked off down the hall and didn't look back. She made her way through the dancing couples to the veranda. Japanese lanterns lit up the trees with a magical glow. In a dark corner, she sat down and took a deep breath. It was quieter out here. Couples swayed together and the night air was warm yet soothing.

Feeling a chill, she ran her hands up her arms. She lifted her eyes and saw Judd standing in the shadows a few feet away. Her eyes locked with his and her heart thudded with the force of a nine pound hammer.

Her first thought was to walk away, but this time pride wouldn't let her. This time she was standing her ground and facing Judd.

CHAPTER TWELVE

"EVERYONE IS EXPECTING US to dance," Judd said in a voice that flowed around her like a warm blanket and wrapped her in memories.

The good ones.

"Yes," she managed to reply.

He held out his hand.

Go to hell. Not in this lifetime ever again. When hell freezes over. The comebacks were right there in her throat. All she had to do was say the words and walk away from him. She could do that. She'd done it before.

Something stronger than her pride moved her forward. She placed her hand in his and he pulled her into his arms. Her soft curves pressed into the hardness of his body and they began to move to "Bluest Eyes in Texas." Her forehead rested against his jaw and his sandalwood scent shot her estrogen levels up a few notches. The tautness of his muscles shot her levels through the roof. But she didn't pull away. She was on autopilot.

Still dancing, they moved out of the shadows and among the other couples. Out of the corner of her eye Cait saw Maddie, Sky, Gran and Renee watching them. Nothing registered but the male body pressed against hers. She had to admit she'd missed his touch. She'd missed him. That part of their relationship had been nothing less than fantastic.

Some couples stopped dancing, but Cait and Judd

danced on. In his arms she felt like a princess—the belle of the ball. He pulled her closer and there was nothing left to the imagination; every muscle, every sinew, she felt. And she floated away to a happy place where fairy tales came true.

"Why wasn't this enough, Caitlyn?" His throaty voice broke through the clouds to reality.

She pulled back slightly to look into his dark eyes. It felt strange to have this conversation after fourteen years. "Because sex and love are two different things."

"They're the same to me."

"They're not to me. Sex is an act. Love is a feeling in here...." She removed her hand from his to place it over his heart. Her eyes holding his, she added, "Sex is fleeting. Love lasts forever."

He glanced down at her hand. "I didn't know I had a heart until you broke it."

Her breath felt heavy at his admission. "You could have come after me."

"You could have come back."

"But that would have changed nothing. It still would have been an arranged marriage without love." She pushed away from him then. "So go ahead and get even. Take your revenge. Hurt me if that makes you feel better. The sad part is that I've hurt myself more." She tore away from him and ran from the room, past startled guests, out the front door, down the front steps and into the night.

She lost a shoe and sank to the ground and began to laugh. Laughter turned to tears. Try as she might she couldn't stop them, so she gave up and howled.

Maddie and Sky eased down by her. She sat on the grass and wiped away tears with the back of her hand.

Her sisters didn't say anything. They just hugged her, which was what she needed.

Maddie held up her red high heel. "Would Cinderella like to try on the magical shoe?"

Cait burst into laughter once more. "Most certainly. Even though I've never heard of Cinderella in a come-hither red dress. She looks virginal, like you."

"Yeah, right." Maddie ruffled her skirt. "That Walker guy had the nerve to ask me to dance. I told him my mommy doesn't allow me to."

"He's a hottie, so I danced with him." Sky nudged Cait playfully. "I told him we only let Maddie out of the attic on special occasions, and that she's a little gun-shy or man-shy."

"Hardy har-har." Maddie made a face at Sky, then linked her arm through Cait's. "Let's go home."

"First Cait has to slip on the magical shoe."

"Hell's bells, Sky, there's no magic in it," she protested.

"I beg to differ," Maddie said, holding it out.

Cait slipped her foot in.

Nothing happened.

Same old heartache. Same old bizarre evening.

"Okay." Maddie wrinkled her nose. "Maybe there isn't any such thing as a fairy tale."

"You got it. Let's load up the Lincoln, pick up Gran and get the hell out of Dodge."

"Good plan," Sky murmured as they got to their feet. "I guess y'all know we're going to have grass stains on these dresses."

"So? After tonight we'll retire the dresses from hell." Cait peered through the darkness at the sea of cars. "Now where is that old Lincoln?"

"Whistle, Cait, like you always do," Maddie suggested. "Maybe that guy who was ogling you will come running."

She put her fingers to her mouth and blew. Nothing happened. They burst into a fit of giggles. "We've had too much champagne," Cait said.

"May I help you?" The young man appeared abruptly, scaring the living daylights out of them.

"Yes. We'd like our car, please. The Lincoln," Cait told him, trying not to snicker.

"The old one?"

"Yes. The old one."

"I'll bring it around."

The Lincoln rolled to a stop in front of them.

"I'm driving," Sky said, and rounded the car.

Cait slid into the passenger's seat and Maddie climbed in the back. "Make a circle so we can pick up Gran," Cait instructed.

"Yes, bossy."

She shot her the finger.

Sky zoomed forward and came to a screeching stop at the front door. Maddie jumped out to assist Gran, who was waiting on the veranda with their hostess.

Gran got in, and Renee waved. Cait did not wave back. Sky tore out of the driveway.

"We're going home, Gran," Sky said, glancing in the rearview mirror.

"Yes, my baby, we're going home." There was a long pause and then Gran asked, "Caitlyn, baby, are you okay?"

"Yes, I'm fine."

"Did Judd hurt your feelings?"

Her gut tightened. "Naw. He just bruised my pride. I'm tough."

"Women shouldn't be tough, Caitlyn." Her tone suggested Cait should mind her p's and q's.

"Come on, Gran," Sky said, negotiating a turn. "Belles are tough. We all are."

"That's why you don't have husbands."

"And that's the name of that tune," Cait whispered to Sky.

They rode in silence for a moment.

"It was a lovely party," Gran said. "I kept waiting for your father to show up."

Cait and Sky exchanged a glance.

"Before any of you say it, I know Dane is dead."

"Yes," Cait replied. And added a private *thank God* for not having to say the words.

THEY WALKED Gran into the house and up to her bedroom. But Cait wasn't ready to close her eyes. Her engine was still running. While Maddie and Sky helped Gran, she went down to the parlor and to her father's wine collection. She pulled out a merlot and uncorked it. Breathing the fragrant scent, she closed her eyes. *Oh, yeah.* This was what she needed. Tipping up the bottle, she walked to the kitchen. She chugalugged right out the door and all the way to the barn.

Within minutes she had a bridle on Jaz. From the refrigerator in the barn, she grabbed two carrots and stuffed them into her cleavage. Then she hitched up her red skirt and slid on bareback, the bottle in one hand. One high heel fell to the ground and she left it there.

She had something she wanted to do, and she rode like hell through the night.

JUDD SAT IN HIS STUDY with a bottle of bourbon and a shot glass in front of him. He should have never gone down to the party. But God, she was beautiful. That red dress was something out of his fantasies. Every man in the room, married or single, had wanted her. He was no exception.

The dancing part was great. Conversing always brought trouble, though. They'd never connected on that level, and it was important to her. Why did women always want to talk and analyze everything to death?

He was an action man and he didn't like any of that intense inner emotional crap. That's why he was sitting here drinking bourbon—alone. Tyra or Jenna would be happy to keep him company, and he wouldn't have to do a lot of conversing, either. Still, he'd left the party soon after Caitlyn. She pretty much put the lid on the night.

For fourteen years they'd managed to stay apart, and in a matter of a few days they were smack-dab in the middle of each other's lives. He wanted her to bend. He wanted her to beg.

And he was going to grow into a lonely old man waiting for that to happen. He threw the shot glass at the wall and it exploded in a burst of amber liquid.

As he watched bourbon trail down the paneling, his cell phone buzzed. It was 2:00 a.m. Who was calling this late? He picked the device up and saw it was Harland. Something had to be wrong.

He clicked on. "Yes."

"Sorry to bother you so late, but we have a situation at the stables."

He stood and ran a hand through his already tousled hair. "What is it?"

"You need to see for yourself."

"I'll be right there." Judd still wore his tux trousers and his white shirt hung loose over them. He didn't bother to change.

Harland met him at the stables. "I heard a noise so I thought I'd check on the new horse. I'll show you what I found."

Judd followed him to Whiskey Red's stall. They'd put blinders on the horse and she'd settled down. The blinders were now off and Caitlyn sat on the floor of the enclosure, her back against a wall, sipping from a bottle of wine. A carrot poked out of her cleavage. She still wore the red dress and the skirt was bunched between her bare thighs. She was barefooted. Disheveled black hair cascaded around her shoulders.

A familiar longing tightened his lower abdomen.

"Hey, Judd." She raised the bottle.

"I'll take care of this," he told Harland.

"I tried to pull her out of there, but the horse gets riled, so I left her alone."

"Thanks." Judd leaned on the stall door. "What are you doing, Caitlyn?"

"Visiting the horse you took from me."

"Looks to me like you're drinking."

"Yep. That, too." She tipped up the bottle.

"Get out of the stall."

She squinted at him. "Nope. Don't think so."

"You're trespassing."

"Yep. I am."

She was sloshed and he didn't want to hurt her by dragging her out. The thought hit him like the bourbon deep in his belly—warm, fuzzy and jolting. Everything he'd done recently had been meant to hurt her. Maybe that hadn't been his intention at all. Maybe all he wanted was her attention.

A sobering thought.

"Come out of the stall, Caitlyn. It's late."

She lifted the bottle. "Make me."

He slid the latch of the stall door open and stepped in. Red immediately threw up her head, fidgeting in an agitated manner.

Judd fully intended to make Caitlyn leave the stall, but once he saw the pain in her eyes, that plan went south. Instead he sank down beside her in the dirt and straw.

She handed him the bottle. "Want a drink?"

"No, thank you."

She took a swig and then peered into the bottle with one eye. "Damn, it's all gone. Someone drank my wine."

"You did."

"No, no, no." She shook her head. "You did. You took my royalties, my horse and—"

"I bought your royalties and your horse. They weren't cheap, either."

"Why? Why did you have to do that?" Her blurred blue eyes tried to focus on him.

"You're drunk," was all he could say.

"Yep." She jammed the bottle into the hay. "And it never felt so damn good." She plucked the carrot from her cleavage. "Here, Red, have a carrot before I have to leave Mr. High-and-Mighty's stables."

The horse munched on the offering and Cait rested her head against the wall. For a moment he thought she was out, but she wasn't. She was close, though.

The overhead light cast shadows across them. The scents of manure, horse, sweet feed and hay radiated through the barn. A horse neighed and another stomped in its stall. All normal scents and sounds, but nothing was normal about this night.

"You didn't have to run away tonight."

"Yes, I did." Cait hiccuped.

"Why?"

"Oh, please." She staggered to her feet. "Your goal in life now is to hurt me. Well—" she clutched at the stall wall for support "—you've succeeded, but you'll never get High Five. Ooh." She grabbed her head. "The stall is moving."

He rose to his feet, not bothering to dust off his clothes. "Why do you keep fighting this? It's just a matter of time."

"Don't... Don't—" she jabbed a finger at him "—say that...." She swayed like a felled tree and he caught her before she crumpled to the ground. He swung her over his shoulder and left the stall, latching the gate behind him.

"Put me down," she yelled, beating on his back.

He kept walking toward his Ford Lariat truck, parked at the garages.

"The shoe had no magic. Poof. It didn't work."

He didn't know what the hell she was talking about. Yanking open the door, he deposited her on the passenger side. He waited to see if she'd try to get out, but she didn't. Her head dropped onto the leather headrest, her tousled black hair a striking sight against the red dress.

"If you'd been a prince, the shoe would have been magical," she muttered. "But you're no prince." She turned toward him, her eyes managing to hold his. "You're the devil."

He closed the door and a chill shot up his spine. Walking around to the driver's side, he said to hell with her. He didn't care what she thought of him. His conscience, something he hadn't been in contact with for some time, chose that moment to awaken and mock him.

From the moment Dane had offered him the royalties, Judd had felt a burst of energy. He would now have his revenge. He would make her hurt the way she had hurt him. But ironically, hurting Caitlyn was harder than he'd ever expected.

CHAPTER THIRTEEN

JUDD TURNED THE KEY and the engine hummed to life.

"My horse. I can ride my horse," Caitlyn muttered as the truck moved onto the road.

"Where is your horse?"

"I tied her to a tree by the barn...I think."

"I'll return her tomorrow."

"I don't need...your help." Her voice was growing weak and sleepy.

He didn't say anything else, just drove toward High Five. No other vehicles were on the road at this time of the morning, so he made the trip in record time. He pulled to a stop in front of the Belle house. The front porch light was shining brightly and a light was on at the barn.

He touched her arm. "You're home."

She sat up straight and grabbed her head. "Geez, Louise." She opened one eye to peer through the darkness. "How did I get here?"

"Guess." His gaze held hers. "You were too drunk to ride a horse."

"Listen..." She winced.

"Get out of the truck. You're home."

Caitlyn stared at him though the darkness. His tousled hair falling across his forehead and his dark growth of beard evoked so many memories. Good memories of when she'd thought he loved her.

Without thinking clearly, she slid a hand around his neck, caressed his roughened skin and pulled his face toward hers. She touched his lips gently, almost reverently. It took a split second for remembered emotions to explode.

He took over the kiss, cupping her face with both hands, and time floated away, as did the years, as they found comfort in a kiss that bound them together. Tongues and lips knew the drill. Memories like this weren't forgotten, just buried beneath the pain.

He tasted of bourbon, and the heady sensation was making her drunk all over again. Or was it just Judd?

He was the first to draw back. "Why did you do that?" His voice vibrated as smoothly as the engine of his fancy truck.

She licked her lips. "To see if my collection of memories is gold plated or the real thing?"

"And?"

Cait would never know what her response would have been because Cooper tapped on the window, and when she glanced up she saw Maddie and Sky hurrying down the sidewalk.

Cait smiled slyly. "You'll never know." She opened the door and almost fell out.

"Everything okay?" Coop asked as he caught her.

"Yep," she replied, staggering. Coop steadied her. "I'm a little drunk, though."

"Cait," Sky called. "Where have you been?"

She glanced at Judd and wasn't sure how to answer that. It had been a bizarre evening. What had possessed her to kiss him? She blamed it on the liquor, and closed the door. She didn't want to see Judd's face any longer. It made her weak.

The truck pulled out of the driveway and Sky and

Maddie rushed to her. "Where have you been?" Sky demanded.

"*Are* you okay?" Coop asked, and Sky shot him a this-is-none-of-your-business look.

"Yes, Coop, thanks." Cait smiled at him to ease any hard feelings. "I got a little sidetracked tonight."

"I saw Jaz was gone and I was worried."

"I took a midnight ride to visit Red."

"You didn't." Sky was aghast.

"Yes, I did, and I got caught." She picked up her filthy skirt. "Now I'm going inside to crash. Night, Coop."

"Night." He strolled back to the bunkhouse.

Maddie and Sky linked their arms through hers and they marched together toward the house, through the door and up the stairs.

"Your dress is ruined," Maddie said, inspecting Cait in the light.

"That's what happens when you wallow in the stables with a bottle of wine."

"Sometimes you're like a loose cannon." Sky opened the bathroom door. "And you stink."

"Shit happens, I suppose," she replied, stepping inside and closing the door on her sisters.

She turned on the bathtub taps, stripped out of the ridiculous dress and sank into the warm water. It felt heavenly, and wonderful to wash away the grime. Washing away the memories was something else entirely. Not a task that could be done with mere soap and water.

Why had she kissed him? Why? Her hand went to her lips and she still felt Judd's soft caress, so different from the strong and powerful man that he was. Liquored up, she couldn't resist or deny the pull she always experienced when she was around him. That was her only explanation. And it didn't change a thing in her life.

He was still the enemy.

She quickly got out of the tub, dried off and slipped on a big T-shirt. Opening the door, she found her sisters standing there with their old sleeping bags.

"We're camping on the veranda tonight, or what's left of the night," Maddie told her. "It might be a long time before we see each other again."

"I'm game." Cait picked up her bag and they trudged out to the porch and got comfy.

"Gran asleep?" she asked, rolling out her bedding between Maddie's and Sky's.

"Yes. The dancing wore her out." Maddie wiggled on top of her bag. It was too warm to slide inside.

There was silence for a moment as they absorbed the warmth and peace of the night.

"What were you and Judd talking about?" Sky asked. "We were looking for you and saw the truck drive up. What took you so long to get out?"

"I was making a fool of myself." She folded her hands behind her head. "Yep. I'm getting good at that."

Sky rose up on an elbow. "What happened?"

"Well, remember I was highly intoxicated…."

"Anyone who would visit a horse in the dead of night has to be intoxicated or insane. Should we take a vote?"

"Shut up, Sky," she said, and moved uneasily.

"So what happened?" Sky pressed.

She didn't answer for a moment. "I just wanted to make sure Red was comfortable. She's very temperamental. I took her a treat, a couple of carrots, and I took a treat for myself—a bottle of wine."

"After all the champagne we consumed!"

"Yes, Betty Crocker, it wasn't a brilliant idea, and my head is pounding. Let's go to sleep."

"Not until you tell us what you and Judd were talking about." Sky wouldn't give up.

"Geez, you're relentless. It was the same old, same old." She moved uneasily again as the truth weaved its way around her heart. "I sat there looking at him through liquored up eyes, but all I could see and feel was the way I used to love him." She watched the moon hanging in the sky like a neon sign, and was sure the fictional man in the moon had a come-on-in sign stapled on his chest. It was that warm. That inviting. Breaking down her barriers. "So I kissed him."

Maddie sat up straight. "You did what?"

"Well, well." Sky rose also, sitting cross-legged. "Now what does that say?"

"It says I was drunk out of my mind."

"It says you still love him," Maddie countered.

Cait sat up and wrapped her arms around her bare legs. "Maybe. Maybe I'll always love him, but that doesn't change a thing. Judd hasn't altered. He's still like his father, needing to have power over a woman because he feels she's less than he is. I can't live with a man who thinks that way. I can't love him, either."

"So, what? You're going to sneak over at night and have sex with him, and during the day you're still enemies?"

"Sky, I didn't have sex with him."

"I'm sticking to my original suggestions," she stated. "As a woman, you have the power to make him beg. Use everything in your arsenal, and High Five and Southern Cross will be yours. Think of it as a contest and the big prize is Judd."

"Judd is not a prize and I don't have an arsenal."

"Well, honey, you should have seen yourself tonight. Judd couldn't take his eyes off you, and when you danced there was not a smidgen of daylight between you."

"Sky…"

"Can we please talk about something else?" Maddie asked. "We only have a few more hours together. Let's don't spend it bickering."

"Okay," Cait said with a smug expression. "Let's talk about Kira. When are you going to tell Gran?"

"When I see fit."

"Gran has a right to see her great-granddaughter."

"I feel awful lying to her, but I have little choice. I've been trying to get in touch with Todd so he can get his parents off my back, but so far no response. Until that happens I have to stay in hiding."

Sky stretched out on her sleeping bag and Cait and Maddie followed suit. They were quiet as crickets serenaded. A horse neighed and a dog barked in response to a coyote howling in the distance. The sounds of High Five. The ranch that Cait loved, but how long would she be allowed to stay here?

As if reading her thoughts, Sky asked, "Do you think you can show a profit in six months?"

"I'm going to give it my best shot."

"But you have no help," Maddie pointed out.

"That's why I work fourteen-hour days."

"The simple solution is just to sell," Sky said. "Gran can still live here, and I'm sure if you ask nicely, Judd will let you stay, too."

"I don't do *asking nicely* to Judd Calhoun." The mere thought made her stomach roll.

"Leave Cait alone," Maddie stated. "We agreed to

six months, and she even sold Red, so stop browbeating her."

There was silence for a moment and then Sky said, "Okay. I'm in for the long haul."

They gave each other the customary high five and snuggled onto their bags, settling down for the rest of the night. But Cait stayed awake long after she heard her sisters' wispy snoring. Tomorrow she would be alone again with Gran, and fighting to save High Five.

Somewhere between lucidness and sleep she wondered if she was fighting a losing battle. In the end, she could lose it all. But she still had to take that risk.

JUDD WALKED INTO THE BARN to check on Whiskey Red. She raised her head with a nervous neigh.

"It's okay, girl." He tried to reassure her, and she seemed to settle down. He saw the wine bottle and opened the stall door to retrieve it. The thoroughbred watched him, but stayed calm. Along the wall, Judd glimpsed a flash of red. He picked up a red high heel. He hadn't noticed it before. It must have been behind Caitlyn.

On his way out he flipped off the lights and tossed the wine bottle into the trash. He glanced at the shoe and started to trash it, too, then stopped.

Caitlyn had said something about the shoe having no magic. That if he was a prince, it would have been magical. Was she talking about a stupid fairy tale? No, she was too mature for that. But it was romantic stuff. Stuff that was important to her.

He strolled to the house with the shoe in his hand. The place was in darkness and endless quiet prevailed—the way he liked it. His study light was on and he headed there for the bourbon.

Placing the shoe in the center of his desk, he poured himself a shot and sank into his chair with a groan. What a night!

He licked his lips, still tasting the wine on Caitlyn's. Magic was there. Why couldn't she see it? Why couldn't she feel it? He downed the amber liquid in the shot glass and gazed at the shoe.

It seemed to taunt him.

The shoe wasn't magical.

Did she honestly think she could slip her foot into a magic shoe and he would love her? He had never loved her, had he? He desired her. He wanted her. Those were the emotions he understood.

Oh, God. He jammed his hands through his hair and then poured himself another drink. Everything was supposed to be simple. With the royalties gone, Caitlyn's only option would be to sell High Five. Even though she wouldn't want to, her sisters would force her hand. He'd have his revenge and she would disappear out of his life forever. He wouldn't see her in High Cotton. He wouldn't see her anywhere.

His mother had warned him that Caitlyn would come back fighting. She'd been right. Now Caitlyn was making his life a living hell.

He downed the bourbon. She was making him aware of how much he wanted her. That was lust, not love. And there was no magic in that.

After opening a drawer, he reached for the shoe and flung it inside.

So much for magic.

And Caitlyn Belle.

CHAPTER FOURTEEN

THE NEXT MORNING SAW a tearful goodbye. After a big breakfast, Etta drove Maddie and Sky to the airport. Gran went along so she could spend more time with her granddaughters.

Cait didn't have time to be nostalgic. There was work waiting for her. She met Coop and Rufus at the barn.

"The baler broke, but Ru and I got it fixed last night," Coop told her. "We're ready to go."

"God willing and the baler doesn't break again, we should be through by the end of June." Ru climbed into his truck. "There's still a lot of hay on the ground, though."

"I'll check the herds and then give y'all a hand," Cait called.

Coop jumped onto the tractor connected to the baler. "Jaz was in the corral this morning. And I found a red high heel in the barn. Don't know where it came from and I'm not asking. I put it on a shelf. See you later," he added, with a twinkle in his eye.

She waved as they rolled out of sight, and then glanced toward the corral. There was Jaz, and her bridle was hanging on the fence. Had Judd brought back the horse or had he sent one of the cowhands? Either way, she just wanted to forget the miserable evening. Her aching head made that a little hard, though—a reminder that was going to be with her for the rest of the day.

Saddling up, Cait found her eyes straying to the red shoe laid haphazardly on a shelf. She had no idea where its mate was. The only explanation was that she'd lost it on the way to Southern Cross, and she'd just as soon forget about that visit.

She headed for the pastures. Water was flowing in all of them, the windmill spinning like a large whirling fan. The stock tanks were getting lower, though. Local ranchers needed rain badly.

In the last pasture, she didn't see Boss, and worried he might be on the Southern Cross again. Cait rode through the herd twice and still didn't spot him. Damn! Then she saw him coming out of the woods, looking a little scuffed up. He'd probably been fighting with the other bulls, which was his modus operandi. But she was relieved he wasn't trying to court the Southern Cross cows again.

At midday she headed back to the ranch house, and was surprised to find Etta and Gran weren't back. Cait checked for messages on the phone and there weren't any. If something was wrong, there would have been a message, so she told herself not to worry.

She made sandwiches and packed a lunch to carry to Coop and Rufus. Afterward, she worked the tractor with the front fork to lift the round bales from the field and place them along the fence. It was a hot, scorching day—the type of weather to be indoors with air-conditioning or in a swimming pool.

But she wasn't an indoor person, and lying around a pool wasn't her, either. She must enjoy cruel and inhuman punishment, Cait decided ruefully. Sweat rolled down her back and soaked the waistband of her jeans.

It coated her whole body, and the warm breeze made her feel as if she was in a sauna.

She lowered a round bale to the ground and massaged the calluses on her hands. *This isn't women's work.* How many times had her father said that to her? And how many times had she tried to prove him wrong?

Was she trying to hold on to High Five for Gran, or trying to prove something to her father? As she removed her hat and wiped sweat from her brow, she thought she might be proving him right.

He'd always said that a woman's place was in the home, making babies and pleasing her husband. None of his daughters had cottoned to the idea, so to speak, but he'd never wavered in his conviction. And neither had Caitlyn.

As the sun sank in the west, Cait suspected she was going to grow old clinging to her beliefs. Nothing would ever change her mind.

Not even Judd Calhoun.

Or her love for him.

That thought stayed with her as they made their way home.

She came to an abrupt stop in the kitchen doorway. Etta was at the stove, and Maddie and Gran were setting the table.

"Maddie, I thought you left." She removed her hat and placed it on a rack.

Her sister wiped her hands on her apron. "I thought about it all the way into town. I now have the cash to pay off my debts, so I stopped and called my mom and wired her the money. She's going to pay the bills and I can stay here and help you. You need it."

"Maddie…"

"Belles stand and fight. Isn't that one of Dad's sayings? And I have a stake in this ranch, too."

"Oh, Maddie!" They hugged tightly.

"Why are you girls talking about such things?" Gran asked, straightening a napkin. "Your father takes care of all that."

Cait and Maddie glanced at each other and knew a response would be useless.

"Here, Gran." Maddie pulled out a chair. "Have a seat. Etta's chicken fried steak is almost ready."

Gran sat as Cooper and Rufus walked through the door.

When Coop spied Maddie, he took a step backward. "Oh, I didn't know we still had company." Before he could take another step, Maddie grabbed his arm.

"No, you don't, Cooper Yates. I don't bite. I promise."

Maddie's sweet smile thawed the cowboy faster than the Texas heat. "I just don't want to intrude."

"You're not," Cait said. "And I'm starving. How about you?"

After supper, Maddie helped Etta with the dishes.

"See you at home, Etta." Rufus shuffled out the door and Cooper followed.

The phone rang and Cait ran to answer it.

"This is Gil Bardwell. I'm trying to locate Caitlyn Belle."

"This is Caitlyn."

"Chance Hardin gave me your number. I'm the foreman of a large road construction company and I need sand and gravel. Chance said you have some to sell."

"Yes. Yes, I do." She took a long breath. This was too good to be true, but she wasn't looking this gift horse in the mouth. They arranged to meet in the morning and discuss a price.

"Was that Sky?" Maddie asked from the doorway.

"No." Cait hugged her. "You're bringing me good luck. That was a man who wants to buy sand and gravel. It's going to help tremendously. I have to make some calls to check on prices." She picked up the phone and glanced at Maddie. "Could you please help Gran? I'll be up as soon as I finish."

"Don't worry about Gran. We're going to watch an old movie. *Giant,* with Elizabeth Taylor and Rock Hudson."

"Thanks. I'll try to catch the end."

By ten o'clock Cait's eyes wouldn't stay open any longer, so she trudged upstairs. But she had numbers and knew what prices to ask. There was a light beaming at the end of the tunnel of her nightmare.

Gran was sound asleep with Maddie curled up at her side, a popcorn bowl in the crook of her arm. Cait clicked off the TV and shook her sister.

"Time for bed," she whispered.

Maddie sat up, stretching. "I didn't realize I was so tired."

"Me, neither," Cait admitted. "See you in the morning." At the door she looked back. "Thank you."

"That's what sisters are for."

"I'm sorry I was on the phone so long. Sky couldn't call."

"I phoned her on my cell. I told her you were making big deals. She made it home safely and said she can't stop holding Kira." Maddie kissed her cheek. "'Night, sis."

Cait showered and fell into a dead sleep, but right

before the hazy, blissful slumber claimed her she saw Judd's face and heard his words.

Why wasn't this enough?

THE NEXT MORNING was hectic as everyone hurried to work. After breakfast Coop and Rufus went to the hay field and Cait rushed to meet Mr. Bardwell. Within an hour, they had hammered out a deal. He explained they would have to dig forty feet deep or more with a dragline excavator, creating some steep hills and deep valleys. He promised to level the land as much as he could and keep damages to a minimum.

She showed him the places on the ranch he could dig, the areas Grandfather Bart had sold from years ago. The pastures with the cattle were off-limits.

Maddie stayed at the house with Gran, and that arrangement worked well. Cait didn't worry about Gran with her sister there.

Maddie had also undertaken the job of cleaning the house from top to bottom. Dust didn't have a chance with her around. And most days she brought lunch to the fields so they didn't have to make the trip to the house.

Several people had called about buying hay, and Cait sold what they didn't need. The ranch was taking a turn for the better. If her luck held, she'd have the books in the black before the six-month time period. She couldn't let up, though. Every day she had to stay on top of things.

It was time to tag the new baby calves and round up the older ones to sell. Maddie saddled up to help. She was a good rider; their father had seen to that. The job was dusty, hot and tedious, but Maggie never faltered.

With the help of the dogs, they herded the cattle from

the pastures into the corral. There, Cait and Coop dismounted and waded into the herd. He caught a baby calf and she marked it, using an ear tag gun. More than once Cait stepped in cow crap, and the scent filled her nostrils. She never stopped, though. They continued until every baby was tagged with the number of its mother.

Then they saddled up again and separated the herd, cutting out mothers and babies into another corral. Rufus worked the gate and Maddie helped; the dogs nipped at the cows' feet. Cows bellowed and the dust was suffocating. Finally, only the older calves were left in the corral. Rufus and Maddie herded the other animals back to the pastures.

"I'll load 'em up later and get 'em to the auction barn for tomorrow's sale," Coop said.

"Good. I'll make sure the cows are settling down." Cait glanced up as she heard riders, knowing it was too soon for Maddie and Rufus to return.

Harland and four Southern Cross cowboys rode into view.

"Uh-oh, I sense trouble." Coop wiped the sweat from his forehead with the sleeve of his chambray shirt.

Harland galloped forward. "Miss Belle, we have a problem with your bull again. I have orders not to shoot him, so you'd better come take care of the situation."

"I'll be right there." She put her foot in the stirrup and swung into the saddle. Coop did the same.

"Yates doesn't come onto Southern Cross property." Harland spit chewing tobacco onto the ground.

Cait rode out of the corral to within a foot of Harland. "Cooper goes where I go." Her voice was sharp enough to cut through a T-bone steak.

"Well, Miss Belle." Harland leaned back in the saddle. "You just might need a man to help you with this problem, so I'll allow it this time."

A round of snickers echoed from the cowboys.

"Just show me where my bull is."

"Yes, ma'am." Harland jerked his bridle and shot away, the cowboys behind him. She and Cooper immediately followed. It was clear the foreman was trying to lose them, or to prove that they couldn't keep up. But she knew every inch of High Five and there was no way she'd fall behind.

They came to a gap and one of the cowboys opened it. It was farther along the fence that Boss had broken through earlier. She wondered why they weren't riding through a broken fence instead of the gap.

She pulled up as Harland and his boys stopped. All eyes were on her. Boss stood alone in the woods, with his head hanging low. He hadn't budged as the riders approached.

Cait dismounted and walked to the animal, Harland and Cooper behind her. She stood in shock for a moment at the sight in front of her. The lower part of Boss's belly was swollen and his split penis was almost hanging to the ground. Blood and pus oozed out of it. Her stomach churned with a sick feeling, but she tried to hide her reaction.

"How did this happen?" she managed to ask.

"Well, Ms. Belle, it seems your bull has taken to jumping the fence. This time he was ready for action, if you know what I mean, and he caught his main feature on the barbed wire, splitting it open. He's useless now. He has to be put down."

A low, guttural sound left Boss's throat. He was in pain and probably had an infection and fever.

"I'm not sure your boy Yates here is allowed to use

a gun—being on probation and all. Looks like you'll have to do the honors."

The cowboys snickered again.

Out of the corner of her eye Cait saw Judd's black horse, and a few seconds later he was standing beside them.

"What's going on here?"

Harland relayed his story and Judd squatted to look at Boss. "Damn. He has to be put down. He's in a lot of pain."

"That's what I was telling Miss Belle."

"She won't do it," she heard a cowboy murmur.

"She hasn't got the guts," another said.

"Shut up or go back to the barn," Judd ordered.

Cait headed for her horse. "I'll do it," Coop whispered beside her.

"You'll get in trouble."

"I don't care."

"I do." She yanked her rifle from the scabbard on the saddle. She always carried one for coyotes and wild dogs that preyed on baby calves. But she'd never used it.

And she didn't know if she could use it now. The men kept watching her with smug expressions. She saw money exchange hands between two cowboys. They were betting she couldn't.

"We'll take care of the animal," Judd said.

The note in his voice that said she shouldn't have to do this ricocheted her courage into high gear. She was a woman and shouldn't be running a ranch. This was where the fictional line was drawn in the sand. She either stepped over it and did her job, or she stepped back and admitted she couldn't run this ranch.

For her, the latter was unacceptable.

"It's my animal. I'll take care of him."

"Caitlyn…"

She walked away, stopping about twenty feet from Boss. He made that gut-wrenching sound again and she knew she had to put him out of his misery.

What was the price of courage? Her pride? Her heart?

Without a second thought, she released the safety and raised the rifle. She took aim at Boss's shoulder through the crosshairs. Everything else faded away. Boss was in pain. She had to do this.

She had to do this.

The rapid beat of her heart pounded in her ears. Her palms were sweaty, and fear like she'd never known before crawled up her spine.

She had to do this.

I'm sorry, Boss.

She squeezed the trigger. The big bull dropped with a thud. He was dead.

The rifle butt kicked her shoulder as the sound of the blast echoed across the landscape. The explosive noise caused a ringing in her ears.

She stood frozen.

After a moment she lowered the gun, walked to her horse and shoved the rifle into the scabbard. Swinging into the saddle, she said to Coop, "Get the tractor and take him back to High Five." Then she rode hell-bent for somewhere other than here.

She kept nudging Jaz on, faster and faster, her stomach churning. When she reached Crooked Creek, she jumped off and threw up until there was nothing left in her but the pain. The pain of having to kill a living thing.

On her hands and knees, she crawled some distance away and leaned against an oak tree, taking deep breaths. Her mouth tasted like bile and she wiped her hand across it. Feeling weak, she rested her head on her knees.

There was absolute quiet here in the deep woods. Just an occasional twitter of a bird, the rustling of leaves and the call of a crow. Through the silence she heard a rider, and thought Coop was coming to look for her.

She raised her head and saw the black horse. Judd.

The last person she wanted to see.

CHAPTER FIFTEEN

JUDD WALKED TO HER and sank into the grass. Plucking a dried sprig, he studied it as if it was a marvel of science.

She didn't speak.

Nor did he.

He lifted his eyes, and their depths were so dark she couldn't even see the pupils. "Why do you have to be so tough? You didn't have to do that."

"A man would have without a second thought, and no one would have told him not to."

"You're not a man."

"Yeah." She faked a laugh. "My father reminded me of that every day of my life. I was never the son he wanted."

"No, you're his daughter—his beautiful, brave and spirited daughter. Why does that make you less of a person?"

It was weird hearing Judd say that. It was even more weird to be sitting here talking to him. Almost as if they were the only two people in the world and he understood her and her feelings.

She took a long breath and tucked a strand of hair behind her ear. "I find it strange that you would say that. You believe every woman is beneath you, the way your father believed...and mine."

"I'm not my father." His eyes darkened to pitch-black.

"But you are. His beliefs have been ingrained into you from birth. You even told me that."

"People change."

"Yeah." *Maybe.* Judd? She doubted it. She ran a hand through the dried grass and knew they had to talk about the past. It was right there between them like a boil that needed lancing. Time to get it over with. "Let's talk about what happened."

An eyebrow darted toward the rim of his Stetson. "We've killed that already."

"No, we haven't. We've danced around the flagpole without ever saluting the flag."

"What?"

"That means we've talked about everything but the real issue—my leaving and the reason I felt the way I did."

He moved restlessly. "I thought we covered that."

"No." She drew a hot breath from the bottom of her lungs. "I didn't leave you for another man. I didn't leave you because I didn't love you. I left because you didn't support me when I learned our marriage was arranged by our fathers. You didn't support me when I wanted to return to college. I left because you didn't love me. I couldn't live with a man who doesn't put me first and treat me as his equal. I wanted it all, and I will never settle for less."

He rubbed the sprig of grass between his fingers. "I told you I'm not familiar with love. I've never had that emotion in my life."

"Bull. Even abused kids know what love is. It's a feeling inside the heart—a special feeling for one certain person. I know you have it. You just won't acknowledge it." She held up a hand. "No. You're afraid to acknowledge it. Once you do, it makes you vulnerable to pain. And I know you suffered a great deal when your mother left you. But she came back. That's what love is. Highs and lows. Joy and sorrow. But it's worth every risk."

Heat suffused her cheeks at the audacity of her words.

She waited for equally heated words to rain down on her head, but none came. He kept staring at the sprig.

"At nineteen I knew what I wanted," Cait told him, "but I couldn't force you to love me, so I ended the engagement. That wasn't easy to do. My father practically disowned me, but I still couldn't give in." She swallowed and said the words she needed to say. "I'm sorry if I hurt you."

He lifted his head and a rare glimpse of a smile lit his face. "I think hell just froze over."

Her mouth twitched in response. "I do remember saying hell would freeze over before I'd ever apologize. But I'm tired of this fighting. You want revenge? Go ahead. Give it everything you've got. But you are not blameless."

"Maybe not," he muttered, and leaned back in the grass. He crossed his booted feet as if he and Cait were having a pleasant relaxing afternoon instead of reliving the engagement from hell. His snakeskin boots were dark brown and bespoke high-dollar comfort. She glanced down at her scuffed, worn ones caked with cow crap. What a difference.

Her eyes were drawn to his long legs and manhood, outlined by the tight Wranglers. It made her acutely aware of the difference between the sexes.

He gazed at her. "The night you visited Whiskey Red you said something about a magical shoe. What did you mean?"

It was hard to look away from the warmth she saw in his eyes, so she didn't. "That was silly."

"I want to know."

She swallowed. "When I ran from the party, I lost a high heel. You know the Cinderella story. Maddie brought me the shoe and, being the romantic she is, said that all I had to do was slip it on and you would love me. Fairy-tale stuff."

"Did you believe?"

Like a fool.

"No. I've outgrown that." She bluffed like a Vegas poker player. A palpable silence stretched, as taut as her nerves. "May I ask you a question?"

"I suppose."

"Why did you ever agree to marry me?"

He sat up and rested a forearm on a knee. "Have you looked in the mirror?"

Astonishment hit her in the face like a handful of manure. "You agreed to the marriage because I'm easy on the eyes."

"Mostly. And the marriage would have been beneficial to Southern Cross and High Five."

"Oh, yeah, that really makes my heart flutter."

"I don't get it. You're fighting tooth and nail to save High Five now, but back then you walked away from it."

"High Five wasn't in trouble then."

"It wouldn't be now if you had stayed."

"But would we still be together?" She fired back the question, her voice as fervent as a preacher's on Sunday morning. "Without love, how would our marriage have survived?"

He lifted his shoulders. "Does any marriage come with a guarantee?"

"No, but love always beats the odds."

"Sometimes. Sometimes it muddles the situation."

"Not in my opinion. It makes it stronger."

"Whatever." He waved a hand. "It makes no difference now. Your father has pitted us against each other and I will honor the agreement I made with him."

Judd rose to his feet and blew out a hard breath. "We can't go back and change the past, and we certainly can't start over. We've hurt each other too much."

"Uh-huh." She waited for an apology from him, something to ease the ache in her heart. She waited in vain.

He held out a hand and she placed hers in his big palm. He pulled her to her feet. "I'm tired of the fighting, too." He gazed off into the distance with a thoughtful expression. "Yes, I admit I wanted revenge in the worst way, and I intended to make you pay for walking away from me and everything I'd offered you. What woman would do that? I knew without a doubt you'd come back begging." His big chest expanded with a sigh. "You never did."

"Did you want me to?" she asked, and held her breath.

His expression changed. "I'm not sure *want* is the right word. I never thought about you or your feelings. My father said you'd come crawling back and I believed him. A woman has to know her place in life."

"Do you still believe that rubbish?"

He heaved another sigh. "No. The years and Caitlyn Belle have slowly altered my mind-set. I can't say I've changed completely. Like you said, those ideas were drilled into me. I'm making progress with my mother. I give in to her because I don't want to hurt her feelings. That has to be progress."

"Yes. I believe it is. It means you care about her, and caring leads to love."

"Ah, yeah, that infamous four-letter word. Keep your dreams, Caitlyn. You deserve them. For me, that elusive emotion is just that—elusive."

"It doesn't have to be."

"Oh, yes, it does. My scars are too deep." His jaw tightened. "But I don't have to live with this anger and resentment anymore. I don't hate you, but like I said, your father has put me in the middle of High Five's affairs, and in six months we'll assess the situation and take it from there."

"You don't think I can make this ranch show a profit, do you?"

"The odds are against you. It's been in debt too long."

She bit her lip to keep words locked in her throat.

"Take the money, Caitlyn, and find the man you want. He's not here."

She wanted to smack him, shake him and, to her surprise, hug him. In a moment of clarity she realized the man she wanted was standing in front of her. And as before, he didn't love her. With her heart somewhere in her crappy boots she walked toward Jaz.

"Caitlyn." She turned back. "Your father would have been proud of you today."

Ironically, those weren't the words she wanted to hear. Her heart had been hoping for so much more. The fairy tale loomed just out of her reach.

She swung into the saddle and headed for home. Love was something he wasn't willing to give or didn't know how to give. The years stretched ahead, lonely and empty. High Five had to survive. That's what she was fighting for. But it wasn't enough.

She still wanted it all.

JUDD WATCHED HER ride away and marveled at what a
sincere apology had triggered in him. He'd mellowed.
Some would say like a lovesick pup, but he knew that
wasn't the case. The honest fact was he didn't enjoy
hurting her.

Maybe there was hope for him.

He wasn't good at sharing, and today he'd shared
more with her than he ever had with anyone. It was a
start, and maybe someday he'd understand what that
love she talked about meant.

He seriously doubted it, though. That emotion hadn't
been ingrained in him from birth. And he didn't know
if it was something a man could learn.

For the first time in his life, he wanted to.

He reached for Baron's reins and headed for Southern Cross. Harland and the cowboys would be quitting
for the day. Caitlyn and the bull would be the topic of
conversation. He had a feeling she'd been elevated a
few notches in their eyes.

It would certainly cut back on Harland's antagonism
of her. Judd was sure the man was responsible for a
lot of incidents that happened on High Five, like the
broken fences and the broken windmill. He couldn't
prove it, but the moment he could, Harland would be
gone from Southern Cross. He'd worked many years
for Judd's dad, and out of respect for those years Judd
gave the man the benefit of the doubt.

He dismounted and handed a cowboy his reins.
"Take care of Baron."

"Yes, sir." The cowhand led the horse away.

"I didn't have to shoot that bull, after all," Harland
said, his tone boastful. "I never thought Miss Belle
had it in her."

"You've underestimated Caitlyn Belle."

The gloating left his face. "Your father wouldn't think so. He wouldn't like a woman running High Five."

"My father doesn't run this ranch anymore."

"I know. But he wouldn't kowtow to no woman."

Judd's body became rigid as he tried to control his anger. "I'm telling you for the last time to leave Miss Belle alone. Southern Cross is your business, not High Five. Do I make myself clear?"

"Yes, sir."

"Then get the stables cleaned out and I'll attend to Whiskey Red."

"I can give the horse a workout," Chuck, an eager young cowboy, volunteered.

"No one touches that horse."

"Yes, sir." The young man stepped back.

Judd didn't have to apologize for his actions. He owned this place, but suddenly his blasted conscience was kicking in again, like a buzzing mosquito he wanted to swat. He wasn't sure why it was being exercised more than usual.

His father had never apologized in his life, and never cared one iota what the cowhands thought of him. He'd hired and fired them at will. It was a plan that worked well.

Until now.

There was something about respect that had to be earned. His father had never cared about respect. He had bought that, too. But Judd wanted to be different. And he started now.

Or maybe he had started earlier, with Caitlyn.

"Chuck," he called as the cowboy strolled away, his head bowed. "Feed Whiskey, lead her into the corral and let her walk around. I'll be out later."

"Yes, sir." The boy seemed to bounce in his boots as he hurried to the stables.

"You can't be easy on these hands." Harland spit chewing tobacco into the dirt. "They'll take advantage."

"That's my business."

The foreman saluted and walked into the barn.

Judd made his way to the house. He should check in at the office, but Brenda Sue would be there and he wasn't in the mood. Ron, his office manager, was hard of hearing and tuned Brenda Sue out without much of a problem.

In his study, Judd grabbed the bourbon and a shot glass. Before he could pour it, the door swung open and Brenda Sue breezed in.

Damn, the woman was like lint—hard to get rid of and aggravating in the process.

"Oh, Judd, glad you're back. Ron wants you to look at these grain prices. The supplier raised 'em because gasoline and diesel are so high, and he thinks they're sticking it to you. I know what he means about that. My ex-husband sticks it to me every chance he gets. He's supposed to have the kids two weeks this summer, but now he says he can only do one week. Bullshit, I told him. They're his kids and he needs to spend time with them. I need a break. And my parents are griping that *they* need a break. I feel like a damn pincushion and—"

"Shut up!"

She drew back. "Oh, you're in one of those moods."

He glared at her and yanked the papers from her hand. "I'll get together with Ron on this."

"I don't know why you have to be so rude."

Did the woman not have a clue?

"You sound like my ex," she continued. "He was always yelling at me to shut up."

Judd bet the man had a constant headache. His skull was ringing in just five minutes.

"I don't know why people are so mean to me."

He sat down, and there went his conscience again, knocking on his door. Damn woman. He didn't care about her problems. He didn't want to hear one more word about her or her life. He just wanted her to do her job. Could she really not know how annoying she was?

He picked up a pen and twirled it between his fingers. "I'm going to tell you something and I want you to listen. Don't speak. Do you understand?"

"I'm not an idiot."

"You talk all the time. You never even take a breath. Everything is about you and your life, and it gets annoying. If you don't want people to be rude to you, stop talking so much, and listen."

"I don't do that, but my ex said something similar. He was always rude, though. That was his personality. I talk a lot, I know, but that's me. I just talk and—"

He held up a hand. "Stop."

She stomped a foot. "I can't." Her face fell. "Oh, no. It's true."

"Judd, are you here?" His mother's voice echoed from the hallway.

"Just ask a question and wait for a response. That's all you have to do. Count to ten or something."

Brenda Sue smiled, and that was the last thing Judd wanted to see. He didn't want her getting any ideas about a personal relationship between them.

"You can be quite nice sometimes."

"Just do your job and try not to annoy me with incessant chatter."

"Judd…" His mother paused in the doorway, her eyes going from him to Brenda Sue. "Is there a reason you always seem to be in Judd's study?"

"Yes, ma'am. I work for him." She said the words slowly, as if talking to a child, and then walked out without saying another word.

Hot damn. Maybe Brenda Sue did have an Off switch.

Renee's eyes narrowed. "You're not getting involved with her, are you?"

"No, Mom, I can honestly say without a shadow of a doubt that I am not."

"Good." She took a seat in a leather chair and crossed her legs. "You haven't said two words to me since the ball."

"And you wouldn't want to hear those two words." He poured the bourbon. "How about a drink?"

"No, thank you." Renee looked at him. "You can act as mad as you want, but I know you enjoyed the party, especially your dance with Caitlyn."

He downed the shot. "I'm not in a mood to talk about that horrid ball."

"What do you want to talk about?"

"Nothing."

"Surprise, surprise."

"Don't be cute." He fingered the glass. Since his talk with Caitlyn, a lot of thoughts had been running through his mind. And a lot of them were about his parents. Their relationship. He couldn't believe the question that mingled with the bourbon on his tongue.

"You told me a number of times how you and Dad got back together."

"Yes."

God, he needed more liquor to ask this question. He

poured another shot and downed it. "Did Dad ever tell you that…that he loved you?"

Her eyes opened wide. Clearly, she was shocked. He was feeling a bit of that himself.

She scooted her chair closer, as if she was going to reveal some deep dark secret. "No. Not in all the years I was married to him did he ever say those words."

"Did it bother you?"

"Damn right, it did. It was the main reason I left the first time. That and his affairs. A woman can only take so much."

"Other than the fact that you would get to see me again, what did he say to make you marry him the second time around?"

"Well." She tapped a pink fingernail against her cheek. "I was working in a diner in Abilene at the time. He just walked in and I almost lost the cookies I'd had for a snack that afternoon. He sat in my section so I had to wait on him. It wasn't like, 'Oh, golly gee, this is my lucky day.' It was more like, 'You rotten, sorry bastard.'"

"So you had words?"

"Hell, no. I wanted to see my son, so I plastered a smile on my face and asked what he wanted in my sweetest, softest voice."

"And?"

"He looked me up and down and said I was still the best goddamn looking woman he'd ever seen. Then he glanced out the window at the motel across the street and said how about a quickie for old times' sake."

"Did you slap his face?"

"Son, I don't think you're getting the picture. It had been seven years since I'd seen you, and he could have demeaned me any way he wanted as long as he let me see my son."

"So you had sex with him?"

"Not before we worked out a deal. I knew he'd divorced Blanche, and I was ready to come home. We spent that evening and the night together. The next morning he asked if I wanted to get married. He made it very plain that was the only way I could see you. We flew to Vegas, did the deed and returned to Southern Cross."

It sounded so cold, so unemotional. Just like Judd was. Just like his father had been.

Judd glanced out the window to the miles and miles of Southern Cross. His heritage, his birthright.

He brought his gaze back to his mother. "Did you love him?"

"At times. At others I hated him, but we were good together. We understood each other and he didn't cheat again. I nursed him in his last days when he was dying of pancreatic cancer. I thought it was love until I saw the will."

His father had left her an allowance, and permission to live at Southern Cross until her death. If she remarried, she received nothing.

"If I had known what he had in mind, I would have wrapped that oxygen tubing around his neck and choked the life out of him before the good Lord could take his sorry soul."

Judd could see so clearly that his and Caitlyn's marriage would have been the same. He would have browbeaten her at every turn until she'd bowed to his every wish. *Oh, God.* A chill shuddered through him. He didn't know much about love, but he knew it wasn't like that.

He swallowed hard and met his mother's eyes and said what he had to, what he should have said years ago. "I'm sorry I was mean to you when you came home."

"Oh, Judd, my son." She jumped up and ran around the desk and hugged him. For the first time, he hugged her back.

"Don't be like him. Please don't be like him."

He made a vow to himself that he wouldn't. But he knew it wouldn't be easy.

CHAPTER SIXTEEN

"How could something like that happen?"

They sat in Cait's office going over the day's events. Maddie was appalled at Boss's injury, and Cait tried to explain it as best as she could. "It was just a freak accident."

"Couldn't you have called a vet? Why did you have to shoot him?"

Guilt scraped across her conscience and her stomach clenched. She knew Maddie didn't mean it that way. Her city-raised sister was not accustomed to the hard knocks and plain bad luck of ranch life. How could Cait make her understand?

"There was nothing a vet could have done. The bull was in excruciating pain. His penis had been split open by the barbed wire. I worked at a vet clinic in college and I know even a prize bull would have been put down."

"How did you do it?" Maddie shivered in her chair.

"I was shaking so badly I didn't know if I could hold the rifle steady, but somehow I managed. No way was I going to back down in front of Harland and his boys. But most of all I could see how much pain Boss was in, and it was up to me to end his misery."

"I could never have done it."

"It's amazing what you can do in a crisis." Cait reached down and pulled off a boot. Her feet were beginning to hurt, along with her backside and every other part of her. She placed both boots to the side. "I'm dog tired, and I need a bath to wash away the trauma of this day. And maybe a bottle of wine."

"Remember the last time you drank a lot of wine," Maddie stated with an impish grin.

"Yeah." She closed her eyes briefly as she recalled the heady feeling of kissing Judd. Today she'd wanted to do the same thing. He was understanding, compassionate—just like the man she knew he was under all that male-superiority rhetoric.

"What did y'all do with Boss?"

"When Coop got back from hauling the calves to auction, we took a tractor and buried him beneath a cottonwood on Crooked Creek. We don't usually bury an animal, but Boss's body was probably riddled with infection, and I thought it best. He can see his herd from a very shady spot."

"Ranching is hard work," Maddie remarked.

"Yeah." Cait looked at her sister. "And I'm going to need your help."

"Anything, just so it's not gruesome. I do not do the gun thing."

On the outside, Maddie acted soft and fragile, but she was a Belle and would do what she had to—just as Cait had.

"This doesn't require a gun. Tomorrow Gil Bardwell's crew will start loading sand and gravel from our property. I'll be elsewhere on the ranch and I was hoping you could keep an eye on them."

"Okay."

"We're being paid by the weight. Mr. Bardwell has a scale at his plant, and they weigh the truck empty, and then again after it's loaded. He seems like a nice enough fellow, but somehow expecting him to be one hundred percent honest about what he hauls out seems a little too trusting. If you could take my truck and check on the operation, keep track of the number of loads you see going out, that would help. He would know we're watching and he wouldn't be tempted to cheat us."

"Now that I can handle."

"No bloodshed at all." Cait removed the rubber band from her hair and wiggled her fingers through the French braid, loosening it. "Gran seemed fine at supper."

"I think she's much better."

"She's happy you're here, and maybe we won't see any more of these dressing up…" Her voice trailed away as their grandmother appeared in the doorway, leaning on the jamb.

"'Come up and see me sometime.'" She wore a frilly short skirt and equally revealing top, with fishnet stockings and heels. Her long white hair tumbled down her back.

Oh, crap! Cait didn't need this tonight.

"Mae West, remember?" Dorie asked gleefully.

"Let's go upstairs, Gran." Maddie took her arm.

"What's wrong with you girls? You used to love playing dress-up."

Cait stood with a tired sigh. "We've outgrown it, Gran." And there was the little matter of the big bad wolf at their door, which made play-acting seem immature.

"Now, that's just sad. You're never too old to remember being young."

Cait took her other arm. "Okay, Gran." But Cait felt she might have to dig deep and use dynamite to retrieve that feeling. Tonight she felt tired and completely used up.

As they made their way upstairs, she wondered if this would be the scenario for the rest of her life. Would she be old before her time and never remember the carefree days of her youth?

Suddenly those feelings she'd had as she'd worn the red dress fluttered over her—she was feminine, young and desirable. She'd experienced an exhilaration that was hard to forget.

Especially when she'd seen the look in Judd's eyes.

Maybe she was just tired, but tonight she would store that memory as a keepsake close to her heart.

Heaven only knew when she'd feel that way again.

JULY SNEAKED IN on sultry waves of suffocating heat, and Texas felt like the bowels of hell. Every day God seemed to stoke that fire a little more as the ground dried and cracked and the grasses turned a dusty brown.

But cattle and horses had to have water and feed, so ranchers had to work. Each day seemed to grow longer and hotter as they settled into a routine. Maddie took care of Gran and the selling of the sand and gravel. She was very organized, keeping notes and numbers in a small notebook. Mr. Bardwell wasn't going to slip a load by her.

Cooper had fixed the transmission on Cait's truck, so she didn't have to worry about Maddie careening off into a ditch somewhere.

Maddie was also getting a tan, and had gained weight from Etta's cooking. She looked healthy again, Cait was glad to see.

Cait worked her butt off most days and didn't have

time to think about anything beyond keeping High Five afloat. She'd received a good price for the calves, but if the county didn't get rain soon, calf prices would drop.

She was actually able to pay Cooper, Rufus and Etta a decent salary this month. That was a satisfying feeling. She had to keep working, though.

Since the bull incident, she hadn't seen Judd. As he'd said, her father had now pitted them against each other. Even in death, Dane Belle was controlling her life. And she had to wonder how long she would continue to try to prove him wrong.

As A BOY, Judd had worked on the ranch as a cowboy, but then he went to college and came home with a degree. His father put him to work managing the business, and he missed cowboying. Jack Calhoun had planned his only son's future, and Judd never wavered from that vision.

Southern Cross was a big responsibility, yet he took it on because it was expected of him. But after talking to Caitlyn and his mother, he found life taking a detour. He now firmly believed Renee had a right to a share of Southern Cross. She had earned it in more ways than he had ever imagined. He also knew that Caitlyn had had good reason to end their engagement.

Admitting that had taken a hefty amount of bourbon, sleepless nights and more soul searching than he was used to. Revenge faded into the background, and his goal now was to be able to live with himself, his choices and his decisions.

After much thought, he offered his mother half of the ranch. With tears in her eyes, she declined. That he'd suggested it was all she needed, she told him, and to know her son thought that much of her—as his mother and as a woman.

Making things right with Caitlyn wasn't so easy. Judd couldn't just gift her the royalties. The big expense of buying the rights was already putting a strain on Southern Cross finances. His conscience, his ever-growing nemesis, knocked on his heart daily with a reminder that he needed to talk to Caitlyn. But he kept putting it off.

He threw himself into working on the ranch, much to Harland's chagrin. The foreman told him repeatedly he could handle things, and Judd had to wonder why his presence made the man so antsy.

One day, watching from a hill, he saw Caitlyn ride across the High Five. There was no mistaking her curved body. She was putting everything she had into making that ranch survive. No man could do a better job.

He also saw the dump trucks going in and out daily. She'd found a way to make money, and he admired her determination and ingenuity. He admired *her*.

Soon he had to tell her that.

THERE WAS A HURRICANE gathering force on the Gulf Coast and rain was expected for the area. It was the best news Cait had heard in a while—not the winds, but the rain.

She dismounted at a stock pond and realized that within a month the pond would be dry. They'd have to move the cows to another pasture or pipe water from a nearby well. Or sell. Her stomach tightened at that prospect.

She'd make that decision later in the week. She swung back into the saddle and took a moment to wipe the sweat from her brow. Damn, it was hot! But it was late afternoon, and the force of the heat was ebbing as the giant fireball sank slowly toward the western horizon. She could almost hear a sigh from the landscape.

Suddenly, she heard riders coming. She was close to the Southern Cross fence line, so it had to be cowboys from there. With an uneasy feeling in her gut, she turned Jaz toward the sound.

She guided the horse out of the clearing into the woods, heading toward the fence. The fact that this might not be a good idea crossed her mind. She was a woman alone, and Harland and his cowboys weren't all that friendly. Just like shooting Boss, though, she had to be able to handle every situation that arose.

Beyond the thicket she could see horses and riders. She pulled up and looked closer. They were gazing at something near the fence. And they were too close for her comfort.

What were they doing?

She pulled the rifle from the saddle scabbard, clicked off the safety and rode forward. Stopping about forty feet away, she took in the situation. A dead Southern Cross Brahman lay right at the fence. A newborn calf had somehow maneuvered beneath the barbed wire and was now on High Five land. It lay prone. She wasn't sure if it was dead or alive. Cait rode closer.

Harland and a cowboy she'd never seen before had dismounted and were inspecting the cow.

"Miss Belle." Harland tipped his hat and looked beyond her. "Your boy Yates not with you?"

"What's going on here?" His nasty remark made her edgy, but she kept it out of her voice.

"This is none of your concern, Miss Belle." He

dragged out her name like a prisoner would a ball and chain—slow and hard.

She pointed with the barrel of the rifle. "That calf is on my property."

"Why don't you go paint your nails or something and leave this to me."

The cowboy laughed.

Anger zigzagged through her. Her hand tightened on the rifle and she kept her eyes squarely on Harland. "I'm asking you one more time…what happened here?"

Harland glanced at the cowboy on his right, and she wasn't sure what was going to happen next. She was just grateful the fence was between them.

"One of our pregnant heifers got out of the corral, and this is where we found her—dead. From the signs of struggle on the ground it must have been a difficult birth, and the calf slid under the fence."

Cait's eyes were drawn to the trembling baby. It was alive. She also noticed something else—the calf was black, not white like the Brahman.

As if Harland read her mind, he said, "Must be an offspring from that damn black bull of yours."

"Must be," she murmured.

"Mr. Calhoun is not going to be pleased about this. The heifer is dead and that calf is worthless. We'll knock it in the head and be on our way." Harland nodded to the cowboy.

What? The mere thought of such a senseless, cruel act ricocheted through her, triggering more anger and a double dose of determination. No one was killing the calf.

The cowhand moved forward, grabbed a fence post and was about to swing himself over when Cait pointed the rifle at him. "Cross that fence and you're a dead man."

The cowboy's boots hit the ground with a thud.

"C'mon, Miss Belle, you're not gonna shoot no-body." Harland glared at her.

"And nobody's killing this calf."

"It belongs to Southern Cross."

"It's on High Five and was sired by my bull."

Harland moved toward the fence with an evil glint in his shady eyes. "Listen, little lady, you're interfering in something that doesn't concern you, and if you value your life, you'll turn that horse around and get the hell out of here."

Fear mingled with her anger, but no way would she turn tail and run.

She nudged Jaz closer, her eyes on Harland, the gun pointed at his chest. "Want to try your luck, Harland? Go ahead and try to cross the fence."

His face turned beet red. "You bitch." He glanced at the cowboy standing next to him. "Kill that calf, and I don't care what you do to her."

A wicked grin spread across the cowboy's face as he again reached for the cedar post.

Cait leveled the gun on him. "I'm not too particular where I place this bullet. And if you think I won't shoot, just keep on coming."

Once again the cowboy slid back to the ground, his hand unconsciously going to his crotch. "I'm not getting shot for a no-good calf."

"You bastard!" Harland shouted at him. "Saddle up, we're getting out of here." He grabbed his horse's reins and swung up, his eyes on Caitlyn. "You haven't heard the last of this. Judd Calhoun will want answers."

"He knows where I live."

She relaxed her grip on the rifle as she watched the riders disappear in a cloud of dust. In case they had a plan of circling back, she kept watching. Satisfied, she dismounted to take a closer look.

She squatted and laid the rifle in the leaves as she looked over the animal. It was a bull calf, still covered in mucus from the birth. His coat was matted with it. The mother hadn't had a chance to lick him dry.

The calf made a croaking sound deep in his throat. Cait grabbed a handful of leaves and started to rub his body to clean it. The newborn shivered, but she continued, trying to evoke a fighting spirit in the animal.

"C'mon, little one, lift your head, root around for milk. Aren't you hungry? C'mon."

He didn't move.

She had to get him back to the barn. But how?

Cooper and Rufus were on the other side of the ranch, and if she left to go get them, she feared Harland and his boys would come back.

A buzzard landed on the fence. Then another.

Damn! She threw a stick at them. "Shoo," she yelled. They flew away, but she knew the vultures would be back, with more of their friends.

She stood and surveyed the situation. If she was a man, she could just lift the calf onto Jaz and ride for home. But she didn't have that much upper body strength. Her mind was as sharp as any man's, though, and she could figure this out.

Jaz was the solution.

She whistled and the horse trotted forward. "Okay, girl." She stroked her face. "I need your help." She pulled on the reins to bring her to her knees.

It didn't work. Jaz threw up her head and backed away.

Damn it! Whiskey Red would have knelt in a heartbeat. But Red didn't belong to her anymore.

She took the reins again. "Jaz, I can only get the calf on your back if you kneel down. C'mon, girl, you can do it." With her booted toe, Cait tapped the back of Jaz's knee. "Down, girl, down."

She kept resisting. Cait kept pushing.

Finally, to her surprise, Jaz's front knees buckled and she went to the ground. "Good girl, good girl. Stay. Don't move. Don't move." She had to hurry. Jaz wouldn't stay in that position long.

Wrapping both arms around the calf's body, she tried to stand up, and fell back on her butt. Damn. The newborn weighed more than she had expected. *Okay.* She got back to her feet, determined to save this calf. It would be her redemption for having to shoot Boss.

This time she counted to three, then lifted with her knees and half dragged, half carried the calf to Jaz. Once again she took a deep breath and hoisted with all her strength. The front legs slid across Jaz's withers and Cait pushed until the calf was draped in front of the saddle. She could get him to the barn like this.

Slowly holding the calf secure, she prompted Jaz to rise. Then she slid her rifle into the scabbard and quickly swung into the saddle, gripping him with one hand.

"Let's go home," she said, and they trotted out of the woods, across pastures and through a hay field. Sweat trickled down her face, but she didn't have a free hand to wipe it away. Soon she saw the ranch buildings, and hoped it wasn't too late to save the animal's life.

JUDD DROVE THROUGH High Cotton on his way home. Walker was at the gas station and he waved for him to stop. Judd pulled in.

The constable strolled to the driver's side. "Have you been home?" he asked.

"No. I'm headed there now. Why?"

"I just got a call from Harland. There's been an incident and he wanted to let me know."

"What happened?"

"One of your heifers that was about to calf got out of the corral, and they found her near High Five. The cow was dead and Caitlyn took the calf."

"What? Why would Caitlyn take it, and why in the hell was the heifer out of her pen? We watch them round the clock when they're about to calf. They're too damn expensive to lose. Something's not right."

"I was on my way over there to investigate when I saw your truck."

"Good. I'll meet you there." Judd turned toward the High Five.

Why would Caitlyn take a Southern Cross calf? That didn't make any sense. She wasn't a cattle rustler. He'd been putting off talking to her and now he had no choice.

He just wished it wasn't under these circumstances.

CHAPTER SEVENTEEN

CAIT RODE INTO THE BARN and Maddie followed her. Maddie had taken to checking on Bardwell's crew on horseback. She was beginning to enjoy riding and the everyday work on the ranch.

Cait dismounted and her sister was right there, staring at the newborn animal. "What in the world? Where did that come from? Is it dead? What are—"

"Stop with the twenty questions and help me unload him."

They both grabbed hold and stumbled backward into the hay. But the calf was safely on the ground.

"Where's Cooper?" Cait asked, checking the newborn. He lay still, unmoving, but he was breathing. She had to keep him that way.

"I guess they haven't come in yet," Maddie replied.

"Keep an eye on this little one. I have to fix some milk." Cait headed for the supply room, where the sink and refrigerator were located.

"What do you want me to do?" Maddie shouted after her.

"Get a rag and rub him. Talk to him."

Cait found the powered milk and a bottle. After mixing the powder with water, she poured it into the bottle and attached the nipple. Hurrying back, she knelt in the hay.

"I've rubbed and rubbed, but he's not moving or

responding," Maddie told her, a note of anxiety in her voice. "I think he's almost dead."

"We have to give him a little incentive." She lifted his head into her lap and attempted to pry his jaws apart.

Judd and Walker entered the barn, but Cait didn't look up. She kept trying to get the calf to open his mouth.

"Caitlyn," Walker said.

"Yeah. What is it?"

"Harland said you took a Southern Cross calf."

She glanced up then, her eyes stormy. "Does this look like a Southern Cross calf?"

"Nope, certainly doesn't."

Judd saw the expression on her face—one of love and determination. Caitlyn always fought for what she loved, except when it came to him.

"Here." She handed Maddie the bottle. "When I open his mouth, put the nipple in."

"Okay." Her sister grasped the bottle, but as hard as they tried, the calf would not take the nipple.

Judd stepped around Walker and knelt by Maddie. "They can be stubborn." He took the bottle and glanced into Caitlyn's glaring blue eyes. "May I?"

"I suppose."

"Sometimes they just need to taste the milk or smell it." He squirted milk around the calf's nose. "Open his mouth," he instructed Cait. When it parted a fraction, he slipped the nipple in and squirted some more.

The little animal's head moved and a grunting sound left his throat.

"He's moving," Maddie cried with excitement.

Judd placed his hand over Caitlyn's and together they worked the calf's jaws around the nipple. His throat moved. He swallowed. They kept working until the calf twitched his head, as if to butt an udder, and sucked on his own.

Maddie leaped to her feet. "Oh, this is so exciting. He's going to live."

Once the calf started sucking, he struggled to get to his feet. Cait scrambled away, holding on to the animal with one hand, as did Judd. The baby was unstable, but finally managed to stand. After a couple of minutes he sank back into the hay, but held up his head, looking around.

Maddie made herself comfortable beside him, stroking him and cooing.

Judd saw Walker eyeing her strangely. Without moving his gaze from Maddie, Walker asked Caitlyn, "Is this the calf Harland was talking about?"

"Yes."

"But—"

"What's going on?" Judd asked before Walker could.

Caitlyn relayed a story that had his eyebrow twitching upward. "Harland was going to kill the calf?"

She nodded. "That's what he said."

"How did you stop him?" Walker asked.

Cait's chin lifted. "With my rifle."

The lawman winced.

"I have a right to protect my property, and this calf is half mine. My bull sired it."

"He's also half mine," Judd stated.

Her eyes flared. "You're not taking this calf so Harland can kill it."

"I didn't say that."

"Then what are you saying?"

"That I need to find out what's going on. Where did you find the heifer and the calf?"

"Near the old Dry Gulch Road."

"I thought that road was closed."

"It's supposed to be, but people still use it."

"I'll check it out in the morning. It's too dark now."

Cait rested back on her heels. "What do you want to do about the calf?"

"You're giving me a choice?"

"Maybe." Her eyes twinkled. "If it's the right choice."

"Figured that." He stood. "Keep the calf for now and we'll talk about it later." His eyes caught hers. "Would you mind keeping this under your hat?"

She reached for her hat in the hay and slapped it against her thigh. "Nothing much in here, anyway. It could use a little company." Her smile made him dizzy, weak and feeling luckier than he had in a very long time.

"Thanks." He strolled toward his truck with a long-forgotten smile.

JUDD PARKED BEHIND WALKER at the Southern Cross. Getting out of his truck, he said, "Let's go inside. We need to talk."

Walker followed him into the study, where Judd grabbed the bourbon and two glasses. "How about a drink?"

"No, thanks," he replied. "With two kids, I've had to cut back."

Judd placed the bottle on the desk and eased into his chair. "I know what you mean. I've been drinking a hell of a lot lately."

"When Trisha left me and the kids, I thought liquor could solve all my troubles. But I soon found out that wasn't the answer. My kids needed me, even though at times my daughter seems to hate me."

"How's the situation now?"

"After living in Houston, my daughter despises Hicksville, as she calls it. My son just wants his mama."

Judd knew that feeling and had an urge to reach for the bottle. He didn't. "That's rough," he replied, eyeing the amber liquid. "Have you divorced Trisha?"

"Yep." Walker folded his hands between his knees. "When your wife runs off with another man, it's a safe bet the marriage is over. I mailed the divorce papers to her sister in Lubbock, like Trisha requested. It's officially over. But it's hell trying to explain that to my kids."

"I'm glad you came home to High Cotton."

"Me, too." Walker smiled slightly. "It's good being back with old friends." The smile widened. "In high school we were something. Judd and Walker—the studs."

"That was just hype."

"Yeah." Walker rubbed his hands. "But as teenagers without a clue, we ate it up."

Old memories mingled with the quiet in the room.

"So what do you want me to do about the calf?" Walker asked, and held up a hand. "And just so we're clear—I'm not taking that calf away from Caitlyn. You'll have to do that one yourself."

"Afraid she'll pull a gun on you?"

"Hell, no. It's that sister of hers and the evil eye she keeps giving me. She's treating that calf like a baby, and she looks at me as the enemy."

Judd laughed. "Maddie's an angel."

"Yeah, right."

Judd leaned forward. "Forget about the calf. I'm

more concerned how that heifer got out of the pen and so far away without anyone noticing."

"You think something fishy is going on?"

"You bet I do. See what you can find out about Brahman heifers being sold at any auction barns across the state, even private buyers. Every one of my heifers has a Southern Cross brand, so it shouldn't take long to find out if they've been sold without my permission."

"I'll get on it first thing in the morning." Walker stood. "I might even make some calls tonight."

"Thanks. I appreciate it."

"Any idea who'd have enough nerve to do such a thing?"

"Harland." Judd pushed himself to his feet and stretched his shoulders. "He's resented me since my father's death. He thought I would give him free rein with the ranch, as my dad had. I told him things were going to be different and I wanted to be consulted on everything. He wasn't happy, and I think he's trying to show me I don't run this ranch. I will now be checking the books and every aspect of this operation."

"Watch your back."

"Will do."

Judd sank into his chair, staring at the bourbon bottle. But what he saw were blue forget-me-not eyes. And they were smiling.

THE HOUSE WAS QUIET as Cait sneaked down the stairs. She tiptoed to the kitchen and slipped out the back door.

At the barn, she sat in the hay, watching the baby calf, which Cooper had put in one of the horse stalls. The animal was sleeping, his head curved to the side. He was going to make it. Some good had come out of this day.

She'd been so scared facing Harland. She still wasn't sure what she would have done if the cowboy had crossed the fence. Shooting a person, even if he was as mean as a rattlesnake, was a whole different deal—and came with a whole different realm of emotions.

It ain't women's work.

A hiccup of laughter left her throat. *Nope.* Glancing up, she saw the red high heel on the shelf, highlighted by the single lightbulb hanging from the rafters. She closed her eyes and envisioned herself in Judd's arms, dancing close together.

She swayed slightly to the music in her head, remembering the touch of his hands, his lips.

"Caitlyn."

She opened her eyes and Judd stood there. She blinked and glanced around. Was she dreaming?

"I saw the light and figured you were here checking on the calf."

"Yeah." Scooting up against the wall, she brushed back her long hair. She should have known he wouldn't just forget about the situation.

"How's he doing?"

"I think he's going to live."

Judd removed his Stetson and eased down by her. She wished he hadn't. A tantalizing woodsy scent pulled at her senses. At her heart.

"What are we going to do about the calf?" he asked, placing his hat in the hay and resting his forearms on his knees.

"He was birthed on my property and sired by my bull, so I believe that makes him legally mine."

"The birthing part is up for question. No one saw that, and his mother belongs to Southern Cross. Custody always goes to the mother."

"The cow is dead," she pointed out.

"So what do we do? King Solomon would suggest cutting the calf in half. At that, you'd fold like a green-horn in Vegas, so that pretty much gives me all the rights."

"Are you saying I'm weak?"

They glared at each other. The glares turned to smiles and then laughter. "Whoever takes the calf has a lot of work ahead, what with feeding and care."

"You're right," he said. "You can keep him."

"Thank you very much." She slapped Judd's shoulder playfully. "We could make a toast, but I forgot to bring wine this time."

"There's a better way to mark the agreement." Judd slipped his hand around her neck and drew her forward, his lips lightly touching, caressing, driving her crazy. She opened her mouth and the kiss deepened to a level they both needed.

"Caitie," he murmured, and her body turned to liquid, flowing only for him, as it had so many years ago when he'd called her that.

His fingers unsnapped her blouse and stroked her breast. Being deprived of him for so long, she felt as if she was drowning and he was the only one who could save her, with his touch, his hands.

"Judd," she whispered, and all her troubles, her worries, floated away.

He pressed her down in the hay and her hands feverishly sought his chest, his muscles. Without a second thought, she pulled his shirt from his jeans, needing more of him.

"Cait." He caught her hands and sank back against the wall. "We have to stop."

She felt deprived, lonely and a little angry. Pulling her shirt together, she sat up.

"We need to talk." He expelled a taut breath.

"Okay," she heard herself say, but her body was still craving something it wasn't going to get.

He ran both hands through his tousled hair. "You made the right choice in leaving me fourteen years ago."

If the ground had opened up and swallowed her she wouldn't have been any more surprised. He was apologizing—something she thought he would never, ever do.

"How do you know that?"

He picked up a blade of hay and studied it. "A lot of things. Getting to know you again and talking to my mom. My father drilled some hardcore beliefs into me at an early age, and I never saw life any differently."

She swallowed. "And you do now?"

He fiddled with the straw. "I'm getting there. Slowly. I never thought I'd forgive my mother for leaving me when I was five." He drew a hard breath. "But I have. I'm finally able to listen and understand her side—why she did what she did."

"Judd, that's wonderful."

"All these years, the resentment kept building inside me, weighing me down, and when you left I thought you were just like my mother, and the weight became unbearable."

"Judd…"

He tucked her hair behind her ear, and at the gentle touch, her voice faded away.

"I couldn't understand why the women in my life wanted to get away from me. I naturally thought it was their fault, but sometimes in life you have to stop and look at the whole picture."

"And what did you see?"

His eyes met hers and she saw he was picturing the years, the good and the bad. A spiral of hope coiled around her heart.

"If you had married me, your life would have been just like my mother's. I would have controlled you, ruined your hopes and dreams, and within a year you would have bolted for freedom."

She trailed a finger down his nose. "You think so, huh?"

He reached up and locked his fingers with hers. "I know so. My father was wrong in his treatment of my mother. I was wrong in my treatment of you."

"I never thought I'd hear you say that."

His hand tightened on hers. "I never thought I'd say it, either. I wanted you to pay for having the gall to leave me."

"And now?" Her breath wedged in her throat.

He released her hand. *No. No. No.*

"As I said before, we can't go back and change things. Now we go on with our lives. I have no doubt at the end of six months High Five will be in the black. Dane was wrong. You can run this ranch."

Any other time, those words would have warmed the cockles of her heart. But not today. They weren't the words she wanted to hear.

"What if the ranch is in the red?"

"Then I'll honor the contract I made with your father."

"So nothing has changed?"

He dropped the straw with a sigh. "In that regard, no. Your father didn't want you to spend the rest of your life running this ranch, out every day in the saddle under a scorching sun or in the bitter cold. He wanted you to have a husband and kids. He wanted you to be pampered and have the best things in life."

She clenched her hands. "I've heard that before."

"Don't take this the wrong way, but what's so wrong with that?"

A hundred responses should have popped into her head, but only one made an appearance. "You think a woman's place is in the home and not as an equal partner."

"No. I think Caitlyn Belle can do anything she wants and stand toe to toe with any man. It's up to you to make up your mind what you really want."

Complete silence followed his words. Judd stretched his long legs out in front of him. The calf made a snoring sound and the night closed around them.

"You know what *I* want?" he asked.

"What?" She looked into his dark eyes and felt their magic.

"I'd like to lay you down in the hay and make love to you."

Her breath caught. "I want that, too."

His eyes held hers. "Are you sure?"

Say no. Just say no. Don't put your heart on the line again. Of its own volition, her hand reached up to touch his roughened cheek.

His eyes darkened to pitch-black. "Sweet Caitie, you're so tempting."

Her pulse accelerated at the passion in his gaze and in his voice.

"But it wouldn't solve anything, would it?"

Her pulse took a nosedive. She'd never expected him to be honorable.

"I guess not," she replied.

He swung to his feet before she realized his intent. "Hang on to your dreams, Caitlyn. You deserve a man who can love you completely."

She stared up at him. "What if you're that man?"

He expelled a breath. "I'm not. As I told you, I don't know a thing about the kind of love you need. The kind you deserve."

"We all know about love, Judd. It's something we're born with, but you have to be willing to open your heart to accept it. And to give it. It's really very simple."

"Not for me."

"As I told you before, love starts by caring. I bet you care about that black horse of yours."

"I sure do."

"You'd be hurt if something happened to him."

"I suppose."

"And your mom. You don't make waves because it would hurt her feelings. That's caring. That's loving. That's how it starts and grows. It's putting someone before yourself. It's trust and respect. It's a special connection between two people and it's felt in the heart—deeply. I know you've felt those emotions."

"Not the way you do, Caitie."

Words hung in her throat and she wanted to hit him, hug him, do anything to change his mind. Sadly, she realized he was the only who could change his way of thinking.

Judd glanced at the sleeping calf. "What are you going to name him?"

She thought for a second. "How about Solomon?"

"That works." He reached for his hat in the hay. Fitting it onto his head, he said, "Goodbye, Caitlyn." Then he turned and walked out of the barn.

She scrambled to her feet and watched as he strolled to his truck. Besides her family, High Five had always been the most important thing in her life. But now she wondered if it really was. A strange feeling settled on her. Had her father been right?

Was the man walking away more important to her than High Five?

Did she love Judd Calhoun that much?

CHAPTER EIGHTEEN

"Cait."

Caitlyn jumped and pushed her palm to her chest. She'd been so engrossed in her thoughts she hadn't seen Maddie walk up. "You scared the crap out of me."

"Who's that leaving?" her sister asked, watching the taillights disappear down the road.

"Judd." Cait turned and went back into the barn.

"What did he want?"

She closed the gate of the stall. "He was checking on the calf."

"Is he going to let you keep him?"

"Yes." Cait flipped off the light and the barn was shrouded in darkness. "We named him Solomon."

"We did, huh?" Maddie remarked in a mocking tone as they strolled toward the house. "That's progress."

"Not really," Cait replied.

"Why not? No, don't answer. Wait."

They walked into the kitchen and Maddie hurried to the stove. "I'll make hot chocolate."

Cait frowned. "It's August in Texas."

She shrugged. "So? I just won't make it so hot."

"Whatever."

A few minutes later, Cait sat with a cup of hot chocolate in her hand, wondering if she should go raid the wine cabinet. She might need it to keep thoughts of Judd at bay.

The two sisters drank in silence.

"What did Judd say?" Maddie asked at last, eyeing Cait over the rim of her cup.

She took a long swallow. "He's not set on revenge anymore."

"Oh, Cait, that's wonderful."

"He's still buying High Five if it's not showing a profit, though."

"Oh."

"But he was different tonight."

"How?"

"He was genuinely sincere. He said Dad was wrong and I can run this ranch as good as any man."

"That was nice."

"Mmm." She placed her cup on the table. "But I didn't want him to be nice. I wanted him to throw me in the hay and make passionate love to me. I didn't want to think about profits, ranches or revenge. I just wanted to think about him and me. I wanted love to make a difference."

"But it doesn't to Judd?"

"No. He says he's incapable of the kind of love I want."

"Everyone's capable of love."

"Try telling that to Judd." She carried her cup to the sink. Leaning against the cabinet, she added, "The last couple of months I've been hoping that Judd and I could work out our differences. I never realized until tonight that I wanted the working out part to come with an I love you." She wrapped her arms around her waist. "I now know that's never going to happen. I'm going to be a lonely old spinster yearning for Judd Calhoun." She walked back to the table, gritting her teeth to keep from bursting into tears.

"Sometimes, and I say this from my vast experience—" Maddie rolled her eyes "—men don't know the difference between love and lust. I mean, you're never going to love anyone the way you love Judd, so wouldn't it be better to be with him than without him?"

"This from the eternal believer in love and fairy tales."

"Life sometimes changes our point of view."

"Mmm. But I can't see myself settling for anything less." Cait stood and linked her arm through Maddie's, pulling her to her feet. "Let's go to bed."

Arm in arm they walked toward the stairs. Halfway there Maddie stopped. "Oh, I came out to the barn to tell you that Sky called, but I got sidetracked."

"What did she have to say?"

"She said Todd's parents hired a P.I. and he was snooping around a diner not far from her apartment. So she and Kira are on the move again. She said she'd call when she found a safe place."

"Did you tell her to come home?"

"I did, and she said she'd think about it."

"Why can't she see this is the safest place?"

"Sky has to make her own decisions."

"Hopefully she'll turn up in the next day or two."

Later, Cait tossed and turned. Her thoughts were on Judd. Tonight was the final goodbye. He knew it and so did she. That's why he hadn't made love to her. He didn't want to complicate the issue.

Tomorrow her broken heart would start to mend—once again. Tomorrow she would continue her quest to save High Five. That was all she had now—a lot of empty tomorrows.

A choking sob left her throat and soon the tears followed. She made no move to stop them. They were what she needed at this moment in time.

JUDD SPENT A RESTLESS night, but was in his office early.
All night he'd kept wondering if he'd lost his mind.
Caitlyn wanted to make love and he'd said no. Why
had he done that?

Make love?

He just caught his choice of words. It wasn't love.
It was sex—nothing but honest sex. Then why had he
made the slip? Did he want her love?

"Judd." Brenda Sue walked in with that nonchalant
attitude that irritated the hell out of him. The woman
didn't know what privacy meant. "Oh." She paused for
a brief second when she spotted him. "I didn't know
if you were in here or not, but Harland's been looking for you. He checked at the house and you weren't
there, and he waited last night for you to come home,
and finally gave up. I asked him what was so important but he wouldn't say. He keeps things pretty close
to his chest, if you know what I mean. You know he's
just a tad too serious and grouchy for me, but then most
men are like that and…"

He held up a hand and she actually stopped running
off at the mouth. "Gave up on taking a breath, huh?"

"Well…" She fidgeted in a self-conscious way he'd
never seen before. Brenda Sue never seemed ill at ease.
"Monty says my talking doesn't bother him and I have
to be, well, myself. I feel awkward when I have to think
about what I'm saying. That's just not me, so if people
don't like it, they can stuff it. Oh…" She quickly back-
pedaled. "I don't mean you. Heavens, no. You were actually nice to me and I'll really try not to be annoying
when you're around."

It wasn't working.

"But Monty likes me the way I am. No man has ever

said that to me before and he was really serious. Some-times you can't tell, but—"

"Monty Crabtree who works here?" Judd inter-rupted, to save his sanity. In his forties, Monty was a quiet, hardworking man who was a cowboy to the core. Conversing was not his forte. He preferred peace and quiet. The thought of Monty and Brenda Sue as a cou-ple was almost comical. Or maybe they were made for each other. What did Judd know?

"Yeah. His mother lives down the road from my par-ents. I had a flat in front of her house about two weeks ago and Monty fixed it. He was so nice. Men usually are jerks, but he actually listens to what I'm saying. I asked if I was getting on his nerves and he said the sweetest thing. He said I could never get on his nerves. Isn't that adorable?"

"Yep." Judd was all choked up. "Tell Harland I want to see him—now."

"Oh." She seemed genuinely upset that he didn't want to hear about Monty. And just to make sure she thought he was his normal grouchy self, Judd added, "And don't distract Monty from his work."

She winked, all bubbly and happy. "You got it. I'll go and find Harland. Who knows, I might see Monty. You wouldn't mind that, would you? I mean, I wouldn't be interfering or anything in what he was—"

"Get Harland!" Judd shouted.

She cleared the doorway in a split second.

He leaned back in his chair, not able to get last night out of his head. His love—that's all Caitlyn wanted. Why couldn't he give her that? She'd said it started with caring. He took care of Whiskey Red for her, not let-ting anyone touch the horse but him. What did that say?

It said he was a flawed individual incapable of accepting the greatest gift of all—love. Was that bull? Cait had said everyone was capable of love. For the first time in his life Judd wanted to experience the emotion, to give Caitlyn everything she wanted. But just like fourteen years ago, he was the one standing in the way of their happiness. Could he continue to live like this?

A tap at the door interrupted his thoughts.

"Come in," he called.

Harland stepped in and closed the door. "Good morning, Judd."

"Morning."

The foreman took a seat in front of Judd's desk. "The Belle woman is a problem again."

"Walker contacted me yesterday about Caitlyn and the calf." He leaned forward slightly, watching Harland's face.

"Good." The man nodded. "Something has to be done. The woman pulled a gun on us."

"Walker and I talked to Caitlyn. She said you threatened to kill the calf."

"Come on, Judd. You're not going to believe that, are you?" Harland moved awkwardly in his chair, the only sign he might be nervous.

"I just know one of my prize heifers was found miles from the corral she was supposed to be in. How did that happen?"

"One of the boys must have left the gate open for a second while he was feeding. As soon as I realized she was gone, we tracked her. But we were too late."

Judd rested his forearms on the desk, his eyes holding Harland's. "That's a damn big loss and I'm not happy about this situation."

"I know. I'll have a talk with the boys."

"*I'll* talk to the boys." His words were clipped.

Harland stood. "If that's what you want."

Judd hated his condescending tone. "Gather them at the bunkhouse in ten minutes."

"Okay. Afterward, do you want me to go over and pick up the calf?"

Judd could see Harland was looking forward to the task. "No. Miss Belle is keeping the calf."

"What?"

He lifted an eyebrow. "You have a problem with that?"

"It's your decision." From his voice he might have been saying, "You idiot."

"That's what I thought."

Harland walked out without another word.

Ten minutes later Judd talked to the cowboys and made it clear he wouldn't tolerate sloppy work and the loss of a prize animal. He was angry and he didn't hide it. He wanted to get his point across.

Later he and Ron went over the books, including gas, feed and supplies. Judd was checking every expense of the ranching operation. Every now and then he was distracted, though. *You can love. You just have to allow yourself to.* Caitlyn's words intruded at the oddest times.

Was she right?

THE DROUGHT WAS CAUSING a problem, but another hurricane was forecasted to hit Galveston by the end of the week. The last storm had missed them completely. Cait was hoping for rain.

She put off culling the herd until the bad weather was over. With enough rain, the ranch could survive the hot summer. They spent the day making sure High Five was ready for whatever Mother Nature threw at her.

Later Cait stood in her bedroom and looked out the window toward Southern Cross. She wondered if Judd had talked to Harland, and what kind of excuses he'd gotten for the heifer being so far away from her corral.

No one had come for the calf, but she knew Judd's word was as good as gold. That's the kind of man he was—honest and forthright. She wished he'd allow himself to express all his other good qualities. But wishing was going to give her a big headache.

She wasn't giving up, though, even if she had to use some of Sky's tactics.

Stretching, she realized how tired she was. Dust and sweat coated her skin and there was dirt beneath her fingernails—not sexy, attractive qualities. The responsibility of the ranch was draining her femininity. Was this what her father had meant?

She caught sight of the red dress hanging on the back of her closet door. Grass stains and dirt marred the skirt. She took the garment down and held it to her, dancing around the room. Closing her eyes, she thought of Judd and his strong arms and tempting kisses. All those feminine feelings resurfaced in a flash and she smiled. Oh yeah, she was still alive, and she knew this was what life was all about.

Somehow, some way, she had to convince Judd of that.

CHAPTER NINETEEN

JUDD SPENT THE WEEK investigating the books of Southern Cross. It didn't take him long to find discrepancies. And they all pointed to Harland. After talking to his gas and diesel supplier, Judd found Harland was taking kickbacks from a guy in the office. He always ordered five hundred gallons of fuel, but the company only delivered four. Southern Cross paid for the five and the guy in the office refunded the difference, splitting it with Harland.

Harland was chipping away at the ranch's profits, a fact that angered and frustrated Judd. It was all done under his nose. He had trusted the man like his father had. But Harland didn't have allegiance to anyone but himself and his pocketbook.

Walker had also uncovered damning evidence. Two Southern Cross Brahman heifers had been sold in Oklahoma and one in Louisiana. The buyers still had the receipts, with Harland's signature. The foreman hadn't even tried to cover his tracks.

"Since I don't have a holding facility for prisoners, I contacted the county sheriff. I'll arrest Harland and transport him to the jail. The sheriff is sending a deputy for backup in case there's a problem," Walker said as they sat in Judd's office. "We have enough to put him away for a long time."

"Yeah, but I want to talk to Harland before the deputy gets here." Judd stood and went into the outer office. "Brenda Sue, tell Harland I want to see him."

She looked up from her desk. "What? I don't know where he is. This is a big place and I step in stuff when I go out there. I have new shoes and I don't want to get—"

"I didn't ask for an excuse. I asked for you to find him—now."

"Oh, okay." Brenda Sue got to her feet in a huff. "I can see you're in one of those moods. I don't understand why men are so touchy. You'd think you were the ones with PMS, but oh, no, you get off easy and still most of you act like a bear with a sore head. I'll never understand men and I've given up trying." She was still chattering as she went out the door.

Judd headed back to his office, but swung around again when he heard the door open. Brenda Sue stood there. Damn it! Today wasn't a day to try his patience. He was in a mood to fire everyone on this ranch, including her.

"Now don't lose your temper," she said in a rush. "Monty was outside and I asked him where Harland was and he said in the bunkhouse. There's no way I'm going in there with all those cowboys, so Monty went to get him. Isn't that sweet?"

When Judd didn't respond, she added, "That's okay, isn't it?"

"He better be here in five minutes." With that, he slammed his office door.

"Calm down, Judd," Walker said.

Judd ran his hands over his face. "I'm just so damn angry. I haven't been this angry since…"

"Since Caitlyn left," Walker finished the sentence.

He sank into his chair. "I forgot you were home at the time."

"Yep. Your father and you were certain she'd come crawling back."

Judd grunted. "I was a fool for listening to my dad."

"Jack had old-fashioned ideas about women." Walker made a steeple with his fingers and Judd could feel his eyes on him. "But I sense you see those ideas for what they are. Rubbish and chauvinistic."

"It's hard to change habits of a lifetime."

"But you and Caitlyn seem to be getting along a little better. I mean, I thought you'd take that calf back come hell or high water. Your father would have."

"Yes, he would, and probably have her arrested, too." Judd drew a long breath. "I'm trying very hard not to be like him."

Walker eyed him observantly. "It's more than that, isn't it?"

A tap at the door prevented Judd from answering, and it was just as well. He didn't have an answer.

"Showtime," Walker said, getting to his feet and moving to Judd's right.

"Come in," Judd called.

Harland walked in and glanced from one man to the other. "Didn't expect to see you here, Walker."

"Didn't expect to be here," he replied.

"Have a seat," Judd said.

Harland eased into a chair, his eyes on his boss. "What's this about?"

Judd pushed a manila folder across the desk. "This will explain everything."

With a frown, Harland stood and picked up the folder. Opening it, he read through the contents and then slammed it onto the desk. "So the jig is up?" he said, his Adam's apple bobbing.

Judd leaned forward, his eyes holding Harland's like a fishhook holds a worm. "You've been stealing from Southern Cross for years."

"Can you blame me?" His face turned beet red in anger. "I repeatedly asked your father for a raise and he repeatedly refused. He said he would deed me land when he died. I worked my ass off for that land, but the bastard lied. He didn't leave me a penny. No one does that to me. No one."

"So you started stealing?" Walker asked.

"You bet." The words came out as a growl. "What better way to get even and stick it to the favorite son. I was finally getting the money I deserved. If that Belle woman hadn't interfered, you never would have found out."

"You've been sabotaging High Five, haven't you?" Judd asked.

"That woman needs to be put in her place. Your father would have made sure of that. High Five would have been a part of Southern Cross by now, but you kowtow to the bitch. Your father must be turning over in his grave."

Judd stood, his hands clenched. He wanted to jump across the desk and strangle the man, or reach for the Colt .45 in the bottom drawer and show Harland who was boss. But he did neither of those things. Mainly because he knew it was exactly what his father would have done. Judd was a better man than that.

Walker stepped forward. "Albert Harland, you're under arrest for—"

"You're having me arrested?" Harland glared at Judd.

"You've stolen thousands of dollars. Did you think

I was just going to let that slide?" He unclenched his hands as some of the tension left him. "Since you're so big on my father's attributes, you should know he would have blown your brains out. Be grateful I'm letting the justice system take care of you."

"You bastard," Harland spat. "You'll pay for this. That bitch will, too."

Before he or Walker could gauge his intent, Harland ran from the room, slamming the door in their faces to slow them down. Walker drew the gun from his belt holster and yanked opened the door. Judd was right behind him.

"What's happening?" Brenda Sue asked.

Neither responded as they made a dash for the front door. Monty stood outside like a lovesick fool.

"Where's Harland?" Judd demanded.

"He ran for the stables."

Judd and Walker hurried there, but Harland was nowhere in sight. Then, Chuck walked up from the tack room.

"Have you seen Harland?" Judd asked.

"He just rode out of here like the devil was after him."

"Which way did he go?"

Chuck pointed toward the High Five.

"Damn it!"

"Was he alone?" Walker asked.

"No," Chuck replied. "Those new cowboys, Ernie and Ray, were with him."

"Thanks, Chuck." Judd moved a short distance away to speak to Walker.

"What do you think?" The constable slid his gun back into his holster.

"I think he's gone after Caitlyn." The mere thought

made Judd's stomach tighten. He reached for the cell phone hooked on his belt, and punched out High Five's number.

Etta answered.

"Etta, this is Judd Calhoun. Is Caitlyn there?"

"Heavens, no. She left early to take care of everything before that hurricane blows through here."

He'd almost forgotten about the hurricane. "Do you know where she went?"

"No, but Maddie might."

"May I speak to her?"

"Who?"

Judd drew a patient breath. "Maddie."

"Oh. Okay."

A second later she was on the line. "Maddie, this is Judd. Do you know what part of the ranch Caitlyn is on?"

"Oh, hi, Judd. Cait left early with Cooper and Rufus, and I have no idea where she went. She did mention something about checking a windmill and all water sources."

"Thanks, Maddie."

"Is something wrong?"

"No. I just need to find Cait." He clicked off and shouted to Chuck, "Get my horse and a horse for Walker—pronto."

Walker was on his cell and turned to Judd. "I was talking to the sheriff to apprise him of the situation. I assume we're going after Harland."

"You got it. We have to reach Caitlyn before he does."

CAIT DISMOUNTED at the windmill, relieved to discover everything was working fine. She glanced south and could see dark clouds rolling in. The area was expecting high winds and heavy rain, and from the looks of the sky she knew the storm would be here soon. Time to head back to the ranch to make sure Gran and everyone were safe.

As she turned she saw smoke coming from the west. It seemed to be in the location of her hay fields. Could they be on fire? She swung back toward Jaz and froze. Harland and two cowboys had come up on horseback. One of the cowboys reached for Jaz's reins and pulled her away.

Cait's heart kicked against her ribs. This was trouble. Without her rifle, she had no way to defend herself against three men, except maybe to bluff her way out of whatever Harland had in mind.

"The hurricane is on its way, so we better get out of the weather," she said, playing it cool.

"You're not going anywhere, Miss Belle," Harland replied in an icy tone. "It's payback day for all the times you stuck your nose in my business. You're the reason my lucrative job is gone, and you're going to pay."

Judd had fired him? At the evil glint in Harland's eyes, fear like she'd never known before inched up her spine and she took a step backward. The man was going to kill her.

She knew that as well as she knew her own name.

Harland dismounted, as did one of the cowboys. She quickly weighed her options and realized she had only one—the windmill. Turning swiftly, she sprinted for the ladder and began to climb.

"Get her," Harland shouted.

The cowboy was right behind her. He grabbed her boot, but she held on tight and kicked back with her other foot. Her boot heel connected with his face.

"Bitch," he shouted, clutching his cheek with one hand. Blood oozed through his fingers.

"Get her," Harland shouted again, from below. "Yank her off there."

She didn't pause to see what the guy was doing; she climbed higher. The wind picked up and she felt the tower sway. Her hat blew off and she held on with all her might. But what good was that if the windmill went down? *Oh, God.* She needed help.

There was no one out here, though, and Harland knew that. He was going to make sure she died here.

JUDD GALLOPED at breakneck speed toward the smoke on the High Five ranch. Walker was right behind. They came into the clearing of the hay fields, noting the scorched, charred ground. Cooper and Rufus were fighting the flames with horse blankets, trying to beat them out.

"Call the volunteer fire department," Judd yelled to Walker.

Cooper heard him. "I already did. They're on the way."

At that moment two fire trucks and a number of firefighters roared onto the site. The men immediately went to work, fighting the conflagration and the rising wind. Judd hoped the rain wasn't far behind.

"Where's Caitlyn?" he yelled.

Cooper paused from beating at the blaze. "She went to check the windmill."

Judd swung his horse in that direction, as did Walker. He knew Caitlyn didn't have a lot of time. After galloping into the pasture, they pulled up short. Judd saw Caitlyn climbing the shaky windmill, a cowboy right behind her. Harland and another cowboy stood on the ground, watching.

Judd drew his rifle from the saddle scabbard and Walker drew his gun. They jumped off their horses at the same time.

Walker took care of Harland and the cowboy. Judd pointed his rifle at the man on the windmill. "Come down," he shouted against the wind, "or I'm going to shoot you off of there."

The man stopped climbing.

"Now!" Judd shouted again.

Slowly the cowboy began to descend. Walker had handcuffed Harland and trained his gun on the two men. A deputy drove up just then and Walker started talking to him, but Judd's eyes were on Caitlyn at the top of the swaying windmill. As the wind tugged at it, she bent her head, her hands clamped tight around the ladder.

A number of options ran through Judd's mind, but none of them seemed right. If he climbed up, the tower might fall with his weight. That was a sure death sentence—for both of them.

He laid his rifle on the ground and cupped his hands around his mouth. "Caitlyn, you have to jump. I'll catch you. Trust me."

Cait heard Judd. *He wanted her to jump! To trust him.* Was he insane? The wind was fierce and she didn't know how much longer the windmill could withstand it. She couldn't jump, though. She was frightened out of her mind.

"Come on, Caitie. We don't have a lot of time. Just push back with your boots and I'll catch you. Trust me, Caitie. I won't let you down this time. Let go and push back...."

That caring, coaxing tone did the trick. The windmill rocked and she knew she had to trust Judd as she'd never trusted anyone in her life. She closed her eyes, said a prayer and then pried her clammy fingers from the rung and pushed out with her feet. The air left her lungs as her body plunged through open space. She heard a scream and realized it was her.

She seemed to lose consciousness for a second and the next thing she knew, strong arms had snatched her from the air. Together, she and her savior tumbled backward. But she was safe on the ground—in Judd's arms.

His hands moved over her body. "Are you okay?"

She drew a breath that scorched her lungs, and then another. "Y-yes. I think."

Walker rushed over. "Wow, Caitlyn, I didn't know you could fly."

She made a face at him and staggered to her feet. Judd was there to steady her, and she leaned on him.

"We have Harland and his boys handcuffed and in the deputy's car," Walker said. "I'm going back to get my car and I'll meet you at the sheriff's office."

By then the deputy had joined them. "You need to sign papers," he said, looking toward the sky. "And we better get out of here. Heavy rain is on the way and that windmill is not too steady."

They moved away from the shaky structure. "I'll make sure Caitlyn is okay and then I'll follow you," Judd stated.

The deputy got in his car and drove away. Walker hightailed it on horseback to the Southern Cross.

Judd looked at Caitlyn's pale face. "Are you sure you're okay?"

She tilted her head. "Well, Judd Calhoun, you keep asking me that and I'm going to start thinking you care." As she said the words, raindrops pelted their faces.

"We'd better take cover," Judd said, grabbing Baron's and Jaz's reins. He led them into a gully, away from the windmill and trees. He yanked a slicker from his saddlebag. Spreading the rain gear over their heads, he hunkered down with Caitlyn to wait out the worst of the storm.

"Wouldn't it be better to make a run for the ranch?" she asked.

"It's too dangerous now with the wind, lightning and rain. Hopefully it will be over soon."

Under the plastic covering, they seemed to be encased in their own private world. The rain beat down and the wind tugged at them fiercely. They held tight to the slicker, which the wind kept threatening to blow away.

Suddenly they heard a loud crash. "The windmill," Caitlyn muttered, grateful she wasn't still on it. The slashing rain kept battering them, but she wasn't afraid. She had Judd.

Under the slicker she smelled rain, sweat and sandalwood. And Judd. He filled every corner of her mind.

"I wouldn't have jumped for anyone else," she murmured. "I trusted you."

He turned his head and she stared into the dark depths of his eyes. "That's what love is," she added. "Trusting another person completely." She unsnapped her shirt, took his hand and placed it over her heart. "Can you feel it?"

His eyes darkened. "Caitlyn—"

"Don't say you don't know what love is. All you have to do is follow the instructions you gave me a moment ago. Let go, open up your heart and trust me. *Trust* me."

His hand moved over her breast and his eyes held hers. Slowly he dipped his head and his lips took hers hungrily. Neither held anything back. The world, the storm, faded away as their hands and lips found a way to ease the pain of yesterday.

Distracted, they lost their grip on the slicker and the wind took it. "Oh," she cried as she tried to catch it, to no avail. Judd pulled her back into his arms and she buried her face in the warmth of his neck. The rain showed no mercy, drenching them both, but then suddenly eased off again. Even the wind dropped. The gully was filling up with water, and Judd helped her to her feet.

Cait stared at the crushed windmill and defeat washed over her as hard as the rain had. It was going to cost a lot to get it back up and running.

"We can make it home now," Judd said, brushing rain from her face.

She wanted to stay in this moment, in this time. He hadn't said he loved her, but he hadn't denied it, either. That was enough for now.

But thoughts of the ranch and her responsibilities came rushing back. She reached for Jaz's reins. "I saw smoke earlier. Do you know what that was?"

Judd seemed to take a long time to answer. "Your hay fields were on fire and I'm pretty sure Harland and his boys set it." Then he told her all he'd learned about the foreman.

She swallowed hard. "I think he was going to kill me."

"No doubt. He blamed you that I found out about his illegal activities."

"Is that why you came looking for me?"

"Yes. When he realized he was going to be arrested, he said he'd make you pay."

She swung into the saddle with a squeaky wet sound. She was soaked, as was the saddle and her horse. "I have to get home to check on my family."

"I'll come with you," Judd called, and jumped onto Baron. Together they galloped toward High Five. As they came over a ridge, Cait pulled up. Puffs of smoke could be seen coming from the house.

"Oh, no!" She kneed Jaz and was off again like a rocket. She had to find out if Gran, Maddie and Etta were okay.

Jaz covered the wet ground with amazing speed. As they reached the barnyard, Cait leaped off and made a dash for the smoldering house.

Please let them be okay, she prayed.

"Cait!"

She swung around at the sound of Maddie's voice, and saw her, Coop and Rufus standing under the eave of the barn. Gran wasn't with them. Cait's heart sank to the pit of her stomach.

She ran to Maddie, her breath catching. "Where's Gran?" she cried anxiously. "Tell me where she is!"

Maddie put an arm around her and Cait realized her sister was as wet as she was. "It's okay. Gran is at Etta's lying down. She's fine, but a little shaken up, as we all are."

Cait glanced toward the puffs of smoke still coming from the house. "How bad is it?"

"The parlor and two bedrooms sustained damage."

Cait swallowed the constriction in her throat. "How did this happen?"

"Etta and I were working in the kitchen and we smelled smoke. I went into the parlor and saw the blaze at the windows. It traveled to the second floor before Cooper and I could get it out with water hoses."

"But how did it start?"

Coop stepped forward, his face etched in anger. "I was getting ready to go check the rolls of hay to make sure they were secure, and saw Harland and two cowboys ride away. I heard Maddie scream, and I ran to the house. While she got Miss Dorie and Etta out, I grabbed the hoses to extinguish the fire."

"Thank you, Coop."

"I wish I could have saved more. I smelled gasoline and knew that bastard had torched the place."

"And the hay fields?" Cait asked, but she already knew.

Coop removed his wet hat and studied it for a moment. "As we finished putting out the fire at the house, I saw the smoke coming from the hay fields. I told Maddie to call the fire department, and Ru and I got there as fast as we could. But it was too late. The dry grasses and the wind were against us. I'm sorry, Cait. We lost it all."

She took a deep breath and wanted to burst into tears. All her hard work and it was gone. High Five was done. There was no way she could recover from this.

She collected herself quickly. She wouldn't cry. At that moment she looked up and saw that half the tin roof on the barn had been blown away. The tears weren't far away, but the thought of the baby calf saved her.

"Is Solomon okay?"

"Yes." Maddie squeezed her shoulder. "He's in there bumping his head, wanting milk. I'll feed him in a little bit."

Cooper tensed, and out of her peripheral vision Cait saw Judd walk up.

"I'm sorry, Caitlyn," he said.

She turned to face him, and all that love and warmth she'd felt earlier seemed to disappear. She was spent and empty.

"We won't have to wait for six months," she said in a voice she didn't recognize. "Harland has beaten me and High Five is finished. You were right—I was fighting a losing battle."

He took a step forward. "Cait…"

"Please leave. I'll get with you later about the details. I can't handle any more right now."

"Cait…"

Cooper stepped in front of her. "You heard the lady. It's time for you to go."

The two men, the same height and weight, faced off. "I don't want to fight with you, Cooper."

"Then leave."

Judd glanced at Cait. "Is this your kind of trust?"

She couldn't answer. Her whole body was frozen in abject misery. She dropped her gaze and he walked to his horse and rode away.

And out of her life for good.

CHAPTER TWENTY

CAITLYN TURNED and walked into the barn. Maddie and Cooper were right behind her.

"Please," she said over her shoulder, "I need some time alone."

"Cait…"

She faced her sister. "Please, give me a moment."

Maddie hesitated. "Okay. I'll go check on Gran."

"Tell her I'll be there in a minute."

Maddie nodded.

With methodical movements, Cait went into the supply room, which still had a roof, and mixed milk for Solomon. It was mundane work and she needed that. She carried the bottle to the stall and opened the gate. Solomon trotted to her, eager for food. He bumped his head against her leg and she sank into the straw and held the milk out to him. As he grabbed the nipple, she gripped the bottle tightly because she knew he'd jerk it out of her hand.

He drank the contents in no time and curled up beside her, satisfied. She wished her problems could be solved so easily. Setting the bottle aside, she drew up her knees and wrapped her arms around them. She glanced toward the end of the barn and the gray sky peeping through the gaping holes of the torn-off tin. Destruction was all around her. But life was, too. Solomon was new life, a new beginning.

She stared at that patch of sky and wondered if her father was looking down and saying those words she hated to hear. *I told you so.* Maybe he was right. Ranching wasn't women's work.

The odds had always been against her, but she'd been too stubborn to see that. Now she had to admit defeat and say goodbye to her beloved High Five. Uninvited tears slid from her eyes. She slapped them away, but more followed. She wasn't sure what she was crying about—losing High Five or losing Judd. Again.

There was no way they'd survive this. Their love wasn't meant to be, and she had to accept that and move on. She took some solace in the thought of Judd rebuilding High Five. It would prosper like in the olden days.

But she wouldn't be here.

More tears followed and she didn't try to stop them. She was a woman, and damn it, women cried.

After a moment she drew a shaky breath. Now she had to find the strength to look at the damages to the house. And she had to find the strength to tell Gran. That was her responsibility.

Cait got to her feet and headed for the house, her boots sinking into the sodden ground. As she opened the door, lingering traces of smoke filled her lungs and nausea churned in her stomach. One wall in the parlor was scorched and the velvet drapes were gone. The fire had spread up the wall to the bedrooms, and those walls were burned, too. They would have to be ripped out and replaced. That would take money—dollars she didn't have.

She did have insurance, but it would take weeks before she received funds. Where would they live in the meantime?

Nothing else was insured. She couldn't afford it.

That meant High Five would not be able to recover from the losses.

Giving up wasn't easy, but this was destruction Cait couldn't beat. Stoically, she marched to her bedroom, which miraculously hadn't been touched, and stripped off her wet clothes. Her wet braid was heavy, so she undid it and towel dried her hair. After that she put on clean, dry clothes and went downstairs and out the door to talk to Gran.

The cabin was small, with a combination kitchen, dining room and living area, along with two bedrooms and a bath. When Cait had the strength, she'd talk to Judd about letting Etta and Rufus stay here.

In the living room, she hugged Etta.

"Lordy, Lordy, it's awful. Just awful," the house-keeper moaned.

"How's Gran?"

"She's resting." Etta wiped away a tear. "Maddie's with her." The woman gave Cait a push toward a bedroom. "You better go in there. She's worried about you."

Caitlyn walked into the room. Maddie sat cross-legged on the bed, talking to Gran, who was propped up with fluffy pillows.

"Hi, Gran," Cait said as she sat beside her. She looked so pale with her white hair hanging around her face. Cait felt a catch in her throat.

Dorie reached for her and hugged her tightly. "My baby, I've been so worried."

"I got caught in the storm, so I had to wait it out." Cait drew back and tucked loose strands of black hair behind her ears. "I got a little wet, but I'm fine."

"I'll go help Etta with supper," Maddie said, sliding off the bed.

Gran picked up Cait's cold hand. "Don't look so worried, my baby."

She tried to wipe her feelings from her face, but couldn't—not even for her grandmother. "I'll try," she made herself say.

"How's the house?" Dorie asked.

"It's going to need a lot of repairs." She didn't lie. The time for that was over.

"I figured," Gran said, surprising her.

It must have shown on her face, because Gran added, "I know you girls think I'm a senile old woman living in the past."

"Oh, Gran." Cait squeezed her hand.

"It's okay, because most of the time I am. But I know what's going on, Caitlyn."

Gran never called her that unless she was serious, so Cait listened closely. "What are you talking about?"

The old woman pushed herself up against the pillows. "I know Dane sold Judd our oil and gas royalties."

"What?" She had her full attention now.

"Dane told me what he had to do. It was his only way out of all his gambling debts." Gran sighed. "I spoiled him terribly and I'm afraid he never learned to live within his means. He had too many bad habits that I ignored because I loved him."

Cait was speechless, so she just kept listening.

Gran twisted her hands together. "He assured me that everything would work out and that he had made the right decision for you, Maddie and Sky."

"Selling our means of livelihood was the right decision?" The words came out angry, but Cait couldn't stop them.

Gran patted her hands. "Don't fret, child. I know Judd will be buying High Five now. I've resigned myself to that. Your father wanted you to have a life, and now maybe you can find the one you want."

"My life has always been here."

"I think that was to defy your father." Gran looked into her eyes. "What do you really want, baby?"

Judd had asked her the same thing.

Instead of answering, she burst into tears. Gran held her as if she were six years old. "Don't cry, baby, and don't worry about me. I'm a strong old woman and I've survived worse. You do what you have to."

Cait brushed away tears—once she started crying she couldn't seem to stop. "I'm not sure what that is yet. But High Five has received a death blow. I'm not certain what to do next."

Her grandmother stroked her cheek. "You'll know, baby."

Cait stood and stared at her. "What else do you know, Gran?"

"Everything," she replied with a secret smile.

"Everything?"

"That's one good thing about spoiling my son. He told me everything."

"You mean…" Cait wasn't sure how to finish the sentence without betraying Maddie or Sky.

"Yes, I know, Maddie has had a fight with cancer and won, but now she won't be able to have children. I also know about Kira. Dane gave me a photo that I'm very proud of. I wish I could say the same about my granddaughters keeping secrets. But I promised Dane I would let them tell me. Sometimes that promise was hard to keep."

Her grandmother was stronger than they had ever given her credit for, and Cait resolved never to keep anything from her again.

Maddie walked in. "Would you like to get up, Gran?"

Dorie swung her feet over the side of the bed. "Yes, I would. I'm ready to handle whatever comes next."

"And that means you," Cait whispered to her sister.

Maddie frowned, not understanding.

"She knows—*everything.*" Cait emphasized the last word.

"Oh." Realization dawned in Maddie's blue eyes.

Cait walked out, leaving them to talk. Maybe now they could come together as a family without secrets.

THE NEXT FEW DAYS passed in a blur, but Cait kept busy assessing all the damages to High Five, which were extensive. Cooper was optimistic that they could regroup and overcome. Cait wasn't.

The sheriff called and she went to his office to file more charges against Harland. That gave her some satisfaction.

By the end of the week, Coop and Rufus had a new roof on the barn. She called a man to get an estimate on repairing the windmill. The rest of the time they worked on the house, trying to eradicate the smoke smell and pull off the burned wood. It was a monumental task, but there was something cathartic about toiling until you were so exhausted you fell instantly asleep.

All the time they were working she kept thinking it was useless. They were wasting time and resources. Soon Judd would make an offer for High Five, as he'd promised her father. He'd keep his word, so it was only a matter of time.

But they went on working.

Gran stayed at Etta's, and Cait and Maddie moved into the bunkhouse with Cooper. The arrangement worked well and it kept them on the ranch—for now.

Cait received the estimate for the windmill and the cost of repairing the house. Her eyes bulged at the figures. The insurance adjuster looked at the house and took the estimate, saying he'd be in touch. She had no idea when that would be. She needed the money right away, and told the man that.

Mr. Bardwell had stopped buying sand and gravel because the pits were too wet. He said he'd try again in a month or so, but that would be too late.

She thought of selling the herd, but that was just putting off the inevitable. At the end of the second week she called Judd. Brenda Sue answered.

"Brenda Sue, this is Caitlyn. May I please speak to Judd?"

"He's not here and I don't know where he is. He pretty much does what he wants and, believe me, I don't interfere. You know how men are, but then you may not. You've always been sorta—"

"I'd like to make an appointment to see him." Cait cut her off, trying not to scream.

"I don't make his appointments. He's funny about that, too. You'll have to call back or whatever. I've got to go. I've got things to do and Judd doesn't like me talking on the phone. Did I tell you I have a boyfriend? His name is Monty and…"

Cait gritted her teeth and shut out whatever Brenda Sue was rattling on about. "Tell him I'll be there at ten in the morning to discuss High Five. You can give him a message, right?"

"Of course I can, and that's just like you, Caitlyn. You always have to have your way. That's why you're still single and—"

"Give him the message," she yelled, and slammed the phone down.

Cait went into her office, which was still usable, and took several deep breaths. Then she sat down and made out a list of points she wanted to negotiate with Judd. She would like for Etta, Rufus and Cooper to be allowed to stay on the property. She, Maddie and Gran hadn't made plans yet. They would decide at the end.

At the bottom she scribbled "I love you. Why wasn't that enough?"

Maddie rushed in, her cell in her hand. She shoved it at Cait. "Sky's on the line."

"Hey, sis, where are you?" Cait asked.

"In this hick town in Tennessee."

"I would tell you to come home, but we don't have too much of a home at the moment. We just about got out all the smoke smell, though."

"Maddie told me. I'm sorry, Cait. I know how hard you've worked."

"Thanks. I guess it wasn't meant to be."

"You sound resigned to the whole thing."

She wasn't. She was dying a little inside, but no one would ever know that.

"Gran's okay with it, so that makes it better for me."

"Speaking of Gran, I hear we haven't kept a thing from her."

"Nope, and I suggest you call her as soon as possible."

"I will, and Cait? Whatever you decide is fine with me."

"Really? Wouldn't you rather have the money?"

"Of course, but you're my sister and I love you and want…" Her voice trailed away.

"Is 'bitchy' getting soft?"

"Not on your life, sister dear."

"I didn't think so." Cait laughed, and it felt good

to talk to her sister. "Call Gran," she shouted before clicking off.

"She sounds great, doesn't she?" Maddie asked.

"Yeah. She's a survivor."

"Just like you and me," Maddie stated. "We're going to make it."

"We sure are." Cait stood. "Now let's go make Cooper nervous."

Maddie grinned. "He does get rattled when we walk around in nothing but a towel."

"Mmm. I guess we need to be more respectful of his privacy."

"Maybe." Maddie made a face. "But then we'd have no fun."

They giggled and went out the door arm in arm.

JUDD SAT IN HIS STUDY staring at a glass of bourbon, but all he could see was Caitlyn's face. He couldn't seem to get it out of his head.

Please leave. I'll get with you later about the details. I can't handle any more right now.

Why couldn't she trust him not to hurt her again? But of course, she couldn't recover from the enormous loss, and he had to buy High Five. He'd promised Dane. Judd couldn't go back on his word.

That would destroy all the progress they'd made in the last few months.

Could he hurt her that way?

So many times she'd tried to tell him about love, and each time he'd resisted.

Love starts by caring.

Well, he cared. When she was on that windmill, he knew if she fell and died, life wouldn't be worth liv-

ing, just as it hadn't been for the past fourteen years.
That was a wad of truth to swallow.

Love is a special connection between two people.

They'd certainly had that from day one, even fourteen years ago. He was just too pigheaded to see it or
to admit it.

Let go, open your heart and trust me. Trust *me*.

She'd trusted him on the windmill, and she probably
had always trusted him.

Love is something you feel in the heart.

When she saw her family home in ruins, the pain in
her eyes had cut through his gut. He'd wanted to take
that pain away, but she'd told him to leave.

Trust me.

"Judd," Brenda Sue called a moment before opening the door.

He clenched his jaw at this intrusion.

"Oh, good, you're here," the secretary said. "I didn't
know if you were back or not, and I was leaving for
the day. I was going to write you a message, but now I
can just tell you. Caitlyn called and wanted to make an
appointment to see you. I told her I didn't make your
appointments and she got huffy. You know how Caitlyn is. She said to tell you she'd be here at ten in the
morning to discuss High Five. You know, I heard there
was a lot of damage there and—"

He held up a hand to stop the endless chatter. "Call
her back and tell her I have appointments in Austin tomorrow. I'll meet with her later."

Brenda Sue pointed to his phone. "Why don't *you*
call her?"

He lifted an eyebrow. "And what do I pay you for?"

"Oh, okay, but Caitlyn's going to bite my head off.
I'd just as soon not go another round with her if you

know what I mean. But if it's my job I guess I have no choice."

Judd leaned back in his chair. "Try not to criticize. That might help. Just give her the message and don't elaborate on anything else. It's that simple."

Brenda Sue scrunched up her nose. "I'll try to be short and brief. I better hurry. I promised to meet Monty and I don't want to be late. It's our—"

"Short and brief," he reminded her, and she hurried out the door.

He flipped through his Rolodex for Frank's number. Before talking to Caitlyn, Judd had to know his legal rights concerning High Five.

Could he take everything she loved?

CAITLYN WAS MIFFED when she got the call from Brenda Sue. She tried to question her, but the blasted woman hung up on her. Was Judd avoiding her? They had to talk. There were no ifs, ands or buts about it.

After the fire, she hadn't been too nice to him. She'd been in shock, but now they had to find a way to communicate. And she had to find a way to let go. Of High Five.

And Judd.

In the late afternoon, Chance drove in with the bed of his truck filled with lumber and building supplies. She and Maddie ran out to greet him.

After hugs, Cait asked, "Are you going into construction?"

"Nope." He removed his hat and bowed from the waist. "I am at your service, ma'am, to help rebuild the house."

"But I don't have any money to pay you. I'm waiting on the insurance money."

"Miss Dorie never asked for money all the times I ate at her table, so I'm just repaying High Five's hospitality."

"Chance Hardin, you're an angel."

"I'll get Cooper so he can help you unload this," Maddie said.

Chance grinned. "I'd appreciate it." As Maddie walked away, he turned to Cait. "Could I talk to you for a sec?"

"Sure." He sounded serious and she wondered what this was about.

He removed his hat and slicked back his dark hair in a nervous gesture. "I've been offered a job—a really good job. I could stay in one place and not be on the road so much. Also, I would be around to help Etta and Rufus when they need it."

"So the job is in High Cotton?"

"Yeah." He shifted from one booted foot to the other and she was taken aback by his nervousness. He looked up. "Judd offered me the foreman's job at Southern Cross."

"So?" She couldn't make the connection. After Harland, she knew Judd would be looking for someone. Chance had worked on Southern Cross for a lot of years before taking off for the oil fields. He and Judd had remained good friends.

"Well, I know there's a lot of tension between the two families and—"

She pinched his arm. "Take the job. Etta would love to have you close." Cait didn't go into High Five's shaky future. That wouldn't be resolved until she talked to Judd, and she had no idea when that would be. But it gave her comfort to know that Chance might also be looking after High Five and its future.

For the next couple of days, Chance, Cooper and Rufus worked on repairing the house. She and Maddie helped when they could. But Cait's thoughts remained centered on Judd. Why hadn't he called? Brenda Sue had said he'd be in touch, yet so far she'd heard nothing. That left her in limbo. That left her angry. That left her testing her patience.

But she waited.

CHAPTER TWENTY-ONE

SOLOMON WAS GETTING so big that she and Maddie had a hard time controlling him. One butt could knock them for a loop. They were now giving him small amounts of sweet feed, which added to his weight. The calf was always greedy, wanting more.

"I don't think we're ever going to fill him up!" Maddie said as she closed the gate.

"He's a growing boy." Cait laughed as Solomon butted the slats. She banged her fist against the railing. "Stop." Suddenly, over the calf's bleating and shuffling, they heard the thunder of hooves. The sisters looked at each other in puzzlement. The guys were working on the house, so it couldn't be one of them. Before they could take a step to investigate, Whiskey Red galloped into the barn.

"Oh, my God," Cait cried, running to the horse and throwing her arms around her neck. "She must have gotten away." Stroking Red, she added, "I have to take her back." As she thought about it, she knew this was the perfect opportunity to see Judd. Time to face him and sort out the future. He wasn't avoiding her any longer.

She led Red to her stall and turned to Maddie. "Please feed her. I have to see Judd."

"Okay," her sister replied, a bit mystified.

Cait ran to her truck, shoved it into gear and drove

steadily toward the Southern Cross. She stopped on
the circular drive. Jumping out, she ran for the front
door and tapped the brass knocker. No response. She
opened the door and went inside, straight to Judd's
study. He wasn't there. She went into the hallway and
ran into Renee.

"Oh. I didn't realize we had company." The woman
smiled at her.

She didn't return the smile. "I'm looking for Judd."

Renee shrugged. "He's on the ranch somewhere, seeing to all the damages the hurricane caused."

"Was the loss substantial?"

"Just minor stuff, but Judd seems to need to work
twelve hour days."

"Oh." Cait knew the feeling. She'd worked so hard
to save High Five and it was all for nothing. Her eyes
focused on the Persian rug in the foyer and it reminded
her of the day when Judd had told her about the sale
of the royalties.

"Renee, how much did Judd pay for High Five's royalties?" She'd never asked that question and she suddenly needed to know.

Renee didn't even pause before answering. "Over
half a million."

OhmyGod! Cait had never imagined. All this time
she'd thought Judd had finagled her father into selling, but with a gambling debt that large her dad really had had no choice. The Belle family was lucky
Judd had bought the royalties. It had saved them from
a worse fate.

"Would you please tell Judd…" Her voice trailed off
as he strolled down the hall.

"I think you can tell him yourself, my dear." Renee
patted her son's arm and disappeared out the door.

Judd looked tired, but it didn't diminish his appeal. "You wanted to see me?" he asked, walking into his study.

"Yes." She clenched her hands at his gruff expression. "I wanted to let you know Red is at my place, in case you were looking for her."

"I'm not," he replied, sinking into his chair and shuffling through papers on his desk.

That shook her. What did he mean? "Well, somehow she got loose and—"

"She didn't get loose." He leaned back in his chair, his eyes holding hers. "I let her go."

That made no sense at all. "Why?"

"She's your horse, not mine."

"You bought her."

"Out of spite." He jammed both hands through his dark hair. "You see, Caitlyn, I find it very hard taking things you love."

That almost blew her out of her boots. "Still…" That was all she could say. Warm feelings suffused her whole body and she couldn't think.

"Consider it a wedding gift."

Her eyes narrowed on his. "Excuse me?"

He leaned forward, his expression keeping her from jumping for joy. Tapping a document on his desk, he added, "I talked to Frank about the codicil. He said it was my choice whether to invoke it or not, so I've thought long and hard about this." He took a breath. "I've decided against taking High Five, for the reason I've already told you. But I have a solution for its future. As my wife you will own half of all my holdings, including the gas and oil royalties. Your half will go back into High Five, the other half will go toward the amount I paid for them. High Five will have funds to recoup."

She could hardly believe her ears. "Is this a marriage proposal?"

Without a flicker of emotion, he answered, "Yes."

Joy wasn't the first thing she felt. Anger was. After all their talks, he hadn't changed. The cold proposal was the same as it had been fourteen years ago—without love. She would not sacrifice her pride, her dignity for anything else.

She walked closer to his desk. "The answer is no."

"What?" He was clearly shocked.

"Are you hard of hearing?"

His lips twitched. "No."

She stared directly at him. "You know my bottom line. It's the same as it was the last time you proposed. Without love we have nothing, and until you can open your heart and accept what you're really feeling, there will be no marriage—not even to save High Five."

He looked stunned.

"You once asked me what I really wanted. I want you. I want your love, not a business deal." She swung toward the door. "You have until midnight to make your decision." She walked out as fear edged its way into her heart.

It was all or nothing. What would Judd do?

Judd stared after her in complete misery. But what had he really been expecting? That she would be grateful…? He ran both hands over his face. For days all he could think about was their situation, and he'd thought he'd found a solution. It was easy for him—he wouldn't have to sacrifice his heart and his soul. He'd protected that part of himself for so long, and was still doing it.

He drew a heavy breath. *Open your heart.* Cait

didn't realize how hard that was for him. But if he wanted her... *I want your love, not a business deal.*

This time, could he give her what she asked for?

His mother breezed in. "What did Caitlyn want?"

"My soul."

Renee placed her hands on her hips. "Well, wrap it up with a pretty red bow and give it to her."

"You have a warped sense of humor."

"Son, it's not humor. It's desperation."

He shook his head. "What are you talking about?"

"Why do you think I gave that ridiculous ball?" She didn't give him a chance to respond. "I wanted you and Caitlyn to remember how happy and in love you were at your engagement party. Whether you believe it or not, you were, until she found out the truth."

"Mom..."

"You loved her. That's why you were so hurt. That's why you were so set on revenge. Can't you see that?"

"Mom..."

"You haven't been happy since she left, so whatever you have to do to bring Caitlyn back into your life, swallow your pride and just do it."

Judd wanted to. He really did. But... He eased open the bottom drawer of his desk and glanced at the red shoe. Had he kept it for a reason?

Did he love her? Had he always loved her?

For a smart man, he was dangerously close to being a complete fool.

"Women like to be swept off their feet, don't they?"

Renee blinked. "What?"

"Women like romantic gestures and the Prince Charming thing. They want magic and love, right?"

"Of course. Every woman wants love—that's the most important thing."

"Did you?" He watched her face.

She wrapped her arms around her waist. "I used to dream of Jack saying, 'Renee, you're one hell of a woman and I love you like crazy.'"

"But he never did."

"No. He equated sex with love." She pointed a finger at Judd. "Don't you make that mistake."

He already had. He rose to his feet, knowing he had only one choice. "I have to see Caitlyn."

AT MIDNIGHT, Cait knew he wasn't coming. So much for that. Now she was going to lose it all.

She trudged upstairs to get clothes for tomorrow before going to the bunkhouse. The repairs on the house were coming along nicely. The wall in the parlor was almost complete. Even that didn't cheer her.

Grabbing jeans and a shirt, she saw the red dress hanging on her closet door. On impulse she took it down and stared at it for a long time.

Why wasn't this enough?

Judd's words came back to her. Why couldn't he see they needed so much more? Slowly, she pulled off her clothes, even her boots, and slipped into the red dress. She wiggled her toes. No shoes, but she knew where one was.

She ran down the stairs to the parlor and grabbed a bottle of wine. After uncorking it, she took a sip and headed for the barn. She hoped Maddie wouldn't come looking for her.

Cait went into the barn and took down the red shoe. Clutching it and the wine in one hand, she used the other to open the gate on Red's stall. She rubbed her horse's face and sank down into the hay to say another goodbye. Tomorrow she'd have to return her.

On that thought, she took a swig of wine and slipped on the red high heel. She lifted her foot. "What do you think, Red?" She gulped a breath. "He didn't come and it hurts. I've loved this man for so long and he keeps breaking my heart. How can he do that? Men are…" She glanced up and saw Judd leaning on the gate.

"Men are what?" he asked with a devilish grin.

"Pigs," she said, her heart beating a little faster at the sight of his handsome face. "And you're late."

"I was leaving when there was a problem with one of the heifers calving. I had to wait for the vet, and it was a long painful birth."

Cait was at a loss for words, so she said the first thing that came to her mind. "I'll return Red tomorrow."

"Red is a gift. Please accept her as such."

Her eyes held his. "I can't."

"Caitie, High Five would be in the black if it hadn't been for Harland, my employee. I take full responsibility for his actions. He only did it to get back at me. You've turned the ranch around with hard work and skill." He rubbed his hand along the top of the wooden gate. "Your father should have never come up with this crazy deal."

"Sometimes I wonder why he did that." She propped the wine bottle against the stall wall.

"I have, too, but we'll never know. You deserve High Five and I'm not taking it. Isn't that what you wanted? And Red?"

She gazed up at him, the dim bulb casting enticing shadows across his angular face. She started to reach for the bottle, but realized she didn't need the wine. All she needed was that look in his dark eyes.

"No. I told you what I want."

The words hung between them.

His eyes held hers and a giddiness swept through her from the warmth she saw there. "I've been doing a lot of thinking about this thing called love, and the difference between slam-damn-good sex and love."

"You have?" She held her breath.

"Um-hmm. Trust and respect—they're important to you?"

"Yes." The word slid from her throat.

"When you were on that windmill, you trusted me. You've always trusted me and I've let you down. That day, I knew if you fell and died, my life would be over. And when your family home burned, I saw the pain in your eyes and I felt it in my gut. I wanted you to trust that I would never hurt you again. That's the main reason I can't take High Five. I can't take anything else you love."

Slowly, he opened the gate and stepped in. Red neighed and trotted out to nibble at the fresh bale of hay Cooper had brought in earlier. Judd closed the gate and Cait's giddiness turned to euphoria.

He removed his hat and knelt in front of her. His eyes darkened. "I'm not sure if I'll get this right, but I trust you, Caitie…with my heart."

She bit her lip to keep from crying out with joy, but she hadn't yet heard the words she wanted to hear.

Reaching behind him, he pulled her red high heel from his back pocket and held it out for her to slip on.

This was right. This was perfect, and she couldn't believe Judd was making such a romantic gesture. She tucked her foot into the shoe, but there was something inside and she couldn't completely get it on. No, no. The shoe had to fit. There had to be magic.

"I can't…" She squirmed and lifted the shoe to investigate. Inside she found an engagement ring—her engagement ring. The one Judd had given her fourteen years ago.

The breath left her lungs. "It's... I..."

He took the ring from her with a grin. "Slip on the shoe."

She did, gladly, and it fit perfectly. Now she waited for the magic. Judd's magic.

He lifted her trembling hand and stared into her eyes. "Caitlyn Belle, I— I..."

This time *he* was stammering and she smiled, still waiting.

He swallowed hard. "I'm no prince, but I... I love you. Will you marry me?"

The words came out in a rush, but she heard every one.

She threw herself at him, knocking him backward into the hay. "Yes. Yes. Yes!"

He cupped her face and touched his lips to hers in a stirring, sweet kiss that was powerful and binding.

"I love you, too," she whispered between feather-like kisses. "I've always loved you and I'll never stop loving you."

"Caitie." His mouth covered hers and their tongues and hands renewed a ritual they knew well. She lay half on top of him, feeling and enjoying the hardened contours of his body.

He suddenly sat up and positioned her on his lap. She wrapped her bare legs around him, picking straw from his hair. "I can't believe this," she murmured, and pressed her breasts into his chest, feeling the power of her femininity as he groaned and kissed her neck. Hot, branding kisses trailed to her cleavage.

"I've dreamed of you in this red dress." He moaned. "I've dreamed more of removing it."

She leaned slightly away and unzipped the back. "I have nothing on underneath."

A guttural sound left his throat, and Cait was beginning to think that Sky was right about feminine wiles. She could never be so uninhibited with anyone but Judd, though. As she slipped the dress down, all her inhibitions floated away.

Her breasts filled his hands and then his mouth tasted each nipple, and tingles of desire shot from her breasts to her navel and below. Judd pulled the dress over her head and tossed it on the hay.

She still sat on his lap with her legs wrapped around him, her tousled hair spread across her shoulders. His eyes glowed as he gazed at her nudity. She'd never seen that look before and she recognized exactly what it was. Love. Love shone in his eyes. There it was—the magic she craved. She needed that and had sacrificed so much for this day. It was worth every pain she had gone through. She had definitely won the prize, as Sky so aptly put it. And the prize was Judd's love.

She slowly unbuttoned his shirt. "You have too many clothes on."

"I was thinking the same thing," he said into the warmth of her neck. "And I really need to remove these jeans."

She giggled. "Yes. I'm sitting on a bulge that needs freedom."

"Don't tease." A lazy grin spread across his face as he jerked off his shirt and threw it on top of her dress. She scooted down and helped to remove his boots, then unbuttoned his jeans. He watched as she slid down his zipper and his erection thrust into her hand.

"Oh," she murmured, and before she knew it he was out of his jeans, pushing her down into the hay. The straw scratched her back, but she hardly noticed as Judd's lips found hers. The kiss was deep, hot, and her body simmered just from the touch of his naked skin against hers.

"Caitie," he moaned into her mouth.

"Yes...now...please."

He slid into her easily, as if they'd never been apart. Once again she wrapped her legs around him, drawing him deeper and deeper until fourteen years disappeared along with the heartache. Each move, each thrust bound them closer, until the world exploded into brilliant sunshine.

Her nails dug into his back as her body welcomed the much-needed release. Judd cried her name as he trembled against her, and then there was quiet—an unbelievably peaceful quiet.

Judd couldn't bear to let her go, and they lay together for a long time, just enjoying the incredible moment. They'd made love before, but not like this. Years ago it had been hot and steamy, but as soon as it was over he'd zipped his jeans and was gone. It was just sex. Now it was so much more.

Today he wanted to hold on forever—hold on to Caitie. This was love—his heart was about to pound out of his chest with it. He needed Caitlyn. Until this moment he'd never realized how much. This was living. This was loving. Every man needed this.

He sat up and pulled her into his arms. Leaning against the stall wall, he brushed her dark hair away from her face and she sighed contentedly.

"Happy?"

"Mmm." She tilted her head to look at him.

He cupped her cheek and kissed her softly. "Good. I want you to be happy."

She nestled against him. "You make me happy."

"Then we can solve all our problems. With this much love it should be simple."

She smiled. "What problems?"

"For starters, I'm a difficult man to live with. I don't open up easily. Fear of losing you once again was the only thing that got me here. And of course, I realized I'd loved you forever."

"That's not a problem," she told him.

"Then there's my mother. She lives with me and Southern Cross is her home."

"Not a problem."

"Brenda Sue works for me and I don't want to fire her, because Harvey and his family are going through a rough time."

Cait touched his cheek. "See? You care about all these people. You're just a softie underneath that stern exterior."

"You think so?"

"Who else would put up with Brenda Sue?"

"Then there's hope for me?"

"Yes, yes." She kissed him and they forgot everything for a minute.

He gently tucked her hair behind her ears again. "The wedding has to be what *you* want, without any interference from our families."

"I can handle that."

"I have no doubt. Next is High Five. It stays in the Belle family. That's the way it should be. But you, sweet lady, I want at Southern Cross with me."

"Okay." She ran her fingers through his chest hairs and lower.

He caught her hand. "Okay?"

"Yes. As your wife I should be at Southern Cross, but as part owner of High Five I will be here some, during the day, only until my sisters, Gran and I decide what to do with the ranch."

"Deal." He squeezed her. "The offer still stands about half the royalties being returned to High Five."

"I accept graciously. Thank you."

"I love you." He kissed the tip of her nose. "And we really have to stop meeting in horse stalls."

"Oh, but it's so much fun." A bubble of laughter left her throat.

He stroked her arm. "I'm sorry I botched up that second proposal. I was protecting myself."

She raised her head from his shoulder. "I know, but I love you, so I was willing to give you a third chance to get it right. And, boy, did you get it right!"

They gazed at each other and then burst out laughing as Red looked over the stall gate at them.

A loud bump sounded from the other side.

"That's Solomon. He hears my voice and wants attention."

"He's not the only one…."

She trailed a finger down Judd's nose and he grabbed it, then nibbled at the tip.

"There's only one person getting my attention tonight. And for the record, you are my prince, my prize."

He pulled her onto his lap yet again. "Ah… I like the sound of that."

After a moment, Cait said, "Maybe we should let Red have her stall."

"In a minute," Judd whispered, and leaned his face against hers.

Neither wanted to move or end this moment—this time out of time—when love had made the difference.

EPILOGUE

Two months later...

CAITLYN WAS MARRYING Judd and the whole family was playing dress-up.

She crept downstairs in her long slip to take a look at the flowers and make sure they were arranged the way she wanted.

She clasped her hands as she gazed at all the beautiful white blossoms adorning the parlor. They were perfect. Two candelabras graced the fireplace mantel, along with a huge arrangement of white roses. This was where she wanted to say her vows—in her family home, which had been completely restored. To appease Renee, the reception and dance were being held at Southern Cross.

This wedding was much smaller than the original was to be, just the way she and Judd wanted it. She chose to wear her grandmother's wedding dress, a gorgeous Italian eyelet-lace-and-silk gown that Maddie had altered to fit. Cait never knew her sister had so many domestic talents.

"What are you doing down here?" Maddie took one arm and Sky the other. "You are not supposed to see all this." They whisked her back upstairs.

Cait was so happy Sky had come home for the wedding. Her joy was complete, and watching Gran and

Kira together was an even greater joy. Cait was hoping Sky would stay, especially since Maddie had decided to run High Five, with Cooper's help.

They all had a stake in the ranch, but Cait would now back away and let her sisters make the decisions. She'd never thought anything would become more important than High Five, but Judd had. He was her life now.

An hour later, she came down the stairs in her wedding dress, her nerves humming like taut wires. Maggie was behind her, holding the long train. Sky met her at the bottom and winked. "Ready?"

"Like fourteen years ready."

Sky straightened Cait's veil. "Didn't I tell you what you had to do from the start?"

"I did, and a little more—Belle style." She laughed and Maddie's "Shh" stopped her.

Maddie squeezed past Cait on the stairs. "We have to behave. This is a special day."

"I always behave," Sky said with a straight face.

The music started and their chatter stopped. Maddie and Sky kissed her. "Good luck, big sis," they chorused. Maddie handed Cait her bouquet of roses and baby's breath, and then she and Sky gathered theirs and started down the aisle.

Cait held her breath and said a silent prayer for dreams that come true. And for love.

"Here Comes the Bride" echoed through the old house. Cait turned and walked to the parlor entrance. Her eyes went directly to Judd. He looked so handsome in his tux, and he looked nervous. But happy. She started down the aisle to marry the man of her dreams.

Thirty minutes later, Mr. and Mrs. Judd Calhoun walked out of the house toward the waiting limo. Frank stood nearby, and came up to Caitlyn and handed her an envelope.

"Congratulations, Caitlyn. In case you married Judd, your father wanted me to give you this."

She stared at the envelope and started to tuck it away to read later.

"Open it," Judd whispered, his arm around her waist. With his support, she could face anything.

She stuck a manicured nail under the flap and ripped it open. Inside was a single sheet of paper. On it was written: "Gotcha. Love, Dad."

The sneaky old devil.

He *did* know what was best for her.

* * * * *

MADISON'S CHILDREN

A special thanks to Kim Lenz for going above and beyond in sharing her hometown of Milano, Texas.

And Melinda Siegert for explaining a nervous stomach.

And Susan Robertson for bringing me up to speed on all things little boys.

And to Luke for answering pesky questions.

And Lara Chapman for kindly offering information on Giddings, Texas.

And Naomi Giroux, RN, for graciously sharing her knowledge of ovarian cancer.

Also, The American Cancer Society for their invaluable information.

All errors are strictly mine.

DEDICATION

I dedicate this book to the wonderful editors at Harlequin who have influenced my work and my life. With the sale of my first book in 1999, I had the good fortune to work with Paula Eykelhof, Executive Editor, who guided me through the new-author nervous jitters with patience, kindness and skill. She is, to me, the very best example of an editor.

And Kathleen Scheibling, Senior Editor, Harlequin American Romance. My good luck held when Kathleen was appointed my editor. She follows in Paula's footsteps with her talent, insight and understanding. She's an exceptional editor, and makes my writing life a joy.

Also, Wanda Ottewell, Senior Editor, Harlequin Superromance. I was nervous when I first met Wanda, but her warmth and friendliness put me at ease. A true Harlequin editor.

Thank you, ladies, and happy anniversary!

CHAPTER ONE

SOMETHING ABOUT BEING the good sister made Madison Belle want to be bad.

Very bad.

She laughed at the thought, the sound snatched away by the late November breeze. Hunching low, she kneed her horse, Sadie, on, faster and faster as they flew over hills and valleys, slicing effortlessly through the wind. They cantered into the barn, the chill nipping at her bare nape above her Carhartt jacket. But it felt great. She was alive and enjoying every minute.

As she jerked Sadie's reins to stop, the horse reared her head, prancing, wanting to keep running. Maddie patted her neck. "Whoa, gal, we're home."

Maddie's heart pounded from the exhilarating ride, and she took a moment to catch her breath. The barn was quiet, and the scent of alfalfa, leather and dust tickled her nose. Swinging her right leg over the back of Sadie, she dismounted. Her knees almost buckled and she had to grab the saddle. Darn!

Her sister Cait didn't tell her that staying in the saddle most of the day made your butt numb and exhausted your muscles. She wasn't that much of a city girl, was she?

Begrudgingly, she admitted she was. She'd been raised in Philadelphia by her mother. Summers and holidays she'd spent with her father, Dane Belle, on the

High Five ranch in Texas. Dane had three daughters, all by separate wives.

Caitlyn, the oldest, had always lived on the ranch because her mother had passed away when Cait was born. Skylar, the youngest, was raised by her mother in Kentucky. Every year the sisters looked forward to their summers together.

Madison was the predictable middle child. Her sisters knew what she was going to do before she did it. Easy, compassionate Maddie—the consummate Goody Two-shoes. Even if she wanted to be different, Maddie knew she'd never change.

She undid the saddle cinch, took hold of the saddle and threw it over a sawhorse. The muscles tightened in her arms and she smiled. Oh, yeah. She was getting stronger. When Caitlyn had called her sisters home to face a financial crisis, Maddie had been skin and bones. Now she was healthy again, or she prayed she was.

After the crisis had been settled, she'd planned to return to Philadelphia. But she'd found peace here at High Five and her grandmother needed her.

Caitlyn had married the man of her dreams and moved to the neighboring Southern Cross ranch. They needed someone to run High Five. Maddie didn't know a lot about ranching, but she was happy to stay and take over the reins.

Removing her worn felt hat, she placed it on the saddle horn and tucked stray blond hairs behind her ears. After the chemo, she'd lost all her hair. It was growing back now even thicker than before. It was long enough to pull back into a ponytail, although her hair had a way of working loose by the end of the day.

Three years and she was cancer-free, but to save her

life the surgeon had taken everything that mattered to her—the ability to have a child.

The ache around her heart pulsed for a moment. She allowed herself to feel the pain, and then she let it go. It was an exercise she'd practiced many times.

Rubbing her horse's face, she said, "Ready for some feed, ol' gal?" The horse nuzzled her with a neigh, and Maddie relaxed in the comfort of something warm and real.

Cooper, the foreman, said the horse wasn't worth much, but with her speckled gray coat, black mane and tail, Sadie looked beautiful to Maddie. Soon she learned that with a little coaxing Sadie could fly like the wind. Finding the good in Sadie was something she never let Cooper forget. She firmly believed there was good in everyone—no matter how flawed.

She led Sadie into the corral and removed her bridle. Cooper had put out sweet feed earlier. Sadie trotted to the trough, knowing exactly where it was.

With a sigh, Maddie turned back to the barn, looking forward to soaking in a hot bath. Her muscles screamed for it. So did her aching feet. Her arches were still getting used to living in cowboy boots.

As she secured the bridle on a hook, she heard a noise. It sounded like a sneeze. Looking around, she didn't see anyone. The open-concept barn had a dirt floor; horse stalls were on the left with stacks of hay on the end, saddles and tack on the right with a supply room. A hay loft with more bales was above—a place where she and her sisters had played many times. The big double doors opened on one end to the corral and the other to the ranch.

It must be the old tomcat that lived in the loft, making the barn his home. Then she spotted the feet barely visible under a horse stall door—two sets of sneakers, one trimmed in pink. They certainly didn't belong to ol' Tom.

What…?

Mystified, she walked over and opened the door. There stood two wide-eyed young girls. One was blonde and about ten, and she had a small boy at least three or four cradled on her hip. His face was buried in her neck. The other girl had dark hair and was older, maybe fifteen or sixteen, and she was very pregnant. They all wore jeans and heavy Windbreakers. Maddie was at a loss for words for a full thirty seconds. This certainly wasn't predictable.

She cleared her throat. "What are you doing hiding in the stall?"

"We're not hiding," the younger girl replied in a defensive tone, "we're waiting for someone."

"Who?"

"Brian Harper," the older girl said.

Maddie frowned. "There's no one here by that name."

"He works for Ms. Belle."

"You mean Caitlyn?"

The girl nodded.

"Caitlyn doesn't live here anymore. She married Judd Calhoun and lives on the Southern Cross."

The girl's face fell. "She still owns this ranch, doesn't she?"

"Yes. She's part-owner with our sister, Skylar, and me."

The girl made a sucking lemon type face. "Who are you?"

Maddie didn't feel she had to keep answering questions, but the worry in the girl's eyes swayed her. "I'm

Madison Belle." Her glance swept over the trio. "What are your names?"

"I'm Ginny," the girl responded readily. "And this is Haley and Georgie."

The boy raised his head. "I'm Georgie."

"Shh, Georgie." Haley cradled the boy closer against her. Even with the winter clothes, Maddie could see the girl was very thin, and she didn't seem to have the strength to keep holding the boy.

"I wanna go home," Georgie wailed.

"Shh." Haley stroked his back.

Maddie watched this with a sense of trepidation. Something was very wrong, and she decided to get to the bottom of what the kids were doing here. They surely had parents, and those parents had to be worried.

"Why do you want to see Brian Harper?"

Ginny rested her hands over her swollen stomach in a protective gesture. "He said if I ever needed anything, he'd help me."

"And we need money to buy bus tickets to Lubbock," Haley added. "My mom lives there and we have to see her."

"Mama," Georgie mumbled.

Maddie listened carefully, but none of it made any sense to her. "So basically you're running away. I assume you have family in High Cotton."

"That's none of your business," Haley spat in a defensive tone.

Maddie lifted an eyebrow. "You made it my business by hiding in my barn."

Before the kids could form a reply, the pounding of hooves caught their attention. Cooper Yates and Rufus Johns rode in and dismounted. The cow dogs, Boots, Booger and Bo, followed. Rufus began to unsaddle and feed the horses, seeming oblivious to the kids. But that was Rufus. He spoke very little and minded his own business.

They were the only two cowboys on the ranch and both were ex-cons. Caitlyn trusted them with her life and Maddie now knew why. They were as honest and reliable as the day was long.

Rufus was in his seventies and had worked on High Five all his life. His wife, Etta, was the cook and house-keeper. In his younger days, he'd gotten into a fight in a bar, trying to protect a woman from her abusive boy-friend. Rufus was a big man and one blow from his fist sent the man flying into a table. He hit his head and died instantly. Rufus spent three years in a Huntsville prison for involuntary manslaughter. He came home to Etta and High Five and never again strayed from the straight and narrow.

"Stay here," Maddie said to the kids, and walked over to Cooper. He removed his hat and slapped it against his leg to remove the dust.

Cooper was a cowboy to the core. There wasn't any-thing he didn't know about ranching, cattle and horses. His passion was horses, and he had worked at several thoroughbred horse farms. The one in Weatherford, Texas, had been his downfall.

Several expensive horses had died from the feed being mixed incorrectly with pesticides to kill wee-vils. The owner pointed the finger at Cooper. In anger, Coop had gotten into a fight with the man, who'd filed charges. Coop had been convicted for assault and kill-ing the horses.

He spent six months in prison before the truth came to light. The owner had mixed the feed incorrectly to collect the insurance money. Cooper was released, but people now looked at him differently. He was an ex-con and people didn't trust him, but Caitlyn and Dane Belle had. At Cait's urging, their father had given Coop a job when no one else would.

Maddie nodded at Cooper's bay gelding. "I told you Sadie could beat that bag of bones." She and Coop had become good friends, and each day after work they'd race back to the barn. Coop usually won, but today she'd outsmarted him. She'd gotten a head start.

He slid his hat onto his head in an easy movement. "You cheated, and that old gray mare can't outrun Boots." The dog lay at his feet. At the mention of his name, his ears lifted.

"I beg to differ since I was here first and that old gray mare is in the corral eating sweet feed."

Coop grinned, and he didn't do that often. His past weighed heavily on him and he was a bit of a loner. Over six feet tall, Coop had sandy-blond hair and green eyes. The townspeople said he was bad to the bone, but Maddie knew he had a heart of gold.

Coop eyed their visitors. "What's going on?"

"They're looking for Brian Harper. Do you remember him?"

"Yep. Dane hired him back in the spring, but he left to work in the oil fields."

"Do you know where?"

"No. Cait might." Coop glanced at Ginny. "God, she's pregnant. How old is she?"

"I don't know, but I'm guessing Brian Harper is the father."

"That kid had a head full of dreams of making big money. If she wants him to take responsibility, I can tell you that's not gonna happen."

"He's not the responsible type?"

"Nope. Far from it. He's out for himself and that's it."

Maddie hated to hear that. The girl was too young to have a baby. Something inside Maddie twisted at life and its cruelties.

"You might try calling Walker," Coop said.

"Why?"

"Those are his kids."

"What?" That shocked her. Walker was the constable and the only law in High Cotton, Texas. She'd met him at a party at Southern Cross. He'd made an offhand comment about her looking as young as his daughter. What he'd really meant was that she looked like a child. No woman wants to hear those words from a handsome man. It still rankled.

"Are all of them his kids?"

"No. Just the two small ones."

She thought about that for a second and what Haley had said about her mother. "Where is Walker's wife?"

Coop shrugged. "All I know are rumors."

"Tell me, anyway. I have to figure out what to do with these children."

"They say she left him for another man."

"What about the kids?"

"She left them, too."

What kind of woman would do that? A child was a gift—the most special gift. Anger simmered inside her. How could a woman disrespect that gift and walk away from the love and care her babies needed?

Coop pointed to her face. "You're getting those little lines around your eyes when you're angry."

"I do not get little lines." She stuck her nose in the air and desperately wanted to look in a mirror.

"If you say so." He glanced at the kids huddled together. "Good luck." He ambled out of the barn, lead-ing his horse, the dogs trotting behind him.

She faced the kids, trying to think of a solution. "Let's go to the house for milk and cookies and I'll call Caitlyn."

"We don't want your cookies," Haley said, and Mad-die realized the girl was angry, probably from every-thing that was happening in her young life. And she had to wonder if the mother even knew that Haley was planning a surprise visit.

"I want a cookie." Georgie raised his head.

"Then you shall have a cookie." Maddie held out her arms. "Want to come with me?"

"No, he…"

Haley's words trailed off as Georgie went to Maddie. His weight in her arms caused her throat to close up. He was adorable with caramel-colored eyes and brown hair. She melted from the contact. Turning, she headed for the house. The girls had no choice but to follow.

THEY WALKED INTO A WARM, big kitchen, and Etta swung from the stove, a spoon in her hand. A spry, thin woman, she was in direct contrast to her big hus-band. Her eyes opened wide when she saw the children.

She zeroed in on Ginny. "Lordy, Lordy, Ginny Grubbs, you're pregnant."

"Yes, ma'am." Ginny removed her Windbreaker and slid into a chair at the table, as if to hide her stomach.

Etta had a lot more to say, but Gran entered the room. Dorthea Belle was a delicate, ethereal creature who seemed to float instead of walk. Her hair was completely white and curled into a bun at her nape. She gave the appearance of being fragile, but Maddie knew her grandmother's inner strength.

Maddie kissed her cheek. "Hi, Gran. We have company."

"I see." Gran's eyes swept over the boy in her arms. And Maddie knew she was thinking what Maddie had pushed to the back of her mind. She would never have a child of her own.

To block those thoughts, she removed Georgie's jacket and placed him in a chair. "Etta, we need milk and cookies, please."

"Coming right up."

"I have to call Cait. I'll be right back." She leaned over and whispered to Gran, "Watch them, please."

Gran winked and Maddie hurried to her office. Judd answered on the second ring.

"Hi, Judd. Is Cait there?"

"She's right here." There were muffled voices and whispers. Then silence. Maddie waited. What were they doing? Now, that was a real stupid question.

Finally, her newly married sister came on the line, sounding out of breath. "Hey, Maddie. What's up?"

"Do you two ever stop?"

"No." Cait giggled. Her sister was happy. Maddie wondered if she would ever be that happy.

"Enjoy, sister dear."

"Oh, I am." There was another muffled silence. Then Cait asked, "Is this important?"

"I found three kids in the barn. Cooper says two of them are Walker's kids. The other is Ginny Grubbs and she's pregnant. She's looking for Brian Harper. Do you know where he is?"

"Good heavens, I haven't seen him since the spring. I have no idea where he is." She now had Cait's full attention. "How did they get there?"

"I don't know."

"Call Walker immediately. He must be worried out of his mind about his kids."

"Do you have his number?" While she waited, she tapped her fingers against the desk, thinking. After making the remark at the party, Walker had asked her to dance. She'd refused. Skylar had danced with him instead, saying something silly, like they only let Maddie out of the attic on special occasions. The tapping grew louder. Her childish behavior was now a little embarrassing. The man probably thought she was insane, just as Sky had insinuated. She'd never acted like that before in her life.

Cait rattled off the number and Maddie quickly jotted it down. "Have a fun evening," she said before hanging up. She paused over the phone for a moment and then punched out the number.

"WHAT DO YOU MEAN YOU DON'T know where they are?" Walker stared at his aunt in disbelief. She wasn't the most reliable babysitter, but she was all he had. He and his aunt had inherited the general store in High Cotton, and they lived next door to each other in homes their ancestors had built.

His aunt had never married and was set in her ways. She wasn't fond of children, either. He was going to have to make other arrangements because this was unacceptable.

"Did Haley get off the bus?"

"Of course." Nell Walker rang up a sale and handed Dewey Ray his change. "She took Georgie to the back room to do her homework. When I went to check on them, they were gone. That's why I called you. They're your responsibility—not mine."

The bell jingled over the door and Frank Jessup came into the store. "Hey, Walker."

Walker nodded. He was too worried to say much of anything else.

"Did that part come in I ordered, Nell?"

"It sure did," his aunt replied. "I'll get it."

"See you later, Frank." Walker charged outside before he lost his temper. God, he was doing a lousy job of caring for his kids. Haley hated High Cotton and skipped school regularly. She didn't fit in with the other kids. Instead she hung out with the Grubbs girl, who was so much older. That was unacceptable, too.

Talking to his daughter was a waste of his breath, though. She had so much anger in her that at times he thought she was going to explode from the sheer magnitude of it. And his son cried constantly for his mother. If he ever saw his ex-wife again he might just strangle the life out of her. Leaving him was one thing, but leaving her kids was something entirely different.

He drew a long, tired breath. High Cotton was small, with barely five hundred people. Someone had to have seen them. First, he'd check with Earl Grubbs to see if they were there. Since the kids made fun of Ginny and her pregnancy, Haley had somehow become her champion. Two outcasts facing the world.

As he reached for his cell, it rang. "Yes," he answered.

"Is this Walker?" a very feminine voice asked. A voice he recognized. *Madison Belle.* His nerves tightened.

"Yes, what is it, Ms. Belle?"

There was complete silence.

"Ms. Belle?"

"I just wanted to let you know that your children are here at High Five."

"What!"

"Haley, Georgie and a girl named Ginny."

"How did they get there?"

"I'm guessing they walked. You really need to keep a closer eye on your children."

He gripped the phone so tight it almost came apart in his hand. "I'll be right there. Do not let them leave."

Running for his car, he cursed under his breath. Madison Belle had taken an instant dislike to him, and now he had to face the woman and see his failings as a father in her blue eyes.

He'd rather take a bullet.

CHAPTER TWO

MADDIE HUNG UP THE PHONE and made her way to the kitchen. On the way she thought about Walker. He was an enigma for sure. She didn't even know his first name and she'd never heard anyone mention it, either. He was just Walker to everyone.

She'd met him four times; at the party, at High Five, at the convenience store, and at Cait and Judd's wedding. Funny how she remembered every encounter. He always said hello, but little else, and she couldn't blame him. *Avoid crazy lady,* she could almost hear him thinking.

He seemed very stern, very disciplined—a by-the-book type of man. Cait had said he'd been in the marines and later had joined a search-and-rescue team in Houston. He'd only returned to High Cotton because of his children. Cait hadn't said anything about the mother, but she must be a fine piece of work.

Her sister Skylar thought Walker was a hunk. Maddie rolled that around in her head for a moment. He was tall and impressive, with broad shoulders, caramel-colored eyes like Georgie's, brown hair that curled into his collar, lean, sculptured features, and a body that rivaled Arnold Schwarzenegger's.

Her taste ran more to indoor guys in tailored suits and J. Crew shirts, who didn't wear cowboy boots, Stetsons or risk their lives in the line of duty.

That described Victor, the man she'd been dating in Philadelphia. Tall and thin, Victor never got his hands dirty. As a doctor, he was very meticulous and fastidious in everything he did, even away from the hospital. He was fifteen years older than Madison and at times he made her feel like one of his children, which irritated her. But he was a compassionate, caring man and that's what had attracted her.

Wasn't it?

Victor wasn't a muscled, gun-toting-hero type like Walker. The constable was all muscle and raw power.

He was too…too manly.

She almost laughed out loud at the description. Could a man be too manly?

As she entered the kitchen, Gran was telling the kids about Solomon, their pet bull. Maddie and Cait had raised him from a baby when his mother had died. Solomon was now quite large, and it wasn't uncommon for him to be at the back door waiting for her in the mornings. He wanted feed and he didn't like waiting.

She never knew how he got over the board fence until she saw him jump it one morning. Solomon's father had had the same bad trait, and it had led to his demise. Maddie wanted to break Solomon of the habit. So far she hadn't had any luck.

"Can I see him?" Georgie asked. His upper lip sported a milk mustache and his cheeks were smeared with chocolate from the chocolate chip cookies. He was so cute. How could his mother leave him?

"No, Georgie," Haley told him. "We're going to find Mama."

"Oh." Georgie stuffed more of the cookie into his mouth.

Ginny saw her standing in the doorway. "Did you get Ms. Belle?"

"Yes," she replied, walking farther into the room. "She hasn't seen Brian since he left High Five for the oil fields and she doesn't have an idea where he might be."

"Oh." Ginny hung her head and Maddie's heart broke for her. It was time for a heart-to-heart and she didn't want Georgie to hear them.

"Gran, would you take Georgie to the veranda? Solomon might make an appearance."

"Oh, boy." Georgie bounced up and down in his chair.

Gran took his hand, which was covered in chocolate, and quickly reached for a napkin to wipe his hands and mouth.

After that, Georgie wiggled one arm into his jacket, but seemed unable to get the other one inside the sleeve. Maddie came to his rescue and zipped the Windbreaker.

"Come on, little one," Gran said, leading him to the door. The screen banged behind them.

Maddie took his seat. "Ginny, I'm not trying to pry, but is Brian the father of your baby?"

"Yes, ma'am." She still hung her head.

"And you think he'll take responsibility for the child?"

"Oh, no, ma'am." Ginny raised her head, her voice sincere. "It's not like that. I mean, Brian dropped me after… well, you know. I just want the money to get us to Lubbock and Haley's mom. I'm planning to keep my baby."

The dream of a young girl who hadn't a clue about life. Maddie wondered how she'd manage.

She looked at Haley, who was playing with her glass. "Haley, does your mother know you're planning a visit?"

Her caramel eyes turned dark. "That's none of your business."

"Watch your mouth," Etta said before Maddie could form a response.

Maddie shot Etta a silencing glance and said, "She doesn't, does she."

Haley clamped her lips together and no response was offered. Maddie had her answer.

She stood. "Haley, you're a minor, and I had no choice but to call your father."

"You bitch." The words were fired at her with such venom that it took her aback for a second.

Etta tapped Haley's head with her wooden spoon. "Any more words like that, young lady, and I'll wash your mouth out with soap."

Haley rubbed her head and glared at Etta.

Maddie took a breath and sent another silent message to Etta to cool it. She'd felt the sting of that spoon many times as a kid and knew that Etta meant well, but Haley wasn't in their family and not theirs to discipline.

She focused on the fury in Haley's eyes. "I'm doing what's best for both of you."

"Dad will take Ginny home and her dad hits her all the time. He'll make her lose the baby and the baby is all she has." Haley's words were delivered with all the fervor of a brokenhearted little girl.

Ginny touched her arm. "It's okay, Haley. We don't have any money so we have to go home."

"It's not fair." Haley crossed her arms over her chest.

"Your father will do what's best for you," Maddie tried to reassure her.

"He doesn't even want Georgie or me, and he bums us off on Aunt Nell all the time."

"Haley…"

"You don't know my father. You have money, so just give us some so we can go to Lubbock."

All kinds of questions tumbled like broken glass through her mind. Was Walker taking the pain of a failed marriage out on his children? Haley seemed to hate him. What had Walker done to warrant that? Did he not want custody of his kids? Maddie now had misgivings about calling him, but if anything was amiss, Cait would have said so.

"I want to help you. I really do, but—"

There was a knock at the front door.

"Please don't make us go home," Haley begged, tears glistening in her eyes.

Maddie's heart dropped like a rock, and she felt like the bad guy. But she had no choice. "Stay here while I talk to your father." As she hurried to answer the door, she wondered how she'd gotten caught in the middle of this. Her predictable world just got blown to hell.

Before she could fully open the door, Walker said, "Where are my kids?"

His attitude got to her. He made to pass her, but she held out her arm. "Just a minute. I want to talk to you."

"Ms. Belle, I don't have time for—"

She stepped out on the veranda and closed the door behind her. Shivering, she wished she'd grabbed her jacket. "Make time."

He frowned at her, and she could see the resemblance to Haley. She sat in one of the old rockers on the porch and looked up at him, then wished she hadn't. All that male testosterone was just a little too close. Her breath caught in her throat.

For the first time, she took a really good look at this strong, rigid man. What she saw was a frightened father. Tiny worry lines crinkled around his eyes. His mouth was slashed into a stubborn line. His well-built body seemed restless. He was dressed only in jeans and a shirt—he had no jacket even though the temperature was in the forties. He must be thick-skinned, too.

His eyes told a different story, though. What he could hide with toughness and bravado, his eyes couldn't. He was hurting, but she knew he would never admit it.

He was the type of man who never showed weakness. That was clear from his strong stance. She also knew he was at a loss at how to handle his own children, but he would never harm them. She understood all of that from the desperate look in his eyes.

She wrapped her arms around her waist. "Do you know what your daughter has planned?"

"No." He pushed back his Stetson. "My daughter has an aversion to talking to me."

"Why is that?" She stared directly at him, and the heat from his stare washed over her. Suddenly she wasn't cold any longer. Her body felt hot, sticky, and the rocker creaked as she moved uncomfortably.

"Ms. Belle, I appreciate you taking care of my kids, but this is really none of your business." The words were calm and direct, not angry like she'd expected.

Even though he was intimidating, she didn't fold like a used wallet ready to be tucked away out of sight. She lifted her chin. "Your daughter made it my business by hiding in my barn."

"What?" He was genuinely puzzled. "Why would they do that?"

"They were looking for Brian Harper. Evidently he told Ginny he would give her money if she needed it."

"Why would they need money?" he asked slowly.

She had to tell him the truth, and she didn't pause

in doing so. "For bus tickets to Lubbock to find Haley's mom."

"Shit." He swung away, his body taut as he gazed at the barn and corrals. "Haley doesn't know where her mother is."

"Why does she think Lubbock?"

He swung back to her, his jaw clenched. "Trisha's sister lives there, so I assume Haley thinks her mother is there, too."

"And she's not?"

"Where are my kids?" The questions were clearly over, but Maddie wasn't finished.

She stood and took a step backward. Standing close to his male heat made her breathless, but she had a point to get across and she was determined to do it. "Before I came to live at High Five, I was a counselor in a hospital. I dealt with a lot of children. Usually when a child runs away and doesn't want to go home, there's some sort of abuse in the home." She paused to gather her courage. "Haley doesn't want to go home, so naturally I heard warning bells. But talking to you I know that isn't the problem."

He tensed. "Very big of you."

She ignored the sarcasm. "Ginny doesn't want to go home, either, and in her case I'm inclined to believe she's being abused."

"Her father's a drunk and gets his kicks by beating his wife and kids."

"Can't you do something?"

Walker was all out of patience, and Madison Belle was treading on his very last nerve. But there was something in her blue eyes that stopped him from giving her a full dose of his anger. *She cared*. She had to have been born under the sign of the Good Ship Lollipop, fairy tales and happily ever after. *Good* was probably her middle name, and she believed in it to the hilt. He avoided women like her because they usually had their head in the clouds with reality nowhere in sight.

He'd seen the worst in people, and when push came to shove, the worst always won over the good. But Goody Two-shoes Madison would never believe that.

He dragged his thoughts back to her. From the first moment he'd seen her, at a party at Southern Cross, he'd thought she was the most beautiful woman he'd ever laid eyes on. At the time, he'd said some off-the-wall remark that had irritated her. As he'd looked into her shining eyes that day, his good sense had taken a hike. That was a first for him.

Her sisters, Caitlyn and Skylar, were beautiful, too, but he had no trouble talking to them. Something about Madison tied him up in knots. He didn't like the feeling. He was in control—always. Over the years he had mastered it, but somehow she had broken through all his defenses with just one look. He didn't like that, either. So he avoided Madison Belle.

Now she was in his face, demanding answers and wanting the good to shine through in this situation. He'd dealt with Earl Grubbs before, and the man didn't have an up-close-and-personal relationship with good. How did he explain that to her, though?

"I'll do what I can" was all he could say. But he was going to make sure Earl got the message this time.

"That's it?" She arched an eyebrow that spoke volumes.

Against his will, his eyes swept over her. Her soft curves were emphasized in the tight jeans and western shirt. Her blond hair had come loose from its ponytail and hung enchantingly around an angel face perfect in every way—smooth, gorgeous skin, pouty lips with a sexy curve and an expression of wholesomeness minimized by pure, come-hither blue eyes. Exactly what every man would want in his Christmas stocking.

He put brakes on his thoughts and took a long breath. "Ms. Belle, I appreciate your concern, but now I'm taking my kids home." He opened the door and went inside with her on his heels like a pit bull.

Hearing voices, he headed in that direction. Haley and Ginny sat at the table eating cookies. Etta Johns was watching them.

Haley looked up and saw him. "Daddy," she said in a guilty voice.

"Let's go. Where's Georgie?" He tried to keep his voice calm, but it came out as stern, probably a side effect caused by Ms. Belle.

Haley rose to her feet, her movements nervous. Her eyes were like his, but her hair was blond like her mother's. Her jeans and knit top hung on her thin body. His daughter had a nervous stomach, and he didn't know how to make her eat without getting sick. The divorce had hit Haley hard, and he wanted to make her world happy again. Maybe with a little of Madison Belle's good.

He didn't know how to accomplish that, since his daughter seemed to hate him and blame him for Trisha leaving. His gut twisted a little more each time he looked into her anguished face.

"He's outside with Miss Dorie."

"I'll get him," Madison said. In a minute she was back with Georgie in her arms, Miss Dorie behind her.

Madison was talking softly to him and Georgie was smiling. Walker was mesmerized by the picture of Madison's face close to Georgie's. She seemed so natural with a child in her arms.

"Daddy," Georgie shouted when he spotted him. He wiggled free from Madison and ran to him. Lifting his son into his arms, he held him tight. His daughter might hate him, but Georgie didn't. He was grateful for that small miracle.

"Daddy, I saw a bull," Georgie said, his eyes bright. "A big bull." He stretched out his arms as far as they would go.

"You did?"

Georgie nodded. "I 'cared of him."

"He won't hurt you," Madison assured him.

"Is he talking about Solomon?" he asked Madison.

"Yes." She smiled, and his heart kicked against his ribs with the force of a wild bronco. "He's getting so big."

Walker had been there the day Caitlyn had brought Solomon home. Back then, Cait and Judd were at odds. High Five and the Southern Cross ranches were adjoined, and Cait's bull was always jumping the fence to get to Judd's registered cows. Eventually, one of Judd's cows gave birth and died shortly after. When Cait saw the calf, she realized it was from her bull and took it home. Walker felt sure there would be a fight over the calf, but Judd had allowed Cait to keep it. That's when he knew Judd had finally forgiven Caitlyn.

The last time he saw the calf, Madison was cooing at it as if it were a child. Somehow he knew she'd make a pet of him.

He forced his eyes away from the light in hers. "Let's go," he said, and glanced at Ginny. "I'll take you home, too. I want to talk to your father."

"You can't take her there." Haley scrunched up her face in anger. "He hits her."

"I'll take care of it."

"No, you won't. You just want to get rid of us." Everything in him screamed at his daughter's attitude, but he was powerless to change it. God knows he'd tried.

"Don't talk back," he said, "and thank Ms. Belle for any inconvenience."

"Thank you," Haley mumbled, grabbing her jacket and running toward the front door.

He slowly followed with Georgie and Ginny. Outside they came to an abrupt stop. A young black Brahma bull stood on the stone sidewalk. Haley seemed frozen.

Madison ran around them and grabbed the bull's halter. "Solomon." She stroked his face. "You're scaring our guests." The bull rubbed his face against her and a deep guttural sound left his throat.

The thought crossed Walker's mind that if she stroked him like that, he might make that sound, too.

"It's okay," she called. "He won't hurt you."

Haley and Ginny made a wide circle around him. Walker stepped close to Madison. "You know, a bull is not a pet. He's male—all day, every day, and potentially dangerous."

Her eyes locked with his. "Yes. I know what you mean."

He had a feeling she wasn't talking about the bull.

CHAPTER THREE

WALKER TURNED ONTO THE DIRT road that led to the Grubbs's trailer house. No one spoke. He glanced toward the backseat and saw Georgie was asleep. Haley leaned in close to him, always there, always protective of her baby brother. But her face was a mask of pain.

How was he going to reconcile with his daughter?

"Mr. Walker." Ginny turned to him in the front seat. "You can let me out here. I'll walk the rest of the way. I'll tell my dad I missed the bus."

"Sorry, Ginny. I need to talk to Earl."

"Why, Daddy?" Haley asked in her usual angry tone. "It's only going to cause trouble."

"Mr. Walker..."

"Trust me, girls."

"Yeah, right." He heard Haley mutter under her breath.

He ran a hand over the steering wheel, feeling lower than sludge. Neither girl had any faith in his abilities to defuse a potentially dangerous situation. He'd have to show them. This time Earl was getting the full brunt of his anger.

Pulling into the lane that led to the Grubbs's place, he made to get out and open the aluminum gate covered with chicken wire.

"I'll get it, Mr. Walker," Ginny said, and hopped out.

Earl raised goats, pigs and chickens. They were all

over the cluttered yard. Ginny shooed chickens and goats away so she could open the gate.

He drove through, and Ginny quickly got back in the car. The old trailer was straight ahead. Not a blade of grass grew in the dirt yard. The aluminum siding was rusted in spots, and the screens were missing. A makeshift porch attached to the front looked ready to collapse. In stained overalls and a discolored flannel shirt, Earl lounged in a chair propped against the trailer. He was raising a jug to his lips. Walker knew it was homemade wine. And *good* was nowhere in sight.

Earl could be a decent-enough guy when he was sober, but those occasions were very rare. He had an aversion to getting a job, and he blamed God, the government, neighbors and anyone who came within his vision for his poverty.

Walker glanced at Haley. "Stay in the car with your brother."

"Like I want to get out" was her clipped response.

Walker opened his door and the stench from the pigpen filled his nostrils. It took a moment to catch his breath. How did people live like this? He shooed chickens away and was careful not to step in goat crap.

Two hunting dogs barked and pulled at their chains at the end of the trailer.

"What you done now, gal?" Earl asked when he saw Ginny, his words slurred. He took another swig from the jug. "If you're in trouble again, I'm gonna beat your sorry ass."

Ginny stood next to him, and he could see her trembling. She was frightened to death. Fueled by anger, Walker started up the steps, the decaying boards protesting under his weight.

"My daughter and Ginny missed the bus, so I

brought Ginny home." It was a lie, but it would suffice for now.

"She got legs, she can walk. There ain't nothing wrong with her but stupidity."

"Go inside," Walker said to Ginny.

"You don't tell my daughter what to do," Earl spit out.

Walker nodded to the girl, and she opened the screen door. A thin woman holding a small girl stood there. Four other children of various ages were behind her. He noticed the woman's bruised face before she quickly pulled Ginny inside.

"You better have supper ready on time," Earl shouted at his wife. "And stop mollycoddling those brats."

Walker had had enough. He jerked the jug out of Earl's hand and flung it into the yard. It hit a chicken and she flapped away squawking.

"What…the hell…?"

Walker kicked the chair forward with his foot. Earl spit and sputtered, but being drunk, his reflexes were slow. Taking Earl's face in his hand, he yanked it up so he could look into his bloodshot eyes.

"Listen up, Earl."

"You…y-ou b-bastard."

Walker squeezed tighter and Earl's straggly beard scratched his fingers. "You're not paying attention, Earl. Now, listen. If you lay one hand on Ginny, I'm coming back with both fists loaded, and I'm going to show you what a beating feels like. You got that?"

"Y-ou…y-ou…" Earl sputtered.

Walker squeezed even tighter. "And lay off the wine."

Earl's eyes almost bugged out of his head and Walker

released him. Rubbing his face, Earl said, "You can't tell me what to do on my own p-property."

"I have a badge that says I can," Walker replied. "And you better listen to me. I'm coming back tomorrow and the day after that and the day after that. If Ginny, your wife or any of your kids have bruises, I'm arresting you and throwing your ass in jail. I'll make sure you get convicted, and Earl, those inmates in Huntsville don't care for child abusers. They'll have a good old time with you."

Earl's bugged-out eyes opened wider. "Y-you can't…"

Walker straightened. "This is a warning. Next time I won't be so nice."

"I can't go…go to jail. I got kids to feed."

Walker looked at this man who had reached the very bottom. "Think about it, Earl. All you have to do is stop drinking and take care of your family instead of using them as punching bags."

"You think you're high and mighty—"

Walker pointed a finger at him. "Get your act together. I'll be returning in a couple of hours to make sure you heed my warning." Saying that, he swung off the porch and headed for his car.

And clean air.

THE RIDE HOME WAS AGAIN in silence. Georgie woke up as he pulled into their driveway. The house was a block away from Walker's General Store. He had no interest in running the store, but Nell had. So they worked out a compromise. They split the profits fifty-fifty and she drew a salary.

Walker had also inherited his father's house and land. Nell lived in his grandfather's house, which was next door. When he'd first brought the kids to High Cotton, Nell had helped him, but he could see now it had been a mistake. Her life was the store, and there wasn't room for anything else. He would have to find other babysitting arrangements when he had to go on a call.

He lifted Georgie out of his car seat, and they went inside the white clapboard two-story house with the wraparound porch detailed with black gingerbread trim. The Walkers before him had taken very good care of the house, so it was in good shape. When he'd returned, he'd had central air and heat installed for the kids.

Since he was an only child, he'd often wondered what he was going to do with the house, land and store in High Cotton. He had no desire to live here. He'd been away too long. But life had a way of mocking his plans. At the ripe old age of thirty-six, this was the only place he wanted to raise his kids now.

He set Georgie on his feet in the big kitchen. "It's about suppertime, what—"

Haley made a run for the downstairs bathroom and he could hear her throwing up. Dammit! He didn't know how to help her. She'd started having problems when she was about six. The doctor thought she might have irritable bowel syndrome, but she didn't. More tests were run and the diagnosis was a nervous stomach. She needed a stress-free environment and a healthy diet void of spicy and high-acidity foods. No matter what he and Trisha had tried, nothing completely cured Haley's problem.

The divorce had triggered a major upset, and Walker could see his daughter wasting away before his eyes.

"Haley sick," Georgie said, twisting his hands.

"Yeah." Walker tousled his son's hair. "She'll be okay." She had to be. "Daddy will be right back. Do you want to watch a movie?"

"Uh-huh."

"How about *Shrek?*" he asked, making his way into the living room.

"No. *Finding Nemo,*" Georgie shouted from behind him.

Walker found the movie and slipped it into the DVD player and pushed buttons on the remote. Georgie grabbed his Curious George off the sofa and settled in front of the TV. Walker hurried to the bathroom.

Turning the knob, he saw that the door was unlocked. He tapped so as not to invade her privacy.

A muffled "Go away" came through the door.

"Haley, sweetheart, it's Daddy."

"Go away."

He couldn't do that. "I'm coming in." He opened the door and glanced around. The bathroom was large and had an antique bathtub with claw feet. Everything in the room was antique from the pedestal sink to the pull-chain toilet. Haley was sitting by the toilet, her back to the wall, her forehead on her drawn-up knees.

Ignoring the horrible smell, he sank down by her. Honestly, he didn't know what else to do.

"Are you okay?" He stared at his boots, searching for the right words.

"Just leave me alone," she muttered against her knees.

"I'm your dad and I'm not leaving you alone—ever."

"Oh, yeah." She raised her head and his heart took a jolt at her pale face. "You leave us with Aunt Nell all the time."

"I have a job, and I'm not leaving you alone here at

the house." They'd had this conversation before. It was the only thing Haley had opened up about.

"Why not?" Her watery eyes suddenly cleared. "I'm ten years old and I can take care of Georgie. If something goes wrong, we live in the middle of High Cotton and I could get help in no time."

"So you think you're responsible enough."

"As much as Aunt Nell."

He mulled this over and wanted to meet her halfway. "I'll think about it."

She placed her head on her knees again.

Several seconds went by. "We need to talk about today."

She didn't respond.

"I don't know where your mother is."

Her head shot up, her eyes filled with something he couldn't describe. It was almost like fear. Was his daughter afraid of him?

"You do, too."

"Haley, I don't."

"You're lying."

"I have no reason to lie." He tried not to raise his voice. "You're old enough to know your mother left of her own free will. I have sole custody of you and Georgie."

"You made her leave." The fire was back in her eyes. "You were gone all the time helping other people and you should have been home helping us."

"Your mother and I had problems for a long time, and yes, a lot of it was because of my job. I can't change that now, but I can be here for you and Georgie." He paused and prayed for a break in her implacable armor. "Please give me a chance."

"I want to see Mama," she sobbed against her knees. "I have to see my mama."

He tried to put his arm around her, but she jerked away. Oh, God, his heart stopped beating and he hurt for her. He felt her pain deep inside him—a place that was created the day he became a father.

The mass in his throat clogged his vocal cords. "Your mother..."

She lifted her head, tears streaming down her face. "I know she left us, and you know where she is. You just won't tell me. I...I..." Sobs racked her thin body, and this time he pulled her into his arms and held her, searching for those magical words that would help them both. But they were elusive, and he hated that he was so bad at being a parent.

"Please, Haley. Give me a chance." His words were hoarse, and he had to swallow a couple of times to get them out.

Before she could say anything, Georgie came running in and wiggled into his lap. "Oh, it stinks in here." He looked up at Walker. "I'm hungry." The odor didn't seem to bother his appetite.

"Suppertime," Walker said, and tried to act normal. "Haley, would you like chicken noodle soup and a grilled cheese sandwich? You usually can hold that down."

"I guess." She straightened and moved as far away from him as she could. That hurt a little more.

"I want peanut butter and jelly." Georgie gave his menu choice. "Grape jelly. I don't like any other kind." Walker had made the mistake of using strawberry one time and Georgie had never forgotten it.

"I know, son." Walker stood with the boy in his arms. "And we can have ice cream afterward."

"Yay!" Georgie clapped his hands. Haley was silent. She was silent all through dinner. She was silent as they washed the dishes. Instead of watching TV, she took a bath and went to bed.

Soon he tucked Georgie in, but Walker couldn't sleep. His mind was in overdrive. His children's well-being was at the front of his mind—always. All he could do was be here for them and maybe Haley wouldn't try to run away again.

Not only was he worried about his kids, but Ginny was on his mind, too. If anything happened to her, he would never forgive himself, not to mention that he'd have no hope of his daughter ever forgiving him.

An hour later, he still wasn't asleep. He got up, dressed and went into Georgie's room and gathered him into his arms. He carried him to Haley and tucked him in beside her.

"Daddy," she mumbled sleepily.

"I'm going to check on the Grubbs family. Take care of Georgie." He handed her the portable phone. "Call my cell if there's a problem." She wanted responsibility, so he was going to give it to her—for a while.

"Oh." Her voice sounded excited.

In less than thirty minutes he was back. Earl was passed out on the sofa. Verna, his wife, said everything was fine. Ginny seconded that and Walker felt a lot better.

He fell into bed exhausted, but the worry over his kids was always there. What was he going to do? He needed help.

Blue eyes edged their way into his subconscious. His eyes popped open. *Madison Belle.* It was hard to explain his reaction to her. When he was a senior in high school, he and his dad had gone on a fishing trip to the Gulf Coast. They'd rented a cabin on a secluded cove outside Rockport, Texas. The cabin was shaded with gnarled, bent oaks, tempered and tried by the Gulf winds. The water in the cove held him mesmerized. It was the purest blue he'd ever seen, as if it had been untouched by nature and its wrath. He thought he'd never see that color again.

Until he looked into Madison's eyes.

She had that same purity. That same quality of not being tainted by the ups and downs of life. It had to be an illusion. No woman could be as pure or as good as Madison appeared.

For a cynical man like himself, he knew it was an illusion. His motto was to avoid the woman in case she could look into his soul and see all his sins.

MADISON SLEPT VERY LITTLE. She couldn't stop thinking and worrying about Walker's kids. And Ginny. She was so young to be pregnant. Her family situation seemed dire, and she wondered how the girl would cope?

A baby.

Maddie would give everything she had for a child. It seemed so unfair, but she'd come to grips with her situation long ago. Every time she thought about it, though, she felt that empty place inside her that would never be filled.

She had a ready-made family waiting for her in Philadelphia. All she had to do was accept Victor's marriage proposal. Victor's wife had died five years ago, leaving an eleven- and a fourteen-year-old who needed a mother in their lives. But Victor was a friend, a very dear friend. She didn't have passionate feelings for him. Hadn't even gone to bed with him. She'd told him how she felt, and he'd said those emotions would come later. She didn't believe that.

Soon she'd have to go home and face Victor and her future. But for now her life was here on High Five. Maybe she was in denial. Maybe she was hiding. Or maybe she believed in miracles and love.

She went to sleep with that thought.

The next morning she dressed in jeans, a pearl-snap shirt and boots, her customary garb. Oh, yes, she was a cowgirl now and she was getting damn good at it.

She hurried to Gran's room as she did every morning. Gran was up and winding her white hair into its usual knot at her nape.

"Good morning, my baby." Gran smiled at her.

Maddie sat on the stool beside her in front of the mirror. Gran called her three granddaughters "baby." At thirty-one, Maddie was past being a baby, but it was useless to mention that to Gran.

"Caitlyn's coming to pick me up. I'm going to Southern Cross for a visit," Gran told her, patting her hair.

Maddie lifted an eyebrow. "So the honeymooners are having company?"

Gran slipped on her comfortable shoes. "I'm not company. I'm the grandmother. Besides, we were all at Southern Cross for Thanksgiving."

"Everyone but Sky." Maddie worried about her baby sister and wished Sky would just come home.

"Sky has a mind of her own."

"Mmm." Maddie linked her arm through the older woman's. "Let's go down for breakfast."

"Yes, my baby. It's the first day of December and we have to start thinking about the upcoming holiday."

Maddie would rather not. But soon she'd have to tell

her mother that once again she wouldn't be in Philly for Christmas.

The scent of homemade biscuits met them in the hallway. "Oh, my, isn't that wonderful?"

"Makes my mouth water," Gran replied.

Etta pulled a pan of biscuits out of the oven as they entered the kitchen. "Good morning, lazy bugs."

Maddie glanced at the clock. It was barely seven, but she saw the dirty plates on the table. Cooper and Rufus had already eaten and gone.

Grabbing a biscuit, she juggled it to the table. It was hot, hot, hot. She opened it on a napkin and dribbled honey over it. Picking it up, she headed for the door. She had to catch up with Cooper and Rufus.

She took a bite of the biscuit and stopped in the doorway. First, she had something else to do.

"I need to make a phone call," she said to Gran and Etta.

On the way to her study, she finished off the biscuit. Damn, she'd forgotten her coffee. Where was her brain? In Worryville.

She licked her fingers and punched out the number Cait had given her yesterday. Walker's number. He answered on the first ring.

"This is Madison Belle," she said quickly.

"Ms. Belle." His deep, strong voice came through loud and clear. "Is there a problem?"

She curled her sticky fingers around the receiver. "No. I was just wondering how the kids are?"

"Mine are fine. Haley's getting ready for school and Georgie's eating breakfast. Anything else?"

Yes. Lose the attitude.

"And Ginny?" she asked without even pausing.

The silence on the other end was loaded with four-letter words, and they weren't nice.

She waited, licking her fingers.

After a moment he replied, "Ginny is fine, too. I had a talk with her father about what was going to happen to him if he hits her again. I checked on her last night and the family was fine."

"That was so sweet of you."

"I'm not sweet, Ms. Belle," he shot back in a voice tighter than a rusted padlock.

"But your gesture was," she reminded him just because it annoyed him so much.

"Anything else, Ms. Belle?" The way he said *Ms. Belle* was beginning to irritate the crap out of her.

"You might try working some of that 'sweet' into your attitude." The words were out before she could stop them. Not that she tried very hard.

"And you might try minding your own business."

"Ginny needs someone to help her, and I'm beginning to think that Haley might, too." After saying that, she slammed down the phone.

She reached up to see if steam was gushing out of her ears. She was so angry. How could he be so…so ungrateful? And stern. And rigid. And infuriating.

Blood pumped through her veins with renewed fervor. She hadn't felt this angry in a very long time. She took a long breath and blew it out her mouth. Mr. Attitude hadn't heard the last of her.

CHAPTER FOUR

MADDIE HURRIED TO THE BARN to catch up with Coop and Ru. A little exercise was what she needed to untangle all the anger inside her. After all, Walker was the children's father and she was sticking her nose into his business. But she cared. Children were her weakness. In this situation, though, she needed to tread carefully. Or not. Annoying Walker might become the highlight of her day.

In the doorway to the barn, she stopped short. Cooper was shoving bullets into a rifle, and Rufus held another one in his hand. Her heart skipped a beat.

"What's going on?"

Coop turned to her. "Ru got a call from Mr. Peevy. Wild dogs killed two of his baby calves last night. We have to be prepared."

"Prepared?"

Coop handed her the rifle, and she just stared at it. "Put it in the scabbard of your saddle."

She shook her head. "Oh, no. I don't do the gun thing, and since you're on probation, you shouldn't, either."

His face darkened. "I promised Cait to help you run High Five, and I'm not going to let a pack of feral dogs slaughter our calf crop."

She could see the anger in his eyes, which was very rare. Ever since he had the fight with the man who had framed him, Coop kept his anger on a tight leash. Although Coop was cleared of all wrongdoing in the killing of the horses, he was on probation for the assault. The man refused to drop the charges. Maddie understood Coop's anger. Anyone would have lashed out at being used as a scapegoat in an insurance scam, but she didn't want him to get into any more trouble.

Gently, she touched his arm. "I know High Five means a lot to you, but you have to be careful."

He took a deep breath. "I'll be very careful. Out here no one knows."

"Let's keep it that way."

"Okay." He raised the gun in front of her again. "Learn to use it. You have to be able to protect your animals."

Against every objection in her head, she took it. The gun felt heavy and deadly in her hands. Her first instinct was to throw it on the ground and say *no way.* But High Five was still struggling and they couldn't afford to lose a calf crop. The last hurricane had ripped through the ranch and had caused tremendous damages. They were still rebuilding. She had to step up and do her job, like she'd told Cait she could.

But a gun?

This is where the city girl and the country girl collided. Who was Madison Belle?

"There are six bullets in the magazine," Coop was saying. "It's already loaded." He pointed to a spot on the gun. "There's the safety. Always keep it on. If you have to shoot, push it to off and line up your prey with this guide on top. Then pull the trigger." He tapped a forefinger against the guide.

"I'm not sure I can do that," she admitted.

"Would you like to practice?"

"No, thanks." Firing the gun wasn't on this city/country girl's agenda. "Hopefully I won't ever have to use it."

"Mr. Peevy's place is about five miles away. The dogs could travel in another direction, but like I said we have to be prepared."

She placed the gun by her saddle, not able to hold it one minute longer. "How do they become feral dogs?"

"People haul dogs they don't want out to the country and leave them. The dogs begin to scrounge for food. They meet up with coyotes or wolves and mate. Suddenly there's a pack of them, all hungry and killing everything they can to survive."

"How awful."

"Yeah, animal activists have tried to change things to no avail. Sometimes you just can't stop people. Animal shelters are full and now charge if you bring in a dog. People who don't want a dog are not going to pay. It's a vicious cycle and ranchers pay the price."

"Miss Dorie used to take in every stray dog that showed up at High Five," Rufus said, shoving his gun into his saddle scabbard, "but since Mr. Bart died she lost interest in a lot of things. If one shows up, I take it to the shelter so they can find it a home."

"Good for you, Ru," Maddie replied.

"And Booger's a stray we kept. He's part Australian blue heeler and learned to work cattle. He's a natural. Wish we could keep 'em all, but we can't."

"If everyone did that, there wouldn't be a problem."

"But we have a problem now," Coop said. "Ru and I were talking, and we think it might be best to round up all the cows fixing to calf and keep them in the pen next to the corral. Except the hurricane took down the fence, so we have to repair it first."

"Go for supplies and we'll get busy." That was an easy decision to make.

Coop hesitated.

"What?"

"Cait always went for supplies. Ms. Nell doesn't want me in her store."

"Well, that's insane." Maddie couldn't believe Cait tolerated such behavior. "Make a list and I'll pick up everything." And she'd have a talk with Ms. Nell, too. Since she was sticking her nose in other people's business, she might make it a trend.

THIRTY MINUTES LATER she walked through the double worn doors of Walker's General Store. A bell jingled over her head, and it reminded her of the summers she'd spent at High Five as a kid. This was a favorite spot of the Belle sisters—candywise the store had everything.

She breathed in the scent of apples, spices and cedar, a hint of the upcoming holidays. The store was the same as it had been when she was a child: faded hardwood floors, a rustic wood ceiling from which sundries hung, and shelves of gallon jars filled with every candy a child could want.

The aisles were cluttered with everything imaginable, from buckets and fishing poles to barrels of apples, pears and oranges. Homemade quilts hung on a wall. A couple of Christmas trees were propped in a corner. A feed and hardware department was at the back. Every now and then the scent of oats wafted through the tantalizing aroma of the holidays.

Maddie walked over to the counter where Nell Walker stood waiting on a customer. Cigarettes took pride of place in the glass case beneath. A gallon jar of jawbreakers sat on the counter among chewing tobacco, gum and tempting candy bars. She always went for the jawbreakers—they were her favorite. She resisted the urge to stick her hand in the jar.

Instead, she studied Ms. Walker. She had aged since Maddie had last seen her. Her gray hair was cut short like a man's and the lines of her stern face were set into a permanent frown. A tall, big-boned woman, Nell Walker exuded a persona of toughness and rigidity, the same as her nephew.

The customer left and Nell swung her gaze to Maddie. "May I help you, Ms. Belle?"

She noticed that Nell's eyes were a cold gray like a winter's day. As she pulled the list from her pocket, she thought that Nell looked very unhappy.

"I'd like to pick up some supplies." She placed the list in front of Nell.

Nell looked it over and then shouted, "Luther."

A man in his sixties ambled from the back.

"Is your truck out front?" Nell asked Maddie while glancing at the list and scribbling it into a record book.

"Yes."

"Give Luther your keys and he'll load your supplies."

"Oh, okay." She'd never done this before so she wasn't sure how it worked. Digging in her purse, she found her keys and handed them over.

As Luther took the list and walked out the door, Nell said, "I'll put everything on your bill. Anything else I can help you with?"

Maddie swung her purse strap over her shoulder. "Yes, there is."

Nell raised frosty eyes to Maddie's, and for a moment, a tiny moment, her resolve weakened. She stepped closer to the counter. "A lot of days I'm busy and don't have time to come in for supplies, so I'll be sending Cooper Yates, my foreman, in for them. I hope that's not a problem."

"I don't want him in my store." The words were delivered like an errant baseball smacking someone against the head. Unexpected and painful.

Nervously, her hand tightened on her purse strap, but no way would she bend. Coop deserved better than this kind of treatment. "Fine. If that's the way you feel, I'll just take High Five's business into Giddings, and I'm sure Caitlyn will agree to do the same for Southern Cross."

A telltale shade of pink crawled up the woman's face. Losing two ranches' business would hurt the store. Evidently hitting her in the pocketbook was talking her language.

"I don't want ex-cons in here. It's bad for business, but—"

"Is there a problem?" Walker strolled from the back, Georgie on his heels. Georgie smiled and she smiled back for a second.

Then she glanced at Walker, tall and imposing in a white shirt, snug jeans and boots. His Stetson was pulled low and hid his eyes, but just the sight of him made her heart go pitter-patter.

She took a breath. "Yes, there is. Ms. Walker refuses to allow Cooper to pick up supplies." She stood her ground when she wanted to take a step backward. The man was just so…so intimidating, frustrating and… handsome. There, she'd admitted it. He was too handsome for her peace of mind. And that sincere note in his voice was sidetracking her.

"Is this true?" Walker asked his aunt.

"We can't have ex-cons in here. Business will drop."

"Caitlyn and I will certainly take our business elsewhere if the status quo doesn't change."

"It will change, won't it, Nell?"

Nell puffed out her chest. "I was just about to tell Ms. Belle that."

Walker swung his gaze to her. "Good, then there's not a problem."

Her insides did a crazy flip-flop. What was wrong with her? Earlier she was annoyed at his attitude, but now she was acting like a ridiculous teenager. Before she could gather her wits, Georgie stuck his hand into the jar for a jawbreaker. Nell quickly slapped his hand with a resounding swat. Georgie let out a wail.

Walker gathered the boy into his arms, his eyes turning as cold as Nell's. "You will not hit my child."

"He eats too many sweets and he'll choke on those things."

Maddie walked over to a jar on the shelf and used the scoop to fill a bag with jelly beans. "Put this on my bill," she said to Nell, and handed them to Georgie. She waited for Walker to say he could pay for his own kid's candy, but he didn't say a word, just looked at her. "It's okay, isn't it?" she asked, to hide her nervousness under that gaze.

"Yes."

"See?" she said to Georgie. "These are smaller and chewy. They're good."

Georgie wiped away a tear and poked his hand into the bag. He popped two into his mouth and nodded with a grin.

The door jingled and Luther came in and handed Maddie her keys. "All loaded and ready to go."

"Thank you." She looked at Nell. "I trust we won't have any more problems."

"No, ma'am."

"Bye," she said to Walker and Georgie, and headed for her truck.

Walker watched her leave with a funny feeling in his gut. God, he was falling for her caring attitude. *No.* It was just a natural reaction to her kindness to Georgie. He had enough problems without even thinking of Ms. Belle and her pure, pure blue eyes.

He had parked out back. His office was next door so it was always easy to leave Georgie with Nell. After resigning from his search-and-rescue unit in Houston, he hadn't planned on going back to work. But Mr. Pratt, the constable, had passed away, and the commissioner's court, by way of Judd, begged him to take the job.

There were two years left on Mr. Pratt's term and Walker thought he could handle that. Then he would decide if he wanted to run for the office or not. He was already a state-licensed law enforcement officer so he'd agreed. After in-service training, he was appointed the constable of High Cotton and the surrounding precinct.

As an associate member of the Texas Department of Public Safety, his job was to keep the peace, enforce traffic regulations, go on patrol, undertake investigations and arrest lawbreakers. Since he didn't have a jail, he coordinated his activities with the sheriff of the county.

At the time he'd taken on the job, he thought he would need something to keep him busy. But now he wished he'd thought it over a little more. He was needed at home.

Juggling his kids was getting harder. He never knew Nell was using physical discipline. That he wouldn't tolerate.

He'd gotten a call that the Grayson brothers were

fighting again. He'd planned to leave Georgie for just a little while with Nell. Now he'd changed his mind. He'd take Georgie with him. He didn't have any other choice. His part-time deputy constable, Lonnie, was in Brenham visiting his parents.

The Graysons weren't dangerous, just idiots fighting over a fence that was ten inches over the line. He had to talk to them about every six months to defuse the situation.

He walked closer to his aunt. "You might try losing that holier-than-thou attitude, because if the Belles and the Calhouns take their business elsewhere, Walker's General Store will be in trouble."

"I handled it, didn't I?" She tucked a receipt into the register and slammed it closed.

"Yes, in a disagreeable fashion."

"Now…"

"No." He held up a hand. "This discussion is over. When Cooper Yates comes into the store, you will treat him cordially."

"People don't know their place."

He gritted his teeth and let that pass. "And you will never slap my kids again—ever."

"They need discipline."

"Ever, Nell. Are we clear on that?"

She raised her chin. "Yes."

"Okay, Georgie." He jostled the boy, who had a mouth full of jelly beans. "Let's go see what the Graysons are doing?"

"Aren't you leaving him here?" Nell called.

"No," he said over his shoulder, "not ever again."

As he strolled toward his car, he thought about Ms. Belle. No one stood up to Nell. Most people in town would rather defuse a bomb than cross her, yet Ms.

Belle had no qualms about speaking her mind. About Cooper.

Although he was appalled at Nell's tactics, he had to wonder if there was something going on between Ms. Belle and Cooper. When the crisis at High Five had been settled, she was supposed to return to Philadelphia. But she'd stayed. Why?

And what did he care?

MADDIE WALKED TO HER TRUCK and saw that the barbed wire, steel posts and bag of steel-post ties were loaded. As she was about to get in, she saw a young girl crossing the street to the store. It was Ginny. The school was just across the highway, but school wasn't out. It was too early.

Ginny sat on the bench in front of the store, huddled in her Windbreaker, which didn't reach across her protruding stomach. Her face was pale.

Maddie walked over to her. "Are you okay?"

Ginny looked up. "Oh, hi, Ms. Belle."

"Why aren't you in school?"

"I felt sick and the nurse said I could go home. My dad delivers eggs here and I'm waiting on him."

"Maybe you should see a doctor?"

"No. I'm okay—just pregnant."

"Still…"

"We can't afford it, okay?" The words were angry, defiant. Ginny rested her head against the wall. "God, I wish Brian had been at High Five and then I could be out of this awful place."

Maddie eased onto the bench beside her, thinking the girl might need someone to talk to. "Haley doesn't know where her mother is, so you could have been stranded, too."

"That would be better than this dump of a town."

"Ginny…"

The girl sat up straight. "Please don't give me a lecture. I've heard enough from the school counselor and the teachers."

"They have a point. You're so young." Maddie had a good idea of what the counselor and teachers had told her.

"And stupid, like my dad is always telling me." Ginny chewed on a fingernail that had been gnawed to the quick. Her greasy hair was pulled back into a limp ponytail. Food stains speckled her jeans, even the Windbreaker, and her sneakers were a dirty tan. The girl needed a bath. Maddie wondered at her home life.

Suddenly Ginny turned to her. "Ms. Belle, please help me. A social worker came to our house and my dad told her I was giving the baby away. He says he can't afford to feed another kid. I want to keep my baby."

"Ginny…"

"I have an aunt who lives in Temple, and she said I could stay with her. She'd let me keep my baby and she'd help, too. I just need money to get there. Please, Ms. Belle, help me."

Maddie could feel herself weakening under that desperate tone, but she had to be careful. So many times she let her emotions rule her head. She had to remind herself that Ginny had a family.

"Why doesn't she come and get you?"

"She's had knee surgery and she's not driving yet. I can help her, too."

"What about your mother?" Maddie kept holding back, trying not to let her emotions get involved.

"My dad hates my aunt. She's my mother's sister

and my mother can't even visit her. My mom won't go against my dad."

This was all sounding very odd to Maddie. "How did you hear from her?"

"I called her from school to tell her what my dad was planning. I need to see a doctor and she told me to come, but not to tell my father."

"You haven't seen a doctor?" This one thing stuck in Maddie's mind.

"No, ma'am. We can't afford it."

"But there are free clinics—if not here, then in Giddings."

Ginny shook her head. "My dad wouldn't let me go. He said if I was so stupid to get pregnant then I could have the baby at home just like my mom had all of us."

Good heavens, this was terrible. The girl needed to see a doctor.

"Do you know when the baby is due?"

"No, ma'am."

Maddie took a deep breath and looked off to the vehicles traveling on the country road, some stopping at the gas station/convenience store across the highway, others at the local café and the rest continuing on to their homes and ranches. A cool breeze wafted Ginny's unwashed scent to her.

Everything in her told her not to get involved with a girl she didn't know, but she couldn't ignore the fact that Ginny needed medical attention and more.

Oh, she hoped she didn't regret this. "What's your aunt's name?"

"Thelma Jenkins."

"Do you have her phone number?"

"Why?"

Maddie bit her lip. "I'll give you the money to get to Temple, but I want to talk to your aunt first."

Ginny smiled and her whole demeanor changed. "Oh, Ms. Belle, thank you." Ginny glanced at the pay phone beside them. "I'll call her now if…if you'll loan me two quarters."

Maddie cursed herself for not bringing her cell, but she'd been in such a hurry to catch Cooper and Rufus that she'd left it behind. Opening her purse, she dug for change and handed it to Ginny. The girl jumped up to make the call.

The traffic was deafening, and Maddie couldn't make out what Ginny was saying. Ginny held out the phone to Maddie and she spoke to Thelma Jenkins.

The lady assured her she would do everything to help Ginny. Hanging up, Maddie felt much better.

"I'll give you the money for bus fare, but you have to tell your parents where you're going."

"Sure. They won't care."

Maddie couldn't imagine a parent not caring.

"And I'd like your aunt's number and address."

Maddie pulled a pad from her purse and handed Ginny a pen. After Ginny scribbled the name and number, Maddie tucked it into her purse. She then reached for her wallet and counted out fifty dollars.

"That should be enough for the fare and a little extra."

"Oh, thank you, Ms. Belle. You're so nice."

"And please check in at the school and let them know you'll be gone for a while."

"I will."

Maddie motioned toward Ginny's stomach. "Take care of that baby."

"I plan to." Ginny hugged her briefly, and Maddie got into her truck and drove away, hoping she was doing the right thing. If Ginny wanted to keep her baby, she should be allowed to. Every woman had that right.

As she neared High Five, she met Walker going in the opposite direction. She would call him tonight and let him know about Ginny. That was the least she could do. After all, he was worried about Haley and her involvement with Ginny. She'd probably get a lot of attitude and a sermon about minding her own business.

She'd call, anyway. He had been nice today, and maybe they had reached a new understanding.

Maybe.

CHAPTER FIVE

BY THE TIME MADDIE'S DAY ended, she was exhausted. They managed to finish the fence around the pen, and her arms ached from stretching barbed wire, but it was done. She was proud she had the strength to keep up with Cooper. As she fell into bed, she relished that feeling.

Before sleep claimed her, she remembered she hadn't called Walker. Thoughts of him caused her to move restlessly beneath the covers. What was it about the man that triggered every feminine response in her? Maybe it was because he was so different from the men in her city life. Or maybe it had been so long since she'd been with a man that her feminine sensory receptors were out of whack. Or whatever. She was too tired to think anymore.

She should call him, but it was late and she might wake Georgie. The morning would be a better time.

AT FIVE MADDIE WAS UP and not so raring to go. She felt as if she'd just closed her eyes. But they planned to round up the expecting cows and wanted to get an early start. This might be just a little too early. Coop said there weren't many cows calving this time of the year, so that was a plus. Births were usually in the spring and fall.

After brushing her teeth, she thought of calling

Walker, but it was too early. She'd call at lunch. She shimmied into jeans and stuck her arms into one of Cait's pearl-snap shirts. Luckily they were close to the same size. After tucking her shirt into the jeans, she zipped and buttoned them, then deftly wove a tooled leather belt through the loops.

She sat down to tug on her boots. Wiggling her toes, she was reminded how different her attire was from her Philadelphia wardrobe: suits, silk blouses and Jimmy Choo heels. Oh, yeah, she missed those shoes, but that was another life. Today she was a cowgirl, and work waited for her. Gathering her hair into a short ponytail, she jogged for the stairs, which she figured was a good way to wake up.

She met Etta as she was going out the back door. "Good morning, lazy bug," Maddie mocked with a smile.

"Don't get smart," Etta replied, handing her something wrapped in tin foil. "Breakfast taco. I made them for Rufus and Cooper and I saved one for you."

"Thanks, Etta."

"Get some juice from the fridge."

Maddie grabbed bottled water. "This will do."

"Now, lunch will be ready at twelve and I expect everyone here. You can't go all day without a proper meal."

"Yes, ma'am." Maddie kissed her cheek. "Please look after Gran. I'll check on her later."

"I always look after Miss Dorie." Etta pushed her toward the door. "Go. Coop and Ru are waiting."

By noon Maddie's butt was numb and her body ached, but they had a penful of expecting mamas. She leaned on the fence beside Cooper. "How do you know these cows are ready to give birth?"

"Look at their udders."

"Oh, they're swollen."

"Yep. Full of milk, and their…"

When he stopped, she glanced at him. "What?"

Cooper removed his hat and swiped back his hair as if he was thinking about his answer. "Their tail ends are swollen, too."

"Oh." She playfully slapped his shoulder. "You thought I'd be embarrassed."

His sun-browned skin darkened. "Maybe."

"Ple-ease." She pushed away from the fence, placed her hands on her hips and bobbled her head in a what's-up-with-you movement. "I really am made of tougher stuff."

"Well, you surprised the hell out of me," he admitted. "I thought you'd do your share of the work from the house."

"Not on your life, buster." She started toward the house. "Let's go have lunch. I'm starving."

She had thought of just doing the paperwork. Cooper could run the ranch without her help, but something about being part-owner made her take an active role. Cait had. And she enjoyed the physical exercise. And she needed to feel useful. And she craved the mind-numbing tiredness that kept her from thinking *what if?* What if the cancer came back?

That fear never left her.

IT WAS A TEACHER'S workday so Walker had both kids at home. He'd received a call from Lois Willham. Her husband had just gotten laid off from his job in Rockdale. He'd bought a six-pack of beer and was in the yard drinking and firing a gun. She was afraid he was going to hit an unexpected bystander.

Walker didn't want to take the kids on that kind of call, so he left Haley in charge. He thought she would be happy, but she seemed more nervous than anything.

He didn't plan to be gone that long, so he didn't worry, which was an understatement. Worry was his constant companion.

When he reached the Willhams', Roy was sitting in a lawn chair, a beer in his hand and a shotgun resting across his lap. Walker took the gun away from him and told him to get his act together. His family needed him. Then he listened to Roy ramble on about the unfairness of life. When Walker left, Roy promised to do right by his family, even if he had to go back to farming.

In less than an hour, he walked through his back door. Everything was quiet. Too quiet. An unexpected chill scooted across his skin. He hurried into the living room. The TV was off and the lights out. His kids were nowhere in sight.

He took the stairs two at a time. Their rooms were empty. That chill began to multiply. He dashed to the general store. They weren't there. He checked all over High Cotton. No one had seen them.

Where were they?

Could they have gone to High Five again? High Five was closer than Earl's, so he headed there first. On the way he called his part-time deputy constable to take all calls.

He had to find his children.

ETTA HAD HAMBURGER STEAKS, mashed potatoes, green beans and hot rolls. Maddie ate her fill, as did Cooper and Rufus. They had worked up an appetite.

Afterward, Coop and Ru left to check the herd. Maddie sat with her grandmother in the parlor.

"How was your visit with Cait? I got in so late last night I didn't get a chance to ask."

Gran clapped her hands. "It was wonderful to see my baby so happy."

"Mmm." Maddie had thought that Cait would never walk away from High Five. Her roots were firmly embedded here, but love had made the decision easy. Maddie hoped one day she could find a love that strong. She shifted uneasily. That was highly unlikely, though. Men didn't want damaged goods. They wanted a wife who could bear children. A sharp pain shot through her.

"I thought my baby would become a lady taking care of the house and things like that, but she's in charge of the horses while Judd manages the cows."

Maddie hugged her grandmother. "It's what Cait loves. I just can't see her knitting or crocheting or throwing parties."

"Sometimes I wonder where I went wrong. My granddaughters are so independent and live in a man's world."

"Oh, Gran." She hugged her again. "You've done nothing wrong. Times have just changed. A woman can clean, cook and make babies, but she can be the breadwinner, too. A woman is good at multitasking."

"I don't have a clue what you're talking about. Women should be pampered and loved."

"Hallelujah." Maddie stood and did a fancy tap dance, her boots clicking on the hardwood floor.

"And you're no better." Gran flung out a hand. "Out there with Cooper and Rufus in the muck and the mud."

It was no use arguing with her grandmother. Her views were from another time, another era.

She lifted an eyebrow. "Good thing I'm a Belle, then, huh?"

A smile fluttered across Gran's face. "Yes, it is, my baby."

Maddie kissed Gran's forehead. "I love you."

"And that covers for a lot of unladylike behavior," Gran replied with a touch of her true Belle spirit.

"I'll see you this afternoon," Maddie called over her shoulder. "We'll watch an old movie."

"One where a lady is a lady."

"Oh, yes, ma'am."

Maddie walked out the back door smiling. She came to an abrupt stop when she saw Walker drive up in a white car with a constable's insignia on the door and a siren on top. Oh, no, she'd forgotten to call him. But she was sure his visit had nothing to do with Ginny.

Or did it?

He strolled to her with long strides, his face set in a stonelike mask. This was not good. "Ms. Belle, are my kids here?"

She blinked, confused. "No. I haven't seen them. Isn't Haley in school?"

"No. It's a teacher's workday. Do you mind if I check your barn?"

"No. Of course not." As she followed him, a scenario was whizzing through her mind and she kept pushing it away. But she had to face it. Children's lives were involved.

After a brief search, it was clear the kids weren't hiding in the barn.

Walker clenched his jaw and she could see how worried he was. "God, where could they be? I'm on my way to Earl's to see if Ginny is home. Damn man doesn't have a phone."

As he hurried to his car, she knew she had to tell him. "Walker."

He turned swiftly, his eyes narrowed. "What? I really don't have time."

"I need to tell you something."

His face relaxed for a second. "Have you seen my kids?"

She shook her head and prayed for courage. And she prayed that she was wrong. "No, but I've seen Ginny."

"Where?"

"Yesterday at the general store."

"So? That doesn't mean anything. My kids were home until about two hours ago."

"Ah…"

"What is it, Ms. Belle? I have to go."

She swallowed the wad of cowardice in her throat. "I…I gave Ginny money for bus fare to Temple."

"What!"

The loud word ricocheted off her sensitive nerve endings. She winced. *Run* crossed her mind, but Belles didn't run. It seemed a whole lot easier than facing the angry man standing in front of her, though.

"Please let me explain."

"It had better be damn good."

She told him about the aunt and everything. "I don't believe your kids are with her. She just wanted to see a doctor about her pregnancy and to get away from her father."

"You said you had the aunt's name and number?"

"Yes. I'll get it and you'll see your kids aren't there." Oh, God, she prayed they weren't.

Maddie ran inside, grabbed her purse and hurried back to Walker, who still stood there with that same stone face, except now he had his cell in his hand.

He poked in the number and raised the phone to

his ear. After listening for a second, he handed her the phone.

"Sorry, the number you've dialed is not a working number. Please try again." The message came through loud and clear. And disturbing.

"That can't be," Maddie said as fear edged its way into her voice. "I spoke to her yesterday."

"Did you dial the number?"

"No, Ginny did."

"I don't know who you were talking to, but I'm guessing it wasn't Ginny's aunt. I have a suspicion my kids are with her, and Ms. Belle—" the caramel eyes darkened "—if anything happens to them I'll…" He left the sentence hanging like a noose, and she could almost feel it tightening round her throat.

He swung toward his car, and even though Maddie had trouble breathing, she quickly followed him, jumping into the passenger's side.

His hand paused over the ignition. "What the hell do you think you're doing?"

"I'm going with you."

"No, you're not."

She stiffened. "If this is my fault, I have to help you find them."

"You've done enough, Ms. Belle. Now, get out of my car."

Her anger fired for the first time. "Stop calling me Ms. Belle. My name is Madison or Maddie."

"'Mad' is more appropriate. Now, get out of the car. I don't have time to argue with you."

She stared into his cold, cold eyes and shivered, but she didn't get out. "Sorry. I'm going with you."

He sighed angrily and started the engine. In a split

second they were flying out of her driveway. For a couple of miles nothing was said.

A police radio sat on the dash, an empty coffee cup was in the console alongside a half-empty bag of jelly beans, a package of gum and a box of Kleenex. She sniffed the scent of the coffee and tried to relax.

Walker's big hands tightened on the steering wheel, and she expected it to snap from his brute strength at any minute.

She slipped her hand into her purse for her cell. She couldn't just leave without letting someone know. As she called Cait's number, Walker didn't even glance her way.

She tapped her fingers on her jeans, hoping her sister would answer and not Judd's secretary, Brenda Sue, who didn't know when to shut up.

Brenda Sue's annoying voice came on the line. This just wasn't her day.

"May I speak to Caitlyn, please?"

"Oh, hi, Madison. I'm in the office and I don't know where Cait is and I have strict orders not to bother her or Judd. They get real angry when I do, so you'll have to just call back later. Did you know I have a boyfriend? What am I saying? Sure you do. I mean, you and Cait talk all the time and—"

"Brenda Sue," Maddie shouted, stopping the endless chatter. "Ring through to the house and tell Cait I need to talk to her. It's an emergency."

"Why don't you just call her cell?"

"Ring her!" Cait rarely carried her cell and Maddie needed to talk to her now.

"Don't get huffy. You Belles are all alike and—"

"Call her this instant." At Maddie's stringent voice, Brenda Sue put her on hold.

She glanced at Walker, and she thought she saw his lips twitch. Was he smiling? Hardly. The man never smiled.

Cait's voice came on. "What's wrong? Brenda Sue said you were rude. And I know my sister Madison is never rude."

"How do you keep from strangling her?"

"I just ignore her. So what's the emergency? Is it Gran?"

"Gran is fine. I need a favor. Could you go to High Five and tell Cooper I've been unexpectedly detained?"

"What? Where?"

Maddie took a breath and looked at Walker, who had his eyes glued to the road. "Walker's kids are missing and I'm going with him to find them."

"Why?"

"Just tell Cooper and check on Gran. I'll be back as soon as I can."

"Maddie, what's going on?"

"I'll tell you when I get back. I just didn't want anyone to worry."

"I'm worried now. Walker is more than capable of finding his kids."

"Cait, please. I have to go. I'll call as soon as I can."

"Mad—"

Maddie clicked off before Cait could do her usual grilling. At the moment she didn't have any answers. Slipping her phone into her purse, she hoped Ginny hadn't lied to her.

She noticed the car was flying down the highway, and a glance at the speedometer told her they were way over the speed limit.

"You're speeding."

That was met with a hard stare as Walker flexed his

fingers on the steering wheel. He turned off the highway, tires squealing, onto a county dirt road. Gripping the door for support, she knew better than to say anything else.

Soon Walker swerved into a lane. Ahead was a dilapidated mobile home with goats and chickens in the dirt yard. Two dogs were tied at the corner and barked agitatedly at them, trying to break their chains.

"What is this?" she couldn't help but ask.

"This is where Ginny lives," he replied, getting out.

"You have to be kidding." No one could live here. The trailer was rusted and falling in.

Walker leaned down to look at her. "You may have noticed I'm not a joking type of guy." He slammed the door on that piece of news and went to open the gate.

She took several deep breaths. What had she done? Ginny would lie, cheat and steal to get out of a place like this. In that moment she knew she'd been had. Now Walker's kids were in danger.

Soon Walker was back in the car and drove up to the mobile home. He quickly got out and shooed chickens and goats away. She didn't hesitate to follow.

A foul smell greeted her. She wrinkled her nose. "What is that?" she asked Walker's stiff back.

"There's a pigpen out back," he said as he walked up the rickety steps. He banged on the screen door. It rattled from his big fist and she thought it might fall off.

A man in greasy long hair and dirty overalls opened the door, but not the screen. "Whaddya want?"

"I'm looking for Ginny, Earl."

"She ain't here."

Any hope Ginny hadn't tricked her vanished.

A woman came up behind Earl. It had to be Ginny's

mother, but Maddie couldn't see clearly through the screen door. A small girl hung on to her leg.

"Where is she?"

"Don't know. Don't care."

"Earl, I'm not in a mood for your lip. I want answers and I want them now."

"She left a note saying she was leaving and for us not to worry about her." The woman spoke for the first time as she picked up the child.

"She say anything else?"

"No."

Walker stiffened beside her. "Do you have any idea where she might have gone?"

"No."

"What about your sister Thelma?"

There was a long pause and then the woman replied, "I don't have a sister named Thelma."

"Thelma Jenkins is not your sister?"

"No." The woman giggled. "Thelma Jenkins is that ol' mama goat in the yard. My boy named her that after a teacher he didn't like."

Walker glanced at Maddie with a you're-so-gullible look. And she was. She'd trusted Ginny and now she felt like a fool. Walker had every right to be angry with her. She was angry at herself.

"Does Ginny have any friends?"

"No, not now. Her friend moved away about a year ago."

"Who?"

"Tara Davis."

"Where did she move to?" Walker kept firing the questions as the dogs kept up an incessant bark. Two boys came from around the trailer and tried to quiet them.

Maddie shivered inside her Carhartt jacket, but that was preferable to going inside the trailer.

"I don't know," Verna replied.

"That's it," Earl snapped. "We don't know where the girl is."

"She's your daughter. Aren't you worried about her?" The words came out before Maddie could stop them.

"Good riddance, I say. One less mouth to feed." Earl slammed the door.

"Oh." Maddie stomped her boot. "What a deplorable man."

Walker wasn't listening to her. He went down the steps and over to the boys, who eyed him warily. Their clothes were filthy, and their long, stringy hair hung in their faces. One boy had a severe case of acne and he picked at a pimple. The other boy held a dog by the collar. The dog growled, baring his teeth, as Walker neared.

"When was the last time you saw your sister? And don't lie to me."

The boy stopped picking at the pimple and his face turned redder at Walker's tone. "She snuck out early this morning before anyone was up."

"Was someone waiting for her?"

"I don't know."

"Did you hear a car?"

"No."

"Did you see lights?"

"No. She packed her backpack and left. I was sleeping on the sofa and saw her leave. That's all I know, mister."

"Thanks." Walker swung toward his car and ran smack into Ms. Belle, literally. He grabbed her before she toppled into goat crap. Beneath the jacket her arms felt soft, inviting, touchable. As annoyed as he was with her, he couldn't quell that reaction. A light scent of lavender didn't help, either.

"Watch where you're going." His words were rough and he didn't bother to sugarcoat them.

"I didn't realize you were going to turn so quickly."

He didn't respond as he hurried to his car and got in. Ms. Belle was still sidestepping crap to get to the car. He should just drive off and leave her here. Why didn't he? She was screwing up his whole life and messing with his emotions. From the first moment he'd met her at the party, he'd known she was trouble for his peace of mind. So drive away, he told himself. Yet he waited.

She opened the door, a frown on her face. "I stepped in it."

"You sure did," he replied, hoping she didn't miss the double meaning.

"I don't want to get this in your car." She danced around on one foot.

He tossed her the box of Kleenex. She actually caught it and then sat on the seat, wiping her boot.

Looking at him with a wad of tissues in her hand, she asked, "What do I do with this?"

For an answer he started the engine and she hurriedly crawled in. He drove to the gate and got out to open it. Once he was back inside, he noticed she'd tossed the tissues outside in the ditch.

"You're littering."

"Arrest me, then, because I'm not holding that any longer."

"Don't tempt me." He turned onto the dirt road.

"Where are we going?"

"To High Cotton. I want to know if Ginny got on a

bus with my kids. The bus stopped there at ten-thirty this morning."

He clenched and unclenched his hands, trying not to think about Haley and Georgie getting on a bus bound for Lubbock to find their mother. He could strangle Ms. Belle, but when he looked at her, "strangle" wasn't exactly on his mind.

"I'm sorry. I really am." That soft, sincere voice weaved its way around his heart. And that made him mad.

"You should be. My kids could be anywhere."

"I was trying to help Ginny. She needs to see a doctor."

"You can't help everybody, Ms. Belle."

"That's very cynical."

Maybe he was. Life had done that to him. And Trisha.

"It's reality, Ms. Belle."

She turned toward him. "If you call me Ms. Belle in that tone of voice again, I'll smack you."

He met the blue heat of her eyes. "You've never smacked anyone in your life."

Her eyes crinkled. "Is it that obvious?"

"Yes."

"Doesn't mean I can't or I won't."

"Listen." His hands were perpetually clenched on the steering wheel. "When we reach High Cotton, you're getting out. I'll be moving fast to catch up with my kids."

"I can keep up."

"You're getting out!"

"Please, I really need to see this through."

That soft voice ran through him like a shot of tequila, warm, tingly and potent.

No, he wouldn't weaken. He'd had enough of Ms. Belle. "You're getting out."

Her chin lifted. "No, I'm not. You'll have a hell of a time getting rid of me."

CHAPTER SIX

NOT ANOTHER WORD WAS SPOKEN on the ride into High Cotton. Walker preferred it that way. He pulled into the convenience store where the bus stop was located. Once a week on Fridays a small bus took people who'd bought passes into Giddings to buy tickets for their destination. The town of High Cotton provided the service.

Ruth was at the counter in the store where the passes where purchased.

"Hey, Walker, what can I do for you?" Ruth was divorced and raising four kids by herself. She tended to be overly friendly.

"Did my children buy a pass for the bus this morning?"

"I wasn't on duty this morning. Woody was but he's not here now."

"Look in the book, Ruth. This is important."

"Sure. Anything for you." She reached beneath the counter and brought out a worn book. "Do you think your kids ran away or something?"

"Are they listed?"

"Nope." She chewed on a fingernail. "Just Opal Hinz, Willard Tobias, Juan Garcia and Ginny Grubbs."

"How many passes did Ginny buy?"

"I don't know. Woody would."

"Why isn't it written down?" He couldn't keep the anger out of his voice.

"Now, don't get your shorts in a bind."

"More than that's going to be in a bind if better records aren't kept around here."

"It's not a crime, is it?"

"It's just sloppy." He took a breath to control his temper. "When will Woody be back?"

She shrugged. "I don't know. He worked from 5:00 a.m. to one, so I guess he's probably home sleeping if you really need to talk to him."

Walker turned quickly and bumped into Ms. Belle again. "Look, call your sister or call Cooper. I'm leaving you here."

"You're not…"

"Madison." Joe Bob Shoemaker walked in and she paused. "I was looking for you. I need hay. Do you have any at High Five to sell?"

"No, I'm sorry. With the hurricane damage and the fire we need all we have."

"Damn the luck." Joe Bob chomped down on his chewing tobacco, eyeing Walker. "What are your kids up to?"

"What do you mean?"

"I saw them get on the bus this morning all huddled in their jackets like they didn't want anyone to see them, but there's no mistaking that gal of yours with that boy on her hip."

Walker hit the door at a run, jumped in the car and headed for Giddings. His mind was in such turmoil he didn't even realize Ms. Belle was in the car with him. He didn't have time to deal with her. He had to get to his kids.

Ms. Belle didn't say a word on the fifteen-minute trip. Walker figured she must value her life because he was in no mood to be patient with her. What was she thinking giving Ginny money?

He swerved off U.S. 290 where the convenience store/bus stop was located. The place was old, decaying from age and wear. He killed the engine and made a run for the front door. The place was just as bad inside, with outdated neon beer signs and dirty chipped tiled floors. He showed the woman behind the counter his badge.

"My name is Walker and I'm the constable from High Cotton." He pulled out his wallet from his back pocket and placed a photo on the counter. "I'm looking for these two kids. Have you seen them?"

The woman pushed her glasses up the bridge of her nose and peered at the photo. "Yes, yes. I saw them earlier. They were with an older girl. She was pregnant."

"That's them. Did you sell them a ticket?" He found he was holding his breath as he waited for the answer.

"The older girl wanted to buy tickets to Temple, but the bus had already left. I told her it would run again tomorrow, but she said that was too late."

"So where did they go?"

"They went outside."

"These were kids. Didn't you think something was wrong?" He held his temper in check.

"I was keeping an eye on them, but I got busy and when I looked up they were gone."

"Why didn't you call the police?"

"Like I said, I was busy."

"Too busy to get involved." His temper snapped.

"Now, listen—"

He cut her off. "Did you see them talking to anyone?"

"The older one was talking to a man. The next thing I knew they were gone."

Walker's blood ran cold. "What did he look like?"

"Probably in his fifties. He was wearing a brown jacket and a Dallas Cowboys baseball cap. That's all I noticed."

"Have you seen him before?"

"No."

He took a breath. "Did any of the kids say anything?"

"The little boy kept saying he wanted Daddy. The girl holding him told him to be quiet, that they were going to see Mama."

Damn! He turned toward the door and bumped into Ms. Belle again. The woman was like gum on his shoe, irritating and hard to get rid of. This time he didn't bother with a response. He was too worried about his kids.

When he got in the car, she was there. Without a word, he backed out and headed for FM 448, where the new sheriff's office was located.

On the way, he called Trisha's sister, Doris, in Lubbock to see if she'd heard from Haley. She hadn't. He told her to call immediately if she did.

When they reached the sheriff's office, he had a talk with Roger, the deputy in charge. He introduced Maddie. Walker knew all the people in law enforcement, so he had no problem getting an Amber Alert issued with Haley and Georgie's pictures. Roger then took more information. Walker gave him everything he knew, including Tara Davis's name. They would do a background check on her to see if they could locate her.

Now he waited. He let the officers do their jobs. Someone had to have seen them and he prayed he got to them before anything happened. His kids were with a total stranger. The dangers were just too many for him to contemplate and still keep his sanity.

Walker was restless. He couldn't sit still, but he knew he had to wait. The deputies were checking the bus stop again. Calls would start to come in. They had to.

He made himself sit in a chair by a water cooler, but he kept glancing at his watch. Where were Haley and Georgie? Who had them?

A hand touched his arm and he tensed, staring into pure blue eyes. There she was. The woman he couldn't shake. Her fingers were warm and he needed that human contact.

"I'm sorry."

"I know." And he did. He really couldn't blame her. "Ginny would have gotten the money somehow for Haley. My daughter was determined to leave, so it was just a matter of time." It wasn't easy to admit that.

"I'm too trusting. My dad always told me that."

His eyes held hers. "I knew that about you from the start when you were wearing that white-and-pink dress and looking so innocent, so trusting."

They just stared at each other, and Maddie didn't know what to say. Did he still see her as a child? What a downer for her ego.

For lack of something to say, she waved toward a counter where a pot and cups stood. "Would you like a cup of coffee?"

"No, thanks. I'm wired enough."

"They'll find them."

"But will it be in time?" The words seemed to come from deep inside him.

She touched his arm again, and he didn't tense like the last time. The stern man she knew had disappeared. This man was hurting and unable to hide it. Even though most of the ordeal was her fault, she felt close to him at that moment.

"I've endangered my life many times in the line of duty. As a fighter pilot the risks were high, and I gladly took every one for my country. After my stint in the marines, I became a police officer in Houston. I put my life on the line every day. Trisha hated my job and was constantly on me about all the risks I was taking, so I quit and took on an air marshal's job. Again Trisha complained about me being gone all the time. I then became a member of a search-and-rescue team in Houston. My life was always in danger, but I never thought about it. I was just doing my job."

He took a long breath. "Now it's so different. My kids' lives are at risk and I feel that pain deep in my gut."

Roger walked over. "We've located Tara Davis."

Walker was immediately on his feet. "Where?"

"She lives in Temple with her boyfriend."

Temple. Ginny wanted to go to her friend's, not an aunt.

"Let me have her address and I'll be on my way."

Roger pulled the paper away. "Walker, calm down. A Temple police unit is on the way to the apartment. We'll know in a few minutes if your kids are there. Take a deep breath."

Walker swung away and gazed off down the hall. Maddie knew he was trying to get his emotions under control. Suddenly he swung back.

"If Ginny put my kids on a bus to Lubbock, I'll…"

She took his arm. "Let's sit. We'll have information shortly."

Like a spring, he bounced up again and paced. She had to get his mind on something else.

"Do you have any idea where your ex-wife might be?"

"No." He stopped pacing. "Her note said she was sorry but she loved this Tony Almada guy, her high school sweetheart, and she had made a choice. The kids would be better off with me because he didn't care for children. She told me to send the divorce papers to her sister in Lubbock. She loved Haley and Georgie but she had to go. At the bottom she wrote 'please forgive me.'" He removed his hat and stared at the creases. "How do you forgive such selfish behavior?"

"By loving your kids."

He raised his head, his eyes filled with pain. "I'm trying, but my kids barely know me. My jobs took me away from them and sadly I was never there." He jammed his hat on his head. "Haley and Georgie should have come first. They should have been my top priority, but I left their raising to Trisha. They have two selfish parents."

"You're there for them now. That's what counts."

He sat beside her and some of the tension seemed to leave him. "When Trisha left, I brought them home to High Cotton. I thought it would give us a new start, but Haley hasn't adjusted. She thinks I don't want them and that I'm only putting up with them because I have to."

"Have you told her differently?"

"Yes. But she doesn't trust me."

"You have to show her."

"I'm trying. I'm really trying." He closed his eyes and nothing else was said.

It was surreal sitting in the sheriff's office and talking to Ms. Belle. His main goal had been to get rid of her, but now he was glad she was here. She had a calming effect that he found strange. Other times she'd been like a steely point of a knife embedded in his last nerve.

Opening his eyes, he noticed her cowboy boots. "Are you really running High Five?"

She turned toward him with a lifted eyebrow. "You don't think I can?"

"No offense, but I see you as an indoor lady."

"Fragile and weak?" The eyebrow arched further.

"Far from it."

"You saved your butt there." She smiled, and his whole world seemed brighter. "Being raised in Philadelphia, I was an indoor person. When I visited my father and sisters at High Five, that changed. I enjoyed the outdoors."

Walker glanced at Roger, who was still talking on the phone. What was taking so damn long? To keep his nerves under control, he concentrated on the woman beside him.

"What did you do in Philadelphia? You said something about being a counselor."

"Yes. At a major hospital in Philly. Before that I was a teacher. I went to an all-girl's Catholic school and then to Duquesne University. Nothing prepared me for public schools. It was a challenge and stressful. With a degree in education and a minor in psychology, I searched for something else. The position at the hospital seemed perfect."

A shadow crossed her face. He waited for her to continue, but she didn't. She just stared at her clasped hands in her lap.

"Walker." Roger motioned him over.

He sprang to his feet. "Did you find them?"

The deputy held his hand over the mouthpiece. "I

have Officer Campbell on the line. He's at Davis's apartment."

"And?"

"Your children aren't there and neither is Ginny Grubbs."

He gulped a breath. "May I speak to her?"

Roger spoke to the officer and handed Walker the phone.

"Ms. Davis, this is Walker, the constable of High Cotton. I'm looking for Ginny."

"She's not here" came the response. "Like I told the officer, she was supposed to be here, but she never arrived."

"Did you speak with Ms. Belle yesterday?"

There was a long pause.

"Don't lie, Ms. Davis. This is serious."

"Yes. I spoke to the lady. Ginny asked me to lie and I did. She said it was the only way she could get the money."

"What did she have in mind for Haley and Georgie?"

"Who?"

"Ginny has my two kids with her."

"She didn't mention any kids. My boyfriend said Ginny could stay until she found a job. That's it. He'll have a fit if she brings anyone else."

He dragged in a breath. "Just let us know when she arrives. That's important if you want to stay out of trouble."

"Yes, sir. I have a nine-month-old baby. I can't get in trouble. I was just trying to help a friend."

"Don't let Ginny talk you into anything."

"Yes, sir."

Walker handed the deputy the phone and started to pace again.

"What happened?"

He turned toward the soft feminine voice that was becoming like a tranquilizer. "They're not at the friend's. At least not yet. She was expecting Ginny, but not Haley and Georgie." Walker turned toward Roger. "Ginny might have put my kids on a bus to Lubbock."

"We'll check it out. And a policeman is watching the apartment."

"Good." He walked to the chair and sat. His fears were ping-ponging off his nerves. Removing his hat, he ran both hands through his hair. "I feel so helpless. I'm used to being in the action. It's hell waiting."

Maddie didn't say anything. Office sounds went on around them. Phones rang, faxes beeped and voices murmured in the background. The clock slowly ticked away precious time.

She got up and poured two cups of coffee. She handed Walker one and he took it. Sitting again, she asked, "What's your first name?"

"Just Walker." He took a sip and leaned over, his forearms on his legs, the cup between his hands.

"Everyone has a first name."

"Not me."

She poked him in the ribs. "You're lying, Mr. Walker."

He glanced at her, trying to hide a smile. "Maybe. But you'll never know."

"Mmm."

"Listen." His eyes went to the window. "It's almost dark. Why don't you call someone to pick you up, or maybe Roger can arrange a ride."

Her eyebrow lifted again. "You're not getting rid of me. I'm sticking to you like glue."

"Yeah. I'm beginning to realize that."

A warm, welcome feeling passed between them.

"Were you raised in High Cotton?" she asked, sipping coffee.

"Yeah. Judd and I were in the same grade. We were friends and had a lot in common."

"Like what?"

"We were both raised by our fathers."

"Oh."

He could almost see the wheels turning in her head, but being a proper lady she wasn't going to ask.

He gripped the foam cup. "When I was born it was a difficult birth and my dad said my mother was never the same afterward. She'd disappear for weeks and come home as if nothing was wrong. My dad divorced her when I was eight. I never saw her again and I lost track of the number of times she was married. I met my half brother and half sister at her funeral fifteen years ago."

He'd never shared his life story, not even with Trisha, yet here he sat as if it was the most natural thing in the world.

"Is your father living?"

He swirled the dark liquid in the cup. "No. He died when Haley was three. He thought the sun rose and set on her. Georgie is named after him."

Until this moment he never realized how much he missed his dad. He could always talk to him. How he wished he was here now. Instead, Ms. Belle…

"Walker," Roger shouted.

He was on his feet like a shot.

"We found them."

"Where?" Walker placed the coffee on the desk as his insides rolled.

The deputy was talking on the phone and raised a

hand. Walker tried to wait patiently, but his heart was about to pound out of his chest.

Roger slammed down the phone and handed him a piece of paper. "A truck driver just called. He picked them up here in Giddings. The older girl told him they were trying to get to their mother in Temple. Then he heard the Amber Alert on the radio and knew she was lying. He couldn't call until he reached Milano. They're at the Shell station there. Hal Tibbetts, the truck driver, said he'd hang around until someone arrived."

"All three of them are there?"

"Yep, Walker, all three of them." Relief ebbed its way through him. His kids were okay.

"Figured you'd want to be the one to pick them up."

"I'm on my way." He turned and ran into Ms. Belle. Somehow he was getting used to that. "Let's go."

"I'm right behind you."

He didn't insist she go home. It felt right having her along. Maybe a little too right.

CHAPTER SEVEN

THE SUN WAS SLOWLY SINKING in the west as they sped down U.S. 77.

"You seem to know where you're going," Maddie said. "And you're not speeding."

"I know they're safe. I just want to get to them as fast and as safely as possible. Being raised in Texas, I know all these roads. It's a straight shot on U.S. 77 to Rockdale. Milano's about eight miles from there. It's about a forty-five-minute drive."

She watched as he clenched the steering wheel with his big hands. "I may be out of line, but please be patient with them when we arrive. They're probably scared to death."

He glanced briefly at her, his eyes guarded. "You want me to be patient with Ginny?"

"I'm sure she's scared, too."

"She kidnapped my kids, and I'm not in a mood to be lenient or patient with her. She'll be lucky if I don't arrest her."

"That's going to help the situation immensely," she said, tongue in cheek.

"She didn't kidnap your kids."

"I don't have kids." At the words, she felt an ache inside but quickly ignored it.

"You know what I mean. Why are you taking up for her? She lied to you and played on your good nature."

"She's just a kid looking for a better way of life."

"You're such a patsy. You're just asking for trouble."

She wasn't offended by his words, because they were playful, almost teasing. "My sisters tell me that all the time."

"They're right."

"Cait, Sky and I have different personalities."

"I don't know Sky very well, but Cait wouldn't let Ginny off easily."

"I'm just thinking about her situation and living in that awful mobile home. She's fighting to survive."

He sighed. "And she's breaking the law and taking my kids along for the ride. When we get there, Ginny's going to get a stern lecture and she's going back to High Cotton."

"Then you won't file charges against her?"

He sighed more strongly this time. "You just don't give up, do you?"

"She's a pregnant teenager."

"If she agrees to leave my daughter alone, I might agree not to file charges. I really don't think she belongs in jail."

"Now we're thinking alike."

"Heaven help me."

Despite herself, she laughed. "That's not funny."

As they rode, Maddie noticed how capable he was, handling the car with very little effort. The temperature was now in the forties, but the car was warm. Maddie felt warm and safe just being with Walker. They'd only been together a few hours, but it seemed as if they'd been together for days. And the feeling was the best thing she'd felt in a long time.

They reached U.S. 79 and Walker turned right.

"We're almost there. The Shell station will be on the left."

When they reached Milano, darkness had settled in for the night. It wasn't long before they spotted the lit-up store with gas pumps. An eighteen-wheeler was pulled to the side and a man stood by it huddled in a jacket and wearing a Dallas Cowboys baseball cap. It must be the guy the woman at the bus stop saw Ginny talking to. Thank God he was a good man and not capable of taking advantage of children.

Walker stopped by him and pushed the button to roll down his window.

The man hurried over. "Are you Walker?"

"Yes." Walker got out and shook the man's hand. Maddie quickly followed. "This is Madison Belle."

"Nice to meet you, ma'am." He tipped his cap.

"I'm so glad you called," she said, shaking his hand.

"Yes," Walker added. "Thank you. I've been worried sick."

"I thought something was a little strange with the young girl's story, but I was headed to Temple so I gave them a ride before she asked some unsavory character."

"I appreciate that. Are they okay?"

"They're fine, but the boy's been crying a lot. He wants his daddy."

Walker's gut tightened. "I'll take it from here."

"I've already lost a lot of time. I need to be on my way. The young'uns are inside eating burgers."

They shook hands again. "Thank you. Do I owe you anything?"

"Not a cent. Just take care of those little ones." He tipped his cap at Maddie again. "Ma'am."

Walker looked toward the entrance to the store. People were going in and out. Maddie placed a hand on his arm and felt his taut muscles. "Just be calm."

"I was in such a hurry to find them, but now I'm not sure how to handle this situation. If it was someone else's kids, I'd know. But I don't want to drive a wedge between Haley and me."

She wrapped her arms around her waist from the chill. "Just take it slow and go with your heart on this one."

He pulled his hat low, but not before she saw his ghost of a smile. "I'm listening to a woman who's a patsy."

As Walker strolled toward the entrance, he was glad Ms. Belle was with him. He needed a woman's touch tonight. His mind rejected the notion that he meant that in every way possible. The last thing he needed was getting involved with a woman, especially a woman like Ms. Belle who believed in good, fairy tales and happily ever after. He'd left that behind a long time ago. He had to concentrate on his kids. They came first.

His thoughts came to an abrupt stop as he entered the store. The place was neat and clean. Aisles with goods were straight ahead. A man was paying a bill at the counter to the left and there was a deli area lit up with neon signs. Coolers wrapped around to the back, where he glimpsed a restroom sign. He glanced right and saw the eating area.

There they were. Haley, Georgie and Ginny sat at one of the white tables. Drinks and half-eaten burgers cluttered the small table.

He took a few steps and Georgie spotted him. "Daddy," he screamed, and jumped out of his chair and ran to Walker.

Walker grabbed him in a bear hug and held on for dear life.

Georgie's tiny arms trembled around Walker's neck. "I 'cared, Daddy."

He swallowed. "It's okay, son. I'm here."

"I wanna go home."

Walker patted Georgie's back, and he was grateful he could touch his son again. "We will, but first Daddy has to talk to Haley."

"'Kay," Georgie mumbled into his shoulder.

Walker turned Georgie's face so he could look at him. His heart took a hit at his son's red and swollen eyes. He had to force his anger down.

He kissed Georgie's wet cheek. "Stay with Ms. Belle while I talk to Haley."

"No. No." Georgie buried his face in Walker's shoulder. "I want my daddy."

Walker rubbed his back to console him. "I'm right here and I'm not going anywhere without you, but I need to talk to your sister. Go to Ms. Belle. She'll buy you some candy."

"Candy." Georgie's head popped up. "I want candy."

Maddie held out her hands. "Come with me, then."

"But…"

"I'm right here. You can see me at all times."

He went to Maddie, his eyes on Walker.

Walker reached in his wallet and handed her a five. Their eyes met. Locked. *Be patient. Be calm.* He saw her message clearly and he banked down his anger again.

Taking a deep breath, he turned toward the girls sitting at the table. Two pair of eyes filled with fear stared at him.

Be patient. Be calm.

He walked over, picked up Georgie's jacket from the floor and took his seat. Removing his hat, he placed it on the table, taking his time, making them sweat. But he was sweating, too, searching for the right words.

"I'm sorry, Mr. Walker." Ginny spoke first.

"You should be. You took two minors and put their lives in danger." He surprised himself by his controlled tone.

"I promised Haley I'd help her get to her mother. Things just didn't go right."

He looked her straight in the eye. "I could arrest you for kidnapping."

"What?" Her face paled. "You mean, like, go to jail."

"Yes."

"But…but I…"

"I wanted to go, Daddy." Haley spoke for the first time. "I have to see Mama."

He clenched his jaw. "Do you know how worried I've been?"

"If you'd just let us go, you wouldn't have to worry about Georgie and me anymore."

Taking a long patient breath, he knew he had to do something drastic to get Haley's attention. She wouldn't listen to him, but she might listen to someone else. This called for some tough love. He reached for the cell on his waist.

He fingered the phone for a moment. "I'll make a deal with you. I'll call your aunt Doris and you can talk to her. If she'll let you stay with her, we'll catch the next flight to Lubbock. If Doris knows where your mother is, I'll take you to her. I'll do whatever it takes to see you happy again."

"Oh." The hope in her eyes twisted his gut. He knew what Doris was going to say, and it was going to break

Haley's heart. But he had no other choice. Her ploy today proved that.

"But—" he held up a finger "—if Doris says no and she doesn't know where your mother is, you have to promise to settle down and give High Cotton and me a chance. You have to stop running away."

The light dimmed for a second. "I promise."

Yeah, right, he thought, but he punched out the number, praying Doris was at home. She was.

"Doris, this is Walker."

"Hi. Have you found them?"

He didn't answer because he didn't want Haley to know he'd talked to Doris. He hoped Doris caught the hint. "Haley would like to talk to you."

"Why?"

His fingers gripped the cell. "She just wants to talk."

"Give me a hint. Oh, she doesn't know we spoke earlier."

"No. Here's Haley."

He handed Haley the cell and watched her face as she spoke to her aunt. Suddenly she slammed the phone on the table and ran into the bathroom.

He stood and jammed his hands through his hair. God, he hated hurting her. Pointing a finger at Ginny, he said, "Stay right there. Don't even think about running or I will arrest you."

"Yes, sir." Ginny shifted in her seat. "Is Haley okay?"

"No, she's not, and I want you to stop giving her hope where there is none."

"What do you mean?"

"Haley's mother has run away with an old boyfriend and no one knows where she is, not even her sister. And her aunt has a house full of kids and doesn't want any more. I'm all Haley has and she has to accept that."

"I didn't know," Ginny murmured.

"Haley's a kid but she wants to believe otherwise, so please stop encouraging her."

He walked off to where Ms. Belle stood with Georgie, who was stuffing gummie worms into his mouth. Juice ran down his chin. He hurried back to the table, grabbed napkins and wiped his face.

"How's Haley?" Maddie asked.

"She has a nervous stomach and I'm sure she's throwing up."

"Oh, my. That's why she's so thin."

"Haley sick," Georgie muttered, seeming very comfortable in Ms. Belle's arms.

He glanced toward the restroom. "I better check on her. Take care of Georgie and please keep an eye on Ginny. Do not let her sneak out."

"I won't."

Georgie grinned, back to his old self. "I'm good, Daddy."

"I see you are." Ms. Belle had gummie worm juice on her Carhartt jacket. Without thinking, he rubbed it with a napkin. The spot was right over her breast, and he felt that softness, that lure of something… He pulled away and headed to the counter, his emotions slipping and sliding like a bar of soap on a tiled floor. But he reined them in quickly.

"My daughter is in the bathroom," he said to the young boy at the counter. "She's sick and I'm going in to check on her."

"What? Oh. Okay, I guess."

"Could you make sure no one comes in?"

"I don't know. Like, I…"

"I'll stand watch," Maddie offered.

"Okay. Cool," the clerk replied.

Walker headed toward the small hallway that led to the restroom. There wasn't a door, just another hallway that angled into the room. Walker then tapped on the wall and called out, waiting in case someone was in there besides Haley. No one answered, so he went in. The stench reached him, but that wasn't keeping him out. Haley was sitting on the floor in a stall with the door closed.

"Haley, it's Daddy."

"Go away and leave me alone."

"That's not happening, sweetheart. Open the door."

"No. Leave me alone."

"Haley…"

"No. I want to die, so leave me alone."

He looked around and went over his options. He had to get inside and there was only one way to do that. Tight places were nothing new to him. He stepped up on the sink and then swung himself over the top of the stall and into it.

"What are you doing?" Haley's eyes looked huge in her pale face.

"You wouldn't open the door so I had to come in."

"Why can't you just leave me alone?" She buried her face on her knees.

The stall was small and he had a hard time just turning around, but he managed to ease to the floor beside her.

"What did your aunt say?" His knees pushed toward his face in the cramped space, but he tried to be the father he should be. The father he should have been years ago.

"She doesn't want me. Nobody wants me."

"I want you."

"You don't have a choice."

"Sure I do." He tried to get comfortable but found that impossible. "I could have walked away just like your mother. You and Georgie would have gone into the system, into foster care."

She raised her head. "Really?"

"Really."

Her face puckered. "Why won't you tell me where Mama is?" Tears streamed down her face and his heart contracted.

"Sweetheart, I've told you all I know. Honest. Let's go home and we'll talk. I'll try to answer all your questions."

She sniffed and stood, wiping at her eyes with the sleeve of her knit top.

He pushed to his feet as best as he could. The stall wasn't made for a big man. No matter how many ways he turned they couldn't open the door.

"We have a problem."

"You're not supposed to be in here," Haley said, and her eyes weren't so sad. "You're a man and you're too big."

"I have a plan." He smiled at her. "I'll stand on the toilet and that way you can open the door."

He placed one foot on the seat and hopped up.

Haley glanced up at him. "You look silly."

"I feel silly. Open the door so we can get out of here."

As she pulled on the door he heard a slight giggle. Maybe there was hope for them. God, he hoped so.

Outside the restroom, Maddie, Georgie and Ginny waited. Ginny ran to Haley.

"Are you okay?"

"Yeah." Haley hung her head.

"Get your coats," Walker said. "We're going to High Cotton."

"Mr. Walker, please," Ginny begged, "let me go to Temple. I can stay with a friend. Don't make me go back to that awful place."

"You're a minor. I have to take you home." He tried to remain strong. "And after what you did, you don't deserve favors." He avoided looking at Ms. Belle because he knew what he'd see.

"Yes, sir," Ginny answered, her voice subdued. She turned toward the table to get her coat. Haley followed. Georgie wiggled from Ms. Belle's arms to get his.

That left him and Ms. Belle alone.

She placed a hand on his arm and he froze. Damn, he didn't want her to touch him. He couldn't think straight when she did that. No way was she going to change his mind.

"Think about what she has to go back to."

"I told you from the start I wasn't inclined to be lenient with her. She put my kids in danger."

"She's just a teenager trying to survive. She needs understanding."

"Listen, we're not going to agree on this. Until you have children, you won't understand my point of view."

She tensed and he sensed something was wrong. Her blue eyes darkened. "I don't have to be a mother to know when a child needs help instead of brute force."

He frowned. "Brute force? I'm not using brute force on anyone."

"No, you're just a brute." With that declaration, she marched off to where the kids stood waiting.

Where the hell did that come from? He was doing the right thing. Following the law. Then why did he feel like the brute she'd called him?

CHAPTER EIGHT

MADDIE GOT INTO THE CAR seething. Why did he have to be so structured, so by-the-book? She clasped her hands and took a calming breath.

While Walker had been in the bathroom with Haley, she'd talked to Ginny and the girl had apologized, even offered to give back what she had left of the money. She wanted to keep her baby, and Maddie didn't see anything wrong with that.

Evidently Walker did. Maybe she should try to see his point of view. No. Why did she always do that? Look for the best in people. This time he was wrong, and wrong was wrong no matter how you looked at it. She was sticking to her point of view. But…no, don't do it. Walker loved his kids and… She pulled her jacket tight around her.

"Are you cold?" Walker asked, backing out of the station and turning onto the highway.

"No. I'm fine."

"I can turn up the heat."

She looked at him. "I think the heat's already turned up."

"Yeah." He didn't miss her meaning as that gorgeous ghost of a smile visited his lips. "You may not believe it, but I'm doing the right thing."

Before she could reply, Georgie said from the backseat, "I'm mad at you, Haley."

"I know," Haley replied.

"I'm staying with Daddy."

There was a long pause and then Haley said, "Me, too."

"Maybe some good has come out of this awful night," Walker whispered to her.

She hoped it had, but she couldn't stop thinking about Ginny and her life. And the life of her baby.

"Oh, oh, oooh…"

Maddie turned to Ginny in the backseat. "What's wrong?"

"My stomach is cramping."

"Are you having contractions?"

"I don't know. I…oh…oh…it hurts."

"It's wet everywhere," Haley squealed.

"Her water has broken," Maddie said to Walker. "You have to stop."

"Dammit." He pulled over to the side of the road and Maddie jumped out to check Ginny.

From the car light she could see Ginny slumped down in the seat, her hand on her stomach and her face etched in pain. "Help me, Ms. Belle, please."

Maddie stroked back a strand of Ginny's hair. "Just relax and take deep breaths. We need to get you to a hospital."

"Daddy, please help Ginny," Haley yelled.

"Daddy, I 'cared," Georgie piped up.

Walker stuck his head in from behind Maddie. "Calm down, everybody."

His face was an inch from hers, his hat brushed her hair and a tangy masculine scent filled her nostrils. Her stomach fluttered with awareness—a welcome, stimulating awareness of the opposite sex. She turned her head, as did he, and their lips were inches apart. For a man, he had beautiful lips, not thin like most men's. His lower lip was full and inviting, and she wondered what it would be like to kiss him.

"What do you think?"

His breath fanned her face, and she soaked it up like a starved woman needing a man. In a split second reality hit her in the gut like a balled fist. What had he said? Oh… "We…we need to get her to a hospital."

"Ginny gets her wish, then. Temple would have a hospital and better facilities than the small towns."

Maddie stroked Ginny's hair again. "Keep taking deep breaths and stay calm. We're going to Temple."

"Thank…thank you…Ms. Belle."

Maddie and Walker jumped into the front seat and Walker turned the car around, heading for Temple. He reached for his cell and called information for the Scott and White Hospital. He then phoned the hospital and informed them they were coming.

As they reached Texas 36, Ginny began to scream. Gut-wrenching sounds bounced off the interior of the car.

"Ms. Belle, please…please help me. It hurts."

"I know. Just hang on."

Haley and Georgie were quiet and pale.

Suddenly, a bloodcurdling scream erupted. "Something's…happening. The…baby…is coming."

"You just think it is," Walker told Ginny. "We'll be there soon."

Another nerve-shattering scream. Maddie couldn't stand it anymore. "Pull over. We have to help her."

Walker swerved into the ditch and stopped. Maddie stepped out into the cold winter night. The moon was full and bathed them in a warm glow. Walker got his kids out and Ginny lay down on the seat.

"Oh, no. It's coming. I feel it," Ginny said.

"Do you know anything about delivering babies?" Walker asked from behind her.

"Absolutely nothing. I'm scared for her."

"There are blankets in the trunk. Get them and wrap my kids up so they're warm and keep them far away. I'll need a blanket and I'll call the hospital for instructions."

Maddie was on autopilot, taking the keys, opening the truck and searching for blankets. She carried one to Walker and hurried to Haley and Georgie, who were standing in the dried grass of the ditch, looking scared. She guided them some distance away, sat them down and wrapped a blanket snugly around their cold bodies.

"Stay right here. I'm going to check on Ginny."

"Ms. Belle. Is…is…" Haley was trembling, so she couldn't get the words out.

Maddie tucked the blanket tighter. "She's having the baby. Take care of your brother. I'll be right back."

As she reached the car, she heard Ginny screaming, "I want Ms. Belle."

"Madison," Walker shouted.

Finally, he knew her name.

She stuck her head in. "What can I do?"

Walker was kneeling on the edge of the seat and Ginny was sprawled, her legs apart with a blanket beneath her.

"She has to take off her jeans and panties and she won't do it."

"I want Ms. Belle."

Maddie crawled in on the floorboard. "Come on, Ginny. We have to remove your clothes."

"It's embarrassing and I…this can't be happening."

"Well, it is, and Walker is here to help you. Let's get rid of your jeans."

Her denim jeans were wet, and she and Walker tugged and pulled until they were off. The panties were next. Maddie removed the Windbreaker, but let Ginny keep on her T-shirt.

"It's dark so don't even think about it." Maddie tried to make Ginny feel comfortable. "Just concentrate on the baby."

Walker had the cell to his ear. "The ambulance is on the way."

"Stay with me, please, Ms. Belle." A scream followed the words as Ginny arched her back.

Maddie stroked Ginny's face. "I will." She glanced at Walker through the darkness. "Can you see?"

"Just enough. I see the head," he shouted. "Damn. This baby is coming—now."

"Help me. I can't do this."

"Stay calm." Maddie gripped Ginny's hand.

"I can't…it's too painful. Do something."

"Ginny, listen to me. This is part of being pregnant, so grit your teeth and bear it. It's time to grow up. You're fixing to be a mother."

A tear slipped from Ginny's eye as cars whizzed by on the highway and lights flashed inside every now and then, offering some illumination. Ginny continued to scream and push.

"Come on, just one more push and the baby will be here. Come on. You can do it." Walker kept coaxing as he talked to the person on the phone.

Ginny groaned and moaned and Maddie's hand grew numb from the girl's grip.

"It's coming, coming and…and there it is," Walker said as he reached for the baby as it slid out.

"It's a girl. I need something to wrap her in."

Maddie grabbed Ginny's backpack from the floor and pulled out a small multicolored blanket.

"That's for the baby," Ginny said, her voice weak.

Walker gently wrapped the bloodied baby, the umbilical cord still attached, and placed her on Ginny's chest. A siren echoed in the distance.

"She's beautiful," Maddie said, and used a blouse to mop Ginny's forehead.

"I have a baby and…"

The lights of the ambulance flashed on the car, and in a second several paramedics gathered round. Maddie slid out and her legs buckled. Walker caught her and she leaned on him.

"The baby's not crying," she whispered for his ears only.

"I know. The medic is clearing her throat."

She reached for Walker's hand and he gripped it with cold, steellike fingers. Suddenly a wail pierced the silence.

"She's okay," Maddie cried, and reached up and hugged Walker. Everything faded away as the night wrapped around them and he hugged her back. His hard, muscled body pressed into her and she soaked up every nuance of this strong man.

"Daddy."

Walker let her go as Haley walked up carrying a sleeping Georgie.

He gathered his son into his arms. "Everything's okay, sweetheart. Ginny had the baby and the ambulance is taking her to Temple. You can say goodbye."

Haley walked to the stretcher. "Bye," she said in a sad tone, staring at the baby in Ginny's arms.

"Bye, Haley, Georgie, Mr. Walker and Ms. Belle. Thank you."

"We have to go," the paramedic said.

They rolled the stretcher into the ambulance, and with lights flashing and siren blaring, they sped away.

Silence replaced the sirens. Cars kept whizzing by, but they hardly noticed. They were spellbound by the events of the night—the birth of a new life.

"Time to go home," Walker finally said. "We have to sit in the front. The backseat is a mess."

Haley crawled in and Walker placed Georgie in her arms.

Maddie hesitated. Oh, she hated this part of her nature. She just couldn't walk away and leave Ginny alone. And Haley needed to see her friend was fine. How did she get that across to Walker?

She moved to where he was standing at the back of the car. "Don't you think it would be best to go to Temple to check on Ginny?"

"No." He swiped his hat from the ground. "She has friends and I'm sure she will call them. I'm taking my kids home and putting them to bed. They've been through enough tonight."

"But Haley needs to see her friend is okay."

"Haley needs to go home."

"You know, sometimes you can be a stubborn ass— an unfeeling stubborn ass."

"Listen, you've been on my case since I've met you. I said something about you looking as young as my daughter and you got your nose bent out of joint. Hell, I thought women wanted to look young."

"Maybe I didn't want you to see me as a girl, but as a woman." Cheeks flaming, she marched to the car and squeezed in beside Haley and Georgie, which was a feat, since they had to sit on one seat.

Walker jammed his hat on his head. What the hell did *that* mean? He didn't care. He just wanted to take his kids home.

The lady was starting to get to him. Why couldn't she see that the world wasn't all lily-white? Oh, no, everything to her had to have a happy ending. Ginny Grubbs was another statistic of teenage pregnancy. There was no happy ending for her. She would now become dependent on the government for her livelihood and she would milk it for all it's worth. That's the way it worked for girls like Ginny.

God, when did he get so cynical, stubborn and narrow-minded? Maybe when Ms. Belle made him so aware of his faults.

See her as a woman? How else would he see her?

He got into the car. Ms. Belle was holding Georgie and he was asleep in her arms. Haley leaned into her, almost asleep. It was against the law for them to ride like that and he worried about their safety.

"Can you buckle up, please?"

She shot him a thousand-watt glare. "Are you serious?"

"Yes."

"Good grief." She struggled with the belt, and he reached over and looped it around all three of them. The glare didn't change. He was getting sunburned.

His hand hovered over the ignition. God help him. No! No! But he was powerless to stop the words forming in his throat. "Haley, would you like to go see Ginny?"

She lifted her head. "Oh, Daddy, could we?" The excitement in her voice told its own story. Maddie was right. He was wrong. Glancing at her, he caught that gleam in her eyes.

Dammit. She knew.

GEORGIE WAS OUT FOR THE NIGHT, so Walker carried him as they went into the emergency room. In the bright light he could see that he and Maddie had blood all over them. He'd worry about that later. Maddie sat with the kids while he went to check on Ginny and to wash his hands. He was told Ginny was being attended to, so he went to wait with Maddie and the kids.

As he relayed the message to Maddie, he gathered his son into his arms. Taking a seat, he added, "I really need to get my kids to bed."

"Just let Haley see her and then we'll go."

He looked at her and quickly glanced away. She was so damn sincere that she was making inroads into a resolve he'd mastered over the years—don't get emotionally involved.

"Mr. Walker." A nurse appeared with a clipboard in her hand.

"That's me," he said, and the nurse came over.

"Are you the responsible party for Ginny Grubbs?"

"No, I'm not. She just happened to be in my car when she gave birth. She's a friend of my daughter's."

"Oh." She scribbled something on the board. "She has no insurance and we can't keep her."

"That's insane. She just gave birth." Maddie was on her feet, ready for battle. Walker felt sorry for the nurse.

"I'm sorry, but that's our policy. We'll keep her overnight, but she has to leave in the morning."

"Surely there are programs to help her."

"I'll notify Child Protective Services. That's all I

can do." The nurse hurried away before Maddie could get in another round.

"That's ludicrous."

"That's the real world," Walker told her. He stood. "CPS will handle it. Now, let's go home."

Maddie placed her hands on her hips. "You're not serious."

"Yes. I am."

"Well, tough. We're not going home. Ginny needs our help and we're going to give it to her."

"Now…"

"We are." Her blue eyes bored into him like a chisel, chipping away at his steely resolve.

"Daddy, please," Haley begged.

Now he had both of them on his case. This just wasn't his night.

"I'm sure you know people you can call who can place her somewhere. There are programs in Philly and there has to be some in Texas." Maddie kept up the pressure. As a man who always knew when he was beaten, he gave in.

"I'll make some calls, but I have to get Georgie to bed first."

"I'll hold him," Maddie offered.

"We'll get a motel room for the night, but in the morning, after we get Ginny settled, we're going home. Am I clear?"

She had the nerve to smile. "As a bell."

He lifted his eyebrow at that.

WALKER FOUND A MOTEL not far from the hospital. He paid for two connecting rooms. Maddie and Haley had one and he and Georgie took the other. He removed

Georgie's clothes, leaving on his underwear and T-shirt, and tucked him under the covers.

Haley came into his room. "Daddy."

"What, sweetheart?"

"I'm sorry."

He turned to her. "I know. We'll talk when we get home. Get some sleep. I'm not mad at you."

Her face lit up. "Night."

He wanted to hold her and reassure her, but he refrained. Tonight was a step forward. They were making progress.

He took a quick shower, then dressed in his same clothes, but he felt less grimy. He had to get the car cleaned before morning. Slipping on his boots, he glanced at Georgie and saw he was out.

He tapped on the connecting door. No response. He opened it slightly and peered in. Haley was asleep in the bed. Where was Maddie? He saw the light beneath the bathroom door and knocked lightly. No response. He waited and knocked again. Still nothing. Had she fallen asleep in the tub or something?

Opening the door, he just stared. She stood there naked, towel-drying her hair. Her body was smooth, curvy and better than anything he'd ever seen in the Victoria's Secret catalogs Trisha had around the house.

At that moment, she glanced up. Her face was suffused with color. "Oh, oh…" She danced around, trying to arrange the towel in front of her. "What are you doing?"

"I…I…" he stammered, feeling like a fool. "I knocked, but you didn't answer. I wanted to tell you I'm going to get the car cleaned out. Please watch the kids."

"Oh…oh. Okay." She clutched the towel tighter.

But he didn't move. He couldn't stop staring at her.

With her disheveled hair she looked sexy, beguiling, alluring, and his body was reacting accordingly.

"You're staring," she said in a breathless voice.

"It's hard not to."

"Try."

"I'd rather not." He knew he was grinning.

She took a couple of steps and slammed the door in his face. It was as effective as an icy-cold shower.

But he certainly saw her as a woman.

CHAPTER NINE

MADDIE SANK TO THE FLOOR and threw the towel over her head, letting her body heat evaporate from Walker's gaze. That might take a while, though. She was sure her skin was pink with embarrassment. But she wasn't looking. The tingles shooting through her told her enough.

She liked the way his eyes turned black as he gazed at her body. If she was a bad girl, she would have pulled him into the bathroom instead of closing the door. They could have steamed up the mirror with hot, passionate kisses and maybe more. Cait would have. Sky wouldn't have even hesitated. Maybe she was Betty Crocker sweet as her sisters called her.

Being bad required a lot more experience than she had. She removed the towel and blew out a breath. Her Christian upbringing was really ingrained in her. Maybe being bad wasn't in her. But when Walker looked at her, she felt more than bad. She felt wanton.

Pushing to her feet, she reached for her panties and put them on. Her T-shirt was all she had to sleep in, so she slipped it over her head and walked into the bedroom.

Haley was asleep. She tiptoed in to check on Georgie. He was, too. It had been a rough night for all of them. Crawling beneath the covers, she got comfy, but all she could see and feel were dark caramel eyes.

Haley stirred. "Ms. Belle?"

"Yes."

"Is Ginny going to get to keep her baby?"

She turned to face the girl. "I really hope so."

"But…"

"Don't worry. In the morning we'll see what we can do for Ginny."

"Ms. Belle…"

"Please, call me Maddie."

"Okay, Maddie. Thank you for standing up to Daddy. Nobody does that. He's like Rambo."

"He's tough, but I'm tough, too."

"Yeah." Haley curled into a ball. "Women can be tough."

"Yes, but don't expect me to leap tall buildings in a single bound."

Haley giggled. "Just Daddy."

"Mmm."

Haley drifted off and Maddie stared at the ceiling for a long time. What was she doing here instead of home running High Five? Darn! Darn! She'd forgotten to call Cait.

She slipped from the bed, picked up her purse and went into the bathroom. The call was short. She just wanted Cait to know what had happened and that she'd be home tomorrow. From Cait's response, she got the impression Cait thought she'd lost her mind.

Maybe she had.

Or maybe she'd stepped out of that predictable mode and was taking chances. Maybe even being a little bad.

She could only hope. A smile played across her lips as she tiptoed to the bed. Closing her eyes, she saw a ghost of a smile and passionate caramel eyes. Sleep had never been this good.

Two hours later Walker was back. Everyone was asleep and he was dog tired. He felt as if he'd been on an all-night stakeout. One glance at Ms. Belle's blond hair against the pillow revived him instantly.

How could one woman turn his whole life upside down and sideways? He'd been out of the dating game too long. But back then women like her weren't on his radar screen. She was sweet, nice and known as a good girl. Girls like her made life a living hell for guys like him.

Maybe that's why he fell for Trisha. They understood each other and wanted the same things. Or so he'd thought. All the times he'd been away from home, he'd remained faithful to her. He didn't do the cheating thing. Obviously she didn't have the same principles.

Looking back, he could see they'd fallen out of love a long time ago. He enjoyed law enforcement. She hated it and bitched all the time. That was the beginning of the deterioration of their relationship. She wanted him to be a nine-to-five man in an office. He couldn't handle that. He liked action.

His unwillingness to give in had been the final straw. A gulf had formed between them, but they still stayed together—for the kids. And that turned into a disaster.

Now he was paying for his selfishness. His kids were, too. Damn, it sucked that he'd failed as a father and as a husband.

He stared at Ms. Belle a moment longer before going back to his room. The sooner he returned her to High Five, the better. She made him forget rules and principles. She just made him want her. And that wasn't happening. He was thinking about his kids this time and not himself.

As he eased in beside Georgie and closed his eyes, all he could see was her nude body. This was not going to be a good night.

WHEN MADDIE WOKE UP, everything was quiet. Traffic hummed outside and daybreak wasn't far away. Had Walker come back? She hadn't heard him.

She slipped out of bed and made her way quietly to the other room. His bathroom light was on, so she could see. She stopped short in the doorway.

Walker was on his cell, talking, with his shirt opened and his jeans unbuttoned. His boots sat by the bed. Not an ounce of flab was visible on his broad chest. Tiny swirls of brown hairs arrowed into his jeans. Her stomach fluttered uncontrollably and she started to back out.

He noticed her and clicked off. Their eyes met, and then he glanced from her feet to her legs, then to her hips and finally up to her breasts beneath the T-shirt.

Self-consciously, she tugged the shirt lower. "You're staring."

His eyebrow lifted. "So were you."

She felt a flush as it stained her cheeks.

"Daddy," Georgie murmured sleepily.

Walker turned to his son and gathered him out of the bed. Georgie rubbed his eyes and looked around the room.

"Where are we?"

"In a motel," Walker told him. "Ginny had her baby, and this morning we're going to go see her and then go home." His eyes dared her to dispute that.

"Oh." Georgie twisted his hands and then looked at her. "Ms. Belle's got no clothes on."

"We were just talking about that," Walker said with a smirk.

"I'm just…going…to…change…" Face red, she backed away.

"I put toothpaste, deodorant and other things you might need in your bathroom," Walker called.

"Thanks."

Maddie quickly dressed before she made a complete fool of herself. She was grateful for the toothpaste and hairbrush. Walker could really be thoughtful. As she brushed her hair, she wondered what had happened between him and his ex. But that was really none of her business, as she was sure he would tell her.

Thirty minutes later, they sat in a diner eating breakfast. Since they hadn't eaten the night before, they were hungry. They all had pancakes and sausages except Walker. He had eggs and bacon.

Haley picked at hers.

Walker watched his daughter. "Sweetheart, you can eat pancakes. They don't upset your stomach."

"I'm not hungry." She laid her fork down.

"Sweetheart, please eat."

Maddie's heart twisted at the pain in his voice. It was obvious he didn't know how to help his daughter.

She drew upon her time at the hospital. Children were all different, but usually they had something that sparked their interest. Haley's was Ginny keeping her baby.

Leaning over, she whispered in Haley's ear, "If you eat, I'll kick Rambo's butt today."

Haley smiled—a big smile—and picked up her fork.

Walker frowned. "What did you tell her?"

Maddie wagged a finger at him. "Oh, no. That's our secret, right, Haley?"

"Right." Haley stuffed a bite of pancake into her mouth.

Georgie had syrup running down his chin, and Walker had to attend to him. He didn't ask again, but she caught him staring at her a time or two.

After breakfast, they made their way to the hospital. Georgie ran ahead and Haley hurried to catch him.

"Did you find out about any programs that might help Ginny?"

"Yes, Ms. Belle…"

"Maddie, please. When you've seen someone naked, you have to call them by their first name. It's a rule, and you're big on rules."

"Didn't know that." She heard a smile in his voice.

"It's a fact."

Haley held the door open and they walked through to the hospital.

"Well, Maddie, I talked to an old friend in Houston, a CPS worker. She contacted someone here and we're supposed to meet her in the lobby at nine."

"That's wonderful." She couldn't hide her joy.

"You better wait until you hear what she has to say. Usually these homes have a long waiting list."

"But you can pull some strings?"

"Haley," Walker called and the girl ran back. "There's a fish tank around the corner. Take Georgie there while we talk to the CPS lady and don't let him get away."

"I won't, Daddy."

"You didn't answer my question."

Walker glanced at his watch. "Let's sit over here. It's almost nine."

They sat by windows looking out to the parking lot. The lobby was almost empty, just people hurrying to make their appointments.

She placed her purse on the floor. The temperature was in the high sixties today, so she didn't wear her jacket. It was stained, anyway.

"I can't pull strings. We'll just have to wait and see what the woman says."

"Would you if you could?"

He adjusted his hat. "That might take a bribe."

"Like what?"

"Like another preview in nothing but a towel." He cocked an eyebrow, the gesture loaded with meaning.

She slapped his arm. "Don't be ridiculous."

"I'm not," he said, deadpan.

"First of all, you should apologize for invading my privacy."

"I'd be lying if I said I was sorry."

She shook her head. "You're hopeless."

"No. Just haven't seen a naked woman in a while." His lips quivered with amusement.

"Will you stop. I was embarrassed."

"I know. You blush beautifully."

She settled back in her chair before she blushed again. It was easy to talk to him and her embarrassment soon left.

A tall, thin woman carrying a briefcase walked up. "Mr. Walker?"

"Yes, ma'am." Walker stood and shook the woman's hand. "And this is Madison Belle."

"I'm Reba Sims. Jennifer Haver phoned about a girl—" she looked down at a notebook in her hand "—Ginny Grubbs."

"Yes. She's sixteen and had a baby last night in the back of my car."

Ms. Sims took a seat, juggling purse, briefcase and notebook. They sat, too, one on each side of the woman.

"Are you related to the girl?"

"No, she's a friend of my daughter."

"Where're her parents?"

"In High Cotton, and they've basically washed their hands of her. Her father wants to give the baby away, and I'm guessing he's hoping to receive some compensation for that. Ginny wants her baby."

"I see." Ms. Sims scribbled notes.

Maddie couldn't stay quiet. "They live in deplorable conditions, and Ginny's just trying to get out and keep her child."

Ms. Sims straightened her glasses. "Are you related to her?"

"No. She's all alone."

"I oversee a home for unwed mothers outside of Round Rock. We take mothers with babies, too, but we don't have any vacancies. We screen these girls to see if they will fit into our program."

"What type of program is it?"

"We offer the girls a home and a job. We have a restaurant and a laundry where the girls work. They have to get assistance from the government, which goes to the home. We help them get their GED and teach them a skill so they can support themselves and their child. We have very strict rules."

"What kind of rules?" Maddie asked.

"No drugs, no drinking, no smoking, no dating. Most of all, good behavior. The girls are there to learn to take care of themselves. After six months we reevaluate them to see if they're ready to leave."

"How long can they stay?"

"Depends on their age. We have a fourteen-year-old who's been with us three years. She'll turn eighteen soon and she's ready for the outside world."

"Oh, my." Maddie couldn't even fathom a fourteen-year-old having a child, but she had seen it in Philly.

"Ginny needs a place now, Ms. Sims," Walker said.

"That's out of the question. We don't have room, and the paperwork will take some time. We have to know she's sincere and willing to work. Most girls don't like that and they leave quickly."

"Ginny'll do anything to keep her baby," Maddie assured her.

"I wish I could help, but I can't."

Walker rubbed his hands together. "Ms. Sims, why are you here if there's not the slightest possibility Ginny can get in?"

"I thought you might want to put her on the waiting list."

"But didn't Jennifer tell you we need something now?"

"Yes." Ms Sims fiddled with the notepad.

Walker mouthed "money" behind the woman's back.

Money? The woman wanted money? Everything in Maddie protested that.

She cleared her throat. "Ms. Sims, how does one get in immediately? And be honest."

"We have a very good reputation. That's why our list is so long. We make an exception if a donation is made. The economy is so bad, and we're struggling to help these girls and keep the home open."

"Oh."

"Why don't *you* take the young girl in?" Ms. Sims asked Maddie.

"I live in Philadelphia and I'm only here for a short while. Ginny needs a stable home."

Walker pulled a check from his wallet. "Do you have a pen?" he asked Ms. Sims.

She dug in her purse and handed him one.

What was he doing? Was he...?

He filled in the check and handed it to the woman. "Will this get Ginny a room?"

Maddie glanced over the woman's shoulder at the check. Five thousand dollars!

"Yes, sir. This will get Ginny a room, but we still have to do the paperwork."

"I'm sure you can breeze through that—by noon."

"Yes, sir. I'll go up and visit with the young lady now."

Ms. Sims gathered her things.

"Wait a minute." Maddie wasn't satisfied. This just seemed unethical and underhanded. "If you have no vacancies, where will you put Ginny?"

"I live on the premises and have a two-bedroom apartment. Ginny will have my spare room until a room on the floor becomes available."

"Oh." Maybe the woman was sincere and cared about the girls.

"Ms. Sims," Walker said. "Jennifer said this place is aboveboard and I'm taking her word on that, but I will be visiting and it had better live up to its reputation or I will close it down."

"You can visit anytime and see the good work we do. I apologize for taking the money, but I'll do just about anything to see these girls get help." She paused for a second. "I was once one of them." She strolled off down the hall.

Walker and Maddie stared at each other. She smiled. "You're just a softie in a big old wolf's clothing." She tapped her cheek with her forefinger. "Too bad I don't have a towel."

AT ONE O'CLOCK THE PAPERWORK was finalized and Ginny and baby were ready to go. The nurse pushed Ginny's wheelchair and they followed it out of the hospital to Ms. Sims's car.

Walker kept thinking he'd lost his mind. What had possessed him to give that much money to ensure Ginny a spot? For his daughter. This was a step in rebuilding their relationship. And, of course, Maddie had a lot to do with it, too. Maybe some of her good was rubbing off on him. Or maybe *she* was rubbing off on him.

CHAPTER TEN

GEORGIE CHATTERED MOST OF THE WAY home. He was mad at Haley, particularly because she'd forgotten his stuffed Curious George when they'd run away, and he wanted her to know it.

"George misses me," he told her. "I'm not going with you anymore."

"You've said that about ten times, Georgie." Haley was getting angry.

"You bad," Georgie kept on.

Maddie waited for Walker to put a stop to the bickering, but he didn't.

"But I love you, Georgie," Haley said, a slight quiver in her voice.

"I love you, too."

Then they were hugging.

Walker glanced at her. "That's the way they fight. The *L* word melts Georgie like a Popsicle in the Texas sun."

Was Walker the same way?

Maddie turned toward the backseat. Haley had her arm around Georgie and her head rested on his shoulder. They were drifting off to sleep.

"They're worn out," she said.

"Mmm. This has been tiring for all of us."

Walker turned off Texas 36 and Maddie just had

to ask, "Why did you pay the money to get Ginny in the home?"

"If I hadn't, I would have had to bring her back to High Cotton and Earl. That baby deserves better than that."

"Mr. Go-by-the-Book relented and did a nice thing. It made me very happy."

He looked at her, a gleam in his eyes. "For five thousand I get to see the towel thing how many times? Quite a number by my calculations."

"There's not going to be a *towel thing* again." She ruined the stern declaration by smiling.

"A pity." His hands tightened on the steering wheel. "But you're right. A woman who looks at the world through rose-colored glasses is not my type."

"I do not."

His eyes opened wide in dispute.

"Oh, okay, maybe a little."

"A lot. No one else would have given Ginny Grubbs a second chance. She tricked you, lied to you, and still you fought for her."

"I want that baby to have the best start possible."

"Jennifer said the rules are strict, and if the girls break one, they're gone. The home is only for girls who want help."

"Ginny will behave. She won't break the rules."

"You hardly know her."

"It's something I feel." Maddie stared at the cars whipping by on the sunny afternoon as they traveled toward home.

"Mmm" was his response.

They didn't say anything for a couple of miles. She kept thinking about what he'd said—*not my type.* Who was his type? Don't go there, she told herself. It was nice flirting with him, but her life was very precarious. If the cancer came back…

"How did you get Haley to eat her pancakes?" he asked, breaking into her haunting thoughts.

"Oh, that was easy. The night before she thanked me for standing up to you. She said you're like Rambo and no one does that."

He moved restlessly. "She thinks I'm a troubled man?"

"I believe she thinks you're strong and don't back down from anything."

"Mmm." His brow creased in thought.

"Haley was worried about Ginny, so I told her if she ate I would kick Rambo's butt to ensure Ginny kept her baby."

He grunted, but his forehead relaxed.

"Will Haley be okay?"

"I don't know. I'm hoping she'll trust me and settle down."

"Have you taken her to a doctor for her nervous stomach?"

"Yes, numerous times. The doctors have run every test imaginable, and they've concluded it's from stress. When she gets upset, it's worse. We watch her diet closely. Spicy and acidic foods make it worse, too. She can tolerate meat if it's not real greasy. Since the divorce she seems to be wasting away in front of my eyes. Most everything she eats comes back up."

"Then you have to find a way to keep her stress-free."

"Don't you think I've tried?" he snapped, and she knew Haley's problem was a touchy subject. His hands tightened again on the steering wheel. "Sometimes life isn't easy."

"I'm aware of that."

He glanced at her. "It's well known that Dane Belle spoiled his beautiful daughters. Even though your parents were divorced, I doubt if there was anything in life you wanted that you didn't get."

Except one thing.

A huge pain balled up like a fist in her stomach. She drew in a deep breath and looked up. They were crossing the cattle guard to High Five.

"You don't know me well enough to say that."

"No, I don't," he admitted. "But my daughter is my business."

"You've mentioned that a time or two."

He pulled into the driveway at the house and she reached for her purse. "We're ending this trip just like we started."

"How's that?"

"You being an ass and me wanting to smack you." On that, she opened her door and glanced in the backseat. "Bye, Haley, Georgie."

Georgie blinked and looked around. "I wanna a cookie." Evidently he remembered the last time he'd been here.

"We have cookies at home, son," Walker replied.

She closed the door, walked toward the house and forced herself not to look back. Goodbye to you, too, Mr. Know-Everything Walker.

You don't know me.

As the car drove away, she stopped. Her companion, loneliness, returned, filling every corner of her aching heart. For the past twenty-four hours she hadn't felt alone. She'd felt needed.

Now she was back to the same ol' same ol'.

Predictable Maddie.

MADDIE STOPPED SHORT in the parlor doorway. Cait and Gran were in tutus, very old tutus with stiff skirts that fell to midcalf. Gran had most definitely been in her trunk from Broadway again.

As a young girl, Gran's father had sent her to New York to train to become an actress and dancer. It was Gran's dream, but a man named Bartholomew Belle derailed it.

Gran gave up her dream for love, but that year in New York left an indelible impression. Play-acting was Gran's favorite pastime.

The two women were bent over, their hands on the floor, butts in the air.

Maddie cleared her throat. Cait jerked up and straightened with a wince.

"Having fun?" Maddie asked with a grin.

"Gran said we needed some exercise, and, of course, she had just the thing in her trunk for us to dance in—" she held out the stiff cotton skirt "—tutus from the forties."

"Don't make fun, baby," Gran said, still in the bent-over position. "I danced *Giselle* in this tutu."

Cait's black hair was in a bouncy ponytail. She'd had it cut after her marriage. Maddie surveyed her sister in the outdated costume.

"I need a camera."

"Oh, no, you don't." Cait grabbed her arm as she headed for the study.

"Someone help me, please," Gran called.

They both ran to her.

"I can't get up."

They each took an arm and helped her stand up straight.

"Oh, my." Gran wiped her brow. "I used to do these exercises all day."

They guided her to the sofa. "You were younger then, Gran," Cait said.

Gran's eyes narrowed. "Are you saying I'm old?"

Cait kissed her cheek. "You'll never be old. You're ageless."

"Yes, I am." Gran stroked the skirt. "Your grandfather used to love me in this. He used to love to dance, too. Sometimes we'd dance until the wee hours." She stretched out on the sofa. "I'll rest for a bit and then we'll start again."

"Gran, I have a husband waiting. I have to go."

Gran waved a hand. "Go. Go. You don't have to watch over me like a mother hen."

"Yes, Gran." Cait kissed her again. "See you tomorrow."

Cait pulled Maddie toward the stairs. "You may have to pry me out of this thing."

"Why don't you let Judd do that?"

"Not on your life." Cait opened the door to her old bedroom. "He'd laugh himself silly." Cait pulled at the tutu. "Gran must have been a tiny, tiny woman back then because this thing is cutting off circulation in some vital areas."

Maddie laughed and helped her sister out of the tutu. Cait quickly dressed in her jeans.

Slipping on her boots, Cait asked, "So what's up with you and Walker?"

"Nothing." She kept her voice neutral.

Cait stopped pulling on a boot and looked at her. "Oh, please, I'm not Gran."

"I helped him find his kids and we did. Ginny

Grubbs had her baby in the backseat of his car, so it's been a very stressful night."

"Wow. Where's Ginny now?"

"We found a home for her."

"That quick?"

"Yes. Now she has a chance and so does her baby."

Cait watched her for a moment. "You know, if you had worked it right, she would have given you that baby."

Maddie bristled. "I don't want her baby. She needs to raise her own child."

"Oh, Maddie." Cait stood and hugged her. "Any other woman would have worked it to her advantage."

"I couldn't do that."

"I know." Cait stuffed her shirt into her jeans. "You're one in a million."

Maddie thought for a minute. "Not a million, I'm sure." She was sure there were a lot of barren women in the world, but sometimes it felt as if she was the only one.

"That's not what I meant." Cait grabbed her belt. "How did you and Walker get along?"

"Like oil and water. He's so…ah…"

"That bad, huh?"

"He's strict and structured. At times I didn't know whether to smack him or to kiss him."

"When in doubt, always do the kissing."

"I'll try to remember that."

Cait reached for her purse. "Walker's a really nice man who's been dealt a bad blow."

"His ex must have been something."

"Yes. He could use a little of Maddie's magic."

She scrunched up her face. "I don't think he wants Maddie's magic."

"Oh, you can fix that. Call Sky. She'll give you some pointers."

"Ple-ease. I don't need pointers."

Cait looked up. "Okay. Now I have to run. I can't wait to see Judd. We'll probably skip supper tonight." Smiling, Cait picked up the tutu and shoved it into Maddie's hands. "Your turn."

"Oh, no..." But her sister was gone.

Maddie sank onto the bed, thinking about the towel incident. Where would she be now if she had pulled Walker into the bathroom? Probably right here wondering how she could have been so foolish. The double standard was ripping her in two.

Walker wasn't in love with her. He might desire her... She stopped her thoughts. She'd been with the man twenty-four hours and most of the time they'd argued. Springing to her feet, she marched toward the door and headed for the barn. Work would get her mind on other things.

SOLOMON MET HER BEFORE she reached the barn. She rubbed his face and led him to the corral for feed.

"Hey, you're back," Cooper said, coming out of the barn.

"Yeah. I'm just going to feed Solomon."

"I did that about an hour ago."

"Well, then. He's not getting any more." Maddie stroked the bull's neck. "How are things around here?"

"Fine. All the cows fixing to calve are in the pen. Rufus and I are checking the herds regularly. Last night the dogs got one of Mr. Carter's calves. Everyone is keeping a lookout for them."

"I guess that's all we can do."

Cooper removed his hat and gazed into the after-

noon sun. "I was thinking in January we could cul-
tivate that piece of land on the west we're not using.
Come spring we could plant corn and sell it or have it
ground for feed."

"Did you talk to Cait?"

"No. I thought it would be your decision."

"Well, dang, Coop. You see me as the boss."

He settled his hat on his head. "Yes, ma'am, I sure
do."

She leaned in and whispered, "I don't know a thing
about planting corn."

"You're in luck. I do."

"Thought you might. If it will cut back on expenses,
I'm all for it. But first, let's work up an estimate of what
it will cost versus the benefits to the ranch."

"Damn, gotta love a woman with a brain."

"Ah, shucks, you gonna make me blush."

He grinned. But Cooper's smile wasn't the one she
was beginning to love.

LATER THAT EVENING, MADDIE WAS wondering how to get
the blood off her jacket. She showed it to Etta.

"Put some hydrogen peroxide on it, and then we'll
wash it and see what happens."

Maddie checked the pockets before tossing it into
the washing machine. She found the change from the
five Walker had given her to buy Georgie candy. She'd
forgotten to give it back.

She thought about it for a minute. "Etta, I have to go
out for a little while. Can you please stay with Gran?"

"Sure. We'll watch a movie, but I'm not putting on
one of those ancient tutus. I draw the line at that."

"You don't have to worry. Gran is worn out."

She dashed upstairs, showered and changed into

clean jeans and a black pullover sweater. She had no idea why she was going to Walker's, but at least she had an excuse. One minute she was mad at him and the next…

Only one problem remained. Where did he live? That was easily solved by asking Etta. She knew everyone in High Cotton.

MADDIE HAD NO PROBLEM finding Walker's house. It was around the corner from the general store, and his car was parked in front of the garage. The house was very similar to the house at High Five—same half Doric columns with a wraparound porch. Walker's ancestors had been here forever, too.

She parked in front and went up the steps. Tentatively she knocked.

A TV blared inside, but no one came to the door at first. Then slowly it opened. Georgie stood there in his underwear and socks, Curious George clutched in one arm.

"Hi, Georgie."

He raised a hand. "Hi."

"Is your father home?"

"Yeah. Haley's locked in her room and Daddy's trying to get her out."

Before she could say anything else, Walker called, "Georgie, who's at the door?"

"Maddie. And she's got clothes on."

She was glad of the darkness. The blush that warmed her cheeks was unnoticeable. Hopefully.

Walker immediately appeared and he was frowning. "Maddie!" She thought of just backing away, but that was silly.

Luckily he noticed his son. "Georgie, where're your clothes?"

Georgie pointed to the TV where they lay in a heap.

"Why did you take them off?"

"I'm hot."

The phone rang, interrupting this discussion. Walker reached for it and she stood there feeling foolish.

Georgie looked up at her. "Wanna come in?"

She stepped in and closed the door.

"I'm gonna watch TV." Georgie went back to his spot in front of the set.

She took in the room. It was functional, Maddie noted. Besides the large TV, there was a bookshelf with an assortment of movies, a sofa, a recliner, some odd tables and an area rug covering hardwood floors. An old piano stood in one corner. No curtains, just blinds. No flowers, no frills, nothing feminine. A man's room, a man's home.

"I'll be right there," Walker said, and hung up. He ran both hands through his hair.

"Is something wrong?"

"I have to go on a call. Haley's locked in her room and I'm at a loss as to how to reach her."

Maddie sat her purse in a chair. "Go on your call. I'll watch the kids and try to get Haley out of her room. I owe you a favor."

"You'd do that for a stubborn ass?" That light in his eye was making her dizzy.

"Yes" came out all squeaky.

He reached for his hat. "I'll make it short. Georgie, Maddie's staying with you for a bit. Behave and put on your clothes."

"'Kay."

Walker paused at the door, his eyes holding hers. "This doesn't cover the bribe. That involves a towel and nothing else."

CHAPTER ELEVEN

MADDIE FELT THE WARMTH in her cheeks, and she knew why she was here. Walker irritated and annoyed her, but she was attracted to him. On their quest to find the kids, she'd seen a different side of him, a side he rarely showed: his soft, compassionate nature. It was evident in the way he loved his kids and would do anything for them, even making sure Ginny had a fair chance at life.

Of course, she might be looking at him through rose-colored glasses, as he'd accused her. But that was okay. She was stepping out of her cautious world. Predictable Maddie would not be here. Predictable Maddie did not take risks.

She noticed Georgie staring at her.

"Where's Haley's room?" she asked.

He pointed to the stairs leading to the top floor. "I show you," he said, darting for the stairs with his Curious George and a blanket in tow.

She trailed after him. With the blanket, he reminded her of Linus from the *Peanuts* cartoon. They reached the landing and Georgie pointed to a door.

Maddie tried the knob, but it was locked.

"She does that a lot," Georgie told her.

"Is she sick?"

Georgie shrugged. "She locks herself in and won't talk to Daddy."

"Oh." Even though the thought of Haley in pain was breaking her heart, she decided to give her some time.

She bent to Georgie's level. "Have you had your bath?"

He shook his head vigorously. "I don't like baths."

This stopped her, but only for a moment. "You have to get ready for bed."

"I don't like going to bed."

This wasn't going to be easy. "If you're bathed and tucked in bed, Daddy will be so happy. You want to make Daddy happy, don't you?"

"Ah…uh-huh, but you can't wash my eyes or my ears."

"Deal." Maddie suppressed a smile. "Let's get your jammies."

Thirty minutes later Georgie was bathed and in his Spider-Man pajamas. She managed to wash his ears and eyes without him really noticing.

"You bath good," he told her. "Daddy gets soap in my eyes." Evidently Walker gave an energetic bath.

Georgie yawned and his eyes fluttered. He was half asleep. She gathered him, Curious George and the blanket and headed for his room.

Pulling back the covers, she tucked him in. "Mama," he murmured, clutching his stuffed animal.

How could Walker's ex leave these precious children? She would never understand that.

She turned and saw Haley standing in the doorway. Her Hannah Montana pajamas hung on her thin body, and her long blond hair was limp around her pale face.

"I can put Georgie to bed," she said.

"He's already in bed and out for the night." Maddie glanced toward Georgie's sleeping form.

"Does he have his Curious George?"

"Yes, and his blanket." Maddie flipped off the light and they left the room.

As Maddie made to close the door, Haley said, "You have to leave it half open."

Maddie did so and they walked out into the hall. "Would you like to come downstairs for a minute?"

Haley didn't answer, but she followed Maddie to the living room. "I'm not sure what Georgie was watching but…"

"*Finding Nemo.* He loves that movie." Haley settled on the sofa. Maddie clicked off the DVD player and picked up Georgie's clothes.

Sitting by Haley, she folded them neatly in her lap, taking her time, hoping Haley would talk.

"Why would a mother leave her children?"

The words were spoken low but Maddie caught them. She juggled them in her head before answering, searching for a magic answer that would help Haley.

"I'm sure it wasn't an easy decision."

"He came to our house all the time when Daddy was gone."

"Who?"

"Tony. Mama's boyfriend. I told her I didn't like him and she got mad and… She said he was only a friend, but when Daddy was gone she'd leave us at the neighbors' and stay out all night. I wanted to tell Daddy, but I…" Tears streamed down Haley's face and she wiped them away.

Maddie gave her a minute. "You're not responsible for what your mother did."

"If I had told Daddy… I needed to tell Daddy."

"What would have happened?"

"Maybe he could have stopped her. I mean, he can do anything. Then we'd still be a family."

"Do you really believe that?"

"I want to." She hiccupped. "But…she left and didn't even say goodbye and… Georgie cried himself to sleep for two weeks."

"Did you cry, too?"

Haley twisted her hands. "Yeah. I thought it was my fault and…that's why I have to see her."

"It's not your fault," Maddie told her.

"But I made her nervous when I threw up and…and I did bad things. I…made Mama mad."

Maddie rubbed her thin arm. "Sweetie, your mother's leaving had nothing to do with what you did or didn't do."

"Aunt Doris said Mama's lost her mind and we're better off with Daddy." Haley gulped a breath. "But he doesn't want us, either. Nobody wants us." A flood of fresh tears followed that statement.

Maddie took the girl in her arms. "I don't know your father very well, but I spent twenty-four hours with a man who was worried out of his mind about his kids. Everything he did showed how much he loves you and Georgie. He even paid so Ginny could get into a decent home. He did that for you because Ginny is your friend and he wanted you to have some peace of mind."

"Daddy did that?" the girl cried into her shoulder.

"Yes. He's feeling his way on being a single father, but I know one thing—he will never leave you. He will always be here for you and Georgie. That's why he brought you home to High Cotton and took the constable's job. He may have not been there in the early years, but, sweetie, he's in your life to stay because he loves you. Please believe that."

More tears followed and Maddie just held her. Haley

seemed to carry the weight of her parents' marriage on her shoulders and Maddie's heart broke for her.

Walker was right. Maddie never had this kind of stress in her life. After the divorce, her parents got along so much so that her mother allowed her only child to spend every Christmas at High Five with her father and her sisters. That must have been a tremendous sacrifice for her mother. But Dane and Audrey always did what was best for Maddie. She never realized what a gift that was until now.

The door opened and Walker stood staring at them.

"Haley, sweetheart, what's wrong?" Worry was carved into every word.

Maddie got to her feet and relinquished her seat to Walker. He took his daughter into his arms and Haley gripped him tightly.

"I'm sorry, Daddy. I'm sorry."

Maddie picked up her purse and quietly left. Walker needed time alone with his child.

THE NEXT MORNING, MADDIE was up early, ready to get back into the swing of ranching. As she was coming down the stairs, the phone rang. She hurried to her office to get it.

"Mornin', Maddie." It was Walker, and her name never sounded so good. So sensual.

"Morning."

"You left so quickly last night I didn't get to thank you."

"You needed time with Haley."

"We had a long talk. I never dreamed she blamed herself for not telling me Trisha was seeing Tony behind my back."

"I got that impression, too. Poor kid has been carrying around a lot of guilt and making really bad decisions."

"I owe you for getting her to open up. I think we're making a turn for the better."

"I hope so. And if you ever need a sitter, just call me."

"Don't you have a ranch to run?"

"Yes, but I can take Georgie wherever I go. Just so long as he's not scared of cows or horses."

"The only thing he's afraid of is a bath. How did you get him to take one last night?"

"I asked very sweetly."

"Ah. That might work on me, too."

Her heart kicked against her ribs. "I don't know if 'sweet' works on you."

"Try it tonight."

"What?"

"I'm doing burgers on the grill. Have supper with us."

"Oh. Okay." He didn't have to ask her twice.

"See you at six. Oh, did you come for a reason last night?"

"Yes. I forgot to give you your change."

"What change?"

"From the five you gave me to buy Georgie candy."

"You can't be serious."

"It's your money."

"Just keep it."

"I'll bring it tonight."

"Fine. See you then."

Walker hung up, wondering if she was for real. It was five measly bucks. But that was Maddie. What was he doing inviting her over? He wasn't ready for a relationship. His kids needed him. A friendly thank-you was all it was.

With the most gorgeous woman he'd ever laid eyes on.

With or without her clothes.

THE TEMPERATURE DROPPED into the thirties, and Maddie froze her butt off helping Coop and Ru feed the cattle. They had to cut off the water to the well pumps so they wouldn't freeze. While they were working, Maddie kept a close eye on the woods, looking for the wild dogs. If she saw one, she didn't know what she'd do. But Coop wasn't far away.

The whole time she worked she thought of Walker and the evening. She couldn't believe how much she looked forward to it.

She had to impose upon Etta again to stay with Gran.

"Don't you worry about it," Etta said. "Dorie, Ru, Coop and I are playing Texas hold 'em tonight. So have a good time. I'll be here."

Maddie had forgotten about their weekly poker game. It was hard to imagine Gran with her Southern manners and attitudes playing poker. But Gran loved it.

Tonight she wanted to look good. No, scratch that. She wanted to look bad. Sexy and unpredictable. She took her time dressing. Since it was so cold, she wore a heavy white turtleneck sweater with black slacks and boots—not cowboy ones. These were made of soft leather and had a three-inch heel. Grabbing a black leather jacket, she was on her way.

Georgie answered the door. He was fully dressed and his hair was neatly combed. He looked so cute.

"Daddy's out back and Haley's in there." He pointed inside.

She removed her coat and followed him into the kitchen where Haley was cutting lettuce and tomatoes for hamburgers.

"Can I help?" Maddie asked.

"No. You're a guest," Walker said as he came through the back door with a pan of cooked burgers. The smell whetted her taste buds. As did the man.

For a moment she soaked up his strong, manly persona. His hair was tousled and his shirtsleeves were rolled up, revealing forearms sprinkled with dark hairs. A smoky, woodsy scent filled her nostrils. He warmed her senses by just being in the room.

She was impressed with Walker's concern for his daughter's eating habits. The French fries were baked in the oven, and he patted her hamburger with a paper towel so it wasn't greasy. Haley only ate the bun and meat with mustard and she seemed to hold it down. It was a fun, relaxing evening.

After dinner, Haley and Georgie ran to watch TV. Maddie laid her napkin on the table. "Have you talked to Ginny's parents?"

"I spoke to them today. Earl said Ginny wasn't welcome at his house anymore. Her mother seemed nervous, so when Earl stomped off I told Verna where Ginny was in case she wanted to write her. But I doubt that will ever happen."

"It's sad."

He reached across the table and lifted her chin. The gentle touch sent a warm sizzle through her. "Ginny is free and so is that baby. They don't have to live in that squalor. Isn't that what you wanted?"

"Yes." Her eyes met his. "Are you looking in on the other children?"

"You bet I am. I even called CPS, so now they're involved."

She leaned over and whispered, "You have a compassionate side."

"Don't tell anyone," he whispered back. For a moment they were lost in an attraction pulling them closer and closer. Suddenly Walker got to his feet. "Time for bath and bed, son," he called to Georgie. She slowly followed Walker into the living room.

"No. I don't wanna go to bed."

"Son…"

"I want Maddie to give me a bath. She gives good baths." Georgie ran to her, took her hand and they went upstairs. He soaked her sweater with the bathwater, but she didn't care. She wrapped him in a towel and carried him to his room. Walker helped to put his Spider-Man pajamas on and laid him in his bed.

Walker kissed him. "Night, son."

"I want Maddie to read George to me."

"Son…"

"It's okay." There was a stack of Curious George books on the nightstand. Maddie picked up *Curious George Goes to the Library*. She had barely begun George's adventure before the boy was out.

"Night," she whispered, and they walked to the door.

Outside the room, Walker said, "You're very good with kids. You should have a houseful."

She couldn't keep her expression from changing and Walker noticed.

"Did I say something wrong?"

"No, no. We better check on Haley." She hurried

down the stairs and went to the kitchen. Walker was a step behind her.

"Sweetheart, you didn't have to clean the kitchen."

"It's all done." Haley turned with a smile, and Maddie thought she was actually very pretty. Too many times sadness marred her features. "I have homework, so I better go do it." She hugged Walker. "Night, Daddy. Maddie."

"Night, sweetheart."

That left the two of them, and Maddie felt nervous and she wasn't sure why.

Maddie sat on the sofa as Walker moved the wrought-iron fireplace screen and placed another log on the burning fire. It crackled and popped and bathed the room in an effervescent glow.

A romantic glow.

Walker stoked the fire and she thought the sparks might burn his forearms.

"Do you ever wear a jacket?"

He placed the poker by the fireplace and sat by her. "Sometimes. In the marines I learned to condition myself against the elements. Mind-over-matter type of thing. But the truth is, jackets are cumbersome and I don't wear one unless it's really cold."

"Like tonight."

"Mmm."

She watched the leaping flames. "Haley seems better."

"I think she's finally realized that I do want her and I don't know where her mother is."

"That has to be hard for a young girl."

He looked at her, and her nerves crackled like the fire. "You helped her."

"I didn't do anything."

"You listened with your heart and saw all Haley's pain. You said everything she needed to hear."

"That ability comes with rose-colored glasses." She felt her mouth lift into a smile.

He smiled that gorgeous grin and her knees felt weak. They weakened more as his eyes traveled over her. "Do you know how good you look?"

"I just put on warm clothes."

"They're certainly warming me up."

She thumbed toward the fireplace. "It's the fire."

"No, I think it's blue, blue eyes, a curvy body and blond hair."

They stared at each other for a long moment. Almost in slow motion his hand circled her neck and pulled her forward. His lips touched hers tentatively at first and then the warmth of the room, the warmth of each other, engulfed them.

Her arms went around his neck and she pulled him closer, their tongues and lips kindling their own hot fire. She knew he'd kiss like this—with heart-squeezing intensity and a body-numbing wildness.

Pressing her breasts into him, she heard him groan. Or was that her? It sounded delicious, evocative. And the moment spun away into feeling, touching and mind-blowing sensations she hadn't felt in forever. Her body needed this desperately.

His hand scorched her skin beneath the sweater and her hands molded the muscles of his shoulders. God, he was strong and...

"Maddie...we...have to stop this." He spoke the words between her lips, but made no move to stop.

"Why?" The one word came out as a smoky whisper. With Victor she'd never been ready, but with Walker she knew she was.

Cupping her face, he rested his forehead against hers. "My life's a mess. I can't get involved with anyone. I have my kids to think about."

His breath was hot against her face and she reveled in it. "We're kissing. Nothing else."

"Ah, when I touch you, I want it all." He pulled away and leaned back on the sofa. "And you're not a one-night stand."

She tugged her sweater down with shaking hands. "You don't know that."

His eyes pinned her. "Oh, yes, I do. It's written right there in your beautiful blue eyes—good girl."

"Looks can be deceiving." Could she tell him her secret? Very few people knew and it wasn't an easy topic to discuss. But she wanted to be honest. She wanted him not to be afraid that she wanted more than he could give her.

"Not in this case."

She tugged her fingers through her hair, fluffing it as she searched for the right words. "I'd like to tell you something about myself."

His gaze stayed on her face and it made her feel shy. But she forced out the words. "When I applied for the job at the hospital, I had to have a physical." She had to take a breath and she was glad he didn't say anything. "They found a small tumor on my left ovary and it was malignant. I won't go into details, but they said it was stage 1a. They removed it and I went through the hell of chemo. Six months later they found a spot on my right ovary. It…it was also malignant. The cancer stage was now 1b. The doctor said they'd caught it early, but to save my life, he recommended removing the other ovary as well as the fallopian tube. There's a history of cancer on my mother's side. I didn't have much of a choice."

She looked at her linked fingers in her lap. "To save my life they took everything a woman my age values—the ability to have a child."

"Oh, Maddie. I'm so sorry." He stroked her face with the back of his hand and she felt its power.

"The cancer affected everyone around me, my mother and stepfather. My friends. I saw the worry in my mom's eyes so I held off telling my dad. But he came one day while I was having chemo and Mom told him. He…"

He reached over and touched her clasped hands and it gave her the courage to continue.

"After that, Dad flew in often and he was there when I got the news of the second cancer. I didn't want to have the surgery. My dad, who was a big risk-taker, said it wasn't the time to gamble. It was time to live. So…so…I did and I've been cancer-free for three years now. But every day I wonder what if…what if it comes back?"

"The doctors gave you a good prognosis?"

"Yes. They said I was one of the lucky ones because they caught it early. Funny, I don't feel lucky."

"You look so healthy. I would have never guessed what you've been through."

"I was thin for a long time, but Etta has been fattening me up." She tried to smile but failed.

"You look gorgeous."

Her fingers were numb from gripping them so tightly. The cancer was hard to talk about, but Walker gave her the strength to say what she wanted to—needed to.

She raised her head to look at him. All she saw in

the soft caramel eyes was concern, not pity. "I haven't been with anyone since then and I'm just…trying to rediscover all those feminine emotions I thought I'd lost."

"Oh."

"I'm attracted to you and I was acting on it. I'm not looking for a long-term commitment. I'm just looking for a decent guy to have fun with. That may make me a slut—"

He laughed out loud, interrupting her well-thought-out speech. The sound released the tension in the room and in her. "Please. Don't go overboard. You're Mary Sunshine and Mary Poppins all rolled into one."

She leaned in close. "You don't think I can be bad?"

"The thought will haunt my dreams tonight, sweet lady." He tucked her hair behind her ear. "I've been burned so badly by love I'm not sure what it is anymore, but you deserve everything it entails."

"But not with you," she added.

He kissed her lips lightly. "I was married for almost eleven years and I've been divorced for seven months. I want to grab at everything you're offering, but I have to take it slow. I don't want to hurt you."

So much for pouring out her heart. She knew when to admit defeat. At least this time. She stood and slipped into her jacket. Her hand felt the money in her pocket and she pulled it out. She placed it in his hand and then kissed his rough cheek. Her lips lingered for a moment.

"Good night," she whispered.

"Maddie…" But she was walking toward the door and she didn't stop.

Rejection hurt like hell.

CHAPTER TWELVE

WALKER HAD TO RESTRAIN himself from tearing out the door after her. But what would that accomplish? They would still have the same problem. He had to focus on his kids. And she needed someone who could give her his full attention.

Then again... No strings, no commitment. Just enjoying each other's company... He was old enough to know that was a recipe for disaster.

Maddie was an emotional, loving and compassionate woman. Why was he trying to talk himself into having an affair with her? As much as she didn't want to admit it, Maddie wasn't that type of woman.

He could still taste her on his tongue, her scent filled his senses, and her touch was like a brand. He'd remember it forever on his skin. Not only from the heat it had generated in him, but from the sheer power of her gentle fingers.

God. He dragged both hands over his face. He needed something cold. He flung open the door and a blast of frigid air almost knocked him off his feet. But it did the trick. The effects the kiss had on his body slowly eased.

He'd been too long without a woman. The last time he'd had sex was with his ex two weeks before she'd disappeared out of his life. He then went on a search mission to find a missing girl. When he'd returned,

Trisha's note was waiting for him. Her betrayal, her deceit, hit him hard, and he wasn't sure he could trust another woman again.

"Daddy."

Haley stood in the doorway in her pajamas and floppy slippers. God, she was so thin.

"Did Maddie leave?"

"Yes. She just drove away."

"She didn't say goodbye."

That was his fault. "She didn't want to disturb you. She told me to tell you bye."

Liar. Liar.

"Oh." Her face brightened. "I like Maddie. She's nice."

"Yes, she is."

Too nice for a jaded man like him.

"I hope she comes back."

God help him. He did, too. But now, that was highly unlikely.

"We'll see. Do you need an extra blanket?" He quickly changed the subject.

"No, I'm fine. Night, Daddy."

"Night, sweetheart."

She stood there, hesitating, uncertainty on her face. So many times he had tried to connect with his daughter and had failed. This time he went on a father's instinct and took her in his arms, kissing the top of her head.

She didn't resist or pull away. Her arms gripped him around his waist.

"Do you think Mama's okay?"

He swallowed. "Yes, sweetheart, and now we have to go on with our lives."

Haley pushed back, nodding her head. "I'll try." She paused. "Is it bad to keep a secret?"

Walker looked into her concerned eyes. "You had nothing to do with your mother's leaving."

"But I...I...was bad...I made her..."

He cupped her face with one hand. "You have nothing to feel guilty about."

"I should tell the truth."

"Stop worrying." He kissed her cheek. "Sweet dreams."

She walked out of the room.

He let out a long sigh and realized he was clutching something in his hand. That damn money Maddie had given him. He placed it on the mantel.

Maddie.

He'd never met anyone like her before. After what she'd been through, she hadn't lost that goodness inside her. There wasn't an ounce of resentment or bitterness in her—only a touch of sadness that she hid very well.

He remembered how she'd looked when he'd told her she was good with kids. An expression of anguish had filled her eyes. He now knew why.

He ran his hands through his hair. He had to stop thinking about her. And he had to wonder if that was even possible.

THE NEXT MORNING MADDIE hurriedly dressed and refused to think about Walker anymore. She'd thrown herself at him, offering him anything he wanted. That wasn't predictable Maddie. That was foolish Maddie.

She had to admit she'd been trying too hard, yearning for Walker's touch. Had she said she was a slut? Surely not. But she remembered saying those words, and she hadn't had a drop of wine. What had gotten into her?

Now she would back off and leave Walker and his kids alone. Maybe she could find her dignity again. She had certainly misplaced it. Besides, she had work to do, and she didn't have time to continue to make a fool of herself. Usually that was Cait's or Sky's role.

Heading for the door, she braced for a new day. Her cell buzzed. Where was it? She searched frantically until she found her purse. Looking at the caller ID, she winced.

Her mother.

She clicked on. "Hi, Mom."

"Oh, Maddie, it's so good to hear your voice. I haven't heard from you in over a week."

"Sorry. But I've been busy."

"Too busy to talk to your mother." The guilt-inducing tone was like a sharp knife slicing off a piece of her backbone.

She drew a breath. "Of course not. I'm busy working. I'm healthy and I'm happy. Isn't that what you want?"

"Yes, darling. I just miss you."

"I miss you, too."

"Victor called and asked about you."

She gripped her phone. "Tell him I'm fine."

"I'm sure he'd rather hear that from you."

"Mom…"

"You were only going to stay a few days, but you've been there months."

"I own part of this ranch. I need to be here. I want to be here."

There was a noticeable pause. "Are you eating well?"

Maddie gritted her teeth, feeling like a ten-year-old.

"Yes, Mom. Please stop worrying." Her mother's concern was out of love and Maddie had to remember that.

"Etta cooks fabulous meals, but you have to watch for too much fat. She tends to overdo it."

"Etta also serves fresh vegetables and fruits."

"I know. I get so angry at this happening to you. You're too young and…"

"Mom." Her head was beginning to throb. "Don't do that. It makes me sad."

"I'm sorry." Another long pause. "Anyway, I called to find out if you're coming home for Christmas."

"No. I'll be staying here with Gran."

"Since Dane has passed, you don't have to stay there."

Maddie had had enough. "Mom, I'm staying for Christmas, and I'm not sure when I'll be back in Philly. Please respect my decisions."

"You sound defensive."

You make me that way.

Maddie decided to change the subject. "Aren't you and Steven planning a Christmas cruise?"

"Yes, but I wanted to make sure you weren't coming home."

"I'm not."

"I guess that's it, then."

"Have a great time and take lots of pictures."

"I will. I know I smother you, but I love you, darling."

"I love you, too, Mom." She took a breath and hated that the cancer had made her mother so paranoid. "Tell Steven hi and that I love him."

Maddie hung up feeling once again as if she'd disappointed her mother. She didn't have a lot to complain about, though. Her mother was really an angel, but she tended to be overprotective and she pushed too hard. So what else was new in the mother-daughter relationship?

Madison slipped her cell into her pocket and headed for the door and breakfast. Cooper was still at the table.

"Morning, Coop." She slid into a chair.

Etta placed a cup of coffee in front of her. "Thanks, Etta. I'll just have one of your whole-wheat cranberry muffins."

"That's not enough to keep you going all day. How about some eggs?"

"No, thanks." She poured milk into her coffee and added sugar.

Cooper pushed a piece a paper across the table.

"What's this?" She picked it up.

"The corn estimate." He came around the table and looked over her shoulder. "If we plant about a hundred acres, we can save a lot of money." He pointed to the paper. "That's the cost of planting the corn, the diesel and such. If we have a good crop and grind it into feed, it should carry us through several months. It's a win-win for High Five."

"I'm impressed." She glanced over the figures. "There are no wages."

"You already pay Ru and me so there would be none. Ru and I can harvest it, too."

"Sounds good. Let's plant corn."

"Great." He beamed a smile she'd never seen before, and she thought Cooper loved High Five as much as Dane's daughters. "Ru and I will start cultivating as soon as the weather's a little warmer. Now, we better make sure the cows have water this morning." He reached for his hat and turned to her once again. "Ru and I are going to put up that fence by the new windmill, another one the hurricane took out. Then we can start herding cattle to that pasture." He reached in his pocket and handed her another piece of paper. "That's the supplies we'll need."

She glanced at the paper but didn't take it. Lifting her eyes, she said, "You pick up the supplies."

"Ru and I have to clear the fence row to install the new fence."

Yanking the paper out of his hand, she pointed a finger at him. "I'll do it, but next time, Mr. Yates, you're going to face Nell Walker."

"Yep." He headed for the door and she thought she heard him mumble, "When pigs fly."

The screen door banged behind Coop and Etta sat a muffin in front of her. "Eat. Dorie's still sleeping."

Maddie glanced at her watch. "Yes, and it's already seven-thirty. She's usually up by now."

"Dorie's going through a little empty-nest syndrome."

"What do you mean?" She took a bite of the muffin.

"Caitlyn's like her daughter, and she misses seeing her every day. Now, she'll never admit that, but she was happy as a child playing dress-up with Cait on Saturday. Dorie was her old self."

Maddie wiped her mouth. "I'll go cheer her up and I'll make sure Cait visits more often."

Etta waved her spoon. "Cait's a grown woman with a husband. Dorie has to adjust."

"Mmm." She took a swallow of coffee and darted for the stairs. When it came to Gran, the sisters were wusses. They loved her too much.

She found Gran lying on her lounger still in her cotton gown, staring out the window.

"Gran," she said softly, and sat by her. "Aren't you coming down for breakfast?"

"I was just thinking about Dane and how proud he'd be of his daughters."

Oh, no. Was Gran sinking into depression again? They went through this right after their father had died. Gran had had a hard time accepting his death.

"Gran, come downstairs. We'll have breakfast together. I'll call Cait and see if she'll join us. That would be fun, wouldn't it?"

"Don't bother Cait. I just want to sit here with my memories."

"Gran…"

"I'm fine, baby." She squeezed Maddie's hand. "You have work to do. Go." Gran waved toward the door.

Maddie had no choice but to leave. She'd give Gran time and then she'd check on her again. She'd even put on one of those tutus if Gran wanted her to—anything to make her happy.

THIRTY MINUTES LATER, SHE opened the door of Walker's General Store. She saw Cait and Judd at the back talking to Walker. Georgie stood beside his father.

Judd's Ford Lariat was parked outside so Maddie knew he was in the store. Seeing her sister was a surprise.

She laid her list and her keys on the counter in front of Nell. She had the ordering thing down.

Nell looked it over. "We'll have it loaded in no time."

"Thank you."

Cait came up behind her. "Hey, sis."

They embraced, and Maddie noticed Cait wasn't dressed in her usual jeans and boots. She wore slacks and a dressy blue blouse. And heels.

"Where are you going?"

"Judd and I have to testify in Albert Harland's trial today."

Harland was the reason High Five was struggling. Angry at Cait, he'd torched their hayfields and their home. He'd even tried to kill Cait. The man needed to be put away for a long time.

"Walker has to testify, too," Cait continued, "but he's having a problem finding a sitter."

Don't even think it. Don't offer.

Walker and Judd joined them and her heart did excited flip-flops at the sight of his stern face.

"Hi, Maddie," Judd said, looping his arm around Cait. Judd was one of those strong males who'd resisted love. It had taken Cait fourteen years to convince him otherwise.

Walker was on his cell. As he clicked off, Cait asked, "Did you get Mrs. Hathaway?"

"Yes. She has the flu."

"Damn."

Georgie looked up at his father and then glanced at Maddie. He smiled and she smiled back.

"I'll have to call and tell them I…"

"I'll stay with Maddie," Georgie said, and reached for her hand.

"Son…"

"Perfect solution," Judd said. "Best babysitter in High Cotton, probably the world."

Maddie made a face at him. "You sweet-talkin' devil."

Cait kissed her husband's cheek. "He is that."

Maddie squeezed Georgie's hand and avoided looking at Walker. Clearly he didn't want her to keep him.

"I don't need a bath," Georgie said, as if that might persuade her.

He was so cute she couldn't say no. His father was another matter.

"I'll keep Georgie."

"Are you sure?" Walker asked, and their eyes met for the first time and she felt light-headed. She was so easy.

"Yes," Georgie answered for her.

"Thank you," Walker said as he followed Cait and Judd out the door. "I have his car seat in my vehicle. I'll drop him at High Five."

"As soon as Luther loads my truck, I'll be right behind you."

They walked off and Georgie looked back, waving, and a warm, fuzzy feeling suffused her—so much for staying away from Walker and his kids. She really was a patsy.

"Cait," she called before her sister crawled into the pickup. Maddie hurried to her. "Do you think that later you could stop by and see Gran?"

"Why? What's wrong?" Cait was immediately concerned.

"She's a little depressed, reliving old memories and thinking about Dad."

"Oh, no."

"She's not doing anything weird like before," Maddie assured her, "but I'm a little worried."

"I'll be there as soon as I finish in court."

"Thanks, and good luck."

Cait lifted an eyebrow. "You, too."

HER TRUCK LOADED, MADDIE sped home. Walker and Georgie waited at the front door and she hurried there.

"I'm here," Georgie shouted as Etta opened the door.

"Oh." Etta looked at Georgie. "Would you like a cookie?"

"Uh-huh."

Georgie followed Etta and she turned to Walker.

"I don't know how long I'll be," he said. Her traitorous eyes soaked him up like raw cotton. In a crisp white shirt stretched across his broad shoulders and his long legs encased in starched jeans, Walker's sheer male presence made her nerves tingle.

"Ah…it doesn't matter. Just pick him up when you're through."

He nodded, but he didn't move away. "I thought about you all night."

"I didn't think about you at all," she lied, but the expression on his face was worth it.

He grabbed his chest. "Ouch." And then he looked closely at her face. "You know you get little lines around your eyes when you lie."

"I do not get little lines."

He cocked an eyebrow at her sharp retort.

"Coop's always telling me that."

He rubbed his jaw. "Mmm. Is there anything between you and Cooper?"

"Friendship."

His eyes held hers, and she couldn't look away from the warmth she saw there. "Well then, if you're willing to take this relationship one day at a time and see where it takes us, I'll meet you halfway."

"I…" She was at a loss for words. She hadn't expected this.

His arm snaked out and he pulled her against him, his lips covering hers, effectively silencing any doubts she had. The kiss went on as he wrapped her tight in his embrace.

His musky after-shave triggered her senses, and the

fire of his kiss melted every other part of her. "Am I forgiven?" he whispered between kisses.

"Maybe. We might have to explore this more."

That ghost of a smile warmed her against the chilly wind.

"Later tonight." It was a promise that erased the rejection of the night before.

He picked up Georgie's backpack at his feet and placed it in her hands. "He has all kinds of stuff in there. Curious George, for sure. He wants it when he takes a nap, and I added an extra change of clothes. If he gets dirty or banged up, don't worry. That seems to be the norm for my kids. They're accident-prone, but since they're getting older, it's getting better."

"I'm such a patsy," she murmured with a smile.

He kissed her briefly. "I'm beginning to like that about you…and the lines." His eyes twinkled as he sauntered away.

She watched until his car was out of sight. She might have *easy target* written on her chest, but this time she was doing what she wanted.

And following her heart.

CHAPTER THIRTEEN

THE MORNING WENT WELL. Maddie put Georgie in front of her on Sadie to help check on Coop and Ru. Georgie was very good. He did exactly what she told him. He talked a lot, but that didn't bother her.

They rode back to the house at one. The temperature was now in the fifties, so it wasn't too cold. When they reached the barn, Solomon was waiting. At first, Georgie was a little afraid, but she let him pet the bull. Soon he was leading the animal around by his halter. She watched closely because animals were unpredictable.

When they reached the house, Etta had lunch ready. She settled Georgie at the table and hurried to check on Gran. She was sound asleep and that worried Maddie. Maybe she should call Cait, but Cait was at the trial.

In the kitchen, Georgie was keeping Etta entertained with tales of Solomon. Etta had made meat loaf and Georgie wanted lots of ketchup, which he got mostly on his face and clothes. She was washing his face and hands when the phone rang.

It was Walker. "How's Georgie?" he asked.

Her heart fluttered. "He's fine. We had a late lunch."

"I hate to ask another favor."

"But you are?"

"Yeah. I'm still waiting to testify and I'm not going to make it to pick up Haley from school. She can walk or ride the bus, but there would be no one home."

"I'll go get her."

"Thanks, Maddie. I'll let the school know you're coming. It lets out at three."

"I'll be there."

"I owe you for this."

"You certainly do." She could see him smiling as she hung up.

She finished washing Georgie's face. "Do you take naps?"

He frowned. "No. I'm too big."

"Oh, sorry, but I have to ask these things." Walker had said something about a nap, but she wasn't going to push it.

"Are we going riding again?" His voice was hopeful.

"We have to go get Haley from school."

"Oh."

"But first I have to check on my grandmother. You stay in the kitchen with Etta."

"'Kay. She'll give me a cookie." He ran for the kitchen.

Maddie headed for the stairs and stopped short. Gran was sitting in the parlor, fully dressed, her hair in a neat knot.

"Gran."

Her grandmother looked up. "Hi, baby. I thought I heard a child."

"That's Georgie, Walker's son. He's staying with us for the day."

"I was thinking about when you girls were little and how laughter filled this old house. Now it's so quiet."

Before Maddie could answer, Georgie came running in. "I got ketchup on my jacket." He held it up. "See?"

She took the coat. "Yes, I see. I'll try to get it out."

"Hi, Georgie," Gran said.

Georgie lifted a hand. "Hi."

"Do you have a Christmas tree at your house?"

Georgie shook his head.

"We need to do something about that. We don't have a tree, either." Gran glanced at her. "Contact Cooper and tell him we need to cut down a tree. Make that two trees. Right, Georgie?"

Georgie nodded vigorously.

"And we'll pick them out." Gran got to her feet.

Gran was throwing things at her from left field. She wasn't ready to put up the tree, but if it made Gran happy, then she was all for it. She just had one small problem.

"I have to pick up Haley from school."

"Then let's get going." Gran reached for Georgie's hand.

The truck was small and Maddie didn't think they'd all fit. Oh, well, they were off on an adventure.

Haley was waiting by the curb. Gran let her get in and then she held Georgie on her lap. Walker would not like this. No car seat for Georgie or seat belts. Every time she shifted the gears Haley had to move her leg. She drove slowly, hoping there were no maniacs on the road.

"We're getting a Christmas tree," Georgie told Haley.

"We are? Daddy didn't say anything."

Daddy was going to be surprised.

The ride was uneventful and they made it safely back to High Five. Gran took Haley and Georgie inside for a snack and she went to alert Cooper.

The change in Gran was phenomenal. She was chatting with the kids and making plans. She just needed an interest.

As they piled back into the truck to go choose their Christmas trees, Walker drove up. Maddie got out and Georgie was off like a bullet to his father.

Walker swung his son high in his arms. Georgie's giggles filled the afternoon air.

"Daddy, Daddy." Georgie could hardly catch his breath. "We gonna get a Christmas tree." He spread his arms. "A big one."

"What?" Walker's eyes went to Maddie. She was like a magnet, pulling him in. God, she looked great in tight jeans, and her blond hair spread out on the collar of her jacket.

He dragged his thoughts back to his son. "I haven't thought about a tree."

"That's okay," Georgie told him. "We gonna do it, aren't we, Maddie?"

"You're back early," she said instead of answering.

"Court started early. I have to go again in the morning. Judd and Cait are still there talking to the D.A."

"I'll stay with Maddie." Georgie bobbed his head.

"Now, son…"

"Gran wanted to put up a tree and Georgie got sucked into the excitement."

"We need a tree, Daddy," Georgie said in his most pitiful voice.

"What does Haley say?" He looked to his daughter standing behind Maddie. She smiled—a real smile.

"Well, Maddie, if you don't mind some tagalongs, we'll go with you."

"Not at all." The light in her eyes sent his blood pressure up a few notches. "Except we're not all going to fit in my truck. Some will have to ride with Cooper. He has a chain saw and he'll lead the way to the cedars."

Coop strolled over and threw Walker his keys. He caught them while juggling his son.

"Take my truck. It's a double cab and has more room. Chain saw's in the back."

"Thanks," he called to Cooper's retreating back. "I think."

Cooper waved a hand over his head in acknowledgment but kept walking.

He could go home and get his truck, but that would take time and his son's patience was short. After cutting down the tree, he'd come back and get it. That way he wouldn't spoil the kid's excitement. Lord knew they had very little of that lately.

The air was beginning to get chilly again. "Let me get my jacket and we'll be on our way."

Slipping into his lined sheepskin coat, he hurried back.

Maddie smiled. "You do own a jacket."

He nodded. "Comes in handy every now and then." It was hard to look away from the teasing light in her eyes.

The group made their way over to Cooper's truck. Miss Dorie sat in the front with him, and Maddie crawled into the back with Haley and Georgie. They were off to find a perfect tree, which took more time than he ever imagined.

Georgie ran from cedar to cedar, Haley a step behind him, searching for the right one. Miss Dorie found hers quickly, and he had it in the bed of the truck in no time.

His kids had to have Maddie's opinion on everything, the same with Miss Dorie. Maddie was very patient guiding them to the perfect tree. Soon he had it in the truck, and the kids scurried to get in the warmth of the cab, as did Miss Dorie.

He made sure the trees were secure and jumped to the ground. Maddie stood there, her arms wrapped around her waist, her nose red.

He lightly touched her cold skin. "I want to kiss you so bad my lips are tingling."

"That's from the cold, silly."

"No. Don't think so. Other parts of my body are warm…very warm."

She giggled.

"Let's go before you get hypothermia. I must have been out of my mind to cut a tree in weather like this."

Or in love.

Those three words immobilized him. His wife had been gone eight months. He couldn't fall in love again so quickly. But then there was Maddie and her loving nature that went all the way to her soul. She cared about his kids. And they responded to her. Hell, who wouldn't respond to her? He felt a little giddy himself.

He had to take this slow. But everything in him was already going full speed ahead.

When they returned to the house, Miss Dorie insisted on putting up the tree. His kids begged to stay, so he attached the stand while Maddie gathered the boxes of decorations out of the attic.

The next hour was a lively affair as Miss Dorie and the kids decorated the tree. Etta made sandwiches and hot chocolate and placed them on the coffee table. Thankfully she brought him a cup of coffee.

Maddie sat at his feet looking wistfully at an ornament.

"What is it?" he asked.

She held up a crystal angel. "It's my first Christmas ornament from my father. See—" she held it up "—my name and the day I was born is inscribed on it." She was silent for a moment. "Cait was his baby. I was his angel and Sky was his princess. That's what he called us. Although most of the time he called Sky Spitfire." She fingered the ornament. "I miss him."

He squeezed her shoulder and her hand covered his. They were quiet for a few seconds and then she smiled—a stellar one he was sure could move mountains. It sure moved his frozen heart.

"May I please have cheese and crackers?" Haley asked, staring at the sandwiches.

"You certainly may."

Haley was watching what she ate and she hadn't thrown up in days. He hoped they could keep the status quo going.

"Oh, peanut butter and jelly," Georgie cried. "My favorite." He looked at Etta. "It is grape jelly, right?"

"Of course. Don't make it with anything else."

"Daddy does. He used strawberry." Georgie made a face. "It was yucky."

"He's never going to let me forget that," he said for Maddie's ears only.

She laughed, and it felt good to be with her and in this warm family environment. He'd never seen his kids this happy. Looking into her eyes he had to wonder if he'd ever been this happy.

THE NEXT MORNING, MADDIE called Cait to let her know Gran was much better. Last night Cait hadn't made it by because she and Judd were busy with the D.A. going over details.

After a brief conversation, she hurried downstairs, hardly able to believe how excited she was that Georgie was coming. She'd fallen in love with the little boy and Haley, too. Most of all, though, she…

The doorbell rang and she ran to get it. She barely had the door opened before Georgie darted in.

"Whoa." Walker grabbed his son. "Manners, please."

"Bye, Daddy. I'll be good. I gotta go. Etta has something for me I know." Then he was gone.

"One day and you'd think he's lived here forever."

"He really is very good and everyone loves him."

"Gets that from his dad, huh?"

"Maybe." She stared into those warm, warm eyes.

"I never did get that kiss last night. Georgie was asleep on his feet."

She went into his arms as if she belonged there. Slowly he turned his head and their lips met in a fevered kiss that went on and on.

"Damn." He sighed heavily, resting his forehead against hers. "I have to go."

"I'll pick Haley up from school and we'll get started on the decorations for the tree."

"Georgie was whining this morning about the tree, so I have to get it up tonight. I don't have any decorations, though. When Trisha left I sold what I didn't want out of the house and gave the rest to our neighbor."

"We'll raid the general store."

"Oh, that should make Nell cringe."

He seemed not to want to leave, and she didn't want him to. It felt strange and right that their relationship was taking off so quickly.

"I'm going in my truck so I can bring the tree home as soon as possible."

"We'll be waiting," she called as he strolled away.

THE DAY WAS UNEVENTFUL. Georgie chattered nonstop and asked a million questions. After checking the wells to make sure they were flowing, she let him feed Solomon. Coop and Ru were installing the new fence, so she and Georgie went to the house. He entertained Gran with his childish antics.

Later they went to the school to get Haley. She was waiting in the same spot. Haley smiled when she saw them and hopped in. Maddie thought that was a good sign. Haley was better.

They drove to the general store and bought just about everything Nell had for a Christmas tree. Maddie gathered construction paper, glitter and glue so they could make decorations, too.

"We're putting up a Christmas tree, Aunt Nell," Haley said. "Would you like to come over?"

"I'm too old for that kind of stuff."

"How old are you?" Georgie asked.

Maddie quickly intervened. "If you change your mind, please come over."

"Where's Walker?"

"He's testifying at a trial."

"Shouldn't he take care of his own kids?"

As always Georgie had something to say. "I like Maddie. She doesn't hit me."

A look of anxiety crossed Nell's face.

Maddie shuffled him to the door. Unable to resist, she turned back. "If you change your mind, please come." She couldn't help herself. Nell seemed so lonely.

When they reached the house, Haley let them in with her key. They paused in the doorway. The tree was standing in the front window. Walker came from the kitchen.

Georgie ran to him. "Daddy, Daddy. The tree is up."

"Yep. Now we have to decorate it."

Maddie and Haley laid their bags on the sofa. "We have plenty. Did you get through early?"

"Yes. And I don't have to go back." He winked at her and the world was suddenly brighter.

"Oh, boy. Oh, boy." Georgie jumped up and down. "We have our very own tree."

The next hour was a hive of excited activity. Walker put on the lights while Maddie made popcorn. She and Haley made strands for the tree and cut rings out of red construction paper to make a garland.

Maddie created an angel out of construction paper, glue and glitter. She used a pipe cleaner for the halo.

Georgie in the meantime was throwing icicles on the tree in fits of giggles. Finally it was finished.

"Oh, it's pretty." Georgie clapped his hands.

"Wait," Walker said. "I have something else." He went into the kitchen and came back with a small bag. "Since I got out early, I thought I'd pick up something to remember our first Christmas in High Cotton." He pulled out two boxes and gave Haley one and Georgie the other.

Haley held up a heart ornament. "Oh, it has my name on the back and the date." She hugged her father and hurriedly hung it on the tree.

Georgie dropped his and Walker had to help him. "It's George. Oh, boy," he shouted, staring at the Curious George ornament.

Walker held him so he could hang it high on the tree, his eyes catching hers. He wanted them to remember this Christmas the way she'd remembered her father's one-of-a-kind ornament. Walker was such a special man, but she'd known that for a while.

"Now we have to turn on the lights," Haley said. "Everybody sit. I'll turn off the living room lights and then turn on the tree."

Maddie took her seat by Walker. Georgie crawled

into her lap and she squeezed him gently. The lights went out and the room was in total darkness. Then the lights of the tree came on, beautiful and spellbinding.

"Oh." Georgie's voice came out low and breathless.

Haley slid into the spot next to her and they just sat in the warmth of the crackling fire and the beauty of the lights.

Haley rested her head on Maddie's shoulder and Walker's hand reached for hers. All that loneliness inside her dissipated. Ever since they'd told her she would never be able to have children, she'd been adrift. Now she was anchored and felt more love than her heart could contain.

She'd found everything she'd wanted here in High Cotton, Texas.

She'd found Walker, the man with no first name.

CHAPTER FOURTEEN

IN THE DAYS THAT FOLLOWED, Maddie was involved in Walker's life more and more. She juggled ranch duties with keeping Georgie and picking up Haley from school when Walker couldn't make it. After a day in the saddle, she'd shower and change and hurry to Walker's. She cooked dinner a lot of nights at his house, working on menus that Haley's stomach could tolerate. They were like a family except for one thing. They had no time alone.

When the kids were in bed, it was time for Maddie to go home to Gran. She couldn't continue to impose on Etta. Hot kisses at the door were creating a lot of repressed sexual tension—for both of them.

"Come on, Georgie. We have to go," she called, saddling Sadie.

"I have to give Solomon more feed. He's hungry." Georgie now considered feeding the bull his job.

"Solomon has had enough. Come on. We have to catch up with Coop and Ru."

"I'm coming. Be a good boy, Solomon. I'll be back."

Georgie was attached to the bull and the feeling was returned. Solomon was so docile with Georgie. Probably because the boy fed him anything he wanted.

In his cowboy boots and hat that she'd bought him, Georgie was too adorable for words.

She lifted him into the saddle first, which wasn't

an easy thing to do since he was a solid boy. Putting her foot in the stirrup, she climbed up behind him and they were off.

Holding on to the saddle horn with both hands, Georgie said, "I like Sadie." And that started his childish chatter. She just let him talk as they galloped across the pastures.

They reached Cooper and stopped. He was putting out round bales of hay with the tractor. The cows were milling around ready for food.

Seeing them, he drove over and killed the motor. "Hey, Georgie."

"Hey, Coop." Georgie lifted a hand.

"Are you through feeding?" she asked.

"Yep, for the day. We're low on salt and minerals."

"I've already ordered them."

"Damn, can't get anything past you."

"You can pick it up at the general store."

Coop removed his hat and replaced it in a nervous gesture. "I was going to check the fence over there." He pointed. "That big Brangus cow was poking her head through the barbed wire to eat Judd's grass. I wanted to make sure she hasn't broken the fence."

Sadie moved restlessly and Maddie patted her neck to soothe her. "I'll check the fence. You pick up the minerals." Coop had to stop hiding on the ranch. People had to learn he was a good man, not a criminal. "If there's a problem, I'll sort it out."

"Yes, ma'am." Coop tipped his hat with a frown. "Bye, Georgie."

Coop started the tractor and drove away. Georgie kept waving.

"Okay, partner, let's check the fence."

"I'm helping."

"Yes, you are."

The fence was through a thicket, so Maddie dismounted and lifted Georgie to the ground.

"Oh, look." He pointed to some rocks in the grass. "I'm gonna pick out the pretty ones." The boy had a fascination with rocks. He'd done this several times when they'd been out. Maybe he'd become a geologist.

"You stay right here," she told him. "I'm going to walk through the woods to check the fence."

"'Kay." He was already sorting through the rocks. It was strange how a simple thing could make a kid happy.

She checked the fence with one eye on Georgie. She didn't want him to wander off. The Brangus had broken a wire. They'd have to fix it tomorrow before the cow broke through.

Starting back toward Georgie, she heard a deep growl and glanced to the right.

Her blood froze. The wild dogs were on the edge of the thicket about forty yards away. The lead dog bared his teeth, growling. The other dogs answered with hair-raising howls. Their attention was on Georgie.

Oh my God!

She had to get to the boy. If she ran, the dogs would most certainly attack. If she screamed for Georgie to run, they would also attack. How much time did she have?

What should she do?

The gun!

That was the only solution.

No. No. No!

Despite her hatred of firearms, she eased slowly toward Sadie. The horse reared her head, sensing a threat. Maddie stroked her neck and saw the rifle was in the scabbard where Coop had put it.

What did Coop say? Remember, dammit! Georgie's life depended on it.

Gently sliding out the gun, she watched the dogs. They hadn't moved, but they were growing more agitated. The other dogs milled around, tossing their heads. The lead dog never took his eyes off Georgie. Thank God the boy was oblivious, engrossed in the rocks.

A light breeze stirred and danger hung in the air. Sadie neighed and sidestepped nervously.

What had Coop said?

Turn off the safety.

She was shaking inside, but her hands were steady.

Where was the safety?

In her mind's eye, she saw where Coop had pointed and she flicked it off.

Raise the rifle and line up your prey through the guide.

She did.

Coop's words played in her head. *It's automatic with six bullets in the magazine. Just pull the trigger.*

Could she do that?

She swallowed, and it felt like a golf ball going down her throat. Her eyes on the dogs, she prayed they'd retreat into the woods.

Suddenly the lead dog let out a bloodcurdling howl and leaped through the air, heading straight for Georgie. The pack howled behind him at a dead run.

Georgie jerked up his head.

"Lie flat," she shouted, and Georgie immediately fell to the ground.

Pull the trigger. Pull the trigger.

The dogs bounded closer.

Now!

Without thinking, she fired. She missed. The loud sound echoed through her head and her insides cramped, but there was no time to think. Just act. The dogs were a few feet away.

It's automatic.

Looking through the guide, she squeezed the trigger again. The lead dog flipped and lay on the dried grass, but the other dogs kept coming. She fired again and again and again, until there were no more bullets. When the last dog went down, the rest scurried into the woods.

She threw the gun on the ground and ran to Georgie. She lifted him, then headed for Sadie, who had trotted some distance away. With one hand, she reached down for the gun, jammed the rifle into the scabbard and swung into the saddle.

Not until she was in the saddle did she realize she'd mounted with Georgie in one arm. If adrenaline wasn't pumping through her veins like a gushing well, she would never have been able to do that.

Or fire the gun.

"I 'cared," Georgie mumbled into her breast. She held him against her instead of the other way. She needed to hold him.

"I got you. You're safe." She kissed the top of his head and realized he'd lost his hat. They'd get it later. In case the other dogs came back, they had to leave here fast.

"That doggie was gonna get me."

She took a much-needed breath and turned Sadie toward High Five. "Let's go home."

"I want my daddy."

She did, too.

WALKER DROVE TO THE BARN. Cooper and Rufus were inside. "Hey, Coop, where's Maddie?"

"She's—"

Gunshots echoed through the landscape.

"What the hell!" Cooper glanced out the door. "That sounds like it's coming from where I left Maddie and Georgie."

Fear shot through Walker's heart. "Rufus, may I borrow your horse?"

"Sure thing."

He jumped into the saddle and Cooper ran for his horse. They galloped through the cool winter's day, but Walker only felt fear. Reaching a ridge, they stopped. Dead dogs lay everywhere, and Maddie was steadily headed to High Five with Georgie clutched against her.

"Shit," Cooper said at the sight.

Kneeing the horse, Walker took off at a run. Maddie pulled up and waited for him.

"What happened?"

"Daddy." Georgie held out his arms and Walker took him. "Bad doggies were gonna get me. Maddie shot 'em."

His eyes held hers. "Are you okay?"

She nodded, but he could see she was trembling.

Cooper rode over. "Damn, Maddie. You *can* use that gun."

"They...they were after Georgie and there are more. About five ran off into the woods."

For a moment there was silence. Walker sensed she was about to burst into tears. "Cooper, can you take care of this? We're going back to the house."

"Yep."

They cantered back to the barn. Georgie rattled on,

but he heard very little. He was worried about Maddie. She dismounted and began to unsaddle her horse.

"Son, go to the house and Etta will give you something to eat."

"'Kay." He sprinted away.

"Maddie." He caught her hands. She flew into his arms and he held her in a firm grip. "You and Georgie are fine. You did what you had to."

"I was so afraid. Georgie could be—"

"He's not. He's fine, thanks to you."

"I should never have let him pick up rocks. I—"

"Maddie, look at me." She raised tear-filled eyes and his heart jerked with pain. "You did nothing wrong."

"I did." She pulled away, eyes blazing. "I did. He's four years old and I should have never taken him with me. I put him in danger."

"That's life."

"No." She turned and ran for the house.

"Maddie." But she was gone.

MADDIE WENT THROUGH THE FRONT door and up the stairs before anyone could see her. She needed time alone. In her room she sank onto the bed, trying to ease her shaky nerves.

That Georgie could have died today kept running through her mind. A precious child was put into her care and…she stopped those thoughts. They were destructive.

Cait had once told her that in a crisis you did what you had to. She had. She could still hear the loud sound of the gun, feel the sting in her shoulder, see the dogs falling, blood everywhere, and then the enormous quiet that echoed through her shaking body.

She did what she had to for Georgie. She'd give her

life for him. At that moment she realized how much she loved Walker and his kids.

There was a tap at the door. It had to be Gran. She had to pull herself together. Wiping her eyes, she called, "Come in."

Walker stood there looking worried. She ran into his arms. "Don't do that to me again."

"What?" She pulled back.

"Run away from me."

"I've never known fear like that before. I'm a city girl."

He stroked her face with the back of his hand. "I don't think so. You're a true country girl from where I'm standing. A beautiful, courageous…"

"Maddie, where are you?" Georgie called a moment before he entered.

"Right here."

"We're never going to get five minutes alone," he whispered.

She picked up Georgie. "You okay, partner?"

He bobbed his head. "I want my hat."

"Coop will bring it."

He wrapped his arms around her neck and she melted. "I love you."

Her throat closed up. "I love you, too," she managed to say, trying very hard not to shed any more tears. She failed.

Walker rubbed his son's back, his eyes on her. "I called Judd and we're getting together some guys to track down the rest of the pack. When they start attacking our kids, we have to do something."

"I agree. They're not dogs anymore. They're predators."

"Can you watch Georgie a little while longer?"

"Yes, and I'll pick up Haley."

"I'll meet you at my house." He kissed her cheek. "Thank you." That one touch eased all the fear inside her.

BY THE TIME SHE PICKED up Haley she was in a better mood. She didn't have to go home early as Gran was having dinner with Cait. She assured Gran she was fine before she left so she wouldn't worry.

Georgie played with his Spider-Man figures while she helped Haley with her homework. Haley's hair was shiny and her complexion smooth. The sparkle was back in her eyes, too. She looked so different from the defiant girl she'd found in her barn.

"When was the last time you had a spell with your stomach?"

Haley looked up from her book. "Not since Ginny had her baby, and I've gained four pounds."

"You look great."

"Thanks for helping with my diet."

"I didn't do anything. Your father told me what the doctor said, no greasy or spicy or acidic foods, and that's what I cook when I'm here."

"I love your cheesecake and baked potatoes." She looked thoughtful. "It's strange that cheese and hamburgers don't upset my stomach."

"Your father buys low-fat cheese and pats the grease off the burger. Spice and grease are your enemies." And stress, which trigged most of her upsets.

"Did I tell you I got a letter from Ginny?"

"No."

"She's doing great and so is the baby. She named her Haley Madison. Isn't that cool?"

"Very." Maddie was touched.

"After she gets her GED, she's going into nursing. The government will pay for it. Isn't that neat?"

"Yes."

"Daddy said we can go see her at Christmas. You have to come with us."

The doorbell rang, interrupting her answer. Georgie jumped up to get it. Nell stood on the doorstep with a bag in her hand.

Maddie got to her feet. "Come in."

"I don't want to intrude, but I have something for the kids. Is Walker here?"

"No. He's with some men who are tracking the wild dogs."

"I heard about that."

"What you got, Aunt Nell?" Georgie was anxious.

"Haley was curious about my quilting, so I made two ornaments for you." She pulled out two quilted hearts edged with sequins and beads; the back was red satin. One had an *H* stitched on it, the other a *G*.

"They're beautiful," Haley said. "Thank you."

"They are lovely," Maddie echoed.

"We have to put them on the tree." Georgie bounced up and down.

Once the ornaments were in the right spot, Nell said, "Haley, I have my quilting frame up if you'd like to see how it's done."

"Can I, Maddie?"

"You've finished your homework so I don't see why not."

"I'm staying with Maddie." Georgie leaned against her.

Haley whispered something in his ear.

"I gotta go."

"Are you sure, Georgie?" Maddie felt he would be in the way and get on Nell's nerves.

"I'm sure." He nodded his head.

"I'll watch him," Haley said, and then they were gone.

She stood there for a moment and wondered why they hadn't asked her, which was silly. She saw Haley and Georgie all the time. Nell just wanted to spend some time with them. The woman was really lonely. Maybe she would be more lenient with them.

Plopping onto the sofa, she thought about the horrendous day and was so grateful it had turned out well. She got comfy and it suddenly hit her—she was alone. The one thing she and Walker had been waiting for. But Walker wasn't here.

She curled up and drifted off. The door opening woke her. Walker strolled in with a rifle in his hand. "Hey, gorgeous," he said, locking the gun in a cabinet.

She sat up. "Did you get them?"

"Yes, there were six more. Now we don't have to worry about them attacking our kids."

"It seems so sad."

"Well, Ms. Bleeding Heart." He sat by her and a woodsy outdoor scent stirred her senses. "The town is going to do something about that. I spoke with Judd and we're going to have stricter leash laws in High Cotton. Strays are going to be picked up, spayed or neutered free by a vet who lives here, and then Mrs. Finney is going to keep them until someone wants to adopt them. Mrs. Finney loves dogs and she's eager to help."

She rubbed his arm. "Wow. You've accomplished a lot tonight."

He watched her hand and then glanced around the room. "Where's my brood?"

"At Nell's."

He lifted an eyebrow. "What?"

"She's being nice. She even brought ornaments for the kids." She pointed to the tree.

"Well, I'll be damned."

"Evidently Haley is interested in quilting and Nell is showing her how to do it."

"And Georgie?"

"He went, too."

"Really?"

"He didn't want to go at first and then he changed his mind."

He put his arm around her and she snuggled into him. "You mean we have the house to ourselves?"

"For a little bit."

Removing his arm, he reached for his cell. "Let's see if I can stretch that."

He talked to Nell for a minute and then hung up. "She's going to keep them until I call." He placed his arm around her again. "Now, what should we do?"

"Play Scrabble?"

He made a face.

"Cards?"

"Oh, no." He shook his head, his eyes darkening. "This is where the towel thing happens."

She jumped up and ran for the stairs, laughing all the way to the bathroom.

CHAPTER FIFTEEN

MADDIE RAN INTO THE BATHROOM and stripped out of her clothes, almost falling on her head trying to remove her boots. Quickly stuffing her things into a drawer in case the kids returned unexpectedly, she grabbed a tan fluffy towel and held it in front of her. Her heart bounced off her ribs as she waited for him.

Slowly the door opened and Walker stood there, his warm eyes holding hers with a sensual, sexual gaze.

As he devoured her with his eyes, Maddie realized being bad was easy and natural with the right man. She let go of the towel and it fell to her feet in a soft swish. She didn't think twice about the scars on her stomach.

Walker's gaze shifted from her face to her breasts and down to her legs. His eyes, darker than she'd ever seen them, came back to her face.

"Are you sure about this?" His voice was husky.

"Yes." She stepped over the towel and moved until she was almost touching him. "But I can't make love with a man unless I know his first name."

He sighed. Deeply.

"What is it?" She waited.

And waited.

She gently began to unbutton his shirt.

He moaned and then said, "Valentine."

She lifted an eyebrow. "What's wrong with Valentine?"

"Trying being a boy and defending that name. I learned how to be tough very early."

She touched his face. "I like it."

"Good" came out as a groan, and he pulled her naked body against his. "You're giving me heart palpitations. You're so beautiful." His hand slid up her back and cupped her neck, his fingers stroking her skin, driving her wild.

His lips traveled from her shoulder, to her neck, to her cheek. She was hardly breathing when he captured her lips. She opened her mouth, giving and needing to taste and feel everything that was Walker. Needing more, she pulled his shirt from his jeans.

"Wait," he said in a ragged tone. "Let's go somewhere more private." Swinging her into his arms as if she weighed no more than Georgie, he carried her down the hall to his bedroom. He kicked the door shut, then locked it.

The light was on, which was good. She wanted to see every inch of him. His lips caught hers again and she frantically finished unbuttoning his shirt. He threw it aside and whipped his white T-shirt over his head.

Her hands splayed across his broad chest, her fingers soaking up the rough texture of his skin, the strength of his muscles and the lure of the dark spirals of hair arrowing into his jeans.

At the feel of him, liquid warmth permeated her stomach and centered between her legs. This is what she wanted. This is what she needed. Walker. Brazenly, her hand went to his jeans.

"Boots," he breathed between hot kisses.

He sat on the bed and she knelt to remove them. Yanking on one, she fell back on her butt.

He laughed—a sexy, throaty sound that rippled through her.

"Oh. I'll get you for that."

"Come and get me." His laugh deepened as he quickly jerked off the other boot, unzipped his jeans. In less than a heartbeat he was standing nude in front of her. Her breath caught in her throat. He was magnificent, muscle and sinew, strong and powerful and more man than she...

He gently lifted her to her feet, then they fell backward onto the bed. She lay on top of him, feeling the power of those muscles, feeling their effect on her. Her body tingled and yearned and...

Walker pushed the blond hair from her face and kissed her deeply. Between heated kisses, he murmured, "You said you haven't been with anyone since..."

"No. Not since the cancer scare." She kissed his chin, the corner of his mouth. "And very little before then."

Walker wanted to take it slow for her, but he was way past that. The sight of her body and the feel of her satiny skin had sent his hormones into overdrive. And it had been eight long months. He wanted her with a vengeance. Not just the sexual part. He could have that with any woman. He wanted Maddie...the sweet, kind, good woman that drove him crazy. He wanted to be in her, deep and tight.

He rolled her over onto her back and took her lips in a fierce need. His hand caressed her breasts and traveled to her stomach and below. Oh, it was evident she wanted him, too.

Moaning, she slid her hand over his chest and gently stroked his bulging manhood. Her touch sent him into orbit and he groaned, taking her lips and sliding between her legs.

One thrust and he was inside her and the world floated away. It was just her and him, their bodies conversing in an age-old way. He heard her cry his name a moment before the top of his head almost blew off with pleasure. He'd had sex before. He'd made love before, but never like this. His life depended on pleasing her, making her realize how special she was. And in return his pleasure was tenfold.

He wanted to stay joined for a little while longer. Forever, if possible. He never wanted to be apart from her again. Finally, he eased to the side and just held her.

He stroked her hair. "I love you," he whispered.

She took his hand and kissed it. "I love you, too. And thank you."

"For what?"

"After the cancer treatment, I was afraid to find out if everything was still working." She smiled. "It is… wickedly."

"Good girls do it best," he teased.

"You bet," she murmured sleepily.

He gathered her closer. "I'm so sorry for all you had to go through, but you don't have to worry about kids. We have two who need you almost as much as I do."

She jerked up. "Oh my gosh, the time. The kids. We have to get dressed."

He pulled her back into his arms. "In a minute."

She sighed and lay against him. His world was slam-damn good for the first time in his life. Happiness was within his reach. All because of her.

His Maddie.

THIRTY MINUTES LATER they were in the living room, trying to keep from smiling as they waited for the kids.

The door opened and Haley walked in carrying Georgie. Nell was behind them.

"He fell asleep," Haley said as Walker took him.

"I'm not sleep," Georgie mumbled, and scrubbed at his eyes. Looking at Maddie, he held out his arms and she took him.

"We made you something, Mommy."

Her heart stopped. She glanced at Walker and he shrugged. Georgie was just asleep and got her name mixed up. That's all. But next to Walker saying I love you, it was the very best thing she'd ever heard.

"We made you this." Haley held up a quilted heart ornament with an *M* on it. "Aunt Nell helped us. It's just like ours."

Her heart wobbled. "It's lovely." With Georgie in her arms, she placed it on the tree and hugged Haley. Haley hugged her back with a smile.

She then hugged Nell, who stiffened. "Thank you." And she meant that in more ways than one.

"I'm really not a bad person," Nell whispered.

"I know," she whispered back, and hugged Nell again. This time she made an effort to return the embrace.

"Time for bed," Walker said.

"Mommy has to give me a bath."

There was that word again. Maddie looked at Walker, but neither knew what to do about it.

"Son…"

"I'll give him a bath." She kissed his soft cheek. "And then I have to go."

"'Kay."

"Bye, Maddie," Nell called.

"Bye, and thanks." She winked.

"Anytime."

Georgie went to sleep as she dried him. Walker helped her get his pj's on and then Walker carried him to his bed. They tucked him in.

"He's had a rough day," Walker said.

"Yeah."

His arm slipped around her. "None of it was your fault."

"It's hard to get it out of my mind, except…you know… when we were…"

His hand slid up her side to her breast. "We'll have to 'you know' more often."

She smiled, feeling warm, safe and loved. He flipped off the light and they went downstairs.

"Why do you think he's calling me mommy?" she asked, slipping into her coat.

"Is that a problem?"

"No. It's just…"

"What?" He looked into her eyes.

"Too good to be true."

He grinned. "I thought it was impossible to fall in love again and I resisted like hell, but now I'm accepting everything that you and happiness can bring."

"Daddy." Haley walked through from the kitchen eating an ice cream bar and they drew apart. "I'm going to bed."

Walker hugged and kissed her. "Night, sweetheart."

Maddie embraced her, too. "Ace that test tomorrow."

"I'll try." She darted up the stairs.

Walker watched her go. "It's so good to see her eating."

"Her life isn't in an upheaval and neither is her stomach. And now I have to go. I have to pick up Gran at Cait's." She reached for her purse and Walker's arms slid around her waist.

"That bed is going to be awful lonely now."

She turned in the circle of his arms. "I'll be back tomorrow." Standing on tiptoes, she kissed him lightly, but one kiss led to another and then another.

She ran from the room laughing, feeling young, alive and so in love.

THE BUSY DAYS OF LATE December were the happiest of Maddie's life. She took time to call Victor and wish him a Merry Christmas. The conversation wasn't an easy one since she had to tell him about Walker. He advised caution, but wished her the best.

Hanging up, she knew she was taking a risk. She was Dane Belle's daughter, though, and he'd always told her if she wasn't taking risks she wasn't living.

Every now and then *what if* would run through her mind. Then she'd remember her father's words. But still that anxiety was there. What if the cancer returned? Predictable Maddie would certainly turn away from this happiness. But the new Maddie held on to it. Cherished it. Embraced it.

With Nell's help, she and Walker continued to have time together, which they both needed. It was getting harder and harder to leave. And *what if* faded into the background.

Nell was helping Haley make a baby quilt for Ginny, and Georgie had to help because the gift had to be from both of them. Maddie knew Haley was tricking her brother so she and Walker could have time alone.

A week before Christmas they went to see Ginny and the baby. Maddie was impressed with the home. It was up-to-date and clean, the girls and babies very well taken care of.

Ginny was different, more mature. She'd cut her

dark hair, and she seemed to have shed her childhood. Her parents were not mentioned. The future and her daughter were her focus.

They took her out to lunch and then shopping, buying clothes for her and the baby. It was a happy day for all of them.

But the tears came when it was time to leave. Ginny hugged her tightly. "Thanks, Ms. Belle. I'd be stuck in High Cotton if it hadn't been for you. And—" her voice broke "—I wouldn't have my baby."

"You're welcome, and call me Maddie."

Ginny turned to Walker. "I'm sorry I made you worry. And thank you for delivering Haley Madison."

He should be angry at this young girl for putting his kids' lives in danger, but he didn't feel anger. He was relieved Ginny now had a life worth living.

Clearing his throat, he said, "Just don't do anything like that again."

"I won't."

Maddie was holding the baby and his eyes were drawn to her as always. A look of rapture was on her beautiful face, and he hated what had been taken from her. She deserved a child of her own.

When they drove up at High Five, an old car Walker had never seen before was parked out front.

"Oh, Skylar's home," Maddie shouted, and jumped out and ran for the house.

"Who's Skylar, Daddy?" Haley asked.

"Maddie's sister."

They got out and followed more slowly. Maddie was hugging Sky in the parlor. A little redheaded girl about three sat on Gran's lap. Maddie gently lifted her into her arms and motioned for them to come in.

"Sky, this is Walker, Haley and Georgie."

"I remember you," Sky said, shaking his hand. "I danced with you at the ball at Southern Cross. Mainly because Maddie wouldn't and I never miss dancing with a handsome guy."

"Maddie and I got off to a bad start."

Sky glanced from him to Maddie. "But that's changed, huh?"

"Yes, it's changed," he admitted with a grin.

"He's mellowed," Maddie added, sitting on the sofa with the little girl.

Georgie eyed the girl in Maddie's arms. "Who's that?"

"This is Kira. She's my niece."

Georgie frowned. "Why you holding her?"

Georgie didn't like for Maddie to hold anyone but him. He took after his father.

Maddie reached out with one arm and pulled Georgie onto her lap beside Kira. "There's room for both of you."

"No," Georgie shouted, and pushed Kira with his hand.

Before anyone could react, Kira pushed back.

Sky scooped Kira into her arms. "What can I say? She takes after her mother."

Walker knelt by Georgie. "Son, we don't push girls."

Georgie twisted his hands. "She sat on Mommy's lap."

The room became quiet. Very quiet.

Maddie kissed his cheek. "That doesn't mean I don't love you."

"It doesn't?"

"No. You're my partner."

"Now, apologize," Walker said.

"Sorry." Georgie eyed Kira. "But you can't sit on Mommy's lap."

Walker lifted the boy into his arms. "This may take more time than we have." He looked at Maddie. "Visit with your sister. I'll take the kids home. Nice to see you, Skylar, Kira. Bye, Miss Dorie."

Maddie followed them out. When Haley and Georgie were in the car, he lingered outside, staring into her beautiful eyes.

"I'll call you later," she said. "Don't punish Georgie."

"Mmm. You've spoiled him, just like you've spoiled me. We can't live without you."

She linked her fingers with his. "The feeling is mutual and I'll miss you tonight."

"Roughing it is going to be hell."

She squeezed his hand. "I love you." She waved to the kids and ran into the house.

Cait arrived and they talked until after midnight. It felt good to be back together.

"How long are you staying?" Maddie asked Skylar.

"I don't know. I just wanted to be here for Christmas." She flipped back her red hair. They sat in the parlor with the fire crackling and the Christmas lights burning. "A detective showed up asking my neighbors questions in the apartment complex where I lived, so I got the hell out of there."

"Sky, why don't you just stop running and fight this?" Her sister had been on the run since Kira was born, trying to keep her out of her boyfriend's parents' clutches.

"With what? I don't have any money and Todd's parents are loaded. They'd hire the best attorney possible and I'd lose Kira. I can't let that happen. She needs me."

"I can't tell anything's wrong with her," Cait said, curled into a corner of the sofa. "But when she falls I notice she winces."

"The doctor said she might outgrow the juvenile arthritis, but she might not. I have to be there for her."

"You've come to the right place. No one will get near Kira," Maddie assured her. "Cait and I will see to that."

"Hey, I hear you've become Annie Oakley…or Cait." Sky grinned. "They're the same woman, I believe."

"Shut up, Sky."

"You shut up."

They burst into giggles as if they were teenagers.

Sky sobered. "Gran seems a whole lot better than the last time I was home."

"She has some bad days, but Walker's kids have had a positive effect on her. She's just lonely and misses her baby Cait."

"Don't start, Maddie."

Sky turned to Cait. "I guess you know about Walker."

"Oh, yeah."

"Betty Crocker has found her man." Sky poked Maddie in the ribs, and for the life of her Maddie couldn't stop the smile that played across her face.

"Whoa. That looks like Betty Crocker sweet is being oh so bad," Cait added.

"And bad never felt so good." Maddie laughed.

Sky leaned her head back against the sofa. "I haven't had sex in so long I've forgotten what it's like."

"It's like riding a bicycle," Maddie told her. "It comes back to you quickly, in Technicolor and surround sound."

Sky looked at her. "Are you for real?"

Cait's cell beeped. "That's my hubby. I have to go." She rose to her feet, said a few words to Judd and clicked off. "I'll be back tomorrow and we'll talk about the ranch."

"Do you ever stop worrying about High Five?"

"No, dear sister." Cait hugged Sky, blew Maddie a kiss, and she was gone.

Maddie and Sky walked up the stairs arm in arm.

"I'm glad you're home," Maddie said before going into her room.

"Me, too."

MADDIE COULDN'T SLEEP and it was ridiculous. She just wanted to see Walker. Fifteen minutes later she opened his front door with the key he'd given her and let herself in. This was bad, but it felt delightful.

She tiptoed through the dark house, hoping not to bump into the old piano and wake the whole house. She slithered up the stairs like a thief. Quietly, she opened his door and went in, locking it behind her.

Sliding into bed, she curved her hand under his T-shirt and across his stomach and lower.

He caught the wandering hand. "This had better be who I think it is or I'm going to arrest you."

"Oh, Valentine."

CHAPTER SIXTEEN

MADDIE SNEAKED THROUGH her back door at five in the morning. Sky was leaning against the kitchen counter in her T-shirt, terry-cloth bathrobe and fuzzy slippers. Her arms were folded across her breasts.

"Have a good time?" The words were laced with humor.

"Why isn't the light on?" Maddie asked instead of answering.

"I saw your headlights and didn't turn it on. I wanted to see what you were up to and the moon is full tonight. I can even see the color creeping into your cheeks."

Maddie grabbed her face. "You can not."

Sky laughed. "Oh, Betty Crocker, if you're going to be bad, you have to do it with bravado."

"As Cait said one time, I missed that course in college."

"Mmm."

"What are you doing up?"

"Kira woke up crying and I came down to get her some warm milk. Sometimes that helps her sleep."

"Is she hurting?"

"I never know. I just watch for the swelling and try to keep her comfortable."

Of the Belle sisters, Sky was the party girl, the outgoing, outspoken, fun-loving one. And she had a mouth on her that could curdle milk. *Fight* was her middle name. Maddie spent most of her summers on High Five separating Cait and Sky. Two strong sisters, neither willing to bend. It was wonderful to see this caring, motherly side of Sky.

"Where's Kira?"

"She's in my bed with her Elmo. She loves that ugly-looking thing."

"Georgie has a Curious George."

Sky turned from pouring milk out of a pan. "You're really in love."

"Yeah." She wrapped her arms around her waist. "It happened so quickly. I'm afraid my bubble's going to burst."

Sky poured the milk into a glass. "The way Walker looks at you, I don't think so."

They went upstairs together, and Maddie fell into her bed for an hour's sleep.

MADDIE WAS IN THE KITCHEN at seven drinking coffee, lots of it. She and Coop talked about the day's work. In the wintertime it was constant feeding.

"Ru and I are herding the cows in the pen back to the pastures. The wild dog threat is over."

"I'll find you later," she said.

"There's nothing much to do. I still have to pick up the minerals and put some out." With a twinkle in his eye, he added, "You have my permission to take the day off."

She threw a biscuit at him. He fielded it like a pro, took a bite and was gone.

Maddie went to the study to get the books ready for Cait and Sky. An hour later, they sat together, the door closed.

Walker had called and dropped off Haley and Georgie. They were in the parlor with Kira and Gran. Georgie was in a better frame of mind, and she felt sure he wouldn't hit Kira again. But she kept her ears open.

Cait crossed her legs. "The D.A. called late last night and said Harland was found guilty on all charges."

"That's great." Maddie clapped her hands.

"The sentencing is later, but the D.A. said he'll be put away for a long time."

"Glad we have that behind us." Sky scooted forward in her chair. "Let's get this meeting started."

"The ranch is struggling, but we're managing to keep our heads above water." Maddie opened the books. "Oil prices have dropped and that's cutting into our cash flow."

"Judd's not happy about it, either," Cait said. "The economy sucks."

"It's not all bad," she continued. "We received the insurance money from the fire in the house. It went toward the new windmill, which is up and running. Coop did a lot of the work and it saved money, but this month we're breaking even." She glanced at Sky. "Sorry, but there won't be a check this month."

"Damn. What the hell happened?"

"The economy. Winter. Taxes. Life." She pushed the book toward Sky. "There are the figures."

"Maddie, you're the most honest person I know, and I'm not double-checking the figures." She sighed heavily. "I guess I'm stuck here."

"Next month should be better. The expenses won't be so high and Coop purchased more cows so the calf crop will be larger. And in the spring we're planning to plant corn. Maybe even sorghum. I checked this out on the Internet and this could be good for High Five."

"I hope you're not letting that ex-con make decisions."

Maddie bristled at Sky's tone, but she tried not to let it show. "Coop knows more about ranching than I do, and I trust his instincts. I trust him."

"I do, too," Cait said.

"Well, isn't this dandy? You're ganging up on me."

"I manage High Five and I'm doing what's best for it," Maddie stated.

"That can change," Sky fired back.

"Like hell." Cait shot to her feet. "Maddie agreed to run this ranch and that's the way it will stay."

"You're not the boss, Cait."

"I gave my life to High Five, and if you think—"

Maddie picked up a glass paperweight and threw it at the wall. It hit a lamp, which crashed to the floor. No one made a move or spoke.

Maddie rose. "I'm tired of you two constantly bickering. I run High Five and what I say goes. Got it?"

Her sisters stared at her, as if they'd never quite seen her before.

"Damn," Sky said. "When did you get balls?"

"When I constantly have to put up with Bossy and Bitchy." Those were nicknames for her sisters.

"Well, I think you had a little tequila with your oatmeal this morning."

"I could use some now," she shot back, and they started laughing.

"Okay, okay, do not sidetrack me," she said. "This month there are no profits to split. Next month there will be. We just have to roll with it."

Sky looked at Cait. "I think we have to change Betty Crocker's name."

"Yeah. Maybe Brave."

"Bad," Maddie said.

This caused another round of laughter.

But they were feeling better and agreeable.

"I'm not cleaning up that mess." Sky pointed to the lamp.

"Would you like Maddie to make you?" Cait asked.

"No. I'd like for her to make you."

"Let's all do it." Maddie walked toward the lamp and her sisters helped. Then they went into the parlor. They stopped and stared.

Everyone was in costume. Gran wore a long gossamer dress and held a wand in her hand. Haley's hair was in pigtails and she wore an old gingham dress with red shoes. Georgie had on a lion's suit and Kira a dog suit. "Over the Rainbow" played on the stereo.

"Hi, my babies," Gran said. "We're doing the *Wizard of Oz*. We need a tin man, a scarecrow and a wicked witch."

"Why did she look at me when she said 'wicked witch'?" Sky whispered.

"If the shoe fits…"

"Shut up, Cait."

Before they knew it they were pulled into make-believe.

WALKER RANG THE DOORBELL, but no one answered. He knocked loudly, but still no one came to the door. Music vibrated through the walls, so he knew they were here. He tried the doorknob and it was unlocked. He went inside.

In the parlor he stared at the show that was going on. Everyone was in costume. Haley was lip-synching the words to "Over the Rainbow" and dancing in red shoes. Georgie growled, leaping around the room, followed by Kira barking.

He'd never seen his kids so happy. They were having the time of their lives. His eyes zeroed in on the scarecrow. His Maddie.

"I love you," he mouthed

"You better," she mouthed back.

CHRISTMAS ARRIVED AND Maddie had presents to wrap, plans to make. Nell watched the kids so she and Walker could go shopping. They bought Haley a new computer system with video games. They settled for a motorized truck for Georgie, one he could drive himself, a Thomas the Train set, books and more Spider-Man toys. They picked out clothes for both of them.

On Christmas Eve Maddie planned to spend the night at Walker's. She wanted to be there when Haley and Georgie opened their gifts. Sky was with Gran, so she didn't have to worry. They would exchange gifts and eat dinner at High Five on Christmas Day.

The kids were in their rooms, supposedly asleep. They carried all the presents she'd wrapped into the house and put them under the tree. Walker drove the small truck from the garage. They were ready.

Sitting on the sofa, they snuggled together in front of the fire. Walker picked up a cookie Haley and Georgie had left for Santa and handed it to her.

"We better eat these."

Nibbling on a cookie, she enjoyed the quiet moment of being together. Walker reached for the milk and took a swallow.

"I know this is quick, but I thought we should make it official."

"What, Valentine?"

"You love saying that, don't you?"

"Yes." She took the milk and drank.

"Now I'm not going to tell you."

"Ah, please." She kissed him with a milk mustache and then licked it off his lips.

He groaned. "You're driving me crazy, you know that?"

"Yes." She giggled and placed the glass on the coffee table.

His arms went around her and he kissed her deeply. He tasted of milk, winter cold and heat…hot melting heat that made her limp.

"Do I have your attention?" he whispered against her lips.

"Y-yes." She sat up and tucked her hair behind her ears. "What?"

He stuck his hand behind a cushion and pulled out a small gold-wrapped box.

She stared at it. Could that be a…?

Her heart pounded. "Christmas is tomorrow."

"I wanted to do this tonight when we were alone."

"Oh." Suddenly she was nervous. For so long she'd resigned herself to a single life. She never thought she'd find a man to love her the way she was. Then she'd found Walker.

He pushed the box into her hands. "Open it."

What if… No. Don't listen.

"I'm a little nervous."

What if…

He leaned over and kissed her slowly. "That help?"

"Yes." She ripped off the paper and paused a moment before she flipped open the lid. She gasped at the sight of the white-gold ring with a round solitaire diamond.

"Will you marry me?" he whispered.

What if...

"Maddie?"

She fingered the diamond. "I can't help but think what if the cancer comes back."

"Oh, honey." He cupped her face. "It won't. But if it does, we'll face it together."

"Walker..."

He kissed the tip of her nose. "Dane took risks every day of his life. Now I'm asking you to take one—take a risk on me. On us."

The promise of his words buffeted her, gave her strength. "Yes," she breathed, afraid to move or speak loudly. The moment might disappear.

He took the box and removed the diamond. Taking her left hand, he slipped it on her third finger. "I love you."

She threw herself into his arms then. "I love you. I love you." He gathered her close and they lay entwined on the sofa. The fire crackled, and the warmth of the room enveloped them in a cozy world of their own. Only love and happiness lived there.

He lifted her into his arms and strolled to the stairs and his bedroom.

CHRISTMAS MORNING arrived early with screeches of delight. Haley and Georgie tore into their packages like little hurricanes. There were a lot of "ahs," "ohs" and smiles. They were so different from the kids she'd first met.

Walker helped Georgie drive his truck out in the yard and she helped Haley set up her computer.

"I can't believe I have my own computer." Haley hopped around with glee. "I made a new friend. Her name is Cara and she has a computer. Now I have one. Wow!"

Georgie came running in his pj's and slippers, his nose and ears red. "It's cold outside, but I drive good, huh, Daddy?"

Walker ruffled his son's hair. "Like a pro."

"You need your coat and cap," Maddie said. "They're by the door." She waved a hand toward them.

"What's that?" Haley asked, pointing to Maddie's diamond ring.

"Well—" Walker sat down and pulled Georgie onto his lap "—I asked Maddie to marry me and she said yes."

"Oh, boy. Oh, boy," Haley shouted. "I got my Christmas wish. Oh, boy."

Haley and Georgie danced around the room holding hands. Nell walked in. "I see the excitement is over."

"Aunt Nell." Haley grabbed her hands and pulled her into the room. "Daddy and Maddie are getting married."

"Go figure that."

Maddie walked over and sat by Walker. He pulled her close and Georgie crawled onto her lap. They would become a family—the family Maddie always wanted.

It wasn't a risk at all.

It was a rush to get to High Five on time. They dressed for Christmas. Maddie wore a black dress trimmed in red, and high heels. When she came downstairs, Walker stared at her for a long time.

"You look gorgeous."

"So do you, Valentine." Her gaze slid over his body in Dockers and white shirt and came to rest on his cowboy boots. "Mmm, sexy."

"Later," he murmured.

Haley came down in her new plaid skirt and sweater. Georgie trailed behind her in his slacks and a new blue shirt.

Haley hugged Maddie. "Don't we make a good family?"

"Yes, we do, sweetie." Her gaze caught Walker's and she'd never been happier in her life.

The whole family was at High Five for dinner, including Nell and Renee, Judd's mother, Chance, Judd's foreman, and Etta and Rufus's nephew. They opened gifts and enjoyed the company and the holiday.

They were exhausted when they returned home. Haley ran to her computer and Georgie played with his train set. Maddie made ham sandwiches, but no one was really hungry.

"I'm playing with my computer all day tomorrow," Haley announced.

"I'm driving my truck," Georgie said, taking a bite of sandwich.

"Daddy has to be home for you to drive your truck," Walker told him.

"'Kay."

"Can I have cheesecake, please?" Haley asked.

Maddie opened the refrigerator and placed it on the table. It was one of the things Haley could eat, and it was loaded with calories, so Maddie cut her a big piece.

As she placed it in front of Haley, the doorbell rang, interrupting the quiet evening.

"I'll get it," Maddie said. "Georgie, eat your sandwich."

"I want cheesecake."

"In a minute."

She swung open the door and a pregnant blond

woman stood there. A woman she'd never seen before. Her hair was in a ponytail, and she held a hand
over her stomach. She wasn't beautiful, but she was
pretty with a natural look. She seemed nervous and
looked past Maddie as if she was looking for someone.

"May I help you?"

"I'd like to see Walker."

Maddie thought it had to be someone in trouble,
needing help.

"He's in the kitchen." She stepped aside so the
woman could enter. She smelled faintly of cigarette
smoke.

Walker stood in the kitchen doorway, Haley and
Georgie behind him.

"Hello, Walker."

"Trisha."

CHAPTER SEVENTEEN

TRISHA!

Walker's ex.

Maddie's happy heart fell to her feet and she had trouble breathing. She closed the door and realized her hands were shaking.

"Mama," Haley breathed, but made no move to go to her mother.

Georgie wrapped himself around Walker's leg and buried his face against Walker.

"What do you want, Trisha?" Walker's voice was cold enough to freeze water.

"It's Christmas. I want to see my kids."

"Maddie, please take Haley and Georgie outside."

Maddie quickly grabbed their coats and herded them out the door. The kids didn't hesitate or look back.

They sat at the picnic table in the backyard. The late evening bite in the air was echoed in her heart.

A barbecue pit and redwood chairs sat among live oak trees, their gnarled roots poking through the ground. A few feet away Georgie's bright red truck rested in the brown, stiff winter grass. But Georgie had no interest in it now. He was glued to her lap, his face buried in her chest. Haley shivered beside her, and Maddie wrapped an arm around her. This was no way to end Christmas.

Haley leaned against her. "Why is she here?"

"She said she wanted to see you."

"I don't want to see her," Haley said, her hands clenched tight in her lap.

"Me, neither," Georgie muttered, not raising his head.

Maddie knew this was a normal reaction. Their mother had hurt them and they were leery of her feelings. But that would change. Kids forgave easily.

"She's pregnant," Haley whispered almost to herself.

"Yes." Maddie certainly recognized that. What did the woman really want? She wished she could hear what was being said inside.

"YOU'RE NOT SEEING HALEY or Georgie," Walker said, trying to keep his anger under control.

"They're my children. I have that right."

"You have no rights. You signed those away when you ran off with your boyfriend. You didn't even have the decency to say goodbye to them."

"I couldn't." Trisha looked down at the floor. "Once I made the decision, I just had to go."

Her selfish attitude angered him more. "Then you don't deserve any consideration. Georgie cried for two solid weeks for his mama. Haley, God, Haley threw up so much she was wasting away before my eyes."

"She only does that to get attention."

Get attention! Had he ever really known this woman?

"Get the hell out of my house! You've seen the last of them."

"I think you'll change your mind once you calm down and hear what I have to say."

"I don't want to hear anything you have to say."

"Damn, my back is killing me." Trisha walked to

the sofa and sat down as if they were having a normal conversation. She removed her coat and pushed up the sleeves of her knit top. His eyes were drawn to the butterfly tattoo on her forearm. That was new. As was the pregnancy, which he was trying to ignore.

"Don't get comfy. You're leaving," he warned.

"Who's the blonde?"

"None of your business."

She looked around the room and wrinkled her nose in distaste. "I can't believe you brought the kids to this hick town."

"I wanted to give them some stability. A new beginning."

"I take it you gave up your job, which I begged you to do for years."

He gritted his teeth. "How else would I be able to care for Haley and Georgie?"

"And it helped that your dad left you a bundle."

His patience snapped. He wanted her out of his house, out of his life. "You have five minutes to tell me what you want."

"Well." She leaned back, the mound of her stomach very evident. "Tony and I were having Christmas with his mother in Houston."

"How nice. Get to the point."

"She was surprised I was pregnant. Seems Tony had a bicycle accident when he was a kid and he wasn't supposed to be able to father a child. The bitch." Her face darkened in a way he'd seen many times. "She just had to bring it up. That put the wheels in Tony's head to spinning, and he wanted to know if the baby was his." She paused and raised calculating eyes to his. "Or yours."

A sucker punch hit him in the gut and he had to

catch his breath. His hands balled into fists. "And?" came out as a groan.

"I'm not sure." She shrugged. "Tony knew the diagnosis from the accident, but he figured over the years that it had changed. Now he wants the truth. I want it to be Tony's, but I did sleep with you before I left." She shifted uncomfortably. "Tony's pissed about that."

"I know the feeling."

"Walker—"

"He kicked you out?" Walker cut her off, feeling his insides coiling into knots.

"Not exactly. We decided to part ways until the baby is born and a paternity test is done."

"Which is…?"

"Any day."

"God." He swung away. "I can't believe your audacity. Your gall. You selfish, selfish bitch."

"Damn, Walker, you love kids so much I thought you'd be happy to learn you might be a father again."

He pointed to the door. "Get the hell out of my house."

She pushed to her feet. "What about the baby?"

"When it's born and the test is done, give me a call. Until then I don't want to see you."

"I can't go through this alone." Her voice quivered and he didn't feel one ounce of sympathy.

"Haley and Georgie felt the same way when their mother bailed on them."

"Why do you have to keep bringing that up?"

"Because you have to realize what you've done to their lives. You destroyed them. They're in a stable, secure home now and that's the way it will stay."

"I want to see them."

"No." He remained firm.

"Walker…"

"The only way that's going to happen is if they ask to see you. Then I might relent."

She frowned. "You always were hard and unrelenting. You never cared about us. It was work, work—"

"Get out of my house."

She reached for her coat and purse. "I'll call when the baby comes. Please bring the kids."

On the entry table at the door she placed a small sealed box. "This is a DNA swab testing kit. Just follow the instructions inside and mail it. The address is on the return packet. When the baby is born, we can get the results quickly." She pulled a piece of paper from her purse. "That's my phone number. Whether you believe it or not, we have to talk about our children. And the future."

WALKER SANK ONTO THE SOFA and buried his face in his hands. Could it be his child? No. No. Not now. He rejected the mere possibility.

He felt Maddie's presence and glanced up. She was everything he'd ever wanted in a woman. But he'd known from the start that he shouldn't get involved with her. She was special and needed someone special. He couldn't resist her, though. Now his life was messed up and it was worse than ever.

How did he tell her?

How could he break her heart?

"Is she gone?" Maddie asked, her voice anxious.

His eyes met hers. She looked great in that black dress. It brought out the blue of her eyes and the shine in her hair. He cleared his throat. "Yes."

Haley and Georgie charged around her and into his arms. He held them in a viselike grip.

"Daddy…"

"Let's talk," he said, settling back. "Your mother wants to see you, but I told her it was up to you. It's your decision."

"No," Haley said rather too quickly. "I'm going up to play on my computer."

"I need a bath," Georgie said to Maddie.

"Since when do you like baths?" Walker ruffled his son's hair.

Georgie shrugged and took Maddie's hand. Together they bathed his son and soon tucked him in.

"I don't want to see Mama," Georgie mumbled as he dozed off.

Walker and Maddie went downstairs. He could feel the tension in her. Sitting on the sofa, she straightened her skirt over her knees. He thought how beautiful she was and how it permeated everyone around her. She deserved everything that was good on this earth, just like she was.

"What did she really want?" Maddie asked.

He wanted to take her in his arms, but he refrained. He had to tell her the truth.

"She wants to see Haley and Georgie and…"

The blue wave of her eyes caught his. "And what?"

"This isn't easy, Maddie."

"But we have to face it whatever it is." His sweet Maddie was holding on to her control very well. It was evident in the way she clenched her hands and kept her gaze on him.

"First, I want you to know how much I love you. How much the kids love you."

She bit her lip. "It must be bad if you have to preface it with that."

"Maddie." Her sad face broke his heart.

"Tell me."

He ran both hands through his hair. "She said I might be the father of the baby."

"Oh…" The one word seemed ripped from her throat.

He went to her then, but she wouldn't let him take her in his arms. "Is that a possibility?"

His stomach churned. "Yes."

Getting up, she walked into the kitchen to get her coat. As she shrugged into it, she said, "I don't think we should see each other anymore. It's too hard. Your kids need you."

"Maddie, I don't even know if the baby is mine."

"But you have to prepare yourself and Haley and Georgie. It's better if I'm not in the picture."

"They don't even want to see Trisha."

"That will change. She's their mother." She reached for her purse. "I have to go."

He caught her before she reached the door. "I don't love Trisha anymore."

She leaned against him, her face beneath his chin. A faint hint of Chanel teased his senses. He kissed her forehead, her cheek and took her lips with all the passion he was feeling. She returned the kiss with equal fervor for a moment and then tore out of his arms and ran out the door.

He sighed heavily as the chilly air surrounded him. But he didn't feel it. All he felt was her pain. A pain he had caused.

"Goddamn it!" He slammed the door so hard the sound echoed through the house with a ring of goodbye.

He wanted to go after her, to tell her they had a future. But he didn't know what the future was and he couldn't keep her hanging on. He wouldn't do that to her.

Goodbye, sweet Maddie.

MADDIE REFUSED TO CRY. She refused to think. It was too painful. She drove steadily home. When she went inside, the house was quiet. Good. She couldn't talk to anyone.

As she headed for the stairs, she heard voices. Sky and Kira were in the parlor. Kira was playing with a baby doll she'd gotten for Christmas, dressing and undressing it. Sky patiently watched her daughter.

A mother's love. A mother's... Maddie stared a long time, lost somewhere between a dream and a nightmare. Unable to speak to them, she ran to her room.

Stripping out of her clothes, she reached for her big T-shirt and curled up in the bed. When she stayed at Walker's, she didn't even need the T-shirt.

Walker.

A whimper left her throat, but she stoically held back the tears. From the moment she knew who the woman was, she inexplicably knew life would never be the same.

Trisha might be having Walker's baby.

No. *She* should be having Walker's child.

But that was impossible. She couldn't have any man's child. And she couldn't claim Trisha's kids, either. Maddie loved Walker. She probably always would. That's why she knew she had to walk away. Walker and Trisha had to have the opportunity to reconnect—for their children and especially for the baby.

Trisha didn't deserve her consideration, but Haley and Georgie did. She couldn't break up a family if there was the slightest chance for reconciliation. Her Christian upbringing was kicking in big-time. This was no time to be bad.

She hated that side of her personality.

Clutching a pillow, she saw her engagement ring. It

sparkled with the promise of tomorrow. But there was no tomorrow. She should have given back the ring. When she felt stronger, she would.

There was a tap at the door and Sky stuck her head in. "Hey, what are you doing home?"

Maddie pushed up against the antique headboard that had been hers since she was a child. Their father had let them choose from a collection of furniture that had belonged to their ancestors. She'd loved the dark oak and intricately carved headboard that seemed to reach to the sky. Her father had said she would get lost in the bed.

How she wished he was here now. She needed his shoulder to cry on.

"Are you crying?" Sky asked when Maddie remained silent.

"No." She wiped away a tear and realized she was.

Sky sat on the bed in flannel pajamas. "You're wearing flannel?" Maddie hiccupped. Flannel and Sky did not go together. Her sister was known to prefer silk and cashmere. Or she used to.

"Yeah. So what? I have to get up so much during the night with Kira and they're warm."

"Remember that time we went shopping in Austin and you bought that sexy teddy? It was black with white lace and you wore it to bed. Dad had a fit and made you throw it away." She dropped her voice. "No fifteen-year-old daughter of mine is wearing something so skimpy."

"I loved pushing his buttons." Sky ran her hand over the soft flannel. "I miss him. I miss his calls."

"Me, too."

There was silence for a moment as they remembered

a father they both loved. All the pain in Maddie welled up and tears stung her eyes.

"Walker's ex is back."

Sky's head jerked up. "What?"

"She's pregnant and she says it might be Walker's."

"Shit!"

"It's Christmas. How could she ruin our Christmas?" She didn't want to cry, but she was slapping tears away like crazy.

"You didn't just walk away, did you?"

"Yes." She sniffed. "What else was I supposed to do? I can't come between Walker and his family."

"That bitch abandoned those kids. She doesn't deserve your selflessness."

"But Haley and Georgie do."

"You're such a bleeding heart. If you want Walker, fight for him."

"I have to give them a chance to reunite. I couldn't live with myself if I didn't."

Sky narrowed her eyes. "If it were me, I'd be hiring a hit man."

Despite her pain, she smiled. "You're crazy."

"But I made you smile."

Maddie pulled up her knees. "My life was so bright, but now I feel as if I've been drop-kicked through the goalpost of life. I don't know what I'm going to do."

"The last I heard, and very strongly I might add, is that you're running the ranch. Pick yourself up and go on. That's what Belles do. Isn't that what Dad said?"

"Yes."

"And Cait and I will be there to catch you when you land on the other side of that goalpost."

Maddie leaned over and hugged her sister. "I know. That's what I love about coming to High Five. Family, love and sisters. Though we weren't raised together we have a strong sister bond."

She twisted the ring on her finger. "I forgot to give Walker my engagement ring. It has to be the shortest engagement in history. Twenty-four hours." She couldn't keep the quiver out of her voice.

A wail pierced the silence. "Kira. I have to go." Sky paused at the door. "Keep the ring until you know the baby is really Walker's."

Maddie lay back on the bed. Something about being the good sister made her angry. She should refuse to step back and let Trisha reclaim her family. She didn't deserve it, but Haley and Georgie were her children. They weren't Madison's children.

That one thought kept running through her mind. It kept her from charging back to Walker. It kept her embedded in the worst misery she'd ever felt.

She pulled the pillow into her arms and held it against her. "Walker," she murmured as she fought the waves of sleep tugging at her.

CHAPTER EIGHTEEN

LIFE WENT ON. MADDIE FOUND that out quickly. Even though she had a broken heart, the world had the audacity to keep turning. She had only one option—to throw herself into running High Five.

She made sure all the fences were in good shape and repaired those that weren't. The new windmill worked like a dream and the cattle had plenty of water, though they didn't drink much in the winter months.

Coop and Ru were busy cultivating the hayfields so they'd be ready to plant when the worst of the winter was over. In Harland's anger at Caitlyn and Judd, he had burned their fields and now they had to start over. They could wait to see if some of the coastal and alfalfa sprouted, but that was taking a risk. They needed hay, so their best course was to make sure they had it.

One day as she was crossing Crooked Creek, she dismounted and sat in the grass. The ground was hard and cold and the wind seemed to go right through her. But she didn't move as she tried to piece together her broken life. She'd survived cancer. Surely she could survive this.

Her mother and stepfather had put their lives on hold to help her deal with the debilitating process. She had great family support. She had it now, too. But she just wanted to be left alone. That's why she worked fourteen-hour days. She had to. It was the only way to deal with everything she was feeling.

As she sat there, she noticed the towering pecan trees that grew along the bank. She walked over to investigate. The ground was covered with pecans. Cracking two in her hand, she noticed they were paper-shell ones and they tasted great.

When she reached the house, she made several phone calls to see if she could sell the pecans. She found a buyer. The next day she filled two twenty-pound sacks and took them into Giddings. Even though the pecan season was over, people were still buying.

As long as the store wanted the pecans, she kept gathering them. Cooper started to help her. Once they had the truck loaded, he leaned against it, looking at her.

"You're killing yourself," he said.

She dusted off her jeans. "I'm stronger than you think."

"You Belle sisters are going to kill me with your love lives."

She slammed the tailgate. "Ah, you can take it."

"Maddie, please talk to Walker."

She ran her hand along the top of the tailgate. "Do you see him here?"

"No."

"That should tell you a lot." She walked around the truck. "Walker's a go-by-the-book type of man. He'll do the right thing by his ex and his kids. That's just who he is. We love each other, but that doesn't matter. Walker has to do what's right and so do I."

"Sounds complicated when it should be simple."

She pointed a finger at him. "Wait until you fall in love."

He grunted. "When pigs fly."

"Yeah." She hopped into the driver's seat. Coop slid into the passenger side. "For a man who hardly ever leaves the ranch, you'll never find a woman."

"That's what I'm hoping. Love is highly overrated and I think you'll agree with me."

"You'd be wrong, buster."

Love was the best thing that had happened to her. Soon she'd have to find the strength to let go of Walker and all the love she felt for him. And soon she'd have to return his ring.

Soon being eons from now.

WALKER TOOK THE DNA test and mailed it. After that he spent his days listening for the phone. And missing Maddie. He missed her smile, her touch, her sweetness. He wanted to call her so many times, but he forced himself not to. It would only hurt her more.

He was caught between two women—one he loved, the other he detested. The one he detested was the mother of his children. He couldn't ignore that, although neither Haley nor Georgie wanted to see Trisha. He asked every day and he got the same answer. A sharp "No."

He didn't understand that. Haley had run away so many times to find her mother, but now that they knew where Trisha was, Haley had done a complete one-hundred-and-eighty-degree turn.

Sorting this out was taking more patience than he had. His kids asked about Maddie every day and he thought about taking them to visit. But that wasn't fair to Maddie.

Haley was in her room and Georgie was outside driving his truck in the backyard. Walker glanced out the kitchen window and saw Georgie ramming the small vehicle into a tree over and over.

He ran outside and yanked Georgie out of the truck and turned it off. Georgie started to scream and cry, flailing his arms at Walker.

Grabbing his hands, Walker walked stoically to the house and sat Georgie on the sofa. He pointed a finger in Georgie's face. "Stop it." Georgie cried louder.

Haley darted down the stairs. "What happened?" She went to Georgie and picked him up. "Did you hit him?"

He was taken aback by the question. "No. I've never hit you or Georgie."

"It's okay, Georgie." She patted his back. "Haley's here."

As they went up the stairs, Walker ran his hands through his hair. What the hell had just happened? His kids were changing right before his eyes. They were becoming sullen and defiant, similar to the kids he'd picked up from his neighbor months ago.

He had to do something, but he wasn't sure just what yet.

New Year's Eve arrived and he spent it nursing a glass of bourbon, wondering where Maddie was, what she was doing. He took a couple of sips and went to bed.

The call came the first week in January. The baby had been born and it was a girl.

"She looks just like Haley," Trisha said.

His last vestige of hope seemed to squeeze from his lungs. He took a deep breath. "Is the baby okay?"

"Yes. The doctor said she's healthy."

"When will they do the paternity test?"

"It's already been done. We should know something in a week or so."

"Call me then."

"Walker?"

"What?"

"I want to see Haley and Georgie."

He hung up, not able to deal with her request. Right now his kids weren't in a mood to see her and he wasn't going to push them. School started on Monday and he couldn't wait for that. Maybe they could get back into a normal routine.

He might have another daughter. The pain and joy of that ripped through him.

That night he told Haley about the baby.

"I don't care," she said, and ran to her room. She wouldn't talk about it and that was the problem. No one was talking.

Oh, God, he needed Maddie. They all needed Maddie.

MADDIE WORKED HER BUTT off until she couldn't think and she couldn't feel. That's the only way she could get through each day.

Cait and Sky tried to talk to her, but she resisted. Talking wasn't what she needed. Gran was worried about her, and she made a point of reassuring her grandmother that she would be fine. They both knew she was lying.

The one thing that kept her going was the ranch. She had to make it succeed. The pecans brought in a good chunk of money, and Mr. Bardwell was going to start buying their sand and gravel again. By the end of January, High Five would be in the black.

Even though that was her goal, it wouldn't make the pain in her heart go away.

WHEN THE CALL CAME, he didn't want to answer, but he forced himself.

"Walker, I have the results." He could tell Trisha was crying.

"And?" He hardened his heart.

"You're the father."

And just like that the life he wanted came to an end. It took a moment before he could speak.

"Give me the name of the hospital. I'll be there as soon as I can."

After rattling off the name and address, she added, "Please bring the kids."

He hung up without answering. His kids had to make that choice, not him. And the mood they were in continued to get worse. Haley was throwing up again. Their lives were turned upside down and they were reacting out of fear. He had to do something about that, but first he had to see his new daughter.

He called Nell for help. She knew the turmoil the kids were going through and she agreed to take the day off and stay at his house so Haley and Georgie could be in their own home.

In the past few weeks Nell had changed. Because of Maddie. That good in her spilled over into others.

His job was now a problem. He couldn't keep the peace to the best of his abilities. He put Lonnie on full-time until he got himself sorted out.

Then he dressed and headed for Houston and the nightmare that was his life. But first he had something he needed to do.

MADDIE, CAIT, SKY AND GRAN sat in the parlor.

She looked at them. "What? I have work to do."

"That's the point, my baby." Gran patted her hands. "That's all you do."

"It's what I need right now. Please respect that."

Sky crossed her legs. "You start throwing around the word *respect* and it makes me nervous 'cause you know I'm going to ignore it."

Cait shot Sky a glance. "Don't listen to her, sweetie. We just want you to be happy again."

Maddie shuddered. "It's almost an alien emotion to me now. Without Walker…" Her voice wavered and she jumped to her feet. "See. I don't want to go through this. I'm going back to work."

As she swung toward the hallway, the doorbell rang. "I'll get it."

"Maddie…"

She ignored Cait's call and opened the door. Walker stood there with his hat in his hand. Her heart hammered so hard against her ribs it resonated in her ears. Oh, how she'd missed him. She just wanted to throw herself in his arms and hold on until the pain stopped. But the somber look in his eyes prevented her from doing that.

"May I speak to you, please?"

"Yes." She stepped out and closed the door, remembering another time they had talked on the porch—when Haley had run away. He was stiff and unyielding then and she felt it in him now.

She was two feet away from him, and his tangy after-shave pulled her into a vortex of memories, him touching her, kissing her, making love to her. She'd been keeping them at bay, but now they were free and running rampant.

Walker twisted his hat. "The baby's been born. It's a girl."

"Oh." The word scratched her throat.

"I wanted to tell you before you heard from anyone else."

"Thank you."

"The paternity test has been done." He squeezed the hat until the brim creased. "I'm the father."

"Oh." This time the word was barely audible, but it scorched her throat with a burning finality.

"I'm on my way to Houston. I'm sorry, Maddie. I don't have any choice now. I have to do the right thing."

"I understand."

"I don't want you to understand," he shouted. "I want you to be angry. I want you to be furious at what I've done to your life. At what I've done to us."

She bit her lip and pulled off her beautiful ring. Without a word, she handed it to him.

"Maddie…"

She shoved it closer. He stared at it for a moment and then he took it. Their fingers touched and an electrical shock bolted through her. The tears weren't far away.

I love you. The words were in her heart, but she didn't say them. It would only complicate things.

"Goodbye, Maddie," he said, and slipped the ring into his pocket. Turning, he placed his hat on his head and walked to his car.

Goodbye.

It was over.

MADDIE RAN INTO THE HOUSE, up the stairs and into her room. Slamming the door, she slid down the wall like a wet noodle.

Pulling her knees up, she wrapped her arms around them to stop her body from shaking. And to keep from crying. It didn't work. The tears burst forth like a fountain and she cried for everything she'd lost, for everything that would never be.

From the moment Trisha reappeared in their lives, Maddie had known Walker was the father. Walker had known it, too. And so had Trisha. That's why she had come on the pretense of seeing the children. She was paving the way to get Walker back in her life.

Who would tell a man he *might* be the father unless the woman knew the truth? Trisha had a devious plan and it had worked. She gave Walker time to let the news of a new baby sink in. Trisha knew Walker as Maddie did. He would not abandon his child even at the expense of his own happiness.

The door opened and Cait and Sky slipped in and sank down by her. Sky lifted a bottle of wine. "Want to drink away your sorrow?"

"It won't help."

"We saw Walker drive away," Cait said. "What did he want?"

Maddie grabbed the bottle and took a swallow. "The baby is his."

"Dammit." Sky stretched out her legs, and Maddie noticed the Crocs she was wearing. Maddie had a pair in Philly, and that's where she wished she was now. But…

Taking another swallow, she added, "He's going to do the right thing by his kids. He wouldn't be the man I love if he didn't. It's just…"

"Hard," Cait said, finishing the sentence.

Maddie nodded, took another swig and handed the bottle to Sky.

"I can't. I have a three-year-old downstairs who depends on me being in my right mind."

"Kira's out of luck on that one," Cait said tongue-in-cheek.

"Don't push your luck, big sister." Sky made a face at Cait.

Maddie tipped up the bottle and handed it to Cait.

"No, thanks. Judd and I are trying to get pregnant and that damn sperm is taking forever to get to the egg, so that means no liquor. I'm on good behavior."

Maddie took a big swig and burst out laughing, spewing wine all over them. "Sorry," she muttered.

"You can't get drunk that quick." Sky brushed wine from her clothes with a frown.

"It just hit me that you two have finally grown up. I'm the only one still in limbo, so I guess I'll drink myself silly."

Sky jerked the bottle from her. "It's time to face some hard facts. The ex is a bitch. She left Walker and the kids and she doesn't have any right for a second chance." Sky dropped her voice. "It's time to be a Belle and stand and fight for what you want."

Maddie yanked the bottle back. "Dad said that when I was sixteen and Becky Thomas ran against me for class president. She was my friend, or I thought she was, and I didn't want to run against her."

"But Dad made you," Cait said. "And you won."

"And lost a friend."

"You didn't lose squat," Sky snapped. "But you will now if you let the ex take control by using the baby."

Maddie stared at the bottle and saw a lonely empty life ahead of her.

"I don't say this often." Cait linked her arm through Maddie's. "Hell, I've never said it. But Sky makes sense. If you want Walker, you have to make some hard choices. Just like the Becky incident, it's a matter of what you want. And I personally believe you're best for those kids. Think about it, Maddie, that's all we're saying."

"Hot damn, Cait." Sky raised her hand for a high five. "You're right for a change."

They slapped hands like they did when they were kids. Maddie raised the bottle. "Here's to shattered hearts, lost love and whatever the hell comes next."

She didn't really know, but with her sisters' help she could now face it. The more wine she consumed, the more an idea began to take hold.

Was she willing to fight for what she wanted?

CHAPTER NINETEEN

WALKER DROVE STEADILY toward Houston. Countryside of gently rolling hills, farms and ranches flashed by, but all he saw was the pain in Maddie's eyes. He'd probably see it for the rest of his life.

As he neared Houston, traffic became congested and slowed to a crawl. He was glad to see the Bel Air exit and turned off the freeway, heading for the medical center.

He parked in a parking garage and walked through to the hospital. It didn't take him long to find the nursery floor. The curtain on the picture window was open and he could see the babies inside, six girls, two boys.

His eyes scanned the name plates until he found Baby Walker. He moved closer. She was sound asleep, and the only thing visible was her face. Her head was covered in a pink cap and her tiny body was lost in a sleeper covered by a white-and-pink blanket.

He stared at the precious round face, bow mouth and upturned nose—just like Haley's. She was the spitting image of her sister.

His hand touched the glass. *Hey, little one. Your daddy's here.* His heart contracted, and he had a hard time looking away.

A nurse waved at him and mouthed something he didn't catch. She then closed the curtain. Otherwise, he probably wouldn't have moved from the spot.

He took a long breath and walked down the hall to Trisha's room. A woman at the front desk had given him the number. He tapped on the door and went in.

Trisha sat up in bed flipping agitatedly through a magazine. Her blond hair hung limply around her face and she wore a hospital gown. She looked up.

"Walker." She glanced past him. "Where are the kids?"

"At home."

"Dammit." She threw the magazine across the room. "You're doing this to hurt me."

"It's their choice. I've asked every day and they say they don't want to see you."

"You could make them." She jerked her fingers through her already tangled hair.

"I'm not going to do that."

"Oh, yeah. Mr. Perfect who never does anything wrong."

He let that slide and sat in a chair not far from the bed. Removing his hat, he studied the texture of the beaver felt for a second. "I don't understand why the kids don't want to see you. Haley ran away so many times to find you. It doesn't make sense."

"I just need to see her, talk to her. Can't you understand that?"

"Frankly, no I don't."

She glared at him with a look he knew well. She was about to lose her cool.

"I saw the baby," he said to segue into something they needed to talk about.

"Isn't she adorable?" Trisha's whole demeanor changed—the tense lines of her face eased.

"Yes. She favors Haley a lot."

A shadow crossed Trisha's face, and he was becoming more and more puzzled at her reactions and her attitude.

"I want to see the paternity test."

Her eyes shot open. "What? Don't you trust me?"

He looked her straight in the eye. "No."

"And you have to have those i's dotted and those t's crossed?"

"Yes."

She waved toward the door. "They're at the nurse's station."

He stood. "If everything checks out, you and the baby can come back to High Cotton with me. We can try to put our family back together." The words tasted like sawdust, but he meant every one.

"I'm not living in that hick town," she declared.

"That's your choice." He placed his hat on his head. "But the baby comes with me."

"No, Walker, please. She's all I have. Let me think about this." She jerked the sheet to her neck, her hands trembling. "I need a damn cigarette."

"You're still smoking?" She'd quit years ago. Or at least he had thought she had.

"Don't preach. I don't need a lecture. Tony said he was bringing them, but he hasn't showed."

Tony was back in her life. Walker was making a huge sacrifice and she was playing him and Tony against each other.

Before he could form a reply, the door opened and a man he'd never seen before stood there. Instinctively, he knew it was Tony.

The man was completely different from what Walker expected. Medium height, slightly balding with a long ponytail and full beard, Tony wore faded jeans and a black T-shirt. The short sleeves of the shirt were rolled up and a cigarette pack was hidden in one. Tattoos covered his arms, a snake on one and a dragon on the other. Biker man screamed through Walker's mind.

"What took you so damn long?" Trisha yelled.

Tony eyed him for a moment, and then walked over to Trisha. "Calm down. You can't smoke in here."

"Like hell." Trisha reached for Tony's hand. "C'mon, baby, I need a smoke. I'm coming apart at the seams."

Tony reached for the pack in his sleeve and tapped out one against his palm. "Be quick."

Walker watched this scene in a daze. He played by the rules and did what he was supposed to. There was a right and there was a wrong. This was wrong. He could clearly see that—wrong for him and for his kids.

He'd been willing to do the right thing, but… He moved toward the door on feet that felt like concrete.

"May I have a word with you, please?"

Walker turned to look at Tony. "You have nothing to say that I want to hear."

"Listen, man…"

"Tony, no." Trisha took a drag on the cigarette and pulled on the man's hand, stopping him.

Walker stared at the woman who used to be his wife and wondered if he had ever known her. "I'm going to confirm the paternity results and then I'm calling a lawyer. I'd advise you to do the same."

"Walker, Walker…" Trisha screamed after him.

But he didn't even pause in his stride.

He spoke to the nurse at the station, and he had to show his driver's license and sign before he could see the test. Ninety-nine point nine. The baby girl was definitely his. He thanked the nurse and then strolled to a small sitting area.

Having lived in Houston many years, he had a lot of

friends here. One was a lawyer, and Walker sat down to call him. He fingered the cell in his hand, staring at the beige tile on the floor. There was no way he and Trisha could reconcile and become a family again. Too much had happened. And he didn't love her.

He loved Maddie.

Thinking back, he wondered if he'd ever really loved Trisha the way he loved Maddie. He'd met Trisha when he was on leave from the marines. They had a whirl-wind week of hot sex and then he received a letter say-ing she was pregnant. Of course, since doing the right thing was his modus operandi, he had married her. God, how could one man get his life so screwed up?

He called his friend and told him what he wanted— full custody of the baby. He wanted the papers at the hospital as soon as possible. Come hell or high water, Trisha was not getting his daughter. Once he made that decision his life seemed to right itself.

"Hey, man." Tony ambled in and sat across from him.

Walker clipped his phone onto his belt. "I don't have one thing to say to you, Tony, except get a lawyer. This is going to get nasty."

"Trisha said you were going to get back together."

"For one insane moment I was willing to, for my kids. Trisha knows the kids are my weak spot, but she's not playing me anymore."

Tony nodded. "I think you're doing the right thing. The kids need to be with you."

He frowned. "Why? Because you don't want them?"

"Man, I'm not good with kids." Tony shook his head, a vein working overtime in his neck. "I had a stepson once and I took him riding on my motorcycle. A car slammed into us and he died instantly. He was seven years old." He took a deep breath. "That was it for me. I'm not taking responsibility for anyone else's kids."

"Then convince Trisha to let go of the baby and things will go a lot smoother."

Tony ran his palms down his thighs. "Man, I don't want to get into this, but I think you need to know."

"What the hell are you talking about?"

Tony clasped his hands between his legs. "Trisha and I have been friends since grade school. We were going to get married, but I wanted to see the world on my motorcycle and she didn't. I ended up in California and I have a motorcycle shop. I sometimes do stunts for some of the studios. But no matter how far away I got, Trisha and I stayed in touch."

"Funny she never mentioned your name."

"There was nothing but friendship between us then."

"Evidently that changed." Walker couldn't believe he was talking to this man. He should just walk away. But he found he couldn't.

"After my divorce, every time I came to Houston to visit my mom, I'd see Trisha. I love Trisha, but she didn't feel that way about me until last year. My mom was ill and I stayed in Houston for a long time." He paused. "Things just happened—you know."

"It's called adultery."

Tony moved restlessly. "Yeah. But Trisha needed me and I was glad to help her with her problems. We've always been kindred spirits."

Walker's frown deepened. "Problems?"

"I don't know how to say this."

"Then maybe you shouldn't."

"Yep. I should get up and walk away. Trisha's going to hate me for this."

An icy chill slid up Walker's spine. Yet he waited.

Tony flexed his hands and the snake tattoo seemed to wiggle up his arm. Walker watched as if fascinated.

"Man, have you ever noticed your kids have a lot of accidents?"

The question took him by surprise. "Kids are kids and they get bumps and bruises."

"That's one way of looking at it." The snake wiggled faster and Walker knew something bad was coming. "Have they had any lately?"

"No, why?"

Instead of answering, Tony said, "They seemed to have a lot when they were with Trisha."

"What are you getting at?"

Tony raised his head. "I made Trisha leave to protect your kids."

Walker clenched his jaw. "You'll have to explain that."

Tony clamped his hands onto his knees. "Okay, man, here it is. Trisha has a temper. You know that."

"Yes."

"Haley didn't fall off her bike and break her arm. She was whining about something she wanted. Trisha told her no, but she kept on. Finally Trisha slapped her hard and she fell against the kitchen table. That's how she broke her arm. The bruise on Haley's shoulder happened the same way. As did Georgie's concussion. The boy's always yakking and not listening and it makes Trisha angry. His head bounced off the tile floor. That's how he got the concussion. Your kids were being abused. It's not all the time but lately it's gotten worse. Trisha can't control her temper."

Walker leaped to his feet, his hands locked into fists. Everything in him denied what he was hearing. But he knew it was true. The bruises on the kids when he returned from a mission. When he'd questioned Trisha, she'd say, "Haley fell again today," or "Georgie jumped off the swingset and hit his head. He's clumsy." *And he'd believed her!* Everything started to make sense.

Did you hit Georgie?

I don't want to see her.

But one thing didn't. "Haley ran away many times to find Trisha. Why would she do that?"

"Trisha told Haley if you ever found out, that you would have her arrested and thrown in jail. Then Haley and Georgie would be put in foster care because you didn't want them."

"But once Haley was with me and her mother out of her life, she never said a word."

"You'll have to ask Haley about that."

"And the school watches for signs like that. A teacher would have noticed." He was searching for excuses. It couldn't be true.

"She did, but Trisha told the teacher that Haley gets really weak when she throws up so much, and she falls. The teacher believed her because Haley was throwing up at school."

Oh my God!

I have to see Mama.

You know where Mama is. You just won't tell me.

You don't want us.

Is Mama okay?

Haley's words tortured him. It had been a cry for help and he hadn't heard it. His legs felt weak and he sank back into the chair. The hell his kids must have been going through and he'd been oblivious to it all. Believing Trisha. Their mother.

The chill turned to an icicle that pierced through to his heart. It was clear now why Haley had befriended

Ginny—because of the abuse. Haley knew how that felt.

He'd blamed Ginny for putting his kid's lives in danger. But he had done much worse. Every time he walked out the door of his home and went on a mission, he'd threatened Haley's and Georgie's lives by being oblivious as to what was happening in his own house.

How could he not have known? Not suspected? He was their father and should have been looking out for them, seeing the signs.

You were helping other people when you should have been helping us.

Haley's words drove the icicle further into his heart. He'd failed his kids. He'd let them down. What kind of father was he?

"Man, I'm sorry." Tony's voice penetrated his thoughts. "But Trisha was very good at covering up, and she was so sorry afterward. She really didn't mean to hurt them. She just loses control every now and then."

Walker raised his eyes to Tony's, anger shooting through him like an electric current. "That bitch will pay for making their lives a living hell."

"Ah, c'mon, man, take your kids and leave her alone. Despite her faults, I love her and I'll take care of her."

Walker stood. "She will never see her kids again, including the baby."

Tony got to his feet, rubbing his beard. "Well now, Trisha's gonna fight that. She sees this baby as her redemption."

"It's not going to happen."

"I can talk Trisha into letting go, but you have to promise not to press charges."

Walker stepped closer, his body rigid. "You're not in a position to make deals."

Tony took a step backward. "You need me, man. Admit it. Leave Trisha alone and I'll make sure she gets help."

"All I see is a man who stood by and let her abuse my kids."

Tony held up his hands. "Whoa, man. I was in Hollywood most of the time. Trisha called when something bad happened and she was always sorry and promised it wouldn't happen again. Just like you, I believed her."

Walker took off at a run. He had to get away from Tony, Trisha and the guilt that was ripping through him.

As he ran from the hospital, his boots thumping on the tiled floor, people stared at him. But he kept going.

His heart pounding, his lungs tight, he sank onto a bench, realizing he was never going to outrun the guilt. It was branded on his heart.

Failure as a father.

Maddie.

The one word brought calm to his shattered mind. He'd never needed anyone in his life. He was strong, able to handle whatever life threw at him. But he needed her.

What would she think of a man who failed to protect his children?

MADDIE WOKE UP ON HER BED fully clothed in the afternoon. What? She sat up and her head pounded with a reminder. Jeez! She'd drunk too much wine. And she wasn't a drinker. Holy moly.

She swung her feet to the side and sat there for a moment as she thought about the conversation with her sisters.

Fight for what you want. That was easy for them, but she was different. She was raised to be kind, gentle, loving and to never hurt anyone. That was her nature and it sucked most of the time. People took advantage of her, just like Becky had in high school. She knew Madison would not run against her friend.

Becky had been wrong.

Maddie's father had made her.

But Maddie had not felt good about the situation. The tension, the catfighting and the ugly words got to her. But she was a Belle and would not bow to adversity. Those were her father's words and she'd always thought he was right and that he knew everything.

This time he didn't. She couldn't stay in High Cotton and watch Walker with his wife and kids. It would be too painful. She had no recourse but to return to Philadelphia. Her mother was home now and would be excited to see her.

She walked to the closet and pulled down her suitcase. Methodically, she neatly placed undies and bras inside.

You're running.

Belles don't run.

She glanced at the photo of her father and her sisters on her nightstand. "Stop talking to me."

Gathering blouses, the voice kept taunting, "You're running. You're running."

She sank onto the bed, the blouses in her arms. She was running. From the pain. And she was letting everyone down, including herself.

The cancer had taken her ability to have children, but it hadn't taken her ability to love. She loved Walker. And she loved Haley and Georgie.

Could Trisha love them more than her? She'd been

Walker's wife and she was Haley and Georgie's mother. But she'd tarnished that love when she'd left them.

Walker didn't love Trisha. Maddie was certain of that. So what kind of marriage could they have without love? A turbulent one, she surmised. And that wasn't good for the kids.

Without even realizing it, she was hanging the blouses back in the closet. She wasn't leaving. Trisha couldn't make her leave. This time Madison Belle was fighting for what she wanted. And she wanted Walker, Haley and Georgie. The new baby was another matter. But until Walker told her they had no future, she was still in the game.

She quickly dressed in black slacks and a cobalt-blue cashmere sweater. Nell would know where Walker was in Houston, and Maddie planned to find him there. She might get her heart broken all over again, but it was a risk she was willing to take.

Hot damn, her fighting spirit had finally been awakened. Sometimes certain things were worth fighting for.

Grabbing her purse, she headed for the door with a spring in her step.

There was something about being bad that made her feel very, very good.

SHE KISSED GRAN AND TOLD her where she was going and for her not to worry. Sky had gone into Giddings, and Maddie didn't have time to wait for her. Gran would give her the message.

Her head was still aching and she'd meant to take some Tylenol, but she didn't have time. She had to talk to Coop. He was probably wondering what had happened to her.

Coop wasn't in the barn, so she had to leave him a note. It would take too long to find him. She searched for a pen and pad in her purse and was scribbling an explanation when she heard a noise. Was that ol' tomcat chasing a rat?

She finished the note and propped it by the bridles where she knew Coop would go when he unsaddled for the day. Turning, she heard the noise again and glanced toward the horse stalls. Two sets of sneakers were visible under one. Her heart picked up speed. She knew exactly who they belonged to.

Haley and Georgie.

Before she could move, the door flew open and Georgie ran to her. "It's me. It's me, Mommy."

She caught him and just held him. Oh, how she'd missed them.

Haley leaned into her and Maddie wrapped an arm around her.

"We miss you," Haley murmured.

"I miss you, too." She set Georgie on his feet. "Does your father know you're here?"

Haley shook her head.

"Let's talk." Maddie led them to a bale of hay and sat down, one child on each side of her.

As she started to speak, her cell buzzed and she fumbled in her purse for it.

"Maddie, have you seen Haley or Georgie?" Nell's frantic voice came on the line. "Georgie and I were watching a movie and I fell asleep. When I woke up, they were both gone. Walker's going to be so mad."

"They're here, Nell, and they're both fine."

"Oh, thank God."

"Where's Walker?"

"He's still in Houston seeing Trisha."

"Which hospital?"

Nell told her and then said, "I'm so relieved. They've been so deviant lately and it's hard to deal with them. I'll be right there."

"It's okay. I'll keep them."

"Are you sure?"

"Yes, and I don't think Walker will mind. If he does, I'll explain it to him."

"Okay. I know you'll take good care of them."

Maddie looked at Haley. "Now Haley would like to say she's sorry for worrying you." She handed the girl the phone.

Haley talked for a minute, tears swimming in her eyes, and then handed the phone back. Maddie slipped it into her purse.

"I am sorry, Maddie, but I didn't know what else to do. Daddy is going to make us see Mama."

"And you don't want to?"

Haley shook her head.

"Tell me why, sweetie. When I first met you, you were running away to find her."

"Do I have to?"

Georgie crawled into her lap and buried his face in her chest. Maddie patted his back, and Haley burrowed into her as if she wanted to disappear. It wasn't hard to recognize that they were both afraid.

"Tell me, sweetie."

"You can't tell Daddy," she murmured against Maddie.

Maddie stroked her hair. "We don't keep secrets from Daddy. Tell me and I promise I will help you. Trust me, sweetie."

All her life Maddie had been a calm, patient person, but as Haley talked, anger consumed her and she wanted to physically hurt Trisha. For them she kept her emotions in check, wondering how they'd managed to survive.

She clutched their small bodies, telling them that no one was ever going to hurt them again.

"Sweetie." Maddie rubbed Haley's arm. "When your mother left, why didn't you confide in your father? You knew the foster care threat was over."

"I was scared," Haley hiccupped. "I didn't know if Mama was really with Tony or in jail. I came home from school and she was gone. Georgie and I stayed at the neighbors' until Daddy arrived. He wouldn't tell me anything and I asked and asked. Mama said he didn't want us and I thought he didn't."

"But later when you knew your daddy loved you and wanted you, why didn't you say something?"

"I was too scared. If Daddy found out, he might hurt Mama 'cause…'cause…"

"She did a bad thing."

"Uh-huh."

"And you love your mother?"

Haley nodded. "And it was my fault. I threw up and made her nervous and angry…and I didn't behave. I…"

"No. No. No. It's not your fault."

"It's not?" Haley's eyes opened wide.

Maddie hugged her. "No, sweetie. You did nothing wrong."

"But…but I don't want to live with Mama anymore and Daddy might make us."

"He won't, but you need to see your mother and tell her how you feel."

Haley drew back, wiping at her eyes. "Will you go with me?"

Maddie tucked wet strands of hair behind Haley's

ear. "Yes. But you need to see her with your daddy. Do you think you can do that?"

Haley nodded.

"Then let's go find your father."

A few minutes later, they were in Gran's old Lincoln headed for Houston. First they had to stop by Nell's for Georgie's car seat and then they were off.

To find Walker.

CHAPTER TWENTY

AFTER WALKER HAD HIMSELF under control, he went back into the hospital. He wanted to talk to Haley, but he couldn't do that on the phone. He had to do it in person. His lawyer called and he met Mike in the cafeteria.

They had coffee and he listened to his options as he watched people eating, laughing and talking as if his world hadn't been shattered for the third time.

"Walker."

He looked at his friend, who was starting to go bald and had a spare tire around his middle. But to Walker he was the guy in the marines who'd always had his back. With effort, he brought his attention to the conversation.

"I only have one option. No way am I letting Trisha walk out of this hospital with the baby."

"Well, then." Mike patted his briefcase. "Let's see if you can get Trisha to sign papers relinquishing her parental rights. As the father you will have full custody."

"Can you get a court order to prevent her from removing the baby from the hospital?"

"You bet I can."

Now Walker just had to persuade Trisha to sign the papers.

How in the hell was he going to do that?

ON THE WAY TO HOUSTON, Georgie fell asleep and it wasn't long before Haley did, too. Two young lives torn apart by a mother who couldn't control her anger. She knew Walker wasn't aware of any of this, and he had to know as soon as possible.

Again, she was sticking her nose into his business, but this time she hoped he didn't mind. It was almost five when they reached the hospital. She asked at the desk for Trisha's room number and she kept looking for Walker. He was nowhere in sight, but it was a big place.

She got snacks for the kids from a vending machine. Since she couldn't find Walker, she was unsure of what to do next.

Settling the kids in chairs down the hall from Trisha's room, she said, "Stay here and I'll see if I can find your father."

"I'll be good," Georgie replied around a mouthful of an Oreo cookie.

"I'll watch him," Haley told her.

"Do not leave this spot."

"Maddie…"

"And don't worry."

Haley nodded, but Maddie could clearly see the worry in her eyes.

She tapped on Trisha's door and heard a faint "Come in."

Trisha sat up in bed, her hair hanging around her face. She'd aged since Maddie had seen her a few weeks ago. Dark rings shaded her eyes and her face was drawn.

"What do you want?" Trisha asked in a defensive tone.

"I was looking for Walker."

"He just had to call you, didn't he?"

"No. I haven't heard from him."

"Then what are you doing here?"

Maddie took a seat in a straight-back chair, even though she hadn't been asked to. Her knees were feeling weak. Trisha's anger was hard to confront, but it didn't stop her.

"I had a talk with Haley."

Trisha's features tightened. "So?"

"Do you really have to ask that question?"

Trisha pleated the sheet with her fingers. "It's not as bad as she said."

"When you hit a child hard enough to break her arm or give him a concussion, it's bad any way you look at it."

"They were accidents."

Maddie set her purse on the floor. "I firmly believe every woman has a right to raise her own children, but you don't deserve Haley or Georgie."

Trisha pointed a finger at her, her eyes blazing. "You're not getting my kids."

"I'm just trying to protect them, something you should have been doing since the day they were born." It crossed Maddie's mind that she shouldn't be talking to Trisha without Walker. But if she was going to fight, this was where she started.

"No one understands me," Trisha said in a low voice.

"Help me to understand." Heavens, what was she doing?

To Maddie's surprise, Trisha wiped away a tear. "I love them, but I have a hard time controlling my temper. I...I—" she blinked away another tear "—had a rotten childhood. My father died when I was little. I don't even remember him. After that, my mother was an angry woman who went into violent rages. My sister and I lived in fear every day of our lives. I swore I would never do that to my kids but..."

Maddie tried to harden her heart, but she couldn't. She felt sorry for the woman.

"I can be a good mother. I just need a chance."

Maddie took a moment before she replied. "You've had your share of chances. Do what's best for your kids."

Trisha looked straight at her. "Do you want them?"

She reached for her purse and stood, knowing she'd already said too much. "I would love them, care for them and protect them with my life."

"But they love me," Trisha said in that same low voice, the anger not so evident. "Walker said when I left Georgie cried for two weeks for his mama."

"Kids are like that. They love you no matter what, and you're the only mother Georgie has known. He missed you and he didn't know where you were."

As if Maddie hadn't spoken, Trisha added, "Walker said Haley ran away trying to find me."

"Yes, she did. She was scared. She thought Walker had put you in jail and it was her fault because she threw up and made you nervous and angry. She thought it was her fault that you hit her repeatedly. And you made it worse by forcing her to lie."

Trisha pleated the sheet into a knot. "I had to. If Walker found out…"

"He would have insisted you get help and made sure that you did. He would have been there for you and the kids."

Trisha looked up, her eyes skeptical. "You don't know that."

"Yes, I do. I know Walker. He would be angry, but he would do the right thing by you."

The door opened and a man in a leather jacket strolled in. He looked as if he rode with the Hell's Angels. She thought he had the wrong room until Trisha screamed at him.

"Get out of here, Tony. I told you to leave. I thought you loved me, but then you went and told Walker behind my back. Get out, you bastard."

The man glanced at Maddie, seemingly unmoved by Trisha's tirade. "Hi, I'm Tony Almada."

"I'm Madison Belle."

"She's Walker's new love," Trisha said. "And she's trying to make me feel guilty."

"Is it working?" Tony quipped, and Maddie instantly liked him. But she had to wonder what he was doing here.

"Go away, Tony," Trisha shouted again.

Tony walked to the bed. "C'mon, babe, you know I'm not going anywhere."

"How could you tell Walker?" Trisha's voice was softer. Relenting. Maddie knew it was time for her to go.

"I have to find Walker."

Trisha scooted up in the bed. "I know you think I can't change, but I can."

"How many times have you told yourself that?"

Trisha hung her head.

"How many times have you told Haley and Georgie you were sorry? How many times have you told them you'd never hit them again?"

"Get the hell out of my room," Trisha yelled, her anger now turned on Maddie.

"Calm down, babe. She's only trying to help," Tony said, trying to soothe her.

Maddie slipped the strap of her purse over her shoulder. "Do what's best for your kids. That's a promise you can keep."

Before she could open the door, Trisha called, "Madison."

Maddie turned back.

"Please talk Walker into letting me see Haley and Georgie."

"That's Walker's decision."

"Bitch," Trisha shouted as Maddie walked out of the room.

As SHE CLOSED THE DOOR, she saw Walker coming down the hall. The kids noticed him at the same time as she did. They leaped to their feet and made a dash for him. Haley reached him first, wrapping her arms around his waist. Georgie attached himself to Walker's leg.

"Hey, where'd y'all come from?" Walker squatted as both kids barreled into his chest.

"I told Maddie, Daddy. I'm sorry. I'm sorry…" Haley's brokenhearted cries were echoed by the anguish on Walker's face.

"Let's sit over here." Walker stood, both kids still clinging to him. "We need to talk."

"Haley told me some shocking news that I thought you needed to hear, but—" Maddie waved over her shoulder "—I was looking for you and had a chat with Trisha. Evidently you already know. I…I'll leave you alone.…"

"Maddie."

She looked into his pain-filled eyes. "You need to talk to the kids alone."

Walking off down the hall, she didn't know if he was angry with her or not. He might not even want the kids here, and she'd taken it upon herself to bring them. At the time, she'd thought he hadn't known about Trisha hitting them. But he had. That must have caused him inexplicable pain. She wanted to be with him, to help him through this. But her presence would only be an added complication.

For now...

WALKER WATCHED HER LEAVE, his heart so tied in knots he couldn't even think straight. But one thought was very clear. What must she think of him? A man so consumed with his own life he hadn't seen the signs of abuse. He'd let his kids down. He was supposed to protect them. He...

"Daddy, I'm sorry." He had his arm around Haley and her face was buried in his side. Georgie sat on his lap.

"Sweetheart, you have nothing to be sorry about."

She raised her head. "You know, don't you?"

He nodded.

"I should have told you."

"When Ginny's baby was born and we got home, one night you tried to tell me, didn't you?"

"Yes."

"Why didn't you?"

"I was scared. I knew you'd be angry, and if Mama wasn't in jail and with Tony then...then... I didn't want you to put her in jail so I kept quiet."

"Is that why you were so angry with me?"

She nodded. "I was just so scared and I thought you didn't want us."

"Oh, sweetheart. I do, always remember that." He hugged her. "I'm so sorry you've been put through this, but please don't ever keep things from me again, no matter how painful."

"Okay. Maddie said I needed to talk to Mama."

Trust Maddie to get them to do something he

couldn't. He had done it out of fear. She'd done it out of love.

"Are you ready to do that?"

"If you go with me."

Walker jostled his son. "How about you, Georgie?"

Georgie bobbed his head in agreement.

"Let's go see your mother, then." Walker knew Haley was ready. Thank God Maddie had brought them.

When they entered the room, Trisha and Tony stopped talking. Arguing was more like it.

Trisha sat up and clapped her hands. "Haley and Georgie, you're here. Oh, I've missed you. Come give your mother a hug."

Haley stepped forward, but Georgie did not. He was glued to Walker's leg. Haley took his hand and pulled him toward the bed. She had to lift her brother so he could hug Trisha, but they both hugged their mother.

"Oh, my, Haley, you're getting so pretty."

"Maddie tells me that all the time."

Trisha's face tightened and she turned her attention to Georgie. "I think you've grown a couple of inches."

"I'm big." Georgie raised his hands above his head. "I'm a cowboy. Maddie lets me ride her horse and she bought me boots and a hat."

"Well, good for Maddie," Trisha said in a sarcastic tone.

"Maddie cooks all kinds of food that I can eat," Haley told her. "I've gained four pounds."

"She gives me a bath and she even shot some doggies that were going to get me. She…"

"Shut up. Shut up. Shut up," Trisha screeched, holding her hands over her ears.

Both kids ran to Walker. Both were trembling.

"I'm sorry. I'm sorry," Trisha apologized. "Just don't

talk about her, okay? Come back to Mama. I love you guys."

Neither child moved.

Then Haley said in a quiet voice, "We love you, too, but we don't want to live with you anymore. You hurt us."

Georgie nodded vigorously in agreement.

"Oh, oh, oh." Trisha began to cry and Tony reached for her hand.

"Take Georgie into the hall," Walker said to Haley. "I'll be there in a minute."

"Walker, no…"

He stepped closer to the bed, his anger on a tight leash. "As I told Tony, hire a lawyer. You're going to need one. My attorney is filing an order with the court so Baby Girl Walker will not be moved from this hospital until custody is decided."

"You can't do that."

"Watch me."

WALKER PACED, WAITING ON HIS attorney. He wanted something settled tonight. The kids were looking at the baby. He wondered where Maddie was. Why hadn't she come back? God, he needed her.

Finally, Mike stepped off the elevator. They shook hands.

"Sorry to keep you working so late."

Mike grinned. "You saved my life a time or two so I think I owe you. Now let's see if we can get Trisha to sign away her rights."

"Let me check on my kids and I'll be right with you."

Walker made sure Haley and Georgie weren't being a nuisance, and then they made their way to Trisha's room. She was sitting in a chair still in the gown, but now she had a white terry-cloth robe over it. She looked old beyond her years. Pain and sorrow filled her eyes, and it was the only thing that kept Walker from strangling the life out of her.

Tony stood between him and Trisha. Mike waited behind Walker.

"I'm sorry, Walker. I…" She began to cry again and Tony rubbed her shoulder.

"It's all right, babe."

"I love my kids," she wailed.

Tony knelt in front of her. "But you can't be a mother to them. You know that, babe."

"I can."

"No," Tony said. "You've already proved you can't. If you love your kids, you have to do what Madison told you—do what's best for them. Their father will give them a great home."

"I can't," she sobbed.

"Yes, you can," Tony persisted, and Walker was beginning to think the man was an okay guy. "It'll be just you and me, babe, against the world. I love you. Do the right thing here."

Trisha remained stubborn.

"If you don't, that's it for me. I'm gone from your life for good. Kids aren't my thing, you know that."

"You're just saying that."

"I mean it."

"What if the baby had been yours?"

"Then we'd have a problem. My mother probably would have raised it because, babe, as much as I love you, you don't need to be around kids, especially a baby."

She grabbed Tony and sobbed into his shoulder. Tony whispered something to her. After a minute, Trisha got to her feet, brushing away tears. "What do you want me to sign?"

Mike laid the papers on the eating tray and Trisha stared at them. "I want the right to see my kids."

"It's in an agreement Mike has drawn up. You can see them three times a year, but only if you're in counseling and I will always be present."

"That's fair, babe," Tony said. "Walker's a good guy."

Trisha choked back a sob and signed away her rights. Walker let out a sigh of relief.

He left feeling drained, empty and so very alone. He had his kids, thanks to Tony. That was the most important thing.

But he didn't have Maddie.

He sank into a chair in the hall and pulled out his phone. Where was she? All he had to do was call her, hear her voice and his world would be normal again. Guilt slammed into his chest.

What must she think of him now?

His Maddie was a very understanding person, though. His Maddie... Her ring burned a hole in his pocket and he placed his hand over it. God, he had two kids and a baby. He needed her—a woman like Maddie.

But did she need him?

He sighed in torment. Closing his eyes, he could see her face. It was right there, giving him courage.

"Walker."

He opened his eyes and there she was. Beautiful as ever in a blue sweater that made her eyes brilliant. Her blond hair bounced around her perfect, sweet face.

"Walker," Maddie said again. What was wrong with him? He looked confused, worried.

She took a step toward him and he jumped to his feet. "Maddie, where did you go? I thought you left."

"I went to the chapel to pray that Trisha would do the right thing for her kids."

He ran a hand through his already tousled hair. He looked so down, so beat, and she just wanted to hold him.

"I thought you might be angry with me."

He frowned. "Why?"

"For bringing the kids and talking to Trisha."

That ghost of a smile touched his lips. "I don't think there's anything you can do that would make me angry."

She wanted to sink into his warm smile and voice, but she couldn't. Not yet. "After a lot of thought and coaxing from my sisters, I decided I wasn't going to let you go so easily. I was going to fight for our love. Then I talked to Haley and…"

"And?" The one word was barely a sound.

She swallowed. "I'm going to fight for us until you tell me not to."

He sighed heavily, as if he was expecting another answer. He slipped a hand into his jeans and pulled out her ring. "There's no way I can live with Trisha again. Will you marry me with all my faults and my problems?"

"Yes," she whispered, barely breathing. She held out her hand and saw that it was trembling. As he slipped the ring on, the trembling ceased and she threw herself into his arms.

Holding her in a bearlike grip, he cradled her head with one hand. "You came when I needed you the most. God, I love you so much it hurts."

She kissed the warmth of his neck, soaking up the scent and feel of him. "I love you, too."

His lips captured hers, and she wrapped her arms

around his neck and went with the moment and everything she was feeling.

"Well, I never." A woman's voice drew them apart, but only slightly. "This is a hospital. Some people have no decency."

"Now, Mable. I think it's kind of nice."

"Herman," the woman shrieked. "Get on this elevator and stop gawking."

Maddie spluttered with laughter and Walker drew her to a chair.

He buried his face in his hands. "I feel like such a failure. I wasn't there to protect my kids, and I thought you might want to get as far away from me as possible."

She stroked his arm. "No way, and you can't blame yourself. You had no idea what Trisha was doing, and she hid it very well by making Haley lie."

"I'm always going to feel guilty."

"I'll help you with that." She kissed his cheek. "We already have Haley and Georgie. Now we have to fight for the baby."

He smiled, a real honest-to-God smile, and gathered her into his arms. "I'm way ahead of you. Trisha signed away her rights a little while ago."

"Oh, Walker."

"Are you ready for what's about to happen—a life with three kids."

"I've never been more ready." She laughed, a happy sound that erupted from her throat.

He stood and pulled her to her feet.

"Wait." She wiped away an errant tear. "I don't want the kids to see me crying."

Walker kissed away her tears just before Haley and Georgie came running. He held his children as if he couldn't bear to let them go. "I love you," he murmured. "And we're starting a new life with Maddie."

"Oh, boy," Georgie shouted, and leaped for Maddie.

"And with your new baby sister."

Haley leaned away. "Really?"

"Yes," Walker replied. "It's time for Maddie to meet her."

The kids darted ahead and Walker reached for her hand. The curtain was open. Haley pressed her face against the glass.

"I can't see," Georgie cried. "I can't see."

Walker lifted him and pointed to a crib on the right. "There she is." His eyes were on Maddie.

Maddie could only stare at the beautiful baby wrapped in pink. Her breath caught, and she looped an arm around Walker. All her dreams were right here just waiting for her. How lucky she was. How incredibly lucky.

She thought she would never have a family, a child of her own, but now… Her eyes filled with tears. Haley moved to her side and Maddie hugged her, feeling so much happiness she was about to burst. These were her kids. Madison's children. She may not have given birth to them, but it didn't matter. She loved them with all her heart.

She'd always thought a woman had a right to raise her own children. But not in this case.

"We have to give her a name," Walker said.

As she stared at that precious face she knew there was only one name that would fit. "Valentine," she whispered.

"We can call her Val," Haley said, her voice excited.

Walker groaned and set Georgie on his feet. "Maddie…"

He stared into her beautiful blue eyes and gave in without a protest. This day had been the worst of his life, but because of her he saw a rainbow so bright that he now believed there was a little good in everyone. Even Trisha. She had given the ultimate sacrifice for her kids' happiness. He and Maddie would protect them with their love and their lives.

EPILOGUE

Three months later.

THERE WAS SOMETHING ABOUT loving a good woman that made Walker feel good about himself. And his ex. He honestly believed she never meant to hurt the kids. She just couldn't control her temper.

That helped him sleep at night and kept the bad thoughts at bay. As Tony had promised, Trisha was now getting help. He hoped she found a measure of happiness with her biker man.

Walker put soap in the dishwasher, closed it and pushed a button. Oh, if his marine buddies could see him now. Domesticated. By the sweetest woman in the world.

Placing the dish towel across the sink, he looked out the window to the sunny April day. A scent of freshness was in the air as new leaves adorned trees and green grasses sprouted. Spring. A new beginning.

He leaned back against the counter and folded his arms across his chest. They certainly had a new beginning. Their marriage had taken place in the parlor at High Five, just as Cait and Judd's had. But theirs had been simple.

Maddie had worn a long white dress, and the top had been covered in lace. Her mother had brought it from Philadelphia. Meeting Audrey, he knew where his wife got her loving heart. He couldn't even imagine playboy Dane Belle with the prim and proper Audrey. But he supposed every good girl needed a bad boy in her life. Or else he wouldn't have his Maddie.

Audrey and her husband embraced the kids with open arms and open hearts. Haley and Georgie took to their new grandparents immediately and called them Nana and Pa. They couldn't wait until they visited Philly in May when Maddie had a checkup.

Walker would make sure Maddie never missed an appointment. She had to stay healthy. They needed her too much. *What if* wasn't in their vocabulary.

Since Maddie had segued into motherhood full-time, Sky was now running High Five. There was a lot of tension with Cooper, but Cait and Maddie insisted that he stay. The next few months should be interesting.

"Honey," his wife called. "Get the video camera. We're ready."

He dashed into the living room for the camera. Maddie came down the stairs with the baby on her shoulder, Georgie trailing behind her. The new baby was a big adjustment for his son, but Maddie handled it with love, like she did everything.

She gently laid the baby in the small crib in the living room. It had been Maddie's and Audrey thought she should have it.

Georgie peeked over the railing. "Why does she sleep so much?"

"All babies sleep. She's growing and dreaming." Maddie kissed the top of his head. "Know what she's dreaming about?"

"Uh-uh."

"She's dreaming of her big brother and how much she loves him."

"I love her, too."

Maddie hugged him and kissed his cheek. "I have to get my camera to take pictures of Haley."

"She looks dorky," Georgie said.

Maddie swung back and held a finger in front of his face. "Beautiful," she said slowly. "You don't want to hurt your sister's feelings."

"'Kay."

"Mommy," Haley called from the top of the stairs. "The bow in my hair feels loose."

Maddie darted up the stairs to fix the bow. Haley was going to a girl-boy birthday party of a classmate. Her first. Walker wasn't happy about it, but Maddie assured him it was normal.

Maddie hurried down and grabbed her camera. She glanced at him and winked. "Ready?"

He smiled. "Ready."

Haley slowly descended the stairs and he caught every second on film while Maddie snapped still shots. His daughter looked so different in a denim jumper and a pink knit top that matched the embroidery on the dress. Her blond hair was held up with a pink ribbon.

They worked hard to keep Haley's nervous stomach under control. Very seldom did she have a bad day, and it usually had something to do with school or eating the wrong food.

Haley had put on a few more pounds and he realized how beautiful she was. He didn't know if he was ready for the years ahead.

"Be sure to get a picture for Gran," Haley said. "And Nana and Pa."

"Oh, I have plenty." Maddie clicked away.

When Haley reached the bottom, Maddie lowered the camera. "Oh, sweetie, you look so pretty."

"Beau-ti-ful," Georgie corrected her.

"Oh, yes, very beautiful."

They heard a car in the driveway and Haley ran for the door. "Bye. Remember, Daddy, Cara's mom is taking us, but you have to pick us up."

"What?" He lowered the camera. "I don't even get a hug?"

"Daddy." Haley ran back and hugged him.

He held her for an extra second. "Have a great time, sweetheart."

The door slammed behind her and Walker laid the camera on the coffee table. Maddie went into his arms. She smelled of milk, soap and lavender.

"Haley will be fine," she whispered.

"I know. She's just growing up too fast."

"We have a long way to go."

"It's time for my bath." Georgie looked up at them.

"Yes, son, I believe it is." Georgie had dirt all over him from his face to his jeans. "Have you been playing in a pigpen?"

"Uh-uh. Just outside."

Maddie took Georgie's hand and they headed for the stairs.

"Can we go feed Solomon tomorrow, Mommy?"

"Yes."

"Can I play with Kira?"

"Yes."

A wail sounded from the crib. Maddie stopped.

"I'll get her," Walker said.

By the time they had Georgie tucked in and the baby fed and in her crib upstairs, they were both exhausted.

They sat on the sofa and Maddie curled into his side just as the doorbell rang.

"Damn." He got to his feet and went to the door. Nell stood there.

"Oh, Maddie." Nell walked past him as if he wasn't even standing there. "I just finished a blanket for the baby."

Maddie held up the pink-and-white knitted work. "Thank you. It's beautiful."

That made about the tenth blanket or quilt that Nell had made. How many did one baby need? But it made Nell happy so he didn't say a word. Besides, Nell was part of their family and he would never hurt her feelings.

Nell looked around. "Did I miss Haley?"

"She just left." Maddie patted Nell's hands. "I took lots of pictures, so don't worry, we have it on film."

"Good." Nell stood. "I better go. It's past my bedtime. I'll see y'all tomorrow."

Walker headed for Maddie, rubbing his hands in glee. "Now…"

The doorbell pealed.

"Dammit, if that's Nell…"

"I'll get it." Maddie hurried to the door and glanced back at him. "Be nice."

She opened the door to a man she vaguely recognized. He was her father's attorney from Austin. What was he doing here?

"Hi, Frank," she said, "please come in."

"No, thanks, Madison. I'm so sorry I missed your wedding."

"That's okay."

"No, it isn't. Dane entrusted his affairs to me and I've let him down, but I'm here to correct that." He pulled a letter from the inside of his suit jacket and handed it to her. "I was supposed to give you this at your wedding, but I had no idea you were getting married."

"It was rather sudden, so don't blame yourself."

"I wish you and Walker all the best."

"Thank you."

Walker closed the door, and Maddie sat on the sofa with the letter in her hand. She stared at it a long time. What was inside? With a trembling hand, she slipped a finger beneath the flap and opened it. One line leaped out at her in her father's bold signature.

"Now you're living, sweet angel. Love, Dad."

As she read it over and over she couldn't stop the tears that rolled from her eyes.

"Honey." Walker was immediately at her side. "What is it?" His arms went around her and he glanced at the paper. "What does that mean?"

"Dad always said if you're not willing to take a risk, you're not living. Cait and Sky were his risk-takers, but he worried about me because I was always so cautious." She brushed away another tear. "These are his last words to me and they mean so much."

"Honey." He stroked her cheek.

"I'm happy. I really am." She smiled through her tears. "I took a risk just like he wanted me to and look what I have." She curled her arms around his neck. "I have you. You're my risk, my life, my everything."

He held her for a long time and she breathed in the scent of him. Every empty, lonely part of her had been filled by his strong, compassionate love.

"Are you sure you're okay?"

"Yes." She snuggled into him, her hand slowly caressing his chest. "Are you tired?"

"Not when you're touching me."

She leaned her head back to look at his handsome

face. "We have two hours, Valentine. Well, we're a little short on that now, and if the baby doesn't wake up…"

A ghost of a smile spread across his lips.

She jumped up. "I know where there's a towel." She ran for the stairs with the letter in her hand. She would keep it forever. Some risks were worth taking. Her father had taught her that.

Now she would spend the rest of her life with the man of her dreams.

Valentine Walker.

* * * * *

We hope you enjoyed

HOME ON THE RANCH: TEXAS.

If you liked these stories, then you're in luck—Harlequin has a Western romance for every mood!

Whether you're feeling a little suspenseful or need a heartwarming pick-me-up, you will find a delectable cowboy who will sweep you off your feet.

Just look for cowboys on the covers of Harlequin Series books.

Available wherever books and ebooks are sold.

"You going to take off your dress now? Or later?"

The woman's eyes widened. *"Excuse me?"*

"Don't worry. My friends didn't know I was meeting a man. A project engineer, actually, and you don't exactly look the part. Nice try, though."

"Let me guess—Jet Baron."

"One and the same." He gave her a welcoming smile, his gaze slowly sliding over her body.

"Why am I *not* surprised?" she asked.

Her sarcasm startled him, as did the way she eyed him up and down. So direct. So appraising. So…disappointed.

He straightened. "If you're going to start stripping, you better do it now. I'm expecting the engineer at any moment."

"You think I'm some kind of prank. An actress hired to, what? Pretend to have a meeting with you? Then strip out of my clothes?"

He was starting to get a funny feeling. "Well, yeah."

She took a step toward him, and he would be lying if he didn't feel as if, somehow, the joke was on him.

"Tell me something, what makes you think the engineer in question is a man?"

"I was told that."

"By whom?"

"I don't know who told me, I just know he's a man. All engineers in the oil industry are men."

She took another step toward him. "There are actually quite a few women in the business. I graduated from Berkley with a degree in geology." She took yet another step closer. "I interned for the USGS out of Menlo Park then moved back to Texas to get my master's in engineering. My father was a wildcatter, and it was from him that I learned the business—so let me reassure you, Mr. Baron, I can tell the difference between an injection hose and a drill pipe. But if you still insist only men can be engineers, perhaps we should call your sister, Lizzie, who hired me."

Jet couldn't speak for a moment. "Oh, crap."

Her extraordinary blue eyes scanned him, her derision clearly evident. "Still want me to strip?"

He almost said yes, but he could tell that he was in enough trouble as it is. "I take it you're J.C.?"

"I am."

"I should apologize."

"You think?"

Look for THE TEXAN'S TWINS
by Pamela Britton next month from
Harlequin® American Romance®.

HARLEQUIN®

American Romance®

You Can't Hide in Forever

The minute he lays eyes on Forever's new doctor, Brett Murphy
knows the town—and he—won't be the same. Alisha Cordell is
raising the temperature of every male within miles. But the big-city
blonde isn't looking to put down roots. The saloon owner and
rancher will just have to change the reticent lady doc's mind.

A week after she caught her fiancé cheating, Alisha was on a train
headed for a Texas town that was barely a blip on the map.
So she's stunned at how fast the place is growing on her.
That includes the sexy cowboy with the sassy smile and easygoing
charm. Brett's also been burned by love, but he's eager for a second
chance…with Alisha. Is she ready to make Brett—and Forever—
part of her long-term plans?

Look for
Her Forever Cowboy
by *USA TODAY* bestselling author
MARIE FERRARELLA
from the **Forever, Texas** miniseries from
Harlequin® American Romance®.

Available September 2014
wherever books and ebooks are sold.

HARLEQUIN®

American Romance®

Triple the Trouble

When fertility counselor Melissa Everhart decided to have a baby
on her own, she didn't anticipate triplets…or her ex-husband's
return to Safe Harbor. Three years ago, Edmond's reluctance to have
children tore them apart. But now that he's been made guardian of
his niece, Melissa witnesses how tenderly he cares for the little girl.

Though Edmond doesn't believe he's father material, his sudden
custody of Dawn leaves him little choice. He turns to Melissa,
the warmest, kindest person he knows, for help. They begin to
rediscover the love they once shared, but the betrayals of the past
trouble them both. Can they find the forgiveness they both need
to come together as a family?

Look for
The Surprise Triplets
by JACQUELINE DIAMOND

from the *Safe Harbor Medical* miniseries from
Harlequin® American Romance®.

**Available September 2014
wherever books and ebooks are sold.**

Also available from the *Safe Harbor Medical* miniseries
by Jacqueline Diamond:
A Baby for the Doctor
The Surprise Holiday Dad
His Baby Dream
The Baby Jackpot

www.Harlequin.com

HAR75536

HARLEQUIN®

American Romance®

A Little Bit Country…

Emma Donovan ran off to Nashville when she was
young and full of dreams. Now she's back home in
Colorado with a little more common sense.
And that sense is telling her not to count on
Jamie Westland. He won't be around long—not
with his big-time career in New York City.

Jamie's never felt at home, not with his adopted family,
not with himself. Now, on his grandfather's ranch,
the pieces of his life are coming together in a way that
feels right. And Emma has so much to do with it.
But when an opportunity comes along back in New York,
he has to decide between his old life and the promise
of a new one…with Emma.

Cowboy in the Making
by JULIE BENSON

Available September 2014
wherever books and ebooks are sold.

HARLEQUIN®

SPECIAL EDITION

Life, Love and Family

NOT JUST A COWBOY

Don't miss the first story in the
***TEXAS RESCUE* miniseries**
by **Caro Carson**

Texan oil heiress Patricia Cargill is particular when
it comes to her men, but there's just something
about Luke Waterson she can't resist. Maybe it's
that he's a drop-dead gorgeous rescue fireman
and ranch hand! Luke, who lights long-dormant
fires in Patricia, has also got his fair share of secrets.
Can the cowboy charm the socialite into a
happily-ever-after?

Available September 2014
wherever books and ebooks are sold.